The Divorce

By Nicole Strycharz

First Book in The Relationship Quo Series

"Love must be bottomless, you fall in and you fall out. Either way there's no catching your feet."

~_Acknowledgments_~

A Major thank you to my readers. Every book you buy, every word you read and every review you leave, good or bad, is a constant motivation for me. I send love and luck your way every day because without you my books wouldn't have soul.

I also want to send love out to my book family, my "Write or Die" crew. You guys know who you are, your encouragement and understanding are like sunshine to my inspiration.

A Big hug that squeezes the life from you, to Martha Sweeney. Lady you are a constant light of knowledge and friendship. I'm so glad our passion for the pen brought us together!

To mom because you know you are in this book like all the others, you wrecking ball of magnificence. Your opinion is gold, and your love is everything.

Amo and Donna, my PAs but more importantly my best friends across the Atlantic. You two can't imagine how empowered I feel just knowing you.

To all the members of TRQS group! I would need three pages to name you all, but I thank each and every one of you for your support.

And To someone in Europe…

Text copyright © 2016 by Nicole Paulette Strycharz

All rights reserved. No Portion of this book may be reproduced in whole or in part in any form or by any means without prior written permission from Nicole Paulette Strycharz.

The characters and events portrayed in this book are fictitious. Any similarity to real persons, living or dead is coincidental and not intended by the author.

All Logo Designs by "Covers by Julie"

The Relationship Quo Series

The Divorce

The Friend Zone

The Co-Parent

The Significant Other

Coming Soon... More Awkward Relationships. We are far from done...

**These books do contain mature sexual content and explicit language, making them best suited for readers 18 years of age and up.

Chapter One
JENZY

*I*t was Valentine's Day in 2015 when I realized for sure we were drifting apart. Six years together since college and a holiday about red hearts and candy was the mark of our doom. Chris Clark never *forgot* Valentine's Day.

Still, I got home from work, more stoked than ever to search for my gifts. He normally hides the candy, stuffed animal and flowers in different locations and I have to find them while going about my business. I didn't find them that morning, so I figured they were going to be there later.

When I finished turning my closet inside out I sat back on my heels and sighed. "I give up," I said when I heard him come into our bedroom. "I fully surrender, now, where are they?"

"Where's what?" he asked distractedly.

I turned to look over my shoulder and found him on his phone texting with one hand while drinking coffee. His tie was hanging open under his collar and his first few buttons were undone.

He stopped when I didn't answer and looked up. "Oh, my God, Jenzy! What the hell are you doing?"

I looked down and around at my mess…Chris really liked order. This was like nails on a chalkboard to him. "Well, if you hid my gifts in plain sight we could avoid messes."

"What gifts?"

I rolled my eyes and smiled. "Ha, ha, very funny." Then I mocked his deep voice, *"What gifts?"*

"I don't sound like that and I don't have time for this, what are you talking about?"

I opened my mouth to rail at him for being stubborn but then I saw how serious he looked. Granted, Chris was a master trickster, he could hold face like no one's business, but he'd been different this past year, getting more and more distracted by work and less so with me. Actually, we fought more than we talked.

"Did you really forget?" I asked.

He shook his head and went back to texting, "Never mind, when you feel like telling me what the hell you're talking about, feel free." He walked to his side of the room and fished out a watch from his top drawer.

Meanwhile, the lump in my throat was making it hard to say anything. I heard him go into the bathroom as I started to shove stuff back in my closet.

"Jennifer!"

Uh oh… he never used my whole name unless I was in trouble. Like a parent but he was only two years older. "Yeah?" I winced.

He came back in holding his razor up. He used the hand holding his phone to point to it with wide eyes. "What did I tell you about using my damned razor? It's one thing to use it, it's another to leave it all messy and not where I left it. It took me two whole minutes…just to find it. Two minutes I don't have."

"You already shaved."

"That's not the point! Put it back and clean it, or don't use it. They make razors for women, you know."

Then I computed something. "Wait, are you going out?"

"Yeah, few of the corporate partners want to discuss stuff with me. We're going to dinner. They like my ideas for sales on that mansion on James Way Street."

Wow, more gut-wrenching sadness. He really did forget but this was big for him, so there was no point in bringing it up. "That's great! You think they'll take the ideas? They sound so solid."

"I don't know, that's why there's a dinner," his sarcasm stung. "Can you stop playing with herbs and crystals long enough to put our room back together while I'm gone?"

I nodded, "Sure."

He went to tie his tie and brush his teeth.

At first, I had thought all this was a bad mood but after a year and some pocket change of time, you have to fess up to yourself that the mood has elongated into a steady disposition.

"When do you think you'll be home?" I called back.

He gargled and spit, "Whenever they finish, I guess."

I stood and forced my closet closed. Took all my body weight. Then an idea yanked me from my boredom as he came out of the bathroom. He looked amazing like always. My husband is built like a romance book cover model. Broad shoulders muscled chest and torso and arms that show he lifts. He's also inked up but no one outside our inner circle knows because he wears suits that cover it all up. He has hazel eyes that shimmer and dark sandy hair that glosses into gold in the light. Hottest guy in California. No, scratch that. Hottest guy ever.

He's owned my heart since the day I saw him but now I think it's as important to him as one of his ties.

"I'll wait up," I announced.

His phone rang, and he picked up. While he talked, he put on the last of his things and I handed him his wallet, keys, and jacket. He kissed my cheek before leaving but it was a habit not heartfelt. Then he was gone.

Hours later as we closed in on eleven-thirty, I heard him come into the house. I burned myself with the curling iron in our bathroom when the door downstairs closed. I'd spent every minute he was gone making this magical. All those years of having the pressure of making a perfect Valentine's Day, maybe it was my turn to do it for him. Between candles lighting our entire bedroom, incense burning, a new negligee on my body, and *The Weekend* playing on my phone in the portable speakers, I felt like I had this pretty down.

We hadn't had sex in months since he'd been coming home so dog tired, but maybe I wasn't setting the mood?

When I heard his feet on the stairs I primped a final time in the mirror and gapped the transparent black robe I was wearing so my cleavage showed. My teddy was made of nothing but clinging black lace that ended high across my thighs. The underwire gave me *Victoria's Secret* boobs, which I greatly appreciated and there were pink mini bows lining the bodice. My dark chestnut hair fell in waves and curls and I had on that Vanilla scent he loved.

    The door to our bedroom opened and I almost couldn't contain the excitement. I had run out to get Valentine candy in a heart-shaped box and it was sitting on his pillow with a card. I took a deep breath and opened the door to our bathroom at the same time as he yelled.

    "Jenzy, that incense gives me headaches, you really had to light it tonight?" I opened my mouth to make him look at me but then, "Son of a bitch!" He shouted and rushed to the window where one of the curtains had caught fire. It was dangling too close to the candles and he had to yank them down and stomp the flames out. They hadn't totally ignited yet, but it shook me up to think I could've missed it.

    "I didn't even smell anything," I said as we stood over the damage.

    "Because you don't pay attention to anything! A bomb could drop when you're in the clouds and you wouldn't notice." He bent to gather the ruined curtains and I swallowed the scolding. I deserved it. I did almost burn the house down.

    "I'm sorry Chris, I was-."

    "I warn you about your candles, and your incense, and your wax warmers all the time. Yesterday, it was your damned curling iron. It's like you *want* to burn to a crisp."

    I sided a glance at the bathroom trying to remember if I unplugged the curler. While he bagged the curtains I back stepped into the doorway of the bathroom and jerked the plug out without being noticed.

    "I'm sorry, I really am, I was trying to make tonight special and I just didn't see it."

    He grumbled as he took the bag downstairs and I fought for a way to regain the night. When he came back, he was set for pissed, "I have a freaking headache now. Feels like a high school band on crack are in my head."

"I have stuff for headaches, I'll grab something," I said.

"I don't want herbal shit. I want painkillers." He started blowing out all my candles and turned on a small lamp by the door. "I just really need to go to bed. We'll talk about it later."

He turned down his side of the bed and didn't even see the candy box or the card until it fell near the toe of his shoe.

"I'll get it," I tried to beat him to the stuff, but he picked it up and turned it over like he didn't know what it was.

"What's all this?" he asked.

"Well, it was for you. It's just little stuff…"

He stared at the heart box forever, "Oh, right, Valentine's Day. Is that-? What's today?"

I felt a spark of hope. I would prefer to think he forgot than to think he didn't care, "The 14th."

"Is that what all the candles were for? Wow, okay. I didn't…really think we were doing all that stuff this year. We aren't teenagers; it's just another commercialized holiday."

I wasn't sure how to even respond. "Yeah…that's true…it's not important or anything."

"Especially not if it involves burning the house down," he tapped the top of my head with his card then dropped it and the candy on his nightstand like it was junk mail before undressing. *Ouch, ouch, ouch!* I could actually feel his shoe on my heart.

Yes, it is commercialized. You should love one another every day, blah, blah, blah. I am one of the girls that love the thrill of a 'love day'. A reminder for guys to be dudes from the medieval era, presenting gifts and romantic quests to the supermarket for flowers.

Plus, sex.

I went around to my side of the bed and turned down the comforter in a haze. What just happened to this night? He sat up instead of lying down to look over his notes and I groped for a new way to redeem this. "How did tonight go?"

He took forever to answer since he was on his phone again, "Fine. The commission, if it sells is astronomical."

"Chris," I sat up, "that's too much greatness! Congrats, babe."

He nodded while he texted, and I set my chin on his shoulder to look down at his notes, "You're just getting better and better, I'm very happy for you with this."

"Yeah, all we need now is to find you a real job."

There went his foot stomping the hell out of my heart again, "I have a real job."

"You work for that cranky quack at a holistic clinic, where he treats colds with leaves. You need to finish school for nursing; you'd be good at it."

"I like natural healing and Dr. Mouser isn't a quack, he went to medical school and was an MD for years before becoming an ND. He uses both ways and that's what he's teaching me."

"You're twenty-five, Jenzy it's time to do something steady."

I came off his shoulder and looked up at him, "Twenty-seven."

"What?"

"I'm twenty-seven, not twenty-five."

"No, your birthday is in-."

Yeah, jerk, do the math. His eyes flashed with a little ping then recovered, "December…" he murmured.

I scooted away a little and lay down on my back. Still in this useless nighty that he didn't even notice.

"How did I miss that?" he asked out loud.

"You were in that meeting. It's okay. Just another, 'conventional holiday.'"

He reached out and gave my hand a squeeze and even in my sadness it excited me to be touched by him.

"Sorry, I'll make it up, okay? We can go do that star gazing, museum thingy you like or something." He took his hand away to keep working and I missed the heat.

"Linda Goodman says that Leo men are very busy thinkers, so I understand. Can we-?"

"Yeah, she's a real genius. She sells millions of books to people that think the stars have something to do with your personality."

"I'm one of those people."

"Yeah, and every book of hers on your shelf is paying her way to vacation in Cuba."

"She's not living anymore."

"Did the stars warn her about an oncoming bus or did she read a sign telling her to jump in front of it," he smirked at his cleverness.

"You don't have to agree with how I think or what I believe but you don't have to be an asshole about it either."

He didn't answer, like he thought I was just being stupid. Wow. This was a far fall from two people that needed each other like air. He used to think my 'hippie ways' as he called them, were cute, now he thinks I'm annoying.

I rolled to put my back to him and struggled with that cold feeling you get when you feel utterly alone. Sometime after his stuff was closed up and his phone was plugged in, the soft rhythm of his breathing told me he'd fallen asleep.

I snuck out of bed.

I made my way silently to his side and even though it was totally wrong and totally a breach of trust, I opened the passcode on his phone and checked through his messages for signs of an affair.

I just needed to know. Like knowing he was screwing around would mean I just need to step up my game or something. I could fight for him if I had to. There was nothing in here, though. Only work people and nothing remotely personal. He never smelled like some girl's perfume, he didn't have lipstick stains on his collars. There was no gap between home, work, and the gym.

I looked in our messages and saw how flat they were. We never said I love you, any more or I miss you. All couples have to find a settling point, we found one, years back and it was great. Best friends, that find each other sexually attractive, that was our marriage for years. Now we were roommates and I think he'd almost love seeing me move out.

      But I'm going to keep trying. I'm not giving up. This is Chris. I looked down at him and gently brushed his brow with my fingertips. Chris was and always has been the keeper of my everything; my body, my heart, my soul, and my love. I just have to work harder to remind him. I just have to be better. I can do that.

Chapter Two
Little Over A Year Later
April 2016
JENZY

Coming home from work at Dr. Mouser's, I stopped at a New Age bookstore and took a look around. I love this shop and I've been coming here for years. Besides, it's an excuse not to go home directly. Chris is going to freak when he sees my Crystal collection on the window sills. They've been proven to be more powerful under moonlight, though.

I browsed the spines in the astrology section and found a good one on discovering more about your sign. Nice! This bookshelf was from floor to ceiling against the far wall and it was decorated with all kinds of new agey stuff, candles for sale, sage bundles, rocks, crystals, feathers…I was dying of happy.

"Ma'am," someone said from behind me. I ignored it because there were plenty of people in the store on the other side. "Hey!"

I looked up from my book with a frown in time to see the bookshelf was leaning forward enough for a book or two to fall out. By the time I saw the danger, it was too late, but then someone slid their arm around my waist and yanked me back. We both fell just out of reach of the massive shelf when it landed with a scary *thud* that shook the floor. The weight and solid force of it definitely could've potentially killed me. I took in ragged breaths as the possibilities went through my mind. Then I realized I was lying between a guy's legs.

I looked back into the eyes of a very handsome man, with browned skin and a short-kept beard. His hair was dark and cut close to his head. He had a Scorpio symbol tattoo on his forearm and even in plain jeans and a T-shirt he was pretty hot.

"You okay?" he asked.

I looked back at the shelf and hugged myself. The top of the shelf was just below my brown boot.

What if my leg had been under there? "I think so," I said.

"I told my dad to anchor that thing to the wall a thousand times, he said he did."

A crowd was forming to see if we were okay. He got up from behind me then helped me up.

"Thanks," I shouldered my purse, "that could've been serious. I'm still freaked out. I really can't thank you enough. That was…so scary."

He smiled and touched my upper arm, "You sure you're okay?"

"Yeah," I walked further from the shelf like it was going to drag after me. Never know, "I'm Jenzy Clark," I offered my hand and he took it.

"Moses Livingston," he rolled his brown eyes. "I know, my parents were high when they named me. We aren't even Jewish."

I laughed, and it relieved the near-death experience tension. "You make the name work." Oops. Was that flirting?

"What's Jenzy stand for?"

"Jennifer. I hated people calling me Jenny, though. So, I made everyone call me Jenzy. Funny thing is, my nephew, who is four-years-old, he can't say Jenzy. He actually says Jezzy. My mom started calling me Jenzy first. Anyway, now my friends call me that. I don't…" I pursed my lips. "Wow, I just gave you my life story."

He laughed, "I don't mind. Sagittarius, right?"

I lit up inside, "Yeah, what gave me away? The non-stop talking or the clumsy?"

"I was going to say the hand talking and the little Sag symbol on your wrist."

I winced. I do hand talk a lot, "Good guess. I don't remember ever seeing you in here."

"That's because my dad owns the shop. He's getting forgetful, though so I'm coming in more to handle finances."

"Oh," I tried not to stare but he was pretty. As pretty as Chris but in different ways. "What do you usually do?"

"I teach a yoga class like two blocks down from here."

"Really? The Iron Fitness gym?"

"Yeah, you know it?"

"I go there for yoga but in the early morning class. My teacher is Gerda."

His eyes went wide, "I love Gerda, she actually trained me."

"My-." Huh. Strange reaction. Why couldn't I say the words, 'my husband goes there.' I was always so proud of Chris. He's beautiful and I love him but the idea of driving a wedge between myself and this stranger was depressing. I liked him. I like how he looks at me like he sees me. "My old gym wasn't so great," I lied.

"You should come to one of my classes. I teach in the evening."

"Well, my work keeps me till after the evening classes end."

"Where?"

"The holistic clinic on 7th. I'm one of the new herbalists there with Dr. Mouser."

"You're freaking me out now. That's my doctor."

"What?"

"He's been my doctor for like, five years. I use herbs for everything. I'm also a tea addict."

"Me too! I have so much tea in my house."

"We're going to start selling teas here, you know. I want to get in, at least healing teas."

"Oh, and maybe supplements! You know, Dr. Mouser's herbal remedies would sell in here."

"Great idea! Hang on, I need to write it down," he left me to go behind the counter and make notes. While his head was bent I took him in. So much fineness. Even his hands were pretty.

"If I didn't know any better, I'd swear I knew you in a past life," he said glancing up.

"I believe in past lives with a passion. I think I was Egyptian, Asian, and French once."

"You look regal enough to be Egyptian," his eyes sent that silent message of interest and I felt giddy. He leaned over the counter and tapped the eraser of the pencil a few times. "And elegant enough to be in the Asian dynasty."

I let that wash over me. It felt amazing! Chris used to say things like that. Chris used to shower me with compliments and-. Oh, shit, Chris! "Uh, thanks." I swallowed hard and looked at the door. "I should go. It was good meeting you, even if it was terrifying too."

"Yeah, damn, I need to shut down, so I can clean this place up and anchor that friggin shelf. I'm just glad there were no kids around or something."

"That would be devastating."

"Find anything you want to check out before you go?"

"I did find one book…" I looked back at the bookshelf. "But uh…it's a little buried right now."

"Which one?"

"*Discovering the You in Astrology* by a Charles something."

"I read that one, it's great. I prefer Linda Goodman but-."

"You read her too?"

"She's freakily accurate. I read up on people all the time to better understand them and myself."

"You're Scorpio, right?"

He lifted his forearm and grinned, "Yep. Must be why we're compatible."

I laughed then slowed into silence, "I'm…I'm married." I could've found a better way than that.

"Yeah, you're a hand talker, remember? I saw the ring like ten times." His smile was accepting but maybe a little sad. "Guy can dream, though."

I smiled and bit my lip. All my lady parts were tingling, "I need to go but it was great meeting you."

"Same here. Tell your husband to kiss you for me."

We laughed, and it lightened the mood before I left. That felt amazing.

Chapter Three
JENZY

When I got home, I was accidentally horny. The idea of being noticed like that had me wanting touch. Now it had been two years and a couple months since Chris and I had sex. The last couple times before that lacked intimacy and fire. He was unenthused and almost annoyingly gentle. He was also preoccupied. This is a shocker considering Chris had been the best sex of my life. I had quite a few partners as had he before we dated but sex with him was always an art.

He'd lost that touch these last couple years and I missed it. I set my purse down on our kitchen counter and stopped dead in my tracks to see him sweeping my crystals into a bowl.

"Chris!" I rushed over and tried to wrestle the bowl from him. "Stop it! They'll break!"

"They're rocks Jenzy! They don't belong on the friggin sill. I feel like I'm in a cave."

"You act brutish enough to live in one!" I took the bowl and freaked when I saw my amethyst was cracked. I held it up, "It's broken."

"It's cracked. Don't overreact."

"The energy will be all out of whack."

"Jesus, Jenn! It's a friggin rock!"

"These matter to me."

"Make a career choice that matters half as much as these rocks and then I'll listen."

He walked away, and I breathed past the familiar disappointment. Maybe I was wrong again?

"I'm sorry, they don't belong on the sills," I agreed.

"And what are these big-ass boxes?"

I looked under the dining table where he'd lightly kicked a container.

"Recycling bins," I told him. He interrupted me with an eye roll and a sigh, but I explained. "I want to start being thoughtful toward the environment…"

"Like that time, you wanted to free animals from the zoo, right? Or protest that fast food place for supporting traditional family values, or the time you stopped cosmetics that do animal testing? Stick to a cause so I can keep up, will you?"

"I want to make the world better and do something meaningful-."

"Then stop praying to fat men from mythology that don't exist and making fairy gardens for imaginary people two inches high!"

"I'm not a Buddhist, I said I would like to look into it and lots of people believe in fairies."

"Yeah, people in jackets that make them hug themselves," his phone buzzed so he broke to read the messages.

Geez, I felt low right now.

I braved it, "If you don't like me anymore just say so."

He ignored me while he typed.

"Chris."

Still nothing.

"Could you stop that for just one minute?" I pressed.

"*What*, Jenzy? What?"

"Is there anything about me you still like? You knew all this stuff when you married me, I didn't change."

"I can't do this now," he looked back down at his phone and I felt like there might be an opportunity.

I went up to him and took his face in my hands. I kissed him. I kissed him the way I wanted to be kissed, the way I needed to be kissed and in a scared way. I don't want to think about other men or lose his love, but I can't ever get him to see me.

My lips danced over his even when I felt him drawing his neck back.

Please, please, please, don't, I pleaded in my head. I let go of his face to caress his neck and down his shoulders and chest. He felt so good, like home, and love. His lips weren't in it, though they weren't taking mine like they used to. It was just one of his lazy attempts to brush me off.

I started to unbutton his work vest.

He frowned, "Jenzy, what are you doing?" I silenced him with another kiss and let go to try and pull my shirt up over my head. He caught my arms and pulled my shirt down. "I have to make a call, I can't do this now."

"Don't you remember the time we were both sick with the flu and you randomly got horny? You shoved me down on the countertop here, and," I smoothed my hand over the surface. "You were your best when we had to do quickies and in fits of passion. Let's do it now. Like that, right here. Just something fast and hot. I want you, I miss you."

He opened his mouth to say something when his phone rang. Before I could stop him, he answered. I looked at him in disbelief. He shushed me when I tried to whisper, and the rejection was like a hot poker running me through.

I left the kitchen and went up to our room. I can't take this. It's like he finds me the most invisible person in the world. I felt like crying but that wouldn't solve anything.

Hours later he came up for a shower and I stopped in the middle of folding clothes from our laundry basket to watch him undress. He was facing the bathroom, so he didn't see me but God. He's so beautiful. His shirt came down off his arms and I watched his back work. Tattoos winded from his shoulder blades, then down his arms. He had a thin, long dragon down his spine and when he undid his pants I realized my nether regions were throbbing with desire.

What an ass. A perfect ass. The kind you want to bite and strong thighs to support it. He went into the shower and I decided on a new plan. He's a guy! How hard is it to make a guy want sex? The word sex should be enough.

I took off my jeans and stripped to my satin pink bra and panties. All bought with him in mind, just in case the occasion he wants me should ever arrive. I'm not a conceited person but I know I'm not ugly. I stay in great shape and I have okay boobs, they're C cups. That's good, right?

I snuck into the bathroom as I heard the shower go on and stepped into the shower. Trouble is, my Sagittarius clumsy star made me slip.

Chris heard me and turned in time to catch me before I could take down the shower curtain.

"Jesus Jennifer!" he hissed.

I clung to him when he brought me up against him. Ohhhh this felt good. This felt right being in his arms. He smells amazing and he hasn't even scrubbed yet. I wrapped my arms around his neck and even though I was chilled I felt warm.

"I love you…" I whispered into his neck.

He kissed the top of my head, "Love you too. I need to shower babe."

I went stiff in his arms. I think he felt it. I pulled back enough to see him and set my hands over his chest. "You didn't say it," I said.

"Say what? I just said I love you too."

That hurt worse, "No, you didn't say it the special way. The special way we've said it for years."

"Oh, my God, I said I love you. You want me to build you a shrine? Things don't stay the same forever. It doesn't mean anything."

I felt a tear stinging my eye, "What if I said it does to me? What if I need you to say it like you used to? Like you mean it."

"You make everything so big. You do this all the time. You overdo everything. You're either super excited about stupid little things or super worked up about even smaller things, there's no in between."

"Do you still love me?"

"What kind of question is that?"

"Chris, you never touch me anymore. I went to bed in only a thong, three nights ago, I looked like a hooker and you didn't even say anything."

"Well, your daydreams don't pay for us to have a multi-level townhome style condo, but real estate does. I'm tired. Sorry, I don't stare at you every night to see if you're horny. Sorry, I get worn the fuck out!"

"My job makes good money too, maybe not what you make but we almost split everything. Besides, that's not what this is about. Are you still in love with me?"

He looked at me like I was speaking some other language, "Listen, I don't know what brought this on but let me get done in here and hand me the real soap. The soap that isn't made from hemp, or grass or sand. The one you wash your face at the sink with but never put back in the shower."

I felt my chest cave, "I'm standing in the shower with you, in my underwear, telling you I love you and asking you to say it back, and you're asking me to leave?"

He turned his back to me and started rinsing, "Jesus, never mind."

My heart broke so loud I thought we both heard it. I stepped around the broken pieces and him before stepping out. I changed into an old nightshirt before pulling my hair up into a messy bun and went downstairs.

Am I going crazy? We loved each other once, right? I dug through our Blu-rays and DVDs to find the little ivory envelope that held our wedding disk. I slipped it into the player then sat in front of the TV Indian style and watched.

In the video, I tripped going down the aisle, but my dad caught me. Then I forgot my vows at the front, but Chris repeated them with me while holding my hands to his chest. We'd practiced together even though it's unconventional.

God, he looks good in a tux. Before we were pronounced man and wife he couldn't take the waiting and kissed me anyway. He got impatient on the way out of the courthouse too and threw me over his shoulder to run me to the limo we had waiting.

I laughed at the memory.

The filming picks up with the limo dropping us off at the San Francisco Bay. This is still *my* wedding though, so an awkward clumsy moment was just around the corner. In front of friends and family that was waiting for us there, the limo drove off with my dress caught in the door. It tore it right off my legs, to reveal my lace red panties and garters.

Chris was laughing harder than I'd seen him laugh in years. He was so racked with it he bent over with his hands on his knees. I hid behind him and he hurried to straighten and cover my lower half with his jacket. The camera zooms in on us laughing and kissing.

Chris is whispering reassurances to me and I turned up the volume.

"It's okay, babe," he laughed.

"No, oh, my God, everyone saw my underwear."

"Nah! They aren't even looking at you… the Bay is too awesome."

"Shut up," I laugh into his chest.

"It's okay, baby. Look at me."

"No. My dress is ruined."

"Well, let's be fair, I tore it a little on the way here."

"Gahhh!"

He hugged me so close and kissed all over my face, "You're mine remember? Mine forever, who cares?"

"You married a clumsy idiot."

"Perfect. She's a perfect clumsy idiot."

I looked up to hold his tie, "I love you."

"I love you too…I guess," he teased.

I paused the DVD.
Right there.
That was it.

"I guess," had been our thing. We never said I love you without him saying 'I guess,' at the end. It was like a tradition. There was a whole story behind it and it was ours. To everyone else, it sounded insincere and probably really strange but to us, it mattered.

It reminded us of when we almost let go of each other and held on tighter all at once but now Chris wasn't saying it. Now I'm not sure he even means it.

I shut off the disc, put on the Disney movie *Lion King* and made a bed for myself on the couch. I need something fanciful to dull the pain and Disney is my lifeline.

In the morning, my husband didn't even notice I hadn't come to bed.

Chapter Four
Two Weeks Later
CHRIS

I was standing in the kitchen pouring myself a coffee with one hand and text messaging with the other when it happened. I was dressed for work, ready to go, and she came to sit at the table behind me with her tea.

"Chris," she said my name like a question.

"Hmm?"

"I think we should separate."

"Okay, honey," I kept pouring then set down the coffee pot and took a sip. I didn't really hear her. I was reading this last message and multitasking has never been my strong point.

"I'm going to move in with Todd and Mandy. They have that spare room," she went on.

"Yeah."

"Also…" I still wasn't listening but something in the one word caught my attention. "I'm going to run by the lawyer's office today to file for the divorce."

Divorce…the word radiated through me like heat waves and rippled on my skin until the hair on my body stood up. I turned around with a frown and faced her, "I'm sorry, you what?"

"I want to separate and I'm going to live with your brother for a while. I also said I'm going in to file today."

I stared at her for a whole minute. Maybe this was the first time I'd really seen her in months. She was in a white tank and jeans with a pink, fuzzy, shawl, sweater thingy that wrapped around her. She had like three necklaces on and why three? I know why. She couldn't decide so she went with all three. She's terrible with little decisions. This was a big one though and she looked so sure.

As a guy, I said the first thing that came to mind. We don't have nine million thoughts like women have so it was a simple thought I said out loud, "What the fuck?!"

"We aren't in love anymore, Chris it's the logical step to take. No need in dragging it out. We had seven years, and more than half meant the world to me. It was a good run."

"A good run?" I'm not sure what was worse, her words or her calm, "What is this, a marathon? What the hell do you mean a 'good run?' You're my wife for Christ's sake."

"Chris-."

"Don't *Chris* me! And what the fuck do you mean, 'we aren't in love', I love you like I always loved you."

She took the annoyingly calm role, "Look, you don't need me anymore, but I need you. Or I did. You haven't seen me, except when I do something wrong, for two years."

I tossed my mug in the sink and heard it break.

I blocked her out again to replay what she said before, "You're moving in with friggin Todd?" Todd and Jenzy have been best friends since high school but I never noticed her until college when she showed up on campus. She was also his wife's best friend too. "This is ridiculous, Jenzy! Is this something you're doing to get my attention or-?"

"No, I've been trying for that, it hasn't worked. This is me giving up."

"Giving up?"

"You can't mean to say you haven't noticed we're having problems? We only ever fight or ignore each other. I don't want to be that couple that lives that way forever. We can still be friends-."

I laughed out loud like when I watch *Dude Where's My Car*. My wife just told me a line dating people use when it's not working out.

Then the laughter stopped, and I felt anxiety ridden. She was serious. "Friends? I'm your husband."

"And I love you. You were the best of everything for me, but you don't want me. You haven't for a long time. I annoy you-."

"Are you sleeping with someone?" Yeah, I know. Another typical guy question put in the typical guy way, but excuse me, I thought this marriage was fine. Yeah, we fight a lot but all couples fight. Yeah, I haven't put an effort in with sex. My career has been taking off and we settled into each other.

She set her tea down and sighed, "I could never hurt you like that. Cheating is cheap, and you matter too much to me. I would never stomach letting someone touch me behind your back, but…"

Oh shit! "But what?"

"I met someone I like talking to."

"Are you kidding me?" I came around to stand beside her and bent to turn her chair out. She's so small it's like turning a kid. "Who the fuck is it?"

"Come on, Chris it's not important."

"The hell you say! I'll break his face."

"You can't. You're trained in *MMA* fighting and you'd go to jail."

"Invite him over. I'll do it once he's inside. Law says that's okay."

She smiled and touched my cheek. Whoa. Her touch. I've missed that. I love that. What have I done?

"I never did anything to betray you. He and I just talk. Like friends."

"Invite your *friend* over and we can all be *friends* until one of us goes missing."

"I'm setting you free. This is a good thing. This way it's a healthy break."

"I don't want a break," I held her shoulders and she took her hand away, "Jenzy, divorce is big. It's not a timeout or a-, it's for good."

"Chris, what do I do? What's my job?"

I straightened and looked down at her but kept my hands on her, "You're Dr. Mouser's assistant."

"I'm an actual herbalist now. I work *with* him, not under him. It's been in effect since a month ago. Have any clue what job I've been aspiring for since?"

I couldn't answer. Fuck.

She sighed, "Doula work. I told you Dr. Mouser wanted us to go with him to his cabin in the mountains to celebrate with his colleagues. It's close to my parent's cabin. He wanted to present me…for better opportunities and learning chances. There were esteemed Midwives there. I told you while we were watching a show. Do you know what you said?"

Considering I didn't even remember her telling me I braced for something pretty stupid.

She was fighting it, but I saw water collecting in her gorgeous blue eyes as she went on, "You said, 'funny he's got a place in the mountains… how does he find all the plants for his witch doctor medine*s*…?'"

I could almost see the foot coming out of my mouth. I'd unknowingly buried myself.

She toyed with a necklace, "You didn't congratulate me or even hear what I said you just…teased me. It was the best day of my life, aside from marrying you and you didn't even care."

It's not easy feeling like a colossal dick. I scrambled in my mind for something to retract it all with, but I'd buried myself in a debt of hurts it seemed. Then she went on.

"I've been sleeping on the couch down here, for two weeks. You haven't even noticed."

"I figured you were coming to bed later in the night," lame excuse. Even I heard the awful.

She blinked back the little bit of emotion she'd finally been showing and sweetly took my hands off her. That hurt.

"I try coming to you in sexy things and offering myself to you only, so you reject me. I feel…like…I must be hideous to you or terribly boring like you had your fill of me. I mean, what healthy guy under forty turns down sex? I know you aren't gay, it has to be you feel bored with me."

"That's not true."

"You used to be amazing. Breathtaking. I used to have to hold on to things to make love to you. You would take me with this fire, like, you were afraid to lose me, or like you were dying or something. The last few times you were so far away in your head and you made me feel…like a chore."

I should just hand her the meat cleaver behind me and tell her to gore me with it. Same thing. This felt the same. A chore? I made touching her feel like a chore? Isn't it weird how the body works? Hearing her now made me see her.

Gorgeous. Just like the day we met only better. Body of a dancer but with more ass. I love her ass, it's perfect. Her neck, that's my other favorite spot. I had learned our first time, she loved it when I flicked my tongue over her skin. Dragging it made her pant, flicking made her quiver. Holding her down under me and swirling my tongue in circles behind her ear was like slipping a quarter in a machine to turn it on. It was her trigger. Why hadn't I been doing that? Thinking about it was making me hot. Why had I been waiting?

I nodded, "Well, now we've talked this shit over, let me fix this."

"It's not all you. I'm not saying that. I'm not easy to live with either. I'm flaky with my ambitions, I'm messy, I have unrealistic beliefs, I can be annoyingly positive and let's face it, I'm forgetful as hell and clumsy. I'm your total opposite. We don't like-."

"I like having an opposite. I like you, even with all of that."

"But if you loved me, you'd like me *for* all of that. Chris, I suggested counseling, you laughed and blew that off. You outright refused. I have come to you, hundreds of times to explain how I feel and you either tease me or we argue."

I felt my phone ring before I heard it.

She smiled and picked up her tea as she stood, "You need to get that. It's okay. Really. I'll be out by the time you get home and I'll make sure I clean before I go."

I watched her walk away from me and fought more panic. What had I done?

Knowing she wouldn't be there when I pulled in hours later was making me sick. So, when I got off work, I circled our block ten times then checked to see if her bike was in there. She either walked or biked and on rainy days I took her into work. When I pulled up, though her bike was gone.

I reversed and tore out of our drive to go to the gym. This was really happening? I was losing her. I grabbed my gym bag from the back seat and went in, going directly to change into my workout clothes then to the weights. This would do it. This would help. I stuffed earbuds in my ears and blasted anything that had lyrics I could focus on. *Eminem* is good. That worked for a few pumps…until my phone buzzed. I pulled it from my pocket and checked.

It was a text from *her*.

"I know how you are when you go on a working jag. So, I put a stew in the crockpot. (It's not healthy, I promise) It should last you the week and there're bread rolls in the bread box. Do you need anything else?"

Was that a joke? I messaged back right away.
"Yeah, for you to come home."

She typed forever and a day. Was she writing a book? I sighed. My attitude was what put me in this boat. I needed to stop being an asshole, but it wasn't easy to shake.

Then she came back, and my stomach lurched with curiosity.
"Your clothes are folded on the bed, I think I got everything. Your work shirts are pressed and up in your closet."

She missed me, I could feel it. She never was one for domestic housework. She usually cleaned in bouts when she was nervous, excited, and anxious so if she did laundry and stuff she has to be feeling it. She was also an incredible cook. At least when she wasn't trying to make something healthy out of leeks and wicker.

>I tried again.
>**"Just come home and talk to me."**

>She came back.
>**"I tried that already."**

>I fought impatience.
>**"I'm listening now."**

>Her next message came slowly.
>**"I have nothing to say."**
> Now I'm irritated.
>**"You always have something to say. You could talk the ear off a deaf man. You never stop talking, now I ask you to and nothing?"** I reread that then swore at myself. That didn't sound right. Great. I already sent the fucking thing.

>**"Another way in which you are free,"** she sent back beside a plain, closed mouth, smiling emoji and I wanted to crush my phone. I deserved that one.

>I retreated.
>**"I didn't mean it that way."**

I waited but it never said she read it and she never typed back. Fuck! Fuck everything! I went back to benching and then my other routines. By the time I was out of the shower and packing in the locker room, one of the instructors came around the corner with his bag to change.

Moses was a good- looking guy but a major Granola Breath. Between prayer beads on his wrists and earth day t-shirts, there was no mistaking that.

"Hey, Chris," he said as he unzipped his bag on the bench.

"Hey, Moses, how's life?"

"Good," he pulled off his shirt then yawned as he tugged a muscle shirt on.

I smirked, "Up late texting your *girlfriend*?"

He laughed, "She's not my girlfriend yet, man. We just talk but yeah."

"Better make a move or you'll end up in friend zone. My little brother was king of the zone until he met his wife."

"Well, she's going through a lot right now; I don't want to rush her."

"Hey, if she's talking to you into the wee hours of daylight, she is as ready as she'll ever be."

Not sure I was in the right league to be giving relationship advice but catching women wasn't my problem, apparently, it was keeping them.

Moses shrugged, "She's with someone. I don't want to be *that guy*, ya know? Karma. We both have been really careful not to cross that line. They are breaking up but…"

I sat to tie my shoes and looked up at him, "Then it's all good. Breaking up means it's over. Wait too long, you might miss out."

"That's true…" Moses kicked off his shoes then nodded. "She *is* really hot. Like, I don't get how the guy she's with is even letting her go. Not to mention we have so much in common its crazy. Even the way we met seems like fate or something."

I smiled, "Yeah, a falling bookcase is pretty epic. You were like Batman or something."

"Superman."

"Let's not go here again," we laughed at our superhero debate as we headed out; those could get heated with us because who hates Batman? He was off to teach a class and I was off to my empty house. He paused in the doorway.

"Did you know when you met your wife? Like… was it different or was it obvious she was it? Did a star fall or something?" he laughed a little, knowing I didn't believe in that stuff.

I absolutely hate life for throwing me this blistering reminder that I had sabotaged my marriage to a woman I had forgotten how to love right.

I did my best to answer, "When you meet someone new it always feels the same, I think. You hope it's forever, but it only feels different when you make it that way."

He smiled and nodded, "Good point. Thanks, Chris. I'll see ya around, alright? I gotta teach this class."

I nodded but now a memory was flooding my mind. It was like putting in an old movie I hadn't seen in years. It was new to me and perfectly familiar all at once and I sat down in my car with my eyes shut to see it clearer.

Chapter Five
Fall 2007
CHRIS

"*I* fucking hate you!" Todd screamed at me before he bent over and hurled into our frat house toilet.

I laughed before hiking up the seat of my pants and sitting on the rim of the bathtub beside him. "Come on, initiation isn't so bad."

"Tequila shots, an Irish Car Bomb, and a White Russian? You made me drink all that shit in one night! I probably have alcohol poisoning," he wailed.

I laughed, "Nah, only a little…you'll be fine. Just don't tell mom or she'll be down here in like ten minutes on her jet."

"I told you I don't drink. I can't believe you did this on *your* first night too," he used a washcloth I gave him to wipe the back of his neck.

"Oh, I didn't do this. I hate liquor."

He looked up at me like he was going to pull my eyeballs out and feed them to me, "But you said-!"

"I *said* you had to *be initiated*, I never specified how. There's like two other ways. Sleeping with a senior chick or benching a crazy amount of iron and you know no one lifts like your bro, so I picked that one."

He rallied enough to punch me in the knee and I laughed and rubbed the pain down at the same time.

"I'm gonna kill you!" he snapped.

"Oh, my God! Don't be such a pussy. You'll be almost fine in the morning. Sort of. You'll wanna die but then you'll be fine. Unless you do die. You'd still be fine, though. I would be an only child again, which would be fantastical."

He threw up again and I winced at the sound. I tried focusing on the *boom, boom, boom* of the loudly played music on the other side of the door where our peers are still living it up. When he finished I patted his back. "Isn't college great?"

"You just had to be a year older than me, didn't you?" he shot back.

"I came first so I could take care of your sorry ass."

"You came first because you were an accident. I was planned."

"Just think, you can tell your little girlfriend…what's her name? Jessie? Tell her you're a real manly man now."

"Oh, shit!" he wobbled his way into standing and rinsed his face in the sink. "Oh, she's gonna kill me."

"Who?"

"*Jenzy*! I was supposed to pick her up at the bus station! She's moving into the dorm on campus. Shit!" he dug his keys out of his pocket, but I got up and snatched them "Hey! Come on!" he said making a weak try for them.

Being a head taller I held them way out of reach, "You try driving all fucked up like this and I seriously *will* kill you."

"I probably threw up all the booze by now. I gotta get Jenzy, it's raining and she's alone at a dark bus stop."

"Sure, so get in a car drunk off your ass and crash so you can both die. Hell no. I'll get Jessie, you stay here. I'm taking your car, so you can't try anything stupid and she'll know the car."

"Jenzy. Her name is-," he bugged his eyes before falling to his knees and hurling into the toilet again. "When I get over this, I'm gonna kick your ass."

"Yeah, right around the time pigs fly. I'll get your little girlfriend and you stay here and keep throwing up."

"She's not my girlfriend," he leaned his elbows on the seat. "Chris, hurry up, okay. She's really trusting, she'd get in a car with Hannibal Lecter if he had a 'coexist' bumper sticker."

"I got this."

He gave me the name of the station and I got in my brother's ridiculously old Outback Subaru minutes later. I followed the quiet streets in the rain with wipers that kept jamming. At a stop light, I saw that Todd had several pamphlets and posters that protested everything from the way cattle are treated to global warming. I tossed them in the back, so his friend would have room to sit and drove on when the green light came on.

As I pulled up to the station, I grumbled to myself. There was a girl sitting on the bench in a bright purple raincoat with rain boots that were turquoise with purple polka dots. She was shivering. Now I felt like an ass for getting my brother wasted. I parked and got out to go to her.

When she looked up at me I felt that strong sense of luck. Luck is the only word I can think of when you have to do something you don't want to but then find out the person you're doing it for is unrealistically beautiful.

Her eyes were a soft shade of blue that pulled me in. They were wide and lined underneath with thick liner. Her mouth was pouty, like the kind of lips girls pay to get and her hair was long, so long it was near her ribcage where it hung from under the hood of her coat.

I strode her way, "Hi," I said over the rain.

She jumped up and fell over the bench before stepping over to stand behind it. "Uh, my friend is coming to pick me up so just, you know, stay there," she warned.

"I'm actually here to pick you up."

"Listen, my friend is like seven feet tall and he's trained in self-defense so…"

I laughed, "Sure." My brother isn't trained to do anything but run away.

She pulled a tube from her pocket and held it out. "Look, creep I have pepper spray, okay!"

"Fuck," I backed up a step or two but then I stopped and laughed. "You might want to turn it facing out, hon."

She frowned and looked at the tube, "Oh," she pointed it out but then held it to her chest. "I guess if you were a serial killer or something you wouldn't have told me that. I mean, if I blinded myself that would make your job easier, right?"

"Well, unless I like the sport of a challenge then I'm still not that trustworthy."

She laughed then stopped and thought about it which made me laugh harder.

"I'm Todd's older brother, Christopher…or Chris, rather. He was supposed to text you and let you know I was coming."

She checked her phone, "Well, he didn't so…can I see your ID?"

"It's raining pretty hard," I reminded. Mind you, I had no umbrella and no hood.

"My dad told me when he gave me the pepper spray not to trust anyone. My parents are from New York so they're pretty tough. I also have a rape whistle…just so you know."

"Good for you…"

She crossed her arms, so I rolled my eyes and took out my wallet. I found my ID and stepped carefully over to hand it to her.

She eyed me then took it and a slow smile crossed her face while she studied it. "You look a little like Todd, I see it now. He's shorter, though."

"And *way* less good-looking," I added.

She giggled then grabbed a backpack and a wheeled suitcase. "I'm ready to get out of this weather, then."

I quirked a brow, "That's all you have?"

"Yeah! I like to travel light so I'm always ready for like, an adventure or something."

I took her case and her backpack, so she could get in then I put them in the back and got in with her. "Nice coat," I teased as she set the hood back. Whoa. It was hard not to stare at a girl that pretty.

"Thanks. I'm a Sagittarius and purple is our lucky color. Something lucky always happens when I wear purple."

"Is that so?"

"What are you?"

"Am I what?"

"What sun sign? Like astrology."

"I think I looked it up one time. I'm a Leo."

"Oh, wow! The logical thinker, the planner and the royal lion."

"I don't like to brag."

We laughed, and I realized how enthralled she had me.

She went on, "Linda Goodman says Leo's are proud and very majestic. They have a way of being able to talk to anyone. If I come back and reincarnate, I want to be a Libra, though. They just seem to have it all together."

I even loved her babble. I never listened to women when they babble but her…I could listen all day, especially since she used her hands to describe stuff while she talked.

"I don't believe in all that stuff, I'm more of a, 'I have to see it to believe it' type," I explained.

"Typical Leo. I understand how you feel, though. I just like thinking something magical could happen at any moment. I'm going to study nursing, but I thought about Astronomy."

"That's like, total opposites."

"I have trouble with decisions. What about you?"

"I'm studying marketing and finance. I love it." I felt a rush of excitement and decided to go on. "Don't tell anyone but I actually plan to transfer for a semester."

"Oh, yeah? Where?"

"Sweden. My grades are awesome, and they are *so* cost effective out there. It's been my silent plan for months."

"Does Todd know?" she asked as she set her hands near the heat. I noticed she had an arrow tattooed on her wrist. It was cute. An unprofessional spot but cute. I love tats and intend to get pretty inked up myself. When mom can't beat me for it, so long after I leave the country.

"No, only Mom," why did I even tell her?

"Your secret is safe with me. That's great. You just plan to up and move to Europe, then?"

"Yeah, nothing's keeping me here." We were silent for a long time and then I just had to ask. "So, what's up with you and my brother? He talks about you all the time and you guys have been joined at the hip since I left for college. Are you guys like…" I waggled my brows and she laughed.

"No, no, no, he's my best friend in the world. I even just tried hooking him up with one of my friends."

"Okay…" I turned into campus and slowed down, more than I needed to. I didn't really want her out yet. "I'll help you carry these in," I said when we finally made it.

She said thanks then busied herself with her rings, twisting and turning them. When I pulled up, I hurried out to get her door. However, men don't do that anymore so just as I made it around, she swung the door open with pretty impressive force and it smacked into me so hard I lost my footing in the mud and fell on my back.

I heard her yelp and jump out to check on me, banging it into my knees this time. She bent down by my head and covered her mouth while she panicked.

"Oh, my God, oh, my God, I'm so, so, sorry! I didn't see you come over! Are you okay?"

"Embarrassed, winded, a little turned on but okay."

She frowned, "Turned on?"

"I don't want to sound like a sleaze, but I can see up your skirt."

She bugged her eyes and shot up before slipping back and falling forward when she overcorrected. She fell on my chest which made me laugh harder.

"You have got to be the biggest klutz I ever met," I laughed.

"I know, I think I'm cursed," she came off me and we stood.

"It's cute."

She rolled her eyes as the rain suddenly quit. We looked up as the drops came to a perfect halt.

I looked down before she did and let myself stare. Then I tugged the drawstring of her coat till she looked at me. "Guess this *is* lucky," I said.

"I think you're right."

	We just looked at one another and I actually felt like risking kissing her. Twenty minutes with a stranger and I already just wanted to try tasting her, crazy thing was I sensed she might want me to.

	I broke the moment and turned to get her bags. She pulled a directory out of her deep coat pockets and stared at it for way too long as she pulled back her hood. I stared again.

	"Here," I slung her backpack over my shoulder and held out my hand. She gave it over. "Okay, yeah I know where this is. Follow me." I handed it back.

	"How? It's like a rat maze."

	"I've uh…been around the girl's dorms plenty."

	She caught my meaning and raised her brows, "Boast much?"

	"Proud Leo Lion…"

	We talked more as we went and joked. She was so different and so full of beauty even though she talked like she was racing herself. Funny how I followed fine, she had a zest for everything, so her enthusiasm was refreshing.

	When we came to her door she worked to get it open with her key but kept looking back at me as she talked. Once inside, we found it empty on her half. No furniture except for a bed and nightstand with a single lamp on it and it was so dim the bulb must be dying. Her roommate's side was full, colorful, and decorated.

	I blew out air, "Well, this sucks-."

	"It's perfect!" She went in and took a turn around the place. "Look at all the space on my side."

	"You mean emptiness?"

	"I have a roommate but still!"

	"You didn't bring anything for the room, though you'll have to use the generic covers and you have no blankets-."

	"I'm fine it's easier to clean, really." She looked out her window and I smiled to myself. Then there was a chirping and she screamed bloody murder before leaping ten feet back. "Cricket!" she yelled, just as it jumped out from under the bed, beneath the sill. At seeing it, she turned and collided with me before burying her face in my chest.

"Seriously? It's just a bug."

"I'm terrified of bugs. Even the word *bugs*! Okay! Okay. Gahh, I'm so freaked out, get it, get it, get it, *please* get it. Oh, God is it looking at me? Is it coming?"

My cheeks were hurting from smiling as I set down her things and held her to me before looking past her. "Alright, I'll go get it."

"Wait!" She went behind me but hugged me to her chest and I could feel her trembling. "Wait, promise you'll catch it? Don't tease me with it okay? I'm not being a girly girl to be cute, I'm actually terrified."

"I'm not gonna tease you, I promise."

She held me tighter and I covered her hands over my stomach. They were soft, warm, and full of electricity. She had a few rings on almost every finger.

"I'll be right back," I said.

She slowly released me, so I made my way over to the shiny, dark bug that was chirping away on the floor.

I lifted my foot to stomp it while she huddled against the wall, but before I could come down on it, she gasped, "Oh, no stop!" she screamed, and I froze. She held her chest, "Don't *kill* it. It's a soul. It's not his fault I'm a nut case. It could be Abraham Lincoln reincarnated."

"It could also be Hitler."

"Yeah, but we aren't supposed to deliver Karma, the universe does."

"You're freaked out enough to need an inhaler but not so much you want it dead?"

"No, Mother Nature gave him purpose. I just want him to fulfill it outside. Please…Chris, please just take it outside. Toss him out the window; this is only the first floor, he should be okay, right?"

I licked my lips and held back a laugh as I stooped down to scoop up her nightmare. I caught him on the first try and she freaked out and covered her eyes while making silent squealing noises. I tossed him out the cracked window then shut it. When I looked over she was still muttering to herself about *being okay*, and *please don't let it touch me*.

I stepped light to cross the distance and let myself get very close. I took her hands from off her eyes, but she had them closed tight. I leaned so I could talk in her ear. "Hey, he's gone."

"Are you sure?"

"Yep, he's outside making music."

She opened her eyes and met mine like she'd known exactly where to find them. My heart sped up and took in every detail of her face.

"Thanks," she breathed.

"That will be $800 dollars please."

She laughed but then set her back into the wall and glanced around the dorm.

"Would you check for more before you go?"

An excuse to stay longer? Hell yes! I nodded before leaving to check under everything, including her absent roommate's bed. I rationalized many times while I searched that this was my brother's best friend, but my body was still buzzing. When I turned from checking the closet to see her taking off her coat, I groaned inside.

She had a very short, plaid skirt on that stopped way above her knees with a charcoal sweater. Her black knee-highs made me realized how long and slender her legs were when she stepped out of her boots.

She caught me looking and I took a sharp jerk to my right that caused me to knock my head into the closet door. *Fuck!*

"You okay?" she asked.

"Yeah, just…very off my game."

She giggled.

"That's not helpful," I explained.

She stopped but the mirth was in her eyes. She turned back to the case she had on the bed and sorted things on the mattress. I came up behind her and paused like a creeper. It was like her body had some kind of magnet on it. I had to orbit close.

"Are you all good now?" I tried.

"I think so," she faced me but didn't try to put space between us. Her body was telling me. She even stepped closer.

I set my hands on my hips, "Okay, good. Right. Well. I have stuff…I'm going to go back to my frat house and you'll be here, doing good, right?"

She looked at my mouth and then my eyes, "Sorry, what?"

"I said…" huh…what had I said…? "Something about you being okay now…?"

"Oh," she looked at my lips again. Was that an invite? "I'm sorry, what now?"

I grinned, and we laughed. I tried again, "I said-."

She pushed up on her toes and fell into me to press her lips over mine. There was the strongest surge of reality sweetening her lips, like she was rooting me to the moment so that I felt more alive than ever. I didn't worry about how it might seem, I just wrapped my arms around her waist and pressed her closer into me. Her body was perfect; it felt amazing under my hands and against my front.

"Hey," I said breaking the kiss. "What's going on?"

She looked dazed and dizzy and I wanted to devour her on the spot for it. "Sorry," she held the front of my coat. "I believe in seizing the moment. I'm a little impulsive. I just…I wanted to know what would happen if I tried that. Is that weird? Should I have not-? Ugh, I really didn't think it out, I just felt-."

I put my mouth down on hers. God, she was cute. The most adorable, hot mess on the planet and I had to keep touching her. I slanted and chanced pressing the tip of my tongue into the line of her lips, requesting entry and she surprised me by gripping my coat front tighter and parting her lips. She fed me her tongue as I glided over hers and the taste woke up my entire body. The floor spun as she wrapped her arms around my neck. I crushed her to me and straightened to find I'd lifted her toes off the floor.

Jenzy pulled her neck back and looked at me, "Wanna stay?"

"Yeah," I kissed her again. "No, wait!" I pulled back. "How old are you?"

"Eighteen. You?"

"Twenty."

I kissed her again, at least she was legal. Fuck, she was legal; I set her on her feet, so I could glide my hands down her sides. "Mmm," I moaned. "This is weird."

"Not really, our signs are compatible and-,"

I parted my legs a little and bent my knees, so I could press her into me and push my face into her neck.

She took a breath, "And…"

I nuzzled the skin at her nape and breathed her in. Her scent was making me crazy! Vanilla and rain.

She kept trying, "And the-."

I smiled behind her ear and pressed a kiss there, "Is this what it takes to make you stop talking?" I checked.

"Yeah," she gasped when I dared tasting her here. My tongue made a wet line from the bottom of her lobe to the top and she shivered in my hands. "Again…" she demanded. I moved down her neck and she offered more skin by extending it sideways. I made a fine circle with my tip then flickered over her like she was too hot to linger on. She groaned, and her breathing hiked.

Common sense hit me, "Okay, hold up." I stepped away from her and she wavered on her feet. "We *just met* like an hour ago and Todd is gonna freak. And what's with you? Do you have no sense of stranger danger?"

She formed an 'o' with her lips when she thought of my brother, but the sight was giving me great mental pictures.

She nodded, "Yeah, that's wrong. Besides, like you said, I don't know you, there's the whole stranger danger."

"I *just said*- never mind, whatever, exactly."

"Okay."

She wasn't begging me to stick around like most girls; that was annoying.

"I'm going to head out, then," I said.

"Thanks for the ride."

"Sure." I stared until she laughed at me. I went to the door but then turned on my heel to kiss her cheek. Damn it! Getting too close sucked me into her atmosphere. When she tried to step back I slipped my arm around her waist and laid another one on her lips. She dug her fingers into my hair and breathed into my mouth.

"Okay bye," I let go too fast, so she almost fell again. I took long strides to the door and she started my way. "Nope!" I pointed at her with a look. "Stay over there- stay put."

She giggled. Damn it! When she covered her mouth, I lost control and came back in to grab her face and kiss her. I ran my tongue over her bottom lip, it was so full. I needed to bite it. No! I needed to stop. I needed to get the hell out of this room! I pulled my head back and angled her face up to look.

"You have me spelled or something," I thought aloud.

She laughed and held up her wrist, "No but this is a Rose Quartz bracelet and they say it has an energy that-."

I claimed her mouth again. Her little hippie babble was turning me on. She kissed me back with force and unzipped the front of my coat. I let go of her with my hands but not my mouth to take it off and she helped. When it hit the floor, I held her waist before sliding south to cup her ass over the skirt. Grade A ass! Whoa! What am I doing?

"This is really stupid," I said.

"We can stop."

I groaned like a kid having his bike taken away. "We should," I let go and bent to get my coat.

She watched me with wide eyes on alert for my next attack, I guess. She pressed her lips together and I remembered I hadn't bitten that lip yet. Well, I had to do that. No, I didn't.

"Good night," I clipped.

She gave a short wave and stood on her toes, "Good night."

I walked out with a grumble and shut the door behind me. Good. I made it outside her room. It's clear sailing from here. I was halfway down the hall when I stopped and went back. She opened the door too quickly after I knocked, so she must've been standing there.

    I saw her and my whole existence depended on touching her, "Fuck Todd," I said before throwing myself on her. She tried to laugh but I had her mouth and I sucked her lip into my mine, so I could bite it the way I wanted. Her soft flesh gave way under my teeth.

    When we made it to the bed she took herself away to knock all her things off and onto the floor before laying back on it. Sloppy little thing but I dig it. I fell on her body and held her thighs apart to grind my hips into her.

    "Just tonight," I said as I stripped her of her sweater. She wasn't wearing a bra and I felt my mouth go dry.

    She came up on her elbows under me, to push my shirt up too, "Deal," she gasped.

Chapter Six
Present Day
CHRIS

*O*kay, so after reminiscing I started making a practical list in the car of reasons why she might leave me.

One: It was true we hadn't had sex in way too long, especially after that memory. Why the fuck wasn't I on her nightly or at least weekly? I could change that, I wanted her more than ever now.

Two: I was blocking her out lately. I was so involved in my world I really hadn't stopped to see her unless she was annoying me, which she does do. Often.

Three: Hmm…

I batted angrily at the evil eye charm she had dangling from my rearview mirror. Apparently, it was supposed to "protect" me or the car or whatever.

Okay, so maybe three: was, I'm not respectful of her shit.

I didn't reach four until I got home and went in; lights out and a strange empty echo of nothingness. It ruined my appetite, so I shut off her crockpot and went upstairs. One look at our bedroom and I realized why I hadn't thought up a number four. All traces of Jenzy were gone and all the times she annoyed me seemed pretty petty.

The rocks I chastise her about leaving on every surface are gone. The incense burner smell is gone and replaced with some kind of car-like room freshener. There's no multi-colored quilt of the zodiac on the bed; hair ties that usually pepper my own dresser along with Bobbie pins- gone. She normally has five outfits in the lineup for her day because she's an indecisive creature, but she never puts them away because she's also a messy one.

The chair she lays them all over is empty. No heeled shoes by the closet. It's like a nightmare.

Our bedroom has glossy beige walls and dark furniture. The bedspread is my style, clean and crisp white with gold designs and lots of decorative pillows. Her gesture of folded laundry on the *made* bed was making my head pound.

I went into the bathroom to strip but stopped when I saw a new pack of razors on the sink. Her silent message of 'I'm sorry.' Only one toothbrush, no curling iron, no hemp soap, no wet towel on the floor, no lace panties hanging to dry…

I smacked the razors off the sink and splashed my face with cold water. All these opposites of hers that drive me nuts are suddenly gone and making me feel like I have the flu. Missing her is making my whole-body ache.

Come to think of it, my chest feels tight too. Great. Now I can't breathe. Well, fuck.

JENZY

I got a call at around ten while I was sitting with Todd and his wife Mandy. She'd made a late breakfast dinner and as we sat at the table, I silenced my phone without looking.

"Was that him?" Mandy asked as she slid an omelet onto my plate. Todd's wife Mandy was a sliver taller than he was with bright green eyes and dirty-blonde hair. They looked like family and their duplex home was filled with baby things everywhere. Even in the middle of the table, sat a toy truck.

"I didn't look," I told her.

"Stupid, selfish, son of a bitch," she grumbled.

Todd talked with a mouthful of bacon, "Hey. That's *my* stupid brother you're talking about."

"So?" Mandy challenged him with a look. "He's being stupid. Stupid, stupid, stupid."

I poked at my food, "He isn't stupid, Mandy, we just aren't fit for each other anymore."

"You started moving your stuff out a week ago and he hasn't even noticed! That's ridiculous and it has to hurt, don't lie," Mandy demanded.

"Maybe, I was hoping he would notice but it just proves this was the right decision."

Mandy shook her head, "It's a late one. He's forgotten your birthday twice, he's critical of everything that makes you, who you are, he hasn't been intimate in years, he puts down your work, and he did that horrible thing at the-."

"Don't," I froze at the memory and swallowed hard around the lump in my throat. "Please, don't bring that up."

We all went awkwardly silent. Todd rubbed the center of my back which didn't help because now I want to cry.

He sighed then said, "I know you don't want to talk about it but I really want to know what happened this last time."

I pushed my food away as Mandy sat across from us and flipped on the baby monitor that also allowed us to see the two little ones they had. I looked up at Mandy and gave her the okay with my eyes. I hadn't told Todd the deciding factor of why I was leaving Chris. All the little reasons added up on their own, but this last happening was the breaking point.

Mandy looked to Todd and took down the pissed front to seem more sympathetic, "The week Jenzy called to say she was moving in with us…right after that incident where she started sleeping on the couch…?"

Todd looked between us, "Yeah?"

"Chris had some really important office party. It was a big deal."

"Oh, right," he nodded, "I remember, it was the black-tie affair at that enormous hotel. He was being recognized and all that. No spouses allowed, type a deal."

Mandy checked how I was doing but I didn't look because it still stung pretty badly.

She shifted then went on, "Four days before it was held, she got a call from one of Chris' coworker's wives asking what she was wearing. She wanted to borrow some jewelry… for the event…" Mandy waited to see if Todd would figure it out.

"How come she could go and not Jenzy if it was a no spouse…" he slowly faded out his question then looked at me like I'd lost a race. "Oh, man…"

I shrugged like it didn't bother me anymore, "She flipped when she realized I hadn't heard, the co-worker's wife…." I told him. "I was the only wife in the company that wasn't going. When I asked him about it, I didn't tell him she called. So, he lied again and told me they didn't allow spouses. He really just didn't want me to go."

Todd crossed his arms and exchanged silent looks with Mandy. After too long a silence I laughed nervously, "I mean, let's face it, I probably *would* embarrass him. Look at me. I'm like, a hippie you know? I'm- I wouldn't have fit in."

Todd was about to argue when my phone buzzed again, and I checked it.

It was some weird number I didn't know, so I picked up since this was the second time, "Hello?"

I felt all the blood drain from my face when the woman on the other line informed me, as his wife and emergency contact, my husband was in the ER. I wrestled with a train wreck of feelings and fear as I repeated her words, so Mandy and Todd would know what was going on. We all jumped up and I hurried for my purse on their hall tree.

Todd took his keys from the table, "Mandy stay here with the kids, I'll drive Jenzy up to the hospital."

Mandy kissed his cheek and hugged me quick for encouragement before we darted out the door.

When we got in the car I had to sit leaning forward with my head in my hands. I felt like I might pass out.

"What would be wrong with Chris?" I asked. "Nothing's ever wrong with him, Todd. He's fit and healthy, and, and, holy shit, it's Chris!"

"Alright, just calm down, we'll know more when we get there. He's alright, he's gonna be alright."

Ugh, now I felt bad. Chris was my husband, but he was Todd's brother. I took Todd's hand for him and for myself and we didn't talk the rest of the way. Once at the hospital, we both leaped from the car and ran into the ER. I word vomited all over the nurse at the desk about my husband being brought in. I might have given her his social security number thinking it would make her find him faster. Todd put his arm around me before taking over and she found Chris pretty quickly after.

We had to walk down a long hall, finding him behind one of the many dividing curtains. He was lying on the bed with his shirt open. I rushed over and framed his face in my hands before kissing his cheek and stroking his hair back.

"Chris? Are you okay? Can you hear me? Babe, please…"

Chapter Seven
JENZY

*H*is eyes popped open and he brought his hand up to cup the back of my head, "Hey…" he sounded so out of it and gruff that a tear slipped from my eye.

Todd came up on his other side and touched his shoulder, "What happened, bro? You scared us bad."

Chris pulled his eyes from mine and gave Todd a weak looking fist pump, "I don't know, man I had chest pains and they said it was like a heart attack…like apparently, my heart has issues."

"What?" I asked as my eyes went wide. "Aren't you- what if- I can't even think straight. Is this my fault? Is it because I left? Chris? H-how did-?"

He squeezed my hand tighter, "Don't do that, it's not your fault. I was thinking about you being gone and how empty life was… then my chest like…I mean, he did say broken hearts are real, in a health way…"

"Hello," interrupted the doctor as he strolled in with his clipboard.

We all looked up and I straightened but kept Chris' hand in mine.

The doctor smiled, "How are we, Mr. Clark?"

Chris held my hand tighter, "Okay… now anyway."

I feel really confused. He cares that much? Enough to nearly have a heart attack? Where was all that caring all this time?

The doctor made some notes, "Good, because that was a pretty bad anxiety attack."

I frowned. When I looked at Todd, he was frowning too.

Todd stepped up, "Wait, I thought it was his heart?"

The doctor looked up over wide frame glasses and scratched his thinning gray hair, "Are you, family?"

"I'm his wife," I nodded, "and this is his brother. Go ahead, what now?"

Chris' hand went really still, and I suspiciously slanted him a look.

"Your husband suffered a common anxiety attack is all. With a little relaxation and some of the things I'm prescribing here, he should be fine."

I cut my eyes and looked down at the deceitful little shit.

Chris rolled his eyes and I wrenched my hand from his.

"He said his heart was troubled," I clarified.

The doctor narrowed one eye on Chris then looked back up at me, "Your husband is healthy as an ox, Mrs. Clark, this was just a run of the mill panic attack, which can be scary, especially the first time, but it's treatable."

Todd swore, "Are you fucking kidding me? You just said you had heart problems," he ranted at Chris.

Chris crossed his arms, "The symptoms mirror a heart attack, my chest was way too tight."

The doctor made some more notes, "Well, that's normal…." he murmured.

Chris looked about ready to kill the doctor, but I was about ready to kill *him*.

"Christopher," I looked down at him and set my hands on my hips, "This isn't something to fake or joke about; you put me through hell on my way here."

"I didn't have chest pains because I was out of razors; I had them because you left me for no fucking reason!" Chris argued.

"No reason? Chris, we aren't a couple anymore, you don't even know I exist."

"Sure, right, I don't notice you. Give me one good example-."

Todd bugged his eyes and jumped in, "She's been moving her stuff out for weeks, man! You didn't notice your wife's stuff was slowly going missing? If Mandy stopped laying cosmetics all over my bathroom counter or clogging up my tub with hair, I'd notice."

"Shut up, Todd," Chris threw a swift punch to his brother's midsection and Todd curled and kicked his brother's bed. Chris looked back at me, "What do you want from me? I love you and I married you. I come home every night, I provide, that's not enough to prove something? You don't just give up on a marriage. I'm not one of your Goddamn causes!"

"I didn't just give up!" I shouted back.

He snorted, "Sure, *okay*-."

I angrily came back at him, "I tried really hard to make you see me. You've completely tuned me out and I'm not bitter toward you for it. I understand that people grow apart, we can do this the healthy way."

"Nothing about this is healthy! You aren't even talking to me, damn it!"

"I tried that too! You were either too busy or on the phone or-," I mimicked his deep voice, "*God, Jenzy I need sleep. I'm about to make a call. Do you really think I want to talk about this at this time of night? Go ahead and talk, you're gonna do it anyway. Sure, whatever, fine. I'm going to the gym.*"

"I don't sound like that," he retorted.

The doctor cleared his throat and we all went still. *Shit*, we'd forgotten he was here.

He looked pretty entertained but also pressed for time, "I hate to interrupt this, Jerry Springer moment, but I need to check the patient then be on my way."

Todd stepped out of his way and I just stood and glared down at the man that I'd been avoiding this emotion with.

Anger.

I'd managed all this time to see it as two adults drifting apart and though it was sad, it was something I could heal from. Now I was starting to feel an animosity build. This asshole was willing to defend the fact that he'd been a jerk to live with. I accept all my faults. I know I'm not easy to live with, being sloppy, being unrealistic sometimes, being flighty with career choices; being new age…I understand how I'm not what he needs, why can't he see it too?

He took those gorgeous hazel eyes away and now I could breathe better.

Chris told the doctor, "I felt like I couldn't breathe."

"That's normal, the fear and stress restrict your-."

"But there was a tingling, numb feeling in my whole body. It was weird; you mean that's all…?"

"All normal…"

I gave him an arched brow due to his overreaction and he sighed before telling me off, "Listen, that's all doctors ever say. Oh, my arm fell off. *That's normal.* Oh, I was shot in the eye and can't see, *that's normal.* Hey, my ears bleed when the phone rings, *that's normal.*"

The doctor looked really close to laughing but kept his lips tight. Chris set his head back on the pillow.

"Well, dying is normal too, doesn't mean I want to do it," Chris finished.

The doctor patted his shoulder, "And you won't, not of this, anyway. Maybe an upset family planning mutiny."

The Doc handed me Chris' prescriptions and I shook my head as the man left us, "You don't need to take all these, there are natural ways to counter anxiety," I told him.

Chris snatched the paper, "I'll take the drugs."

Todd leaned his back against the wall and shrugged, "You should listen, the stuff Jenzy gives me for my insomnia works and Mandy cleared up the baby's eczema with one of her lotions."

Chris sat up and put the paper in his shirt pocket, "I think I'll trust the medical system that thousands of people use and still live to tell the tale. I don't need to blow kisses at the moon, light a red candle, and chant a spell."

I shouldered my purse, "The stuff they give you is overkill. It has its place and it *is* a help but for people that need it. You aren't prone to attacks, so you could counter it naturally. It would be better for you. Things like Chamomile tea, Green tea, Hops! Yeah, it's in beer but it won't tranquilize like it would from a tincture. Valerian…is another herb, Lemon Balm in the right amounts…. I can help, and like I said it's better for you."

"I'm not your damn problem anymore so why care?"

I felt the sting of tears but had no desire to show him. I just nodded then looked at Todd. He looked sympathetic but upset.

So, I fled, "I'm going to wait in the car…?"

Todd smiled to reassure then set a pissed off scowl on his brother.

I made it to Todd's mini-van and took in the dark silence of the car. Chris really knew how to rip my heart out from the strings.

My phone buzzed, and I hurried to search for it in my sack purse. I finally found it on the last ring and answered when I saw Moses' name.

"Hey," I ran my fingers through my hair.

"Hey, sunshine."

All the sadness ebbed from my core and was replaced by a warm, glowing feeling.

"I might have bad reception…" I warned.

"That's okay, but are *you*? You don't sound like yourself."

"Just…drama…"

"Want to talk about it?"

"What are you up to?"

"Nothing that can't wait."

I smiled. He really was perfect. Not so perfect it was creepy or made me feel less perfect, he was just perfect for me.

"I'm at the hospital-."

"What? Are you okay? What happened? What hospital?"

"No, it's not me…it was my…" should I call him husband or ex-husband? We are not divorced yet. "It was my husband."

"What happened to him? Is it serious?"

"Well, he'd have me believe so. He told me it was a heart condition…when really it was a panic attack."

Moses' laugh helped me see the comedy in it for once and not the fear or anger. "That's pretty creative," he said.

"Yeah, and morally wrong on every level."

"Cut him some slack, Jenzy losing you wouldn't be easy."

I felt my heart race when he said that. "Still, he's mean when he's out of control and this divorce takes him out of control. I tried giving him alternatives to the medical stuff they'll pump him with. He just threw that in my face."

"Everyone has their opinions and their paths. He doesn't have to see it our way. Let him steer his own ship. You have to respect his choices."

I don't like watching people be stubborn but I also know Moses is right, so I picked at the fringe on my purse. "I have a feeling he isn't going to let this divorce happen without a fight. You should know that. He acts like he doesn't even get why I'm doing this."

"He might not be acting. He might still love you. Are you sure this is what *you* want?"

I thought on that for a long moment, probably longer than I should with a guy who wants to date me. *No.* That word echoed in my head. I didn't want this, Chris was my lover, and my mate, but he also didn't see me. I didn't want to be invisible. If I thought for one minute that he wanted me as much as that first time, then no. I wouldn't go through with this.

"I don't want to be with someone who finds my breathing irritating. Someone who can't even respect my life choices. I feel like," I loathed the lump in my throat. "I feel, small, stupid, unattractive, embarrassing and unwanted with him." Oops. That might've been too much information, but Moses had become my friend; my close friend, almost like Todd. After seeing Chris tonight, I had to tell someone.

"Then it's time to move on," Moses breathed into the phone, "as long as you feel those things and you really don't think you can fix them."

"Does it suck giving a girl you want, marital advice?" I had to laugh about something or I would cry.

He laughed, "It sucks so badly."

"I'm sorry."

"No, it's okay. I just, don't understand how someone would be unable to see you, to want you for all of what you are."

"I'm flawed too, Moses. This isn't all his fault. Two sides to every story. This is a fifty-fifty break-up."

"I know that but when you love someone, you agree to love their flaws too. Even if they drive you crazy. I would absolutely *love* for you to drive me crazy."

I turned red; I could feel how red I was. "Right, the dysfunctional, damaged divorcee. You must be nuts."

"The dysfunctional makes you cute, the damage makes me want to repair, and the divorcee thing…I just see myself having a shot now, and I hate myself for that."

"Would you really date me now…? Even with all this baggage?"

"We all have exes. There isn't a time I *wouldn't* date you. I just don't want to rush you."

"Could we try it? A date I mean? I think it might be good. This divorce is late in coming I haven't felt married for two years. I just don't want to drag you into my mess, though."

"No! Seriously, drag away! Please. I would love to be dragged by you."

We laughed. He was winning me over daily.

"Okay then…"

"Can I ask now?"

I laughed, "Yeah. Go ahead."

"Great, okay, wait for it." He paused, and I covered my mouth, so I wouldn't laugh. "Hey, Jenzy…?"

"Yeah, Moses?"

"I'd like to take you to dinner next week… are you free?"

Classic clumsy Jenzy surfaced and my phone slid from my palm and between the seats. I scurried to reach it, but touch screens are tricky, and I was afraid of hitting the 'end call' button. I recovered, though once I had it to my ear.

"I need to check my schedule, but I think I could pencil you in," I said coolly.

"Dropped me, didn't you?" he asked.

I sighed, "Yes, how the hell did you know?"

Chapter Eight
CHRIS

I just got in from showing a house the next week when my doorbell rang. I threw my work case on the sofa and opened my necktie as I went to check the peephole. Then I rolled my eyes before opening the door.

"Hello, fuck face, the traitor," I said to Todd. "Should I dropkick you on my step or bring you in first?"

"You should hear me out and stop being an ass," he responded.

I gestured for him to get moving and come in, so he did. He sat at my kitchen table and I noticed he had something under his arm. He also kept bouncing his leg on the ball of his foot. A nervous tick he had since mom and our step-dad divorced when we were kids.

I reached into the fridge and opened myself bottled water. I wasn't allowed to have these when Jenzy was here. Save the planet and that shit. Penguins might choke, and polar bears might slip on my empty bottle and drown or something.

"What's your problem, *Thumper*?" I asked Todd.

He rubbed the back of his neck then cleared his throat, "Don't freak, okay?"

"Don't give me a reason. K?"

He paused then took the folder or envelope thing from under his arm and I found getting the water down was hard. I held up my hand and stepped back, "No. Don't. Damn it, Todd!"

"Listen, she said it would be better if *I* did it. You don't want the sheriff bringing them over."

"I don't want anyone bringing them over. You are such a pushover. You're my *brother*!"

"I don't want to do this, but you did this to yourself. You've been a dick to her for way too long. She's done."

"Whose side are you on?"

"I'm not on a side. I'm neutral. Like Sweden..."

"You're gonna be like Atlantis when I drown you in my sink."

"I'm serious."

"What exactly does everyone want from me? I love her, I want her, I need her, and I don't want to lose her, what do I have to do?"

"I don't think you can," he looked genuinely sorry. "She's sure about this."

"But come on," I went over to him and loomed, looming helps break Todd. I used this tactic when we were growing up. I once got him to confess to mom that he put gum in his own hair all by looming. Yeah, I did it but little brother's hair is where you put gum. "Tell me what I did."

"Didn't you guys talk?"

"She's not telling me everything. I mean, I heard about the not seeing her, ignoring her, being annoyed by her, not having sex- or I don't know, not having our usual, hot sex."

"Ugh! Seriously. Filter, Chris."

"Sorry, but just tell me. What else? She tells you all her crap."

"There was like one other thing, but it was…well, I feel like she had to be wrong. I mean, you wouldn't be that stupid."

"What? That stupid to what?"

Todd went on to tell me about the dinner. That damned award thing for best Agent of the year. As I recalled the situation, I felt my throat close up but when he told me that Jenzy had found out, I thought all the blood was going to leave my body. I'd never, ever, ever intended for her to find out about that.

"How could you do that to her?" Todd wasn't being my little brother now he was being Jenzy's best friend. "Do you know how humiliating that is? She found out from other wives. Are you actually embarrassed by her?"

"It's not like that, she just, would never...these are mainstream business people. They don't want to talk about herbs, auras, or witch doctor stuff. I did it to protect her from-."

"Bull shit," Todd stood up and slapped the papers down on my table. "You know that's bull shit. She would never embarrass you. She would turn herself inside out to make you look good. You're selfish."

"Come on-."

"No, *you* come on!" he actually raised his voice at me and though he was a head shorter, I was all ears. He ranted, "You didn't hear what Mandy and I heard. You didn't hear her asking us if she was gaining weight or seeing her go on diets, thinking she wasn't looking nice enough for you. You didn't see her buying books on saving marriages or begging you to do stuff. Take trips! I don't even know what happened. You were both so crazy about each other. You met, and it was like fireworks and cotton candy. You've been that way for years. Then these last two- you just quit? What, did you get bored with her or something? Are you having an affair?"

I leveled a dark look on him, "You really think I'd do that to her?"

"I didn't think you'd do a lot of things."

If I was going to be honest, this talk felt like a kick in the balls. Jenzy once worried she was too fat? She tried dieting? Dieting what? She's freaking perfect! She bought books? What had she been begging me to do? Get bored? I didn't get bored...what exactly did happen within two years that changed all this? I cemented my career two years ago. Was that it? I'd set a closing on the diamond of real estate and gained my reputation and my financial stability. My commission had launched me into greatness and I hadn't come down since... but that was good. What caused this divide?

"What am I supposed to do?" I asked.

"I don't know. Marriage...having a wife isn't like getting a trophy to put up on the shelf whenever. The wooing, and the effort, and the tending never stops. It does settle, and it does calm down, you don't have to hold hands everywhere. Hell, Mandy and I are lucky if we all fit in the same bed with both babies between us but…I do other things, she does too. It's a team."

I went to set my back against the wall between the living room and kitchen. I need support because my legs feel weird. I started allowing myself to see how I'd treated her these years. Jenzy hadn't changed…I loved her the night we met when this started, so if she hadn't changed, I did.

I'd dug myself a deep grave and climbing out was going to suck. I looked at the petition for divorce on my table and wished I could burn holes through it.

Being the neat freak I am, I worked out a list then verbalized it to Todd. "Alright, so…here's what I need to do… one: I need to review my awfulness, so I can stop it. I think it's becoming second nature to be an ass, so that has to stop. Two: figure out what the hell did change with me. I don't know if I even realize when I tuned her out. There's gotta be a trigger. Three: I need to win her back before this divorce shit goes too far. She's too beautiful to stay single long. I need to claim it before the ring comes off or I'm screwed."

I noticed my brother's leg was going at it again and with a sinking feeling I frowned at him, "What?" I asked. "What do you know?"

"Hmm?"

"Spit it out or I'll rip it out."

"There's nothing to tell…except…you know…" he shrugged and drummed his fingers on the table. "She's…really, really sure about this divorce."

"I know she was talking to some dude…as a 'friend,'" I stormed back over and gave him the interrogation look. Three cheers for looming. "Spill it."

He tried to hold his own but under a good two minutes of my Hawkeye stare; he folded like a house of cards.

"She may or may not have a date this Friday," he confessed.

"What?!" I screamed it and Todd startled. "How long has that been going on? Talk. Now. What the hell is she doing?"

"It's the guy she told you about. It's only been a couple weeks. This is honestly the first date. I swear he has only been as close to her as I have. He was like the new Todd…now… things might be changing since she filed…"

"Have you met this home-breaking little shit?"

"No, and that's not totally accurate."

"Where are they going?"

"Like I'm gonna tell you that. Mandy's already going to hang me by my nuts for telling you this much."

"Just tell me where. What time? What's he look like? Is he big? Big as me? Could I take him?"

"Slow down, Hulk. I really don't know. I never saw him, they just talk; they have never been out alone. Hey, I know this is hard, but she gave you her all. She needs a break. Maybe this is just a fling."

"That's worse! I don't want her to fling or be flung! I want her home."

"Then you're outta luck."

Sometime after Todd left I went up to our room. I found a lacy red bra she left behind that fell by her bedside. Not to seem too *Edward Cullen* but I brought it to my nose. She still used vanilla and somewhere between the scent and the sexy cut of the bra I got turned on. I was married to a supermodel look-alike but with better curves and eyes that didn't quit and for some odd reason, I hadn't been screwing her till she was handicapped. What was wrong with me?

I went to the wall where our wedding picture was hanging above her dresser. It was an up-close shot of me holding her face and kissing her forehead. The wind had kicked up, so her hair was swirling all around us and the auburn contrasted with the vibrant white she was wearing.

She left a book behind too. One of her Linda Goodman books about the sun signs. I picked it up.

"Oh look, crap that sells," I said aloud.

I stopped on a dime and rolled my eyes at myself. Wow, I really was an asshole. I didn't have to believe it, but did I have to sneer at it? This little book might not be for me, but it was part of what made Jenzy the woman I loved.

Out of curiosity and boredom, I slung her bra over my shoulder and searched for what this quack had to say about me, a Leo. The more I read, the more frustrated I got. It was like this weirdo knew me. Even the parts of me I wasn't too fond of were in here. My traits, my moods, my way as a worker, even a husband.

Huh…I took the picture off the wall, went to the bed and lay down with my bra, my book, and my wedding picture. If this woman was so right about me, how would she do with Jenzy?

I flipped to look for December and a searing pain in my stomach made me almost ill. I'd forgotten her birthday twice. How could I do that? That was a monumental day for us. Also, she made a big, not to mention, over the top deal about my birthday and I forgot hers. That had to kill her. It was suddenly killing me.

Chapter Nine
CHRIS

When Tuesday came along, I decided I was going to fight. I wasn't going to lose the woman that owned my heart because I'd developed into a prick. I called Todd and decided to make him my inside man, my spy.

When he answered, he sounded like a robot. "Hello…Jim…Jim from work," Todd said.

"Our wives are sitting there, aren't they?" I guessed.

"Why, yes, Jim I'm having dinner with my family."

I sighed, "You suck at lying."

"I'll get those reports in ASAP."

"Listen, you said her date was Friday night, right?"

"They are due on Friday…" A baby screamed in the background and I had to take the phone away till it stopped.

"Where are they going?" I asked.

"I can't tell you that, Jim…Corporate would see me swimming with the fishes."

Corporate had to mean Mandy, "I bet Mandy is so cheering for this guy. She's going to throw Jenzy at him."

"Not gonna lie, Jim…you aren't wrong. Corporate even plans to…redecorate so *it*…sells better."

I frowned and tried to crack that ridiculous code. "Ah ha! Shopping! They are going shopping, right?"

"That's right, Jim."

"When?" I asked.

"Tomorrow."

"Where?" I pressed.

"I don't know, Jake."

"I thought my alias name was Jim?"

"Fuck!" he hissed.

"Okay, just hang up, I got it from here."

"Don't you get me fired, Jim I'll come for you," he warned.

I laughed, "Yeah, okay, sure." Then I hung up. I knew exactly where they'd go. Jenzy dressed like a gypsy but if she was shopping with Mandy they would go to Clair's Boutique. It was a ritzy little shop downtown that looked like a mini-mall.

I finally squeezed the time out of Todd over text messages the next morning and called in sick at work. Then got in my car and drove like a speed demon to the boutique. I parallel parked two shops down and put on my sunglasses, so she wouldn't spot me. Yes, I've reached *that* level now. No pride, it's somewhere under rock bottom and one sliver above hell.

Mandy's mommy van pulled into a spot directly in front and I watched as they got out. Jenzy looked great even casually dressed. She had on a gray t-shirt with a red elephant on it. Her jean shorts were really short which drew attention to the perfect little ass she has.

She also had what I called her, 'Jesus' sandals. They just had that nomad, dessert look; like she just came back from teaching Arabic children, Chinese or something. She graced it all with her multiple bracelets, necklaces, and dangly earrings.

My little hippie.

I missed her so much that seeing her was sucking. I know that body and now I'm not really allowed to touch it.

She disappeared inside with Mandy and I got out and went in behind them. They were so into their browsing they didn't notice me while I edged closer, so I could eavesdrop.

Mandy held up a pair of lacy panties and with their backs to me, I could hear pretty well. I went on the other side of a display and listened.

"What about these," Mandy held up the undergarment and quirked her brow.

Jenzy took them and put them back, "I'm here for a dress, not underwear."

I almost said, 'Thank God,' out loud but caught myself.

Mandy picked up another pair, "Honey, you can't sleep with a guy in underwear another guy has seen. It's bad oogie boogie."

"Well, Chris in all fairness hasn't seen my underwear in two years so…"

Not true. I'm sleeping with your bra. I swallowed that. I really was an idiot.

"That's not the point," Mandy went on, "It will make you feel sexy and this guy…even from the pictures; I can tell you won't make the first date."

I bit my fist to keep from shoving Mandy into a dressing room and keeping her good and locked up. She never liked me, the bitch.

"Nothing is happening on the first date," Jenzy denied.

"You and Chris did it in the first meeting."

"That was different. We…were different. I'm not ready to sleep with someone else. This is just dinner and this guy knows that."

Mandy set her arm around Jenzy, "Okay but you still need new stuff. It's good for the soul."

They migrated away from the evil underwear and started perusing the mannequins dressed in tight sexy dresses. This was like friggin torture.

Jenzy closed in on a skin tone-colored dress that had slits on each side and beading at the low neck. She would look naked; it was that close to her skin color, she would look like a naked goddess. I stretched my neck to look.

"What do you think?" she asked Mandy and pulled out the quarter sleeve.

Mandy came over and raised her brows, "Nice. Very sexy. He said to dress up, right?"

"Yeah…"

"Why aren't you letting him pick you up, by the way?"

"Chris used to do that. I'm trying to make sure it's all different. No similarities so I don't feel weird."

"I understand," Mandy touched the bodice of the dress. "Wear this, though and trust me, you'll get laid."

Jenzy hugged herself and sighed, "Maybe this was a bad idea. It's too soon."

"What? No, you haven't been with Chris in years. You just lived together and fought. It's totally time to move on and this guy is amazing."

Jenzy sucked her bottom lip and stared at the dress. I think I'm begging her in my mind not to do this. She belongs to me, she always has, and I can fix this if she slows down and gives me a chance.

"It's weird," she pushed her hand through her hair and exhaled loudly. "When I married Chris, I didn't ever think I'd be picking out 'first date clothes' again. I thought anniversary dinners, birthday dinners, but not dressing up for someone else."

"Yeah, well Chris forgot your anniversary and your birthday twice. How could you be that important to him if he can't even remember those special times? He has all that technology shit; he didn't think to put the dates down?"

Jenzy's eyes cleared like she was seeing Mandy's point and it felt like taking a one-hundred-foot drop to death.

"Yeah, you're right," Jenzy agreed.

"Can I help you find something, sir?" A woman to my left smiled up at me and I looked at her like she asked if I wanted a trip to Mars.

"What? No, go away," I whispered.

"We have a men's selection on the other side of the storefront," she grinned.

"Shhh!" I growled. I saw the name tag and realized I was dealing with a sales lady. "Listen, *Wanda*, I got this."

She turned on a flirty smile, "We have plenty of suits for men with sharp tastes such as yourself."

Ugh, she was into me. She wasn't ugly, but she wasn't Jenzy. She was also going to alert my wife and sister-in-law that I was here.

I tried again, "Look, I don't need help. Not the kind you can give, anyway. Go fold something, I'm fine."

"Are you sure, sir? We have matching vest and necktie sets for just-."

"Will you please just go away! Shoo! Get away from-!"

"Chris?" Jenzy's voice made me freeze. *Shit*! I looked up over the rack to see her and Mandy glaring at me.

"What-? Oh, my God! What are the chances?" I tried to sound natural, but I think I sounded like I was on some caffeine high. "What are you guys doing here? Are you shopping? A-are ya just, like buying stuff? What's up?"

"Nice try, asshole," Mandy shot at me. "Were you spying on us?"

"Spying? No! I would never do that. That's weird. That's- that would be like crossing a line," I said.

Jenzy came up beside Mandy, "Why are you here?" she asked softly.

"Ties," I said what came to mind. "Ties…and….and…matching vest sets. Yeah, Wanda here was just about to show me these things of greatness."

Wanda frowned, "You told me to go away."

I laughed and loudly, "No, no, you are so funny, Wanda. I told you to go away…and get me those neckties. The ones with the matching vests…I'm really on board for all that."

Wanda gave me a look but then I filled her simple head with my sizes and winked. Somewhere in there, she returned to flirting and dropped it before leaving.

Jenzy looked at Mandy and then me.

I put my hands on my hips, "So what about you guys? What are we shopping for?" I asked.

Jenzy avoided my eyes, "It's personal, Chris."

"A date," Mandy was all too happy to tell me. "Jenzy has a date and she needs a new dress, so we are here to find one."

Jenzy knocked her elbow into Mandy but Mandy was too busy gloating.

"A date?" I tried so damn hard to sound nonchalant, but it sounded really strained even to my own ears. "Wow, so, so, there's… a guy…right? A date," I ran out of air on the word 'date' so it sounded more like 'a day.'

Jenzy was looking at me with a twinge of guilt and some acceptance, "It's the guy I told you about," she clarified.

"I remember." I searched for a recovery plan. "So what dresses are we looking at?"

She frowned, and Mandy made an annoying noise like a snort, "We aren't shopping with you; are you crazy?" Mandy snapped.

I went around it, "But see, Jenzy, made it clear when she told me she wanted a divorce that she wanted to be friends. Friends shop together."

"Not when that friend is her ex-husband," Mandy fought.

"She's not technically my ex yet."

"That's even more fucked up. Her husband, helping her pick out a dress for her date?" Mandy grimaced.

"I can offer valuable advice," I went and turned the mannequin wearing the naked dress, "Like for instance. This particular dress would be all wrong for a first date."

Mandy was about to snap but Jenzy looked at the dress then up at me and asked, "Why?"

"Well, for one," I slung my arm over the dummy's shoulders. "This color is basically skin, so it leaves like, nothing to the imagination. Guys like mystery. You are killing the mystery. Second," I tapped the beading on the low bodice. "This clearly says 'trying too hard' which is a major turn off. The slits? That's just slutty."

Jenzy was eating it up but that damned Mandy.

Mandy shoved my shoulder, "Bull…shit…don't even go there. Men just wanna have sex. You dogs aren't complicated enough to break down a woman's clothes like that. The brain in your heads is tinier than the brain in your dicks."

I shrugged, "It's up to Jenzy."

Jenzy sucked her lip. I suddenly remembered how much I loved sucking that lip.

"This *is* kinda weird," she surprised me with that. "I don't really want you helping me pick this out."

There's a feeling you get when someone is stepping away from you. It reminds me of when you step on an enormous grate in the street and you realize you could drop your keys or your phone and there would be no getting them back. Okay, that was a lame thing to equate your wife falling out of love with you too. Never said I was a philosopher.

"Okay," I used my eyes to bore into her, to beg her not to do this, but I don't think she heard it. I let go of the dummy and pointed to the other side of the store where Wanda was collecting an arm full of useless clothes I didn't plan to buy. "If you need me, I'm over there."

Mandy had to take her cheap shot, "She needed you for two years, that didn't change anything."

Jenzy cut a look at Mandy and I debated retaliating but how do you argue truth? Pretending this wasn't my fault was going to cost me Jenzy and that wasn't worth it.

I looked at Jenzy and drew her in with my eyes. "That's…true," I admitted.

She looked mildly affected to hear me say that. Then I went to pretend to shop while I watched them pull outfits that made me sweat. Jenzy went behind the curtained dressing room while Mandy went to find shoes and I decided to take my chances.

I checked my reflection while Wanda was busy ringing up shit I didn't need. I think I agreed to buy stuff. I don't remember.

My tie was on loose so the tip of the tattoo that crept up my neck was showing, and my jacket was on a hook at the front desk. That worked, though because Jenzy loved my build. I popped open my vest and rolled up my sleeves, so more tats were showing.

I made my way to the women's dressing room area like this was Mission Impossible to avoid Mandy, but she was pretty occupied with shoes. I went to Jenzy's curtain door and actually felt nervous. I had to change her mind on all this.

"Hey, how's it going?" I asked.

She opened the curtain enough, so I could see her face, "Chris! Go away."

"I'm just checking on you. First dates are hard. There's so much tension. If you don't find the right dress, it could set the whole relationship to hell."

"Chris, please don't make this worse."

"I'm not," I caught her looking at my chest and some confidence returned. "I'm seriously trying to help. You said we could be friends, I thought you meant it."

She eyed me a while, "Can you get Mandy?"

"Why, what's up?" I stood at full attention.

"Nothing, I just need her for the zipper."

"I can do it."

She looked at me flatly.

"Oh, come on, Jennifer, I've zipped you up for seven years."

"We can't cross boundaries. We aren't a couple. Speaking of which, our lawyers made an appointment to settle the dividing of stuff, or whatever it's called, did you ever agree on a date?"

"Monday."

"Thank you."

Long, awkward, painful, silence, "Just let me help, it's no big deal."

She reluctantly opened the curtain, so I could come in. I almost high-fived myself. Until I saw what she was wearing. A strapless, sleeveless, mint-colored dress that made her look like a sprite. The skirt ruffled and laid over her legs to stop just above her knee. The front pushed her breasts all the way up. It hurt. It hurt to look.

She turned her back to me and I tried to focus. I need to make this sensual, anything to remind her why she didn't need to do this.

I brushed her hair aside and set it over her shoulder but slow enough to feel her skin. Her hair is thick and silken to the touch and smells amazing. She just washed it, I can tell.

I can see her shoulder blades and the smoothness of her back is making me crazy. If any guy saw this, he'd want her. *Think fast, think fast.*

I pulled up the zipper, dying a little to notice she wasn't wearing a bra. As I grasped the zipper and made the slow climb upward, I saw my chance and took it. With an easy turn of my wrist the dainty gold pull, snapped off.

"Oh, no," I feigned sadness, I'm actually pretty good.

She held the front to her chest, "What? What happened?"

"Zipper broke."

"What?" She turned to see it in the mirror, "How? Are you kidding? I liked this one."

"It's a real shame. It was nice on you."

"Yeah, and the only one in my size."

Cue *Evil villain laugh.* "Damn. What are the chances?" I asked.

She was about to say something when the curtain opened to Mandy, "What the hell are you doing in here?" Mandy whisper shouted.

"She needed help with the zipper," I defended.

Jenzy blew out a frustrated breath, "And look," Jenzy showed her the zipper pull in my hand. "It broke. Just my luck."

Mandy pouted, "That's okay, honey we have six others."

I sided out as Mandy handed Jenzy shoes but then Mandy closed the curtain and slapped at my back and shoulder. "You manipulative, ass wipe!"

I shielded myself then stepped out of reach, "I don't appreciate your accusations, lady."

"You broke it. You're trying to sabotage her date. I'm on to you, ya worm."

"Whatever. Can't prove shit."

"You only have yourself to blame for this. She gave you everything she had."

"What if I get that and I want to fix it?"

"Ha! You just don't like seeing something you consider 'yours' being in someone else's hands. You are as bad as my toddler with his blocks."

Jenzy called to Mandy, "How about this one?"

We both looked her way. She stepped out in a way shorter black dress. This one was sewn by Satan. It was a skater dress with another heart-shape front; propping up her bosom. It was unsuccessfully hidden behind a thin veil of mesh. When she turned, we found it was open backed in the shape of a long and lace diamond. Black stilettos were the cherry atop this wicked Sunday and in my head, I screamed like a teenage girl seeing a spider. That dress was going to be my friggin demise if she wore it out.

Mandy grinned, "It's perfect!"

And I spoke at the same time, "Fat, makes your thighs look fat."

Jenzy turned to stare at me with owl-wide eyes and Mandy turned her neck in a slow, Praying Mantis way to glare. That was my only weapon. My last hand grenade. So, I continued to toss the fucker.

"Yeah, it's flared in a way that…makes your…hips look…wider. You're so slim that… the flare…is misleading…it's…unflattering…" I think I should buy a tux from here, so I die pretty because they both looked ready to kill me.

Mandy faced me, "If you don't pay for your shit and leave in five seconds, she'll be wearing your hide for a dress."

Chapter Ten
JENZY

I knew the second it left his lips that he was just trying to get in my head, but I'm still a girl. He hit the Achilles heel.

Weight.

There was no buying that enchanting dress with that sprouting seed of doubt.

It's okay, though because soon after Mandy threatened him, and Chris left, we found the most perfect dress ever. I even hung it on the back of my closet door, so I could stare at it. Now I was super ready for Friday night, even if I was also terrified. Seeing Chris at the shop had me all jittery. He had this annoying habit of looking hot as hell even when he was a mess. The tease of seeing his hidden tattoos under his suit instantly had me hot, but he wasn't mine anymore and I had to stop letting myself go there.

Mandy took me to the salon on Friday and that was a boost. Manicures and pedicures atop a hairstyle that made me feel ready for the red carpet were all I think I needed. I didn't look like my regular hippie self by the time I got the dress on. I looked like I had come alive.

I imagined Moses' reaction and flushed but then like a gnat in my mind, I imagined Chris if he could see me. I thought of how he used to react when I dressed up and my heart did a free fall. He used to eye me like prey and attack me like we had nowhere to go. Not anymore.

Last few times I tried doing this for him, I got a *"that's not new, haven't you worn it? How much was it?"* Or no notice at all. Not tonight. Tonight, someone was going to notice, and I was going to enjoy it.

CHRIS

I saw my brother on the opposite side of the street from his house as he buckled in his older son, Connor. I sprinted that way while keeping an eye on his duplex. I didn't need to get caught. Mandy was tiny compared to me but mighty.

    Just as Todd was about to get into his driver side I rushed him, "Move over," I whispered demandingly.

    He jumped, "Jesus Christ! You scared the shit outta me! What-?"

    "Shut up and get in the car. Move," I shoved him in and he swore at me as he awkwardly scooted and climbed from the driver to passenger side. I groaned, "Hurry up! Your dad bod is going to get us caught."

    "What are you doing sneaking around my house at eight o' clock at night?"

    I got in the car behind the wheel and shut the door. "Hey, little buddy," I reached back to give my nephew a fist pump. He had to be the coolest four-year-old ever. Even with a speech impediment that made him sound like a jungle creature.

    "Answer me!" Todd huffed.

    I turned my back to him and pulled my binoculars to peer into his house. "I want to see what she settled on dress-wise, where this guy's taking her, and who he is."

    "Have you gone crazy? You can't spy on Jenzy, that's wrong and weird."

    I ignored him and kept watch on the door, "I'm not spying; I'm looking out for her. What if this guy is out to take advantage? What kind of guy dates a woman in the middle of a divorce?"

    "Uh, in college before you met Jenzy, you dated two married teachers and a single mom."

    "Don't live in the past, Todd."

    "He's sending a cab to pick her up. She didn't want to drive with him. Not to mention, he's more a biker like her."

    "Probably broke," I assumed.

A taxi glided down the street and pulled up in front of Todd's. I adjusted my binoculars.

"Where'd you get those?" he asked.

"They are Jenzy's, from when she went through her 'bird watching' phase."

"Okay… I had somewhere to go. Connor and I have father son-."

I interrupted him, "Shhh! I see movement."

He sat back and mumbled as I studied the two women through the heavy glass front door.

I frowned and rushed to turn down the window. I hit the locks a bunch of times in my haste but once the window was open, I held up the binoculars and looked.

I sighed, "Who is Mandy talking to?"

"What?" Todd leaned forward and looked over my shoulder. "There is no one else but her and Jenzy in the house."

"No, the chic in the hall; with her back to us, red dress..."

"I see her. It's Jenzy."

"Jenzy's hair isn't that short. It comes down to her hips."

"No, man she cut it to the middle of her back. They went to the salon today. They made it all shiny and wavy and stuff."

I peered harder. It was down but the sides were braided and pulled back like from a medieval book with a jeweled barrette holding them in place at the back of her head. That wasn't Jenzy. Jenzy didn't wear jeweled shit or red. As she backed toward the door, I tensed. Then she turned around and came out the door.

"*Ohhh… shit!*" I said.

Todd pushed closer, "Holy crap! She looks fan-fucking-tastic," he whispered so Connor wouldn't hear.

I took the binoculars down to stare at my wife. "I am… so… fucking screwed."

Jenzy was wearing a skin-tight, blood-red dress with quarter sleeves and hot red heels. The front was low, and the bottom stopped mid-thigh. Her legs went on for days and her ass! When she turned to blow a kiss at Mandy I developed a twitch in my left eye. Her curves were so hugged and sheathed to perfection that I gained a ravenous desire to tear it right off her body.

My mind went there. That bad place when I realized that the only way to pull off a dress that tight was to wear a thong. Now, why? Why, God would you allow my brain to go there?

She set her little silver clutch under her arm to open the door of the cab. She was still Jenzy, so she didn't so much sit, as fall into the seat.

I turned to buckle my seat and because the car was already running, I pulled it into drive and pushed my seat back since Todd was a shorty.

"Wait, where are we going?" he flipped.

"To follow the taxi, duh," I answered.

"Chris, why agonize yourself. It's over. It's so over. Did you even see her just now?"

"Hello! That's why we're going, too. Safety. There's gonna be more men on that ass than white on rice."

"I have a thing to go to," he whined.

"Connor doesn't mind. Do you, Connor?" I asked my little buddy.

Conner giggled and yelled "Go! Go! Goooo!"

I ripped out after Jenzy's cab, "See, even your kid supports this."

"I'm not buckled, yet! Slow the hell down!" Todd panicked.

"Calm down, *mom.*"

I drove pretty scarily trying to keep up but not be seen. Todd held onto the bar above his door like we were jeeping through Africa and I think he prayed to like five different deities when I raced past an almost red light. Connor was cracking up in the back and clapping like this was the best ride ever.

Todd squeaked, "The speed limit is-."

"Jesus, Todd, don't be such a pussy! It's fine."

Connor squealed when we took a corner and yelled. "Pussyyyy!"

Todd punched my arm, "Damn it, Chris!"

"Sorry."

We slowed down and watched as Jenzy's cab pulled to a stop in front of a really shiny, new-looking restaurant. The front was all glass and you could see inside clearly. The tables were round and covered with a white tablecloth and candles. The lighting was bright but set a mood since it was lit by crystal chandeliers. The staff was wearing black and white uniforms and the place itself bore some fancy French name. There was a long drink bar further back, made of glass and everyone inside was dressed up.

"Snazzy," said Todd. "And you said he was broke." I gave him a look and he shut up. We waited, and I winced inside when I watched her take the steps. That ass. It was over. She was too hot to be loose.

We waited when we lost sight of her behind the doors. "Who is this guy?" I wondered aloud.

"I don't know, she said she met him at a bookshop," informed Todd.

"A bookshop," I mocked. "Probably some sickly-looking nerd, then. Women would screw Quasimodo if he acted understanding."

"Nah, I've seen pictures on Mandy's phone. He's pretty good-looking."

I turned to him, "Mandy has pictures?"

"I think it was to spy for Jenzy's sake, but I don't really want to know as her husband. I think you both border the same crazy."

"He as hot as me?" I asked.

"Ew, that's such a wrong question!"

"Just answer the question. Who is Batman, who is Robin?"

He hesitated, "If it came down to the two of you, it would be more like, who is Batman and who is …like…Thor."

"Why, is he blonde? How did Mandy get pictures?"

"Instagram."

I nodded then Connor yelled, "Auntie Jezzy!"

My head snapped around quickly, and Todd leaned almost on me to look. It was her. She was walking toward a table.

I scrambled for my binoculars to see who she was meeting, "Let's just see who this asshole, trying to ensnare my wife is. Fancy restaurants… what's next? A flying pony? He's probably compensating for-."

My mind went off like the inside of a firehouse.

Big red lights started flashing behind my eyes and a woman's automated voice was echoing one word, *warning, warning, warning…*

When the guy stood up to kiss her cheek I almost crushed the binoculars in my hand. I heard a *snap*. Oops. I didn't crush them, but I sure did snap them in half. I felt a rippling anger go down my spine. "Fuuuuuuck!"

Connor laughed and wiggled around in his seat singing, "Fuck, fuck, fuck…"

Todd punched my bicep again, "Chris! Filter! And why is your bicep so hard?" He cradled his hand like it hurt. "What's the deal?"

"What's the deal? What's the deal? That's Moses! That's the guy at my gym! That's-."

"The yoga instructor?" Todd questioned.

"Yes!" I shouted then went back to staring. Oh, God, this wasn't happening. Maybe I was asleep? I gawked as Moses pulled her chair out for her then sat across from her. He was in a dark suit, looking sharp. The one time I don't wear a suit. Tonight, was a spying night so I was in jeans and a long sleeve t-shirt.

"I'm going in," I said as I unbuckled.

Todd grabbed my arm, "To do what?"

"I don't know," I shoved him off; "I'll figure it out on my way up there."

"Public place, witnesses, and you're gonna what? Threaten him? Kick his ass? You're a kickboxer, it is super illegal."

"Not if I'm defending myself."

Todd snorted, "Oh, sure. Hey, officer, I dropkicked my wife's boyfriend in the throat. Oh, don't worry, he came at me with his soup spoon."

"You really think he's her boyfriend? Has she called him that?"

"That's all you heard me say?"

"He's pretended to be my friend for months! I want him to know I know and that I'm going to stop it."

"Alright," Todd sat so he was facing me and chose his words carefully. "I get how much this hurts. I can't imagine how I would feel if this was Mandy. I'd go crazy. As your brother, I know you, so even with all the sarcasm and the bravado and the muscle, I know this is…it's cutting you up."

I resented hearing understanding words. When you're blocking out pain, understanding is the bulldozer that undoes it all. Yes, this hurt but if I surrendered to that instead of anger I would never recover from this.

Then Todd said, "I also see this from Jenzy's side. If you bust in on her in the middle of dinner, she's going to be embarrassed to the core. So just, use your head, be an adult, be the bigger guy and let this go."

I nodded and stared at my lap folded in his tiny van. "Yeah, I see what you're saying," I agreed.

He smiled sympathetically and patted my back.

I pursed my lips, "It's just…" I raced the other words off my tongue. "Too bad I don't give a shit." I opened the door and slipped out before he could catch me by the shirt sleeve.

"Chris! Get back here, you crazy-," I heard him yell my name a few more times but I was busy sprinting up the steps of the place.

"Excuse me, sir," said the hostess at the desk. "This is a suit and tie-."

I walked past her and stormed further in. Seeing them together up close was making my eyes hurt and he was holding her hand across the table.

He looked up first and when he saw me he smiled before waving at me. Arrogant prick was rubbing it in my face!

Chapter Eleven
JENZY

When I came into the restaurant to see Moses waiting for me, I felt some of my nerves settle. He'd become my friend first, even in the few weeks we'd been talking. I went his way and soaked up the glory of seeing a guy as gorgeous as my husband, fawn over my appearance. He stood and touched his chest before breathing out in a gush.

"Whoa," he managed. "You're like the sun. If I stare I might go blind."

I grinned and went to him. He kissed my cheek and the blood rushed through me.

"Thank you," I hugged him briefly then let go but he kept an eye on me as he pulled out my chair at our small table.

"You nervous?" he asked.

"Does it show that badly?"

"Nothing shows on you, except beauty but I'm sure this feels strange." He really got me.

He sat across from me and I turned the ring on my finger. My wedding rings. I had meant to take them off. I had to ask. "It does…I'm sorry. Are you regretting this, yet?"

"I think if you acted perfectly fine after being with a guy for seven years, I would regret this. It just shows you are committed and not trying to replace him. Are you sure this wasn't too soon?"

"No," I reached across our table and took his hand. "I wanted this. I've been on cloud nine getting ready."

He smiled and kissed the back of my hand before stroking my forearm, "Me too."

"So, enough talk about my husband-, er, ex-husband, tell me how the bookshop is going?"

"I don't mind when you talk about him but yeah, it's going well. The finances are clearing up; dad was just adding wrong and way overpaying certain bills. I think I have it recovering now," he looked sure.

"I can't believe you're his son. I've known him for years and been going there for years, it's the best shop in town."

"We must've just been missing each other; I always go from the gym to there."

The waiter came with menus and I felt myself tense. Chris and I had a ritual for when we went out. I'm always stuck between two things because I'm terribly indecisive, but Chris knows some trick to making me pick in a timely fashion.

"You okay?" asked Moses.

I took my eyes from the menu and smiled at him. "I'm fine. This all just looks awesome," he suddenly looked up past me and smiled. I cocked my head, "What is it?"

"A guy from my gym. He's great. We hang out after and talk sometimes," he gave a little wave. "I've told him about you, this way he can see I didn't make you up."

"Really? Small world," I turned, almost eager to meet one of Moses' friends but what I saw made me want to scurry under the table and hide there for about a month. I turned back around when he set his eyes on me and started our way. "Oh, my God, this isn't happening," I whispered and rubbed my burning cheek.

Moses' brows rose, "You know Chris?"

"Yeah," said Chris. He was beside our table and I could feel the hot anger radiating from his body. "She knows me. We were roomies for like, what was it? Seven years?"

Moses frowned and looked back and forth between us, "Wait?" he said slowly.

I lifted my head, "Chris, not here."

Moses put it together, "Oh, shit."

I saw that Chris was glaring at our table and followed his line of sight. Uh, oh, the hand holding.

I snatched my hand back and turned in my seat, "I told you I was going out with someone; this isn't dishonesty or a surprise."

"You said *someone,* not my friend from the gym." He looked over at Moses and I cringed, "Are you friggin kidding me? You're banging my wife?!"

Moses put his hands up, "Hold on just a minute, Chris, I had no clue this was *your* wife. You never said anything about the two of you splitting up. You even told me this would be okay…I didn't know-."

I asked what suddenly came to mind. "How are you even here?"

Chris looked at me and cooled by a tiny microscopic bit, "I guessed."

I saw a pair of broken binoculars around his neck. "Are those mine? Were you stalking me? What's wrong with you? That's against the law."

"No, it is not." He argued, "Stalking is frowned upon, not illegal. I would have to physically threaten you first. Like," he looked back at Moses, "Like *hypothetically* if you lay one finger on my wife, I'll *hypothetically* break that finger…*hypothetically.*"

"Gahhh!" I groaned and got up before taking Chris by the arm and pulling him toward the door. It was like tugging along a tree, he stayed put and daggered Moses with his eyes before finally uprooting and following me to the entrance hall where fewer people were staring.

We went into the quiet and undisturbed doorway and I slapped his chest with my reticule, "Are you insane?" I snapped.

"Name one man that wouldn't go batshit seeing his wife at dinner with his gym buddy?" he challenged.

"We didn't know! I never told Moses your name. I never even told him you went to the same gym. He's like a guy version of me. I figured the two of you didn't even talk. Not to mention you think yoga is stupid. Plus, it's not like *we* ever talked. I probably don't know ninety percent of your buddies."

He tried to level, "You are ready to date? For real? You're okay sitting with another guy and eating with another guy and-."

"Of course, it's different and a little weird but it's going to happen. It'll happen for you too. You're handsome, and good, and funny, you are going to move on too."

"I don't *want* to move on. This is us, you're talking about. You think he can make you feel like I did?" he stressed.

"I'm hoping he won't because for the last couple years the way you made me feel was really shitty. Do you even know how many times I dressed like this for you? Do you know how hard it is to put yourself together for someone? Worse than that, do you know how awful it is to undo it? To take off the dress you tormented over finding, the hair you took hours styling, the makeup you artistically painted on, and the heels you walked around in pain wearing? All that comes off without ever being noticed, over and over again, and you realize it doesn't even matter because he doesn't see you!"

I realized I was crying and that meant my mascara was going to run. "Damn it, Chris! Stop! Stop holding on to me. You don't want this, you never did. You always want what you can't have and now because I don't want you, you want me. That's what you do. That's what you always do. That's not fair! It's not-."

"Shhh," he pulled me into his arms and held me to him. "Okay," he held me tighter and took in a ragged breath that made me think he really heard me this time, "Easy, easy."

I buried my face in his shoulder and felt my throat strain and pull with pain. I clutched his shoulders from underneath and tried to steady my breathing. This was all I had wanted for years. To feel him and know he cared. The heat of his body against mine was home. His scent.

He pulled my arms back, so he could look at me and those hazel eyes I love drew me back.

"Listen," he started, "I'm sorry. I'm so sorry, that I stopped. I don't know why and I'm not sure how I got this way. Jenzy, you're the only woman that's ever made me stay. The only one I gave my time to. It started that way, remember? Us trying so many times not to but we always did. You call me in every time. I screwed up, I get it. I screwed up big but let me fix it."

"You make me feel too unimportant."

"How?" he sounded annoyed now and let go of me to set his hands on his hips. "I don't know if I get how you ever felt unimportant. I was providing everything you needed and dealing with all your habits and…you know, real love isn't romance movie crap. Girls want to bitch about porn but romance movies and books about guys doing epic acts of love or killing themselves or endangering themselves to prove happily ever after is real, that's *not* real! Those men are as fake as the women in porn. That's why I don't even watch that shit with you. It's not realistic."

As quickly as he'd almost turned my head, he blinded me. Yes, I like romance. Yes, I read it and watch it and maybe he was right. It had given me an unrealistic hope for us. I was, after all, fairly impressionable. That wasn't what hurt, though. It was him putting down yet another part of what made me, me.

I approached it another way, "What if the little things are what matter? What if I don't want big displays, just small ones?"

He looked confused and with shaky hands, I took out my phone and scrolled through our messages. This was actually, easy since he almost never messaged me. I went back four weeks. Then looked up at him, "Do you remember when you went to that conference? The one in Texas? You were gone for two weeks."

"Yeah."

"I messaged you to say good morning your first day, but you didn't message back, so I sent a good night. Still, nothing. Then half the next day went by and still, nothing." I felt the tears dry up and give way to numbness. "So, I sent this. Read all the ones from that day." I handed him my phone and waited while he read. I had this conversation memorized.

It read.

"I guess you aren't getting my messages. It must be the phones. I hope the conference is going well and you get back soon. I just want to make sure you're okay since I hadn't heard from you."

He came back an hour later saying.
"Yeah, the phones are acting up. My service is bad here. I could've called on the room phone, but I thought you'd survive one day."

I looked up to see Chris' face change just slightly and I wondered if he read that part. Then I had come back and said,
"I can survive it. We just usually check in by now. I know conferences are annoying for you. It's not a big deal. I just wanted to hear from you."

Then he came back,
"If there's no big deal, why start an argument? I don't get your point."

Thinking about this messaging was making me feel more and more right about this separation. I had gotten a little weak at seeing him but now I remembered.

He kept reading and I remembered my response.
"You just seem distant. You always used to find a way to talk even if one method wasn't working. You don't like it when I miss your calls or messages either. Would you want me to not notice you are missing for a day?"

Then classic Chris.
"It's different since when I call or message I have a reason whereas you want to talk about nothing. No, I don't mind you noticing. If there was something important or serious you really want to talk about. 'Good morning, good night, how's your day, and did you sleep well,' questions I can live without for 24hrs."

I knew when he finished reading because he was tight-lipped and handed my phone back like it was a contract of silence. I took it and watched the emotions play across his face.

"This is such a little thing," I told him. "You managed to turn that on me and make my caring feel weak and needy. The trivialities of my day were a bother, I guess. Though, I did wonder how many of the husbands you were with spoke to their wives at least once before bed." I swallowed, "Well, now you won't be getting any annoying check ins from me or good nights or good mornings. I won't be asking how your day was and I'm surviving pretty well without your messages whether it's 24hours…" I wiped under my eyes and started toward the door of the restaurant, "or forever." I left him like that and went back to my ruined date.

Chris Clark might have at one time, been everything I wanted but I was never what he wanted. Not unless he thought he couldn't have me. Just like now.

Chapter Twelve
CHRIS

I got back in Todd's car and buckled my seatbelt. He must've known by instinct how it went because he didn't say anything to scold me or lecture. I drove him and his son home at a normal speed, but I was gripping the wheel like it was life. Once they were home, I waited while he got Connor out from the back. I kissed my nephew goodbye. Little guy was tuckered out after his Fast and Furious ride.

I said goodnight to Todd and stuffed my hands in my pockets to start the long walk home. It is roughly a thirty-minute walk, but I didn't mind. I needed to think.

Those text messages back and forth. I remembered them. I felt like she was being clingy or nitpicking. People don't have to talk every single day to know they care but there was a time I would have walked a thousand miles with no shoes in a snowstorm to reach a phone and hear her voice. There was a time we missed one another's call and it felt like a canyon was dropped between us.

I did get impatient when she took too long to get back to me. I hated waiting on calls and not getting them. So why would I write it like that? Why would I spin it on her to look needy?

If she hadn't noticed my absence for a day or more, what kind of wife would she have been? Would I want that?

I reached home and crashed in our bed, fully clothed, again, with my bra, again and the picture, again. I dreamt about what I did last night and saw it a million different ways. I also tried to crack the code on what the hell made me distant with her in the first place. Two years. That was the key, but nothing rang a bell.

When I woke up, the sun was blasting through our window on my side, but I was sleeping on hers. Jenzy usually closed the drapes and opened them. I left them open last night, not thinking but now something that simple was hurting me. She had said that last night, hadn't she? It was the little things… Little things made me fall in love with her and it was little things I did to make her fall out of it.

I looked at my phone for the time. I have forty minutes to look presentable before getting to work but the way the sun was hitting my face made me reminisce. Like memories were going to help. Still, maybe memories would unlock the fuck up I'd created.

2007

I woke to the sound of birds and a really annoying siren from a distant firetruck. Probably the potheads on campus again. There was one dorm hall that always caught fire from their escapades.

I opened my eyes slowly and took in the hardwood floor. My frat house didn't have hardwood floors. Uh, oh. I remembered last night and squeezed my eyes shut.

Shit!

Todd's little friend, Jenzy.

I slept with her.

That didn't bode well. I'm going to Sweden soon and I don't need some girl getting all attached. Especially, a sophomore.

I decided to rip off the Band-Aid sooner rather than later. I rolled from my stomach to my back then turned my head awaiting the sight of a crashed one-night-stand. Instead, all I saw was the bed and a pillow. I frowned and sat up. Poor thing was probably out getting coffee and bagels, thinking this was a lasting thing. Thoughts of the night before went through my head and I almost wished the same thing.

She was sexy, sweet, funny, passionate and deliciously dirty minded like me. I got up to search for my clothes. Looks like we were a little more animal than not. They were flung everywhere. I found her panties on the ceiling fan. Now that's good sex. How the hell did that happen? My belt was tied to her headboard and my boxers were torn where the fly was. Her mini skirt was on the windowsill. I found one of her knee-highs tied to my right wrist and smiled.

We'd gone from, this is fun sex, to one more time sex, to let's try it this way sex, to I've never done that sex. I remember her trying to tie me up with the knee-high stocking, but I got impatient and broke free before tying her up with my belt. We were like a dream team in bed. She was submissive, but a hellcat and I was dominant and gave her the force she wanted.

I stared at the bed and fought a little disappointment that she wasn't there to talk about it. However, my second priority was getting out of her dorm before she got back and got girly emotional. That was when the door opened. Thinking it was her; I turned around and was met with an ear-splitting scream. It was her roommate. Fuck! I was standing in the middle of their dorm butt-naked.

I tried to calm her down and grabbed for a sheet on the bed to cover up, "I'm really sorry! This isn't how it looks."

She screamed with her eyes closed, "Get out! Get out! Oh, my God, a perv! Eww! Get out!"

"I'm trying!" I got my jeans over my arm but when she saw the belt tied to the headboard it didn't look too good.

"What were you going to do to me?" she screeched.

"No, no, that was for your roommate."

She screamed again, "Ewww!" She took the lamp by the door and threw it at me.

Okay, I see where that didn't sound right.

"I'm leaving! I wasn't-," she got me in the eye with a shoe. She took off her shoe and used it as a weapon. All while screaming.

"Owe! Jesus!" I covered my eye which made me drop the sheet, so she screamed louder.

"I'll call campus police! I'll," she whipped her other shoe, "I have a rape whistle!" She pulled it from under her shirt. I tried to go past her to get to the door, but she misread that as an assault and slapped the shit out of my head, shoulder, chest and back all while blowing that friggin whistle. I had to go out the window in the buff. It was a really long walk to my frat house.

Hours later I was in class listening to a half-dead professor explain stuff when I got a text from Todd.
"Go for pizza after class?"

I discretely texted back.
"Sure."

As soon as class was out, and I closed up my books, I started walking to *Its Italy,* a little pizza place right off campus. He was sitting at a table just inside, drinking a soda from a jumbo cup.

I sat across from him and nodded to the drink. "You gonna eat anything?" I asked.

"Nah, just thirsty."

I rolled my eyes, "I'll pay for it, dummy."

"Yeah… you sure?"

"Yeah, it's fine."

Little brothers are a pain in the ass that is always broke, but I also just screwed his best friend, so a pizza was the least I could do. I ordered us a large pie with his favorite toppings. We were talking about stupid stuff when right as the pizza came to us, the door opened, and *she* walked in.

She looked amazing in a flowy, peach, peasant dress that stopped way too short and really high wedges.

"Hey, guys!" she said as she spotted us. I panicked inside. Was she going to tell Todd? Was she going to be needy? Why was it so hot? Why was she so hot? Would she want to talk about it?

"Hey, Jenzy," Todd patted the seat next to him between us and she started our way. "I invited her, you don't mind, right?" Todd asked.

"No," I overtried at indifferent. "She can sit here, she's cool, I mean what I know about her, she's okay. I don't mind. I don't care. It's cool."

He frowned at me while he slurped from his straw. "Whatever," he rolled his eyes.

She sat down and opened her purse, "Here," she told Todd, "In case you feel sick again from last night," she handed him a box of tea.

"Thanks. You sure you aren't mad that I didn't pick you up?" Todd asked her.

I started to sweat bullets.

She rubbed his arm, "Heck no, you were sick and drunk, I would be upset if you drove."

"Alright, so you guys met last night." Todd took a slice of pizza. "What do you think of my lame-ass brother?"

I looked up at her for hidden looks, but she just smiled as she took a slice too, "I think he's cool. Drives a little fast, though."

I frowned and asked, "How are you this morning?" Why wasn't she hinting at stuff or looking at me funny?

"Great! I went and explored campus when I got up, met some teachers, looked for where my classes are," she picked things off her pizza and Todd took them and ate them for her. Strange friendship. Was he in love with her? Did I fuck the girl he loved?

"How was your…night?" I tried.

She smiled at me, but it was generic, "I slept really good. Especially, since you got that cricket out of my room. They just creep me out."

What the hell was wrong with this girl? Did she remember having mind-blowing sex?

We all three talked about stupid shit that I barely heard because I was busy wondering why she was acting normal.

Todd laughed, and I tried to pay attention and not stare at her too much. God, she was gorgeous in the sunlight. Those eyes and the taste of those lips…

"Tell him," Todd laughed. "Please, it's too funny."

"Okay, okay," she sighed. "I *love pizza*," she told me, "I could survive off it for the rest of my life. So, this one time, I was super hungry, and Todd and I went to this really shady pizza joint-."

Todd cut in, "They spelled 'open,' 'opin,' on their front doors. That was a sign."

"Well, yeah," she agreed, "but you know I get adventuresome with food places. Anyway, I was so hungry I ate like a whole pizza to myself, but I eat pizza with a fork."

Todd let out a snicker, "See, she's doing it now. It's like she's ninety-years-old inside."

She laughed and drank from Todd's soda, "Yeah, I'm weird like that. So, I was so hungry I didn't realize that two of the four spokes on my plastic fork was gone until the end."

I didn't connect the dots, so Todd forced the answer out around a laugh, "She ate her fork."

"It was an accident," she defended around a fit of giggles, "I thought it was something crunchy on the pizza."

I laughed and sat back. She was cute. I could see her doing that. Todd stood up still laughing, "Running to the bathroom. I'll be right back, guys."

We nodded and when he left I gave her a minute to bring it up.

"Hey," she turned to me with bright eyes. "Did you know that this school has an animal shelter right on the outskirts? I got a job there!"

"That's great."

"I like animals. It's a Sagittarius thing. I used to have-."

"Do you remember last night?" I talked over her.

She looked surprised I brought it up. "Of course. Why?" She picked more toppings off another slice and dropped them on a slice of Todd's.

"Don't you want to talk about it?" I asked.

"Oh! I'm sorry," she dug in her purse for something and I waited. "Here," she offered me a twenty. "Is that enough for gas. You picked me up for Todd and I really appreciate it. Being stranded in the rain is no fun."

I pushed her hand with the cash away, "I don't want money. I want to know why you won't talk about the sex we had."

She bugged her eyes. "It was fun. I had a blast."

"That's it?"

"What else is there?" she questioned.

"You didn't come back this morning."

"Oh," she smiled and took a bite before answering. "I figured it would make it less awkward for you if I left first."

"Why did you leave at all?"

"You said last night, that it was only the one time. 'Just tonight.' Remember?"

"Well, yeah, I say that every time, but most girls don't mean it back."

"Todd's told me about you and how you are with girls. You don't like long-term and you *never, ever* date. He said you're strictly against public displays of emotion and resent the whole idea of relationships. I took note before I kissed you. Plus, you are a Leo…"

"And you're fine with it. No, pleading with me to do it again and no declarations of love?"

She laughed, "I was raised by really liberal parents. I think sex doesn't always have to mean intimacy, not unless you have a bond with your partner. My parents are real hippies, my *mom* is anyway. You know she almost named me Moon Beam. Sex is good for our spirits because we are spiritual beings on a spiritual journey."

More hippie babble. I love that shit when she says it but she has me at sea here, "Was last night…good for you?"

She gave me a warmer smile, like it was for only me and a queer hope inflated in my chest, "It was amazing. I've never been so free with someone. My body is still vibrating with your energy."

I smiled and bit my lip. She was confusing me. Now I wanted her, "Maybe we should do it again?"

"Nah, it would ruin it. We said just the one night and you don't do steady."

Was she using my line against me? "There's still a lot we didn't try," I baited.

She blushed, and I loved it, "My horoscope said not to rush into anything today. To save big and small decisions for tomorrow. I think we should stick with what we agreed. Besides, you're going to Sweden!" She whispered the last part excitedly, so Todd wouldn't hear.

"Yeah…I am…" Sweden meant the world to me. It would kick start my life and get me out of the predictable life road. I tugged my ear, "so…you are okay with this not happening again?"

"Sure! You should stick by your convictions. Trust me because I suck at it."

Awesome. My whole body was fighting itself. That epic night couldn't happen only once, it would be a crime.

Then I thought of something, "Oh, and you might want to tell your roommate to chill. She thought I was a rapist."

She covered her mouth to laugh, "Oh, no! I forgot about her! She didn't mention it when I saw her before coming here. She's great, though. I *really* like her."

"What's her name?"

"Mandy. I want to introduce her to Todd."

Chapter Thirteen
Present Day
JENZY

I sat at the lawyer's office waiting for twenty minutes on Monday. It was so unlike Chris to be late for anything. My lawyer, Guy Wills was leaned back in his chair clicking his pen open and closed and I was braiding the fringe on my purse.

I was wearing a denim button-down with black tights and a multicolored South Western looking sweater. It was big on me and stopped at my thighs with deep pockets. Since it was cool out I also wore a tan scarf around my neck in a wide loop and my hair was up with bangs and long strands down my neck.

I thought this would be the fast part. Divide our stuff (I didn't intend to keep much), sign the divorce and move on. We have no kids, no dog, no specific thing to tug of war over.

"Where is he?" I asked Guy.

"Probably just trying to show you how little this means to him. Don't let it get to you."

"You think he's talking to his lawyer?" Chris' lawyer had left the room about five minutes ago in haste.

"Yeah, I'm pretty sure that was the call he just got."

I noticed Guy was about my age with a dark brown suit on. He probably wasn't the best, but I didn't intend to take anything from Chris.

We heard an engine and looked out of the office through the white blinds that were openly lined up to see Chris pull into the lot. My heart did an urgent flip like I was excited and nervous to see him. He got out with his sunglasses on and buttoned the front of his navy-blue jacket as he shook hands with his lawyer who had apparently been waiting outside. He looked so hot my stomach curled.

He followed his lawyer in and disappeared from sight. When I heard his voice in the hall I sat up straighter. He came in and locked eyes with me the minute he saw me.

I expected animosity, bitterness, even a little indifference since what happened Friday night, but he wasn't looking at me like that. He was looking at me more like…he had accepted a challenge that he humbly but surely knew he'd win. What did he have up his sleeve?

"Mr. Clark," Guy started. "Glad to see you finally made it."

"Sorry," he was still looking at me. "I had things to get in order."

I looked down at the table to avoid his eyes. They were haunting me.

"Let's start with the…condo…" Guy began.

We filtered everything down. It was almost scary. What makes a marriage is love and trust and devotion, but in the eyes of the law it looked more like things, property, vehicle, furniture. They don't put on paper how much of your heart the other person gets, or time, energy, love, hope, memories, or pain. Just things.

"Now…" Chris' lawyer looked up at me like he was dreading this next one and my mind put it together quickly.

My ring.

Chris' mother adored her engagement ring because she had been very in love with his father. Not the stepdad Chris knew and loved in the divorce… I mean the father he didn't know long enough to make memories with. He passed away right after Todd was born. Chris was only two.

Still, I cherished it because his mother and I were close, and she felt safe knowing it was with me. It was also her way of encouraging Chris to claim me. I spun it on my finger under the table.

His lawyer continued, "Your engagement ring is actually, Mr. Clark's property because heirlooms by law-."

"No," Chris said. I looked up to see he was still focused on me. "She can keep it."

"Mr. Clark," his lawyer kept his voice low, "the ring is an heirloom and worth a great deal. If you release it into her possession there is no getting it back. There's also the chance you might want it back for-."

"I won't marry again after this," he nodded at me. "Mom would want you to keep it."

I took an uncertain breath. We hadn't even told our parents, yet. I would call mine when I left here. I don't know when he'll tell his mom, they aren't that tight. I am the one that keeps her close.

"Thank you," I said softly. He dragged his eyes away and waited while they wrote up the last of it.

Hours later we had the papers sitting in front of us. It was so quick. There were no ties and we were flexible to the splitting of things.

"Now you'll both sign these," Guy went on, but I got distracted when Chris leaned in and whispered back and forth with his lawyer. Guy slowed up. "Are you two with us here?" Guy asked Chris and his lawyer in an annoyed tone.

His lawyer sat facing us again and pointed to Chris with his pen, "Mr. Clark has some last-minute agreements he'd like to address."

I frowned at him, "Agreements? Like what? Aren't we done?"

Chris sat forward and spun his papers around, "I'm contesting the divorce."

"You can't, we just went through everything."

"I still have to sign."

"Why would you sit here for hours working this out if you intended to contest?"

"It will be easy if you still want this later," he explained.

"Later?"

"I have conditions to signing."

Guy looked up from the papers and raised a brow, "Like what?"

"I want time," Chris answered.

I shifted in the chair and narrowed my eyes, "Time for what?"

He smiled but it seemed smug, "Time to change your mind."

My mouth dropped open but then his lawyer started talking, "Actually, Mrs. Clark, Mr. Clark's terms aren't unheard of. He only asks you to be open to doing a few minor things together as a last try-."

"You can't do that," I looked at Guy, "He can't right? I mean-?"

Guy opened his mouth in that paused way like he was trying to find a nicer way to say, 'he just did.' "He…it's complicated. Mr. Clark could put the finalizing of this divorce on hold for a very, very, very long time."

"How long?" I asked.

He looked around at the ceiling, but Chris' lawyer took the words from his mouth, "Till kingdom come, Mrs. Clark."

I looked at Chris and fought a helping of resentment, "You are forcing us to stay married."

"Not forever, Jenzy."

"How long?"

"I can't tell you that."

I felt disappointed and relieved at the same time. I wanted this done before something happened to weaken my resolve… "Fuck you," I stood up and hurried toward the door.

"Jennifer," Guy stood. "What about-?"

"Well, what choice do I have?" I snapped back. "I guess I agree." On my way past Chris, I let my purse whack him in the head, but the imp only laughed.

Chapter Fourteen
JENZY

I was in the parking lot, bent over mumbling curses to turn his dick green and unlocking my bike from the guard when Chris came up behind me. I didn't know until my ass bumped into his, far too close groin. I came up fast and spun on him.

"You're a dick," I said with venom.

"Yeah, I'm starting to realize that too. This time, it's hopefully going to work for me, though."

"I want this over with."

"And it will be," he reached down and unlocked my bike with ease. "Long as you comply."

I folded my arms, "Whatever you're up to won't work. I'm not giving you any more of myself to step on."

"Then it's time I give you something…if you still hate me you can step on it."

"I never hated you." I looked away and took my bike. "Whatever, so what's this first condition?"

"Parents…"

I groaned but he kept talking as I straddled my bike.

"We have to tell them together," he demanded. "No calls; my mom first then yours."

"Your mom is going to contrive ways to fix us and my Dad loves you. That's unfair."

"Too bad, Cupcake, you're in it for better or worse till I sign."

I grumbled some more and kicked up my break.

He held my handlebars and hunched his back to make me look in his cobra eyes. "By the way, I just noticed you straddle bikes the way you used to straddle *me*."

I looked up in total shock and tried to process what he just said but then he was walking toward his car.

"I'll pick you up at four tomorrow to see mom," he said over his shoulder.

I shook my head like it was filled with cobwebs. Did he just come on to me?

Something was different. The way Chris acted since yesterday at the law office was so altered. He picked me up at exactly four and I got in his car to see he still had my protection charm on his rearview mirror. The ride to his moms was an hour and it was a Tuesday night so that meant Todd, Mandy, and the kids would be there for dinner too. We usually went together once every month, but I went myself once every other week.

"Are you cold?" he asked, and I saw that I had been holding myself.

"No."

He was wearing a tight flannel shirt with the sleeves down to cover his tats. His body was so thick and muscular it felt like he was swallowing the car and pulling me closer.

"So how are things with Moses?" he asked.

I gave him a true, 'don't even,' look.

He went on anyway, "Come on, it's no big deal. We're getting divorced and you are falling in love again-."

"I'm not in love," oops. Shit. That asshole just deliberately tripped me up.

He was smiling with his eyes on the road, "Oh, really?" he asked.

"Shut up."

I caught him looking at my legs and tugged my dress down. I was in a brown, bohemian-style, halter top dress with gold zigzag designs across; a long charm necklace, jingly earring and lots of bracelets. He once told me this was my 'sexy, primitive, tribal girl' look.

"You look amazing. My mom's going to love it," he said.

Hmm, a compliment. Aren't we just a real winner?

His phone buzzed, and I turned away to look out the window. He would answer, and the trip would go this way, just like always, but then he didn't answer, and I looked back at him, "Wasn't that important?"

"They'll voicemail."

Interesting.

We made it to his mom's in one piece. No fights, no tuning one another out. When I went inside Mandy hugged me with a crying two-month-old worming around in her arms.

"Colic?" I asked.

"Yes," she huffed, "Girl, please tell me you brought the gripe water."

"It's in my purse," I said as Chris came up behind me. "I'll go measure some out in the kitchen."

"Thank you, you're a goddess."

I stepped around them but then heard them talking when I went around the corner.

"Give her over," Chris commanded over the screaming. I stopped and peeked around to see them.

"She's in a spit-up phase, Chris." Mandy bounced harder with her knees to calm the baby. "I'd rather be the one to throw up on you."

"Ha, ha, very funny. Who used to put Connor to sleep again?"

"Don't brag, you probably bored him to sleep."

"Stop being a bitch."

Mandy tried to kick his shin, but he avoided her and I almost laughed. Then she slowed up to start handing our Niece to Chris. I didn't need to see this. Chris and babies were like female catnip. All the strength, all the muscle, and all the height were so easily bridled around children. He was known in our family as the Baby Whisperer.

 Here was why, even now he was soothing Penny, our Niece in his massive arms like it was a science. Easy swaying and soft but deep murmurs of ease and she was looking up at him in her sleeper like he was a movie she had to watch. Babies loved his face.

Mandy offered him the burp cloth, but he declined with a wave of his hand while keeping Penny's eyes. The human heart is really dumb. This guy has played football with my heart for years now and in this moment, I'm finding him irresistible.

I went to the kitchen and tried to shake it when Nona, Chris, and Todd's mother, met me at the doorway of the kitchen.

"Hello, gorgeous!" she said and hugged me real tight. I love this woman. She's a second mother because mine is great too. She's a head shorter than me with thick brown but graying hair she wears in a low ponytail and wide brown eyes. "I missed your face, sit down," she shooed me to a chair.

I went to sit next to Todd at her super long cedar wood dining table. Her house looked like a log cabin, but it was modern inside with very high windows in almost every room.

"I was supposed to make colic medicine, but I think Chris is putting her to sleep," I said about Penny.

Todd rubbed his face. "Thank, God because she was up all night and I don't even know how we drove here."

I looked around, "Where's Connor?"

Nona jerked her thumb out toward the yard as she sliced some veggies, "Out back in the sandbox."

"Fun."

"Tell me what's new, sweetie. I didn't see you last week," Nona began.

I snuck a look at Todd while she wasn't looking. He was nibbling from a bowl of chips but slowed to listen.

"Um," I stopped when Chris walked in. God Damn! He had the limp, pink-swaddled body of Penny in the crook of his arm and he looked right at me. I realize now that's one of the things different. Ever since my date night with Moses, Chris looks at me like he really sees me. I'm not furniture or wall paint anymore, it's like I have a spotlight on me now.

"What are we talking about?" he whispered for the baby's sake.

Nona smiled as he bent and kissed her cheek, "Jenzy's filling me in on life. Go ahead, hon."

I searched for how to slowly lead to this, topics to climb toward the divorce but then Chris started, "It's been a crazy week. Jenzy and I are splitting up."

She dropped her knife and looked back and forth at us. "I'm sorry, what?"

I tried coming at it softer, "We…are in the process of a divorce but that's not how I wanted you to find out," I glared at him.

"Why?" she stopped and looked at Chris, "What the hell did you do?"

Chris shook his head, "It has to mean *I* did something?"

"If you cheated on Jenzy, I'm going to kill you."

"He didn't cheat, Nona." I corrected but it had crossed my mind. "We just, fell out of love-."

"You," Chris said as he sat across from me at the table. "*You* fell out of love."

I didn't want to argue in front of his family, so I pushed on, "It's actually moving pretty quickly. We just have a few things to…finalize."

"But why?" She came over and slapped the back of Chris' head and I mean hard. "I'm serious, you idiot. What did you do?"

"Mom! I'm holding the baby."

"I don't care! Tell me!" Her eyes were getting wet and I suddenly felt awful.

"Nona," I said, "this doesn't change what goes on between us. I love you and I love this family. I'm not going away and there's no bitterness."

"Oh, yes there is," she slapped Chris' head again. "*I'm* bitter. Christopher, I'm going to wring your neck."

Mandy came in with the diaper bag and grinned, "Can I help?" she said with glee.

"Yes, you may," said Nona.

I got up to kiss and hug his mother and she held me close. "I'm not going anywhere," I said again.

She slapped the back of Chris' head again while we hugged.

"Owe! Jesus, Ma!" he swatted.

"You deserve worse. Take it like a man," she scolded.

Todd laughed before popping another chip, "Guess I'm still the favorite," he teased.

Nona let go and wiped a telling tear from under her eye. "You gave me my first grandchildren, of course, you are. Your brother's a failure."

We laughed but it was hurting tonight. I think Chris knew it would.

There was a mood now. A sad decline in all the togetherness.

After dinner, we all went in different directions. Todd was playing outside with Connor and Mandy was napping since Penny had developed into a colic-ridden handful and Chris was somewhere in the living room still attached to Penny. He'd even eaten dinner one-handed.

I helped his mom clean and we talked, skillfully avoiding the divorce. All until I caught her looking at my ring while I was drying the dishes she washed.

"Chris gave it to me in the lawyer's office the other day," I told her, "but I don't think it was his place to make that decision."

"I don't want it, that part of my life is done," she focused on washing for a time and I worried from what she said that she was mad at me. I felt uncomfortable in my own skin.

She went on, "Jenzy…" I waited. "Please, promise me, I won't lose you. You and Mandy, you are the daughters I didn't have."

Ugh, she was tearing up again and I felt a slash go through my heart.

"I meant what I said, Nona, I'm not leaving, this is my family too now. Todd and Mandy are my best friends. You mean so much to me."

"Did he cheat?" she whispered like I wouldn't tell her the truth if she didn't.

"No, I don't think so…I wondered for a while. This started two years ago so I do…wonder…if something happened but I don't think he would do that. He just stopped seeing me."

"You don't deserve that."

"But neither does he. He needs someone that makes him feel the way I used to make him feel." Saying that out loud grated on every nerve.

Nona dried her hands to hug me close. I think my emotions were showing.

She rubbed my back and kissed my temple, "I know my boys…" she sniffed, "I love them, but I know where they come up short. I also know what feeling alone in a marriage is like. If it's the way I think it is…you need to do this. I hate it, but I can't see you unhappy. You or Chris."

I leaned back into the counter and toyed with my neckless. "He'll see how good this is, eventually. Girls are always looking; he'll be able to be like he was before we met."

She smiled slowly and turned her back to wipe down the counters. "Jen, you've had my boy's heart since the night you met. Then you kept it for years. He won't be giving it to anyone for a long time if ever."

I felt comforted by that but shouldn't.

I sighed, "Love must be bottomless, you fall in and you fall out. Either way, there's no catching your feet."

She chuckled, "Don't worry, honey, sometimes there's a trampoline at the bottom…"

I smiled just as my phone buzzed in my purse on the far end of the counter.

"Okay doll," Nona patted my arm, "this is all cleaned up, thanks. I'm going to go break my back while I play with the Prince, AKA, my first grandchild."

"Okay," I watched her go through the back door to go play with Todd and Connor. Then I went to my purse and checked my phone. It was Moses, and my heart flipped when I saw his handsome face pop up in my mind.

Then I read.
"Hey gorgeous, how is family time?"

I checked around then messaged back.
"It's going well. Chris' mother understands."

He messaged right back which made me feel like a priority.
"How are you feeling?"

I typed back.
"Missing you."

He only took a minute.
"Me too. I owe you another date."

Teenage butterflies in my stomach erupted.
"Maybe just the two of us this time?"

I could hear him laughing.
"Hahaha, we talked about this, sunshine. It's fine. Things happen."

I grumbled.
"It was embarrassing and awful."

His comeback was,
"Just proves you're not easy to get over. I knew that already. I just feel bad I didn't know."

I stared at my phone then typed.
"I'm sorry I didn't tell you who he was sooner. I didn't think you'd know each other."

He surprised me with,
"If I pretend to be upset, will it secure me another date?"

I laughed and shook my head before writing back.
"I'll go either way."

He returned with,
"You just totally took the fun out of it."

I laughed.
"Gasp so sorry."**

Then I waited till he returned.
"Hey, Jenzy?"

I felt nervous.
"Yes?"

He really knows how to woo.
"Will you go out with me again?"

I smiled so hard my cheeks hurt.
"Definitely."

We said our goodbyes and I promised to tell him once I was home safe. That was new to me. Chris stopped caring if I made it anywhere safely. I could have been swallowed by a land shark, he would not have noticed.

I wandered out of the kitchen and into the living room to find Chris asleep and sprawled out on the sofa like a panther. His legs were longer than the couch and his big arm didn't fit but he had it pulled in to secure Penny.

Penny was asleep on his chest, lying on her stomach with her lips parted. Her tiny body looked like a peanut on him, her little rump in the air; even his hands were bigger than her, as they kept her in place.

The closer I walked the more haunted I felt. I wanted this for us. It was out of a dream. The baby smell that I loved was swarming around the room and there he was; my beautiful husband.

I knelt by them and reached to take Penny but as soon as I moved her in the slightest, his eyes opened, and he held her tighter to his chest like it was a reflex.

"Oh, hey," I whispered.

"Hey, did I pass out?"

"Yeah, I was going to take her in case she fell."

"She won't, I've got her."

I took my hands away. He obviously did, "You've always been such a natural with babies."

"They like me cause' I'm hot."

We laughed, "They like you because you're goofy."

"I would make a super dad."

"I guess it is good we waited. Divorce with children would take longer and be hard on them…" I justified.

"On the flip side, knocking you up would be my only hope right now."

"We haven't needed protection in years because we went the one-hundred percent effective, abstinence route." I was reminding him of the complete withdraw of sex he put me through, but he didn't seem to notice.

"Yeah, but condom sex is tragic. I should have burned all the condoms in America. It's not like you would pop the pill so you would be good and pregnant and forced to stick this out."

"Birth control pills aren't good for women. I've told you this before. There's like a billion studies on-."

"Do you remember that one time we couldn't find one, a condom, and you insisted I fuck you anyway?"

I was more than shocked about him bringing this up.

I think I looked as shocked as I felt, "N-no…that was like forever ago, like four years…"

"I remember," he looked like he was recalling it all in his head. "We were on that sailing boat we rented, and you started it by telling me what you wanted to do to me, but you thought I wouldn't act on it because we were out in an open space and it was daylight. So, I threw you down on the deck because I never back down from a dare."

He stretched then went on, "I told you I didn't have condoms, though and you begged me for it anyway. That was a great day, not sure if it was the hot sun on my back when I was doing you, the tiny white dress you had on or the lack of barriers, so I could feel you taking me in."

I sat with really wide eyes; I know they're wide because they feel dry and cold. What did he just say? I felt a sudden ache between my legs that was making my breathing a little too sharp. I took in a slow breath and fought for something to say, but I didn't come up with anything, I just stood and said…

"I think I'll ride back with Todd and Mandy."

Chapter Fifteen
May
CHRIS

I went to the gym on Friday. I had been avoiding it, so I wouldn't kill Moses or put a treadmill on his face. However, I need to work out, it will help. Showing to Jenzy these next few months that I still love her is going to take a toll. Meanwhile, I still haven't even figured out what drove the wedge.

I managed to do my routine without seeing him, but after my shower, while I was getting dressed, he came around a corner and paused when he saw me. I only looked long enough to warn him with my eyes not to approach before I pulled on a shirt.

"Hey," he said as he slowly came in and went to his locker. I didn't answer as I sat to pull on socks. "Listen," he leaned his back into the lockers, "Can we just…talk?"

His phone went off in his locker and I ached inside like I'd never ached before. Was that her? Was that my wife? Was that Jenzy? I made her feel like her calls or messages were annoying, in the way, now some other guy was getting them.

Moses silenced it then tried again with me, "I really didn't know Chris, I swear."

I put on my shoes and kept my eyes on my task.

He tried yet again, "I wouldn't have if I had known."

I stood and shouldered my bag, "Now you know. Plan to stop?"

He swallowed and avoided my eyes.

"Yeah, that's what I thought," I said as I shoved his shoulder with mine, going past.

"Would you be able to? You know what it's like to want Jenzy. Would anything have stopped you?"

That was a fair question. No, nothing would or could, not even Moses.

I stopped to look back. "Hey, I get it. I don't have to like it or support it. I don't have to like you. I believe you if it makes you feel better, I know you're not that kind of guy, I still want to break your face. We aren't friends. That stopped when you took her first call."

He nodded and slung a towel over his shoulder, "I really am sorry, though."

I looked him up and down. I could see how it happened. He was her twin in hobbies and beliefs and living choices. He was equal in appearance with me and he was good.

I hated it, but I knew it. "Just know that if you hurt her at *all*, I'll hurt *you*," I threatened.

He accepted that but then a glint of humor sparked. "But for the law's sake that's hypothetical right?" he asked.

I only gave him a flash of a closed mouth smile, "Yeah," and smile gone. I left.

I went to the grocery store that night and shopped to kill time and because there was very little food in the house. Going to restaurants by myself was feeling more and more awkward and lonely.

I was passing the healthy aisles and stopped to stare. Jenzy always shopped in these aisles. Then I saw a woman with chestnut hair in a French braid coming around, pushing a smaller cart. I knew those brilliant eyes anywhere. Jenzy.

I was leaning like a slouch over my cart but I straightened and backed up so I could U-turn to ride up behind her. I had to walk slow as hell when I got trapped between an old lady moving at the pace of a sloth with Lyme. I bugged my eyes while we crawled along and darted when she pulled over. Why don't carts have car horns?

I took in Jenzy after jogging my way around the store. She was in tight jeans and a white top. They were *tight* jeans, though so

I needed to appreciate that for a second, then I rolled up beside her so the carts were aligned and set my hand on her middle back.

She startled then saw me and took a breath, "You scared me."

"Sorry," I took my hand away, "what are we up to?"

"Shopping." She looked suspicious. "Why are you in the 'granola breath' gangway, as you call it?"

"Well, I don't eat like a pig. Obviously," I patted my abs.

"I know, still…"

I looked in her cart then added up that she was dressed nice, she had heels on. Uh oh. His phone had buzzed at the gym. Fuck.

"Date tonight?" I guessed.

"Like I would tell you after last time."

"I won't crash it, I swear. Just curious."

"You were curious at the dress shop too."

"I can help."

"I don't think I want any more help from you," she started walking so I followed.

"But see, I was married to you for seven years. That means I know all your strong points with cooking and your downfalls."

She skidded to a stop. "Downfalls?"

I peered into her basket then leaned on my cart, "Pasta and meatballs? Playing it safe then?"

She pushed on but with me following and with that thoughtful expression I knew I had her in *3, 2, 1…*

"Safe?" she asked.

Bingo.

"You're cooking him dinner, right?" I questioned.

She reneged on telling me, "This is weird again but yeah."

"For starters…this is a big deal. I mean, this is like the 'men's club approval test'. The NFL of Girlfriends, if you will. It determines everything. Is she a good cook? Will my kids eat well and come back from college to eat on weekends? Does she fail miserably and not know it? That means I must fake liking it till I die. Does she know but secretly wants me to be the cook so if I don't catch the hint we starve?"

"Men think all that?"

"Sure. It's survival. Plus, what you cook says a lot too." I gave her cart contents a 'wow' look.

Her eyes widened, "What? What's wrong with pasta?"

"First off, this isn't pasta," I took the box of spaghetti and shook it. "This is healthy broomstick bristles. Secondly," I put it back and winced at the cold jiggly thing in my hand, "This isn't meat, it's tofu. You're making your date fake meat, that's false advertising. You are an incredible cook but not when you are health conscious."

She argued that, "Moses likes the kind of food I tried making for you. He's as health conscious as I am."

"Again, it's not like I vote for fast food, I don't get this body from eating donuts. I just believe in moderation and physical fitness. I also feel free to eat normal people food."

"He likes what I like, so still, I don't see what's wrong with healthy alternatives and pasta." She turned a corner quickly to lose me, but I caught up.

"It's also lazy. Pasta is the easiest thing ever, if there's no effort, it looks like you don't care."

She slowed around the dairy and took that in.

"Make him your eggplant parmesan," I suggested. "That was the meal that won *me,* back then."

She came to a slow stop and faced me, "My eggplant?"

"Yeah, it was like six months after we met, and Todd was stuck in a night class, so we went out to eat. You like exploring new places so we went to a weird little hole in the wall and I ordered eggplant. It was so bad I couldn't take a second bite, but you bet you could make better. We shopped, went back to my frat house and you made the evilest, good-bestest, eggplant parm on this planet." I looked to see I had her pretty entranced. "You don't remember? I ate the whole thing."

"*You* remember that?" she asked.

"Yeah, I fell in love a little."

She took her eyes away and I mourned the loss of them.

Then she said, "My parents are at their beach house, by the way. They said we could visit next weekend. We need to go so I can tell them, so we can…move things along."

I nodded but changed the subject, "Hey, can you microwave a chicken? Like, a whole chicken, just… stuff it in there? Is there a setting for that?"

She rolled her eyes and suppressed a laugh, "No, Chris, no."

"Well, how does the crockpot thing work? What setting equals three-hundred or whatever?"

"Ask your mother."

"You know I'd rather starve."

I was so sure I had her there, but now the disappointment was crushing even as I teased with her. I guess this was how she'd been feeling for two years. But what happened to cause those two years?!

JENZY

Seeing Chris in the market screwed my nerves big time. He knew what he was doing to me and I had to stop letting it happen. He was getting in my head.

When Moses came to pick me up, I also talked myself out of the silly car thing. Chris might have been the one with car memories but now it was time to make new ones.

Moses pulled up to Todd's in his Prius. I handed him the two bags of things I wanted to make for dinner and he loaded them then got the door for me.

I fidgeted a lot in the front seat but then we talked, and I came down a little. He was so easy to talk to. All the same views, no fights or heated political, medical, or general values debates. The ride was carefree, and he lived outside the city. We were surrounded by trees. Big trees.

"Are you planning to kill me out here?" I teased.

"That goes both ways. I've seen daytime movies where women go psycho. I'm in just as much danger, if not more. Women are smarter," he added.

"I won't kill you till after dinner."

We laughed. When we reached a narrow back road lined with trees on either side, I felt intrigued. I loved Chris and my home but country living just seemed simpler and homey. I saw the lights illuminating in his windows first.

His house was a small, one story that reflected a cottage atmosphere. My inner adventurer was very aware. We got out and he insisted on carrying the stuff. We went inside, and I mouthed 'wow'. I could fit his house in mine, but the warmth and the aura were unbeatable.

His kitchen and living room was one common room and at the middle wall was an old wood-burning stove. His living room had a rounded sage-colored couch positioned under a double-sided window, with different colored throws draped over it.

There was a lamp hanging from the ceiling, and a single bookshelf that went all around up high. He had paintings hung to keep the walls from being bare; a really old tree with deep roots, a seasonal wheel of the zodiac signs, the chakra elements, and a creed about the earth being our mother.

I could smell incense and a faint remanence of sage.

Above the far wall was an open loft with a gabled roof where I could see his bed and window from where I stood.

I followed him to the kitchen where the walls were whitewashed with plants growing or hanging everywhere. His appliances were very clean looking and for a guy on his own so were his countertops and floors. His table was only a two-seater and I felt green with envy. This was exactly my idea of living. That and his windows were all open and felt freeing; receptive to nature.

"This is quite a home," I said.

"You like it?" he asked.

"It's perfect! It really reflects you."

"No denying I'm a hippie, right?"

I laughed, "I'll start this," I opened the bags and started arranging things on his counter. He tried to help a few times, but I made him go away. He only went as far as to sit at his table behind me.

"I feel weird letting you cook."

"Why?" I asked as I washed the eggplants in his sink.

"You're my guest; I think it goes the other way around."

"When I get my own place, you can cook there. Sound fair?"

He smiled, "Sure." He opened some wine while we talked, and I cooked. This felt natural. Actually, it was how I wanted things with Chris. I shook my head. Chris doesn't belong in my head tonight.

Somewhere during our talk, I got distracted, though. Moses came up to get things out like plates, but he would put his chest to my back and reach over me with his hand on my hip. I hadn't felt a man touch me in *two* long *years*. This was sex for me.

Oh no. Did I already put the oregano in? I added some but then he was back to get bowls for the soup I was making and the place between my thighs hurt. I wanted him, and his groin being so close was sending wireless signals to mine.

How many garlic cloves did I just grate…? Shit! I was scooping up red peppers when he went by and my clumsy self, poured way too many out. What was wrong with me?

While it was in the oven I fought the guilt and fear that I'd poisoned us.

Chapter Sixteen
JENZY

I sat with him while we waited, and the more Moses made me talk, the better I felt.

"That's why if I ever have babies, I would do it at home with a midwife, you know? I'm aspiring to be a Doula. I was there when Mandy had both her babies in the hospital, it was amazing! It's-." I caught myself too late. "And I'm really sorry, second date and I'm telling you about babies. I'll just go now."

He laughed that sound that made me shudder, "You can't leave unless I drive you and I'm not done with this night yet. I brought it up, remember? I told you they're starting prenatal yoga at the gym."

"Oh, right," I drank from my glass.

"You're cute when you blush."

"Am I blushing?"

"You really didn't freak me out. I agree. If I ever have kids with someone and she's open to it, I would want to try home birth."

I tilted my head, "You don't think it's crazy? Really? Chris used to say it wasn't safe, or he'd tell me all of why I could epically fail at it."

"It's not crazy, it's how nature intended. Not that hospital births are any less beautiful. Birth is birth but wanting to do it in an environment you trust isn't crazy. It's also perfectly safe; midwives know their limits if things go wrong and you wouldn't fail at anything you set your mind to."

I crushed hard. He said all the right things, except he stayed open about who the woman having his kids would be. I think he doesn't want me to feel pressure and that's honorable.

"Thank you," he surprised me by saying.

"For what?"

"For coming tonight. For giving me a chance."

I stroked the stem of my glass, "Thanks for involving yourself with a disaster."

"You aren't a disaster, Jenzy you're miraculous."

I looked into his eyes longer than I should and felt suddenly nervous, so I got up to check the food. My Sagittarius star ensured a fall from grace when I burned myself with the handle of a pot on the stove. I cried out and leaped back.

Moses got up to look, "What happened?"

"My stupidity," I held my hand to myself and groaned.

"Accidents happen, sunshine," he tried to hold my wrist and look but I fought him.

"No, let me bask in my shame."

He laughed, "We have to put something on it, can I see?" I groaned again and showed him my index finger. There was a long burn that stung and sizzled under my skin and only built to worse.

"Ouch," he said. He let go to pull scissors from the drawer and then went to the window where an Aloe plant sat. He snapped off the tip and brought it over.

"Interesting," I said as he came up to me. "Not many people know about Aloe Vera in the kitchen."

"It's a must," he gave a chin lift to the table and sat but my high heel dragged, and I fell awkwardly in his lap. I hated myself at this point, but his sense of humor was broad, and we only ended up laughing. I tried to get up, but he mistook it and settled me across his lap before taking my hand and applying the aloe. It instantly soothed the pain and I sighed. With my other arm around his neck.

"Thanks."

"No problem," he looked up at me and his face made my stomach turn. He was so pretty. The tanned skin, the beard, the bones in his face were all so masculine.

Moses hadn't kissed me yet. Whoa. How had we avoided that? He'd been so respectful of my space I realized this was the closest to touching we'd ever come.

"You have pretty hands," his words took me out of la la land. "I palm read," he clarified.

"Can you read mine?"

"Sure," he held his hand out again but I took my arm from around his neck and gave him the non-injured one. He observed a minute then explained. "See this line here?" He dragged his finger over a line going directly across, "that's the heart line." He dropped one down, "this is the head line," he made a slow curve under my thumb. "This is…the life line."

I started watching him instead.

"This fourth one is the fate line," he said. "Not all people have this one," he glanced up and caught me not looking.

"Sorry," I looked down and felt my cheeks burn. "S-so, w-which one is the-?"

He tilted my chin up and set his lips over mine. Oh! That was great. I missed that. I forgot how men feel when they kiss you. It's forceful but controlled. I felt the heat all down my body and like an engine I started up. I slanted my mouth and parted my lips to let him know he was welcome and he tasted the inside of my mouth.

Everything in me woke up knowing a man was close. My breasts felt sensitive through my clothes and my skin prickled with goosebumps. His hand glided up my thigh and I broke the kiss to move my head another angle and go deeper. He started to push back with more fire and I moaned. I wanted this so bad. Touch. It's like magic sparking up my veins and making me warm.

"I didn't mean to do that," he said pulling back.

"I did," I pulled him in again. *Don't stop now; you're feeding me life here.* I need this.

My elbow hit his wine glass and it fell and busted.

I came off his lap and covered my mouth, "Oh God, I'm sorry, I don't know why I can't manage to not break stuff or hurt myself, it's like-."

He was up in a flash and had my face in his hands, "I don't care," he kissed me again, gahhh these kisses! "You can break my whole kitchen," he said between kisses, "I don't care."

I laughed, if left alone under the right conditions I probably would break his kitchen. He stopped to bring us into the living room, but I tugged him toward the loft instead.

Um, it's been years, a couch can't handle what I need.

A few short steps and we were up in his bedroom. His mattress is low to the ground but made up neatly. I laid back on it and he came over me. His arms weren't as big as Chris' they were hard and wired with muscle but leaner. Stop thinking about Chris!

"I haven't done this in a long time," I warned. Not sure why.

He was kissing me and using his hips to pin me to the mattress which now had me terribly wet. I didn't understand why I wore jeans now?

"Do you want me to slow down?" he kissed me in a lingering way, "or stop?"

"No, please don't stop," I pulled his shirt up from the bottom and he knelt over me to take it off. His body was Chippendales worthy and now I wasn't just wet, I was soaking my underwear, but I noticed things that made him different.

His skin being tanner than Chris made his nipples a shade darker. It was hot, just different. No tattoos other than the scorpion on his forearm. I loved Chris' tattoos. They told stories and made him seem dangerous, tough, and unpredictable. Stop it! I shouted in my head.

"Jenzy?" Moses' voice brought my eyes to his. "You're sure?" he breathed.

I nodded and set my arms over my head like I was offering myself. He took that and bent to kiss me while his hands worked my blouse front. The buttons came open easily and I wanted him to touch my chest, my breasts are throbbing for his hands. I reached down between us and took my shirt off the rest of the way. He kissed my shoulder and bit at my bra strap which pulled a pant from my lips. He hooked the straps and pulled them down my shoulders.

"Purple," he said in a husky whisper.

I smiled and looked down at him while he kissed the rounded tops of my breasts. My bra was courtesy of Mandy and her push for new undergarments. It was a thin lilac with ruffled edges and sheer cups. There was a silk bow in the middle and though he hadn't gotten there yet, my panties matched.

"You like purple?" I asked as I pushed my hands through his short hair.

"I do, but I mean, it's witty to wear." He moved his bearded chin over my nipple and I felt it even more strongly through the fabric.

I squirmed under him and giggled, "what makes you say so?"

"You're a Sagittarius. Purple is your lucky color."

I felt a drop in my drive. It free fell right out of my body and I was left with a really intense reality that this wasn't Chris touching me. My lucky color. I was wearing my lucky color the night he and I met in the rain at that bus stop.

"Jenzy?" I think Moses said my name more than once but then I looked up at him and he used his thumb to wipe a tear from under my eye. "Hey, look at me, what's wrong?" I couldn't come up with a smart lie or a sly excuse, so I just looked at him. He rolled us, now I was on top. He sat up against his wall. I was straddling his lap and now gravity made more tears fall.

"Shhh," he said and pulled my bra straps back up into place on my shoulders, "Hey, talk to me. Please?"

"I'm really sorry," I managed. He pulled me into his arms and held me there. I bridled the tears quickly enough but only after they told on me. He rubbed my back and kissed my ear and I felt like sleeping. "I thought I was ready," I confessed.

"I knew better, It's my fault."

Wow, what a champ. Taking on my train wreck.

"We need to stop seeing each other, this is stupid," I told him as I sat straight. "I want you so badly, but it's selfish, I'm still healing. You'll end up hurt."

"I know the risks. Can I decide what's best?"

"A girlfriend that cries when you try to have sex. That's romantic."

"It's life," he used his palm to take up more tears. "I don't mind. We can go slower, though we were friends first, right? Let's just step back. Simple and sweet."

"I want to be with you."

"Then we keep dating, sex doesn't have to happen now, I'm not going anywhere. I really didn't intend to let us even go this far. I'm trying to wait for a signed divorce. I don't want you confused or… Even if you changed your mind on us, I'm not going anywhere."

That won me, "You'd do that?"

"I want to be in your life, I don't mind how. Okay? Just, don't cry it's not important now."

I took in some easy breaths. Then tried to smile and kissed his cheek. He hugged me tighter.

"The fact that your eggplant smells like burnt popcorn is important, though," he said cautiously.

"Oh shit!" I leaped up with him.

Chapter Seventeen
CHRIS

I picked up Jenzy that next week at 5:30 on Friday evening so we could make it to her parent's beach house by dinner. There was no visiting for a *few hours* with Jenzy's parents. Edna and Scotty were the types to make you stay overnight. Which is what I wanted. Jenzy and I would be spending the weekend with them, from tonight to early Monday morning.

Jenzy looked at me strangely when I took her bags and loaded them. Then I opened her car door. I hadn't acted this way in a long time. I guess that's why I'm getting looks.

She was in a long summer skirt with a cropped top and her favorite beige sweater. It had a hole in the elbow and a run somewhere, she looked amazing to me.

"Ready for this?" I asked her once we were well on the road.

"I guess," she set her head back, "just don't trap me by siding them with you, okay? I'm not doing this for drama; I just want us to live happy lives in separate directions."

I nodded but I had no intention of holding to that deal. "You look tired," I observed over my sunglasses.

"I just didn't sleep well last night."

"You okay?"

"Did you cheat?" Her question would have caused us a wreck on the road, but I felt something like that was coming from her.

She went on before letting me answer, "I won't be mad, it's over between us anyway, I just would like to know, did you ever have an affair while we were…?"

I knew just saying, 'nope' would be as helpful as telling her 'maybe'. She needed a metaphor. "You know that sweater you're wearing?" I asked.

She looked annoyed that I changed the subject. After all, it probably took all her courage to ask.

"Yeah, what about it?"

"It's old as the hills and it's damaged," I said.

"So?"

"So why keep it? There are better sweaters. We live in California, I think this is like fashion central, isn't it?"

She held herself, "It's my favorite, it makes me happy and to me, those 'other sweaters' aren't so much better. I love this one."

"Then there's your answer."

She frowned at me, "Answer to what?"

I didn't speak; I just kept my eyes on the road. After looking at me for a really long time her eyes softened, and she looked out her window. I had to relieve the tension, so I reached out and tugged her sleeve.

She looked back at me and smiled a little which made my heart freak out.

Jenzy bit her lip, "So, you did mean 'no, I didn't cheat' right? Or were you calling me old and holey?" She teased.

We laughed but knowing that she understood made me feel accomplished.

By the time we reached her parent's, she was asleep. Curled into the door on her side, she looked like that college girl I fell in love with. I had a mini heart seizure when I thought of the fact she was dating someone. How far had they gone? Had they had sex yet? Sex was her and I's language, we synced so well it was like we could hear one another's thoughts during the act. Would someone else make her feel that way? Where had Moses touched her? Did she enjoy it?

I put us in park and rubbed her shoulder. Great excuse to feel her, "Hey, Jenzy?" I whispered it. She stirred but held her sweater closer and let out a quiet sound that went straight to my groin. "Jenzy, we're here."

"Oh," she sat up and blinked to clear the sleep. Her parents were well-off people, so their beach house was no small matter.

White and three stories high and so close to the ocean it was on stilts. The rooftops were all gabled and greenish-blue. The veranda was wide and long, and the steps were in an L shape. There was a palm tree in the center of the circular drive and the gardens surrounding were full of little stone Buddha's and or yoga posing frogs. Jenzy's mom was where the hippie came from.

"Who is that?" she asked squinting out toward the sea.

I looked with her and frowned, "I don't-, I don't know…can't tell from here."

"Is that Dad?"

"No, I don't think-."

She screamed, scaring me out of my wits. "Ew! Oh my God! It's Daddy!"

I looked and then grimaced and covered her eyes. I honked the horn a few times and when he saw us, his eyes went wide, and he dove into the high grass. Scotty was totally naked, and my wife was freaking out.

"Is it gone? Is it gone? Oh my God, ew, ew, ew, ugh! Claw my eyes out, Chris! Claw them out!"

"I'm busy gauging my own! Chill out a minute!"

"*You* chill out!" She held my hand over her eyes. "You're not the one that just saw the hose you were cannoned from!"

"I'm trying really hard not to throw up, now chill out."

"I still see it in my head," she whined.

After collecting ourselves and our stuff, we started up to the house. I had to practically drag her, since she was concerned he might not be dressed yet. Once at the door, we didn't even knock before Edna greeted us in a sarong and lots of jingly jewelry. She pulled us in, one at a time for hugs and a face full of kisses.

She was eccentric, to say the least, but I loved Edna, she didn't age. Also smart as hell. A hippie with one serious IQ, which means I never had long awkward lulls in conversation with her. She was an older version of Jenzy and if she was any indication of what was to come, and I could change Jenzy's heart back to me, I was never going to have a less than hot wife.

"How are you two beautiful people?" Edna asked.

"We're okay, mom just traumatized," Jenzy told her.

"Oh, yeah, ya father's pretty disturbed too," her New York accent always made me smile. "The one time I get em' to sunbathe and you two show up. The odds, right?"

"Mind if I put these upstairs?" I asked.

"Yeah, son, go ahead. You and Jenzy's room is all put together."

Jenzy looked at me but I doubted she planned to tell her mom at this very moment, so I just nodded and started up the stairs.

"You look good, Chris, honey! Ya still pumpin' iron?" Edna called as I went up.

I paused on my way and laughed, "Yeah, you bet."

"Good, then you can help Scotty move that pool table down in the basement. He's so fragile he'd probably fall."

Jenzy rubbed her mom's arm, "If you're worried about dad-."

"Worried? I ain't worried, funerals are expensive."

I laughed but Jenzy just glared at both of us.

"I'll help him out later," I told Edna then went up. I opened the door to the room Jenzy and I always shared and breathed in the fresh air.

This was a very big room with a king-sized bed that had four tall cherry wood bedposts. The floors were wood with a massive tanned carpet under the bed, and a candelabrum hung over the middle. The best part of this room was the floor to ceiling windows. One faced the ocean and beside it, the other faced out with a balcony. Both were wide open right now so there was a cross breeze and saltwater smells assaulted me. As I set our things down, I looked at the bed. We'd made a lot of love in that bed, but the last few times we stayed I hadn't touched her.

I rejoined them all downstairs and followed the sound of arguing. Edna and Scotty were like cage fighters all the time, but you get used to it.

I heard Edna first as I walked in, "I said 'bring ya shorts.' You never listen to me. You gotta hear it from someone else, ya that thick in the head."

"You said they were coming at seven! Seven!" Scotty fought back. "Seven is after six, they rolled up at six-forty-five. That ain't no seven!"

Edna shook her head, "Ya brought ya watch but not your shorts that's smart."

They saw me and stopped, "Hey there, Chris," Scotty said and came up to shake my hand, but I had to laugh that Jenzy was sitting at the island in their kitchen slurping at a Pina Colada her mom whipped up. I know this is stressing her. Her father and I are tighter than hell.

"Hey, Scotty," I smiled. "Found your clothes?"

"I did," he laughed but his cheeks were red, "Wowza, I'm sorry kids. I didn't wanna do it, you know. *She* made me. You know how the women in this family are. Pushy, goddamn broads."

Edna started the blender to tune him out. As time went by I chanced sitting down next to Jenzy. She didn't act weird, but she didn't slow up on the alcohol.

"So," Edna looked excited from across the island as Scotty took a drink from their fridge, "we have a swing couple event," she told us.

I raised my brows, "You guys…swing?"

"Dancing," Scotty clarified. We shared a laugh the girls didn't get.

Edna glowered at him, "Anyway, tomorrow night we go out, we dance, we have a good time. I can feel my aura opening up.

It's very cleansing. Music heals, so you guys should go with us. Go get loose. Feels good."

Jenzy licked her lips, "Uh, probably not mom."

"Why not? It's fun baby! Don't ya remember that belly dancing class we took together? You said Chris loved that. You loved that, didn't ya Chris?"

Ah yes, the belly dancing. Jenzy developed a mind-blowing habit of doing orgasmic figure eights with her hips and stomach when she rode me during sex. All thanks to that class.

I grinned at a flushed Jenzy, "Yeah, why not?" I asked her.

She gave me a pointed look, "We don't really do those things anymore, ma."

"What, ya don't have fun?" Edna rinsed the blender and shoved Scotty out of the way to do so.

Scotty sighed. "Ima go watch the game."

"No ya not, your daughter's here. Socialize!" Edna snapped.

"They know I love em', I love em' just as much with the game on. Chris understands. You understand me, don't ya, Chris?"

"Yes, Sir," I saluted.

"Don't get Chris in trouble," Edna warned. "Televisions hold negative energy that causes bad moods."

"Then you must be a widescreen," Scotty retorted.

Edna whipped him with the towel and daggered him like a hawk, which made me look away like she might eat me too.

She leveled, "Watch it, Scotty, I'm this close to making ya death look like a friggin accident."

"Maybe they have TV in heaven," he countered.

Edna looked back at us, "This is why you two need to go. Don't leave me alone with this putz."

Jenzy shook her head, "It's really not our thing anymore," Jenzy deflected.

Edna backed off, "You wanna be alone here at the house then? You should make love on the beach; the neighbors can't see from here. The grass is too high."

"*Mom!*" Jenzy shouted.

"For fuck sake, Edna!" Said Scotty as he gestured at us. "You think I want visions of that in my head? I remember her learning to tie shoes."

Edna leaned forward to get closer to us, "Tomorrow night is a full moon." She told me, "If you have sex out there, I bet you'd knock her up," she added a wink.

"*MOM!*" Jenzy bugged her eyes, "Jesus! Please!"

"What's Jesus got to do with it? He loved babies too, Bible says so."

"No one is making babies," Jenzy insisted.

"Then I'm gonna die before I see any grandbabies. That's nice to know."

"Ma, it's complicated."

"Are you two having trouble conceiving, because I got a charm for that. There are also certain rites…"

"No, we're divorcing," Jenzy announced.

There was a silence that could've broken glass and I crossed my arms as I sat back on the bar stool. Edna and Scotty looked at us a long minute.

Then Edna straightened, "What happened?"

"Nothing, we just-," she glanced at me knowing better than to claim we both fell out of love. "Things happen and it's time we go other ways."

Edna looked at me and I felt uncomfortable. She was too perceptive sometimes. "Is that what you want too, Chris?" she asked.

I debated how to put it, "I want Jenzy happy." I went safe, but Edna saw through it and Scotty still hadn't spoken.

Edna looked to Jenzy, "There has to be a reason."

Jenzy looked cornered by her mom and I realized I was still making her look bad.

I jumped in, "I've treated her shitty these last couple years, we haven't been okay for a while, I just didn't notice."

Scotty put his drink down, "Jenn, you okay?"

I looked and Jenzy was getting pink in the face. She only did that when tears were at bay.

"I'm fine. I'm going to go lay down," she got up and left and I fought the urge to go with her. That's not really my place anymore, though, is it?

Scotty leaned over the island, "Square with me, Christopher. Ya sleeping with someone?"

I sighed, "I'm really tired of people asking me that. Why does everyone assume that? Why doesn't anyone think she might have slept with someone?"

They both laughed like I told a great joke then Edna reigned it in, "Chris, Jenzy was so head over heel she wouldn't even be able to if she tried."

"Well, she's dating already," I said with a bitter edge.

Her mother turned that too, "That's just proof it wasn't happening before. If you mean Moses, I already know they haven't-."

"How do you know about Moses?" I asked.

"Her friend. She told me when they started talking that she liked him but would never do anything behind your back. They've only been friends. I shoulda seen that could mean there were problems with you two."

I rubbed my face like I meant to take it off, "This is a fucking nightmare," I groaned. "Worse part. I have no clue how it got this way. I've been raking my brain like no one's business. I don't know where it went to hell, I don't know why."

Scotty said, "You know what I would do?"

Edna laughed, "Oh, sure, you're qualified to give relationship advice. I don't think so. Shut up, Scotty.

"We're still married, ain't we?" he argued.

"Yeah, because you're like herpes, you don't go away."

"There you go!" This led to a long and dark battle/rant where they flung dirt and yelled.

Then it came to me, "Hey! Guys!" I whistled, and they stopped to look at me. "This is exactly what I'm saying. This, in a way, is what's wrong with her and I. How have you gone this long if you don't even like each other?"

They creased their brows and exchanged a confused look, "What do you mean?" Edna asked. "Who says I don't like Scotty?"

I snorted, "Come on, you two fight all the time."

"Because he's an annoying fucktard. Not because I don't like em'."

"She nags," Scotty put distance between them, "sometimes I don't like her. Especially, when she makes me eat that healthy shit."

"To keep you alive, moron," she snapped back.

"Low cholesterol food isn't food!"

"When I tried making ya eat right twenty years ago, you shoulda done it! Who salts fried chicken?"

"Why did ya make it fried? Maybe you wanted me this way?" he shouted.

"If I wanted to kill ya, I would have made it quick. Why would I put myself through all this?"

I cleared my throat, "Guys…this isn't answering my question. You fight. This is what I mean. You're total opposites. Why stay together? Why put up with all this? It's the same for Jenzy and I. I contested the divorce because I wanted time to fix us. Am I crazy?"

They watched me, and their silence fell hard again.

Scotty finally straightened and swallowed, "No one can tell you if this is right or not. The heart is where marriage is valid, not paper, not where the government is concerned."

Edna and Scotty actually agreed with one another and mellowed before my eyes.

Edna leaned into the counter, "You wanna know why everyone asks if you cheated?"

No, but I guess I need to, so I waited.

"Because as long as we've all known you, ya want what you can't have. Then depending on what it is, you ain't always happy with-it long. When you want something, I've never seen someone fight harder than you to get it. An affair would be a forbidden fruit, I think we all figured you might cave. If the only reason you want Jenzy back is because you can't, then no. You need to sign and let this go."

Scotty jerked his head to the upstairs, "If Edna saying that makes you feel sick right now, then you need to step up the game, and fast."

"You asked us about opposites…" Edna went on, "nobody is perfect, Chris. What might just be an opposite, you have been looking at as a flaw. If you love Jenzy like you did when you met, you'll see her differences as pieces of her soul. Even if you don't agree or don't understand, you'll want to. You'll accept that. If it's too much, then it's not love."

I considered what made Jenzy annoying to me. She believed in stupid things, when sometimes I wanted her to be logical. But just because she didn't have the same feelings did that make her opinions stupid? How was it hurting me if she believed all deities existed? Or that fairies might be real? What was the big deal if she wanted to use holistic medicine, it didn't mean I had to, but it didn't mean I had to devalue her way. I would deal with all of that if it meant having her back.

Chapter Eighteen
CHRIS

After talking more time with her parents, we ate dinner. Edna loved different ethnic foods, tonight was Indian. She was the best cook in the world, even compared to my mom.

Scotty went upstairs to entice Jenzy to eat but she claimed she just wanted sleep. When I was done, I helped clean up then said goodnight. Upon coming into our room, I saw she had left the enormous windows open. An almost full moon was lighting up the room, and the sound of waves was wrapping around it. She was in a ball on the bed with her back to me and she was still in her clothes.

I tiptoed around, getting my bags.

"Where are you going?" she asked in a thick voice. She'd either been crying or asleep.

"Your mom has another guestroom downstairs."

She looked over her shoulder, "Isn't it bare? There are no lights and no bed in it yet."

"I'll be fine."

"The floors are hardwood, Chris."

"I'll crash on the couches then."

She rolled to face me and sat up on her elbow. "There isn't a couch long enough. Just stay, it's fine."

I shouldered my bag, "You don't want to sleep with me."

"I don't want to touch, that's all," she explained. I stood and debated for a minute. "You drove us all the way here, you need to sleep," she offered.

Still worrying about me and I wasn't her problem anymore. I don't think she knows what she wants and that annoys me. "How would Moses feel about that?" I asked.

She paused, then murmured, "Fuck you," and rolled to put her back to me again.

Damn it! My mouth should wear shoes to make the foot in there comfortable.

"I'm sorry," I tried. That wasn't going to do it. "Jenzy?"

"What, Chris?"

I set my bag down, "I'm sorry."

She shrugged, "Whatever, stay where you want."

I realized there was the smallest chance she wanted me to stay and I blew it. I started unbuttoning my shirt and stripped to my boxers. I got in and she scooted to the far end of the mattress like I had an illness. We had nothing but the sound of waves after a while but then I felt her constant fidgeting and smiled to myself.

"It's too hot to sleep in your clothes," I said.

"I'm fine," she snapped.

My smile widened, "You only ever sleep in t-shirts and didn't you tell me sleeping with bras on was unhealthy?"

"Drop it!"

I bit my lip to keep from laughing. Jenzy had to strip at night, she *had* to. She would sleep nude if she could, but her mom told her once that if the house caught fire she wouldn't have time to get dressed and that's how the fire department would find her.

She groaned heavily then sat up, "Just don't look."

"K," I closed my eyes tight and folded my arms behind my head. I could feel her staring at me. I know what my body does for her, especially when the tats are showing. My arms and chest are covered in them. If only she knew her body did the same for me.

"It's not like I haven't seen you naked," I reminded with my eyes still closed.

"So?" I felt her get off the bed. "You haven't *wanted* to see me naked in years. I'm just as unattractive as I've been to you before this divorce."

My eyes opened, and I turned my head to look at her, "Where the fuck did you get that idea-."

"Chris! Don't look!" She screeched as she held her sweater over her chest.

I turned my head back and closed my eyes again, "Why would you think I find you unattractive?"

"I don't know… must've started after the hundredth time you rejected me for sex. My favorite memory was me waiting naked for you in our bed and you telling me if I kept up with laundry I would have something to wear. Then there's the time I tried kissing you at the park and you told me to grow up."

I cringed, I have been *that bad.* It was like being Scrooge and seeing yourself do things to hurt people. I chanced a peek at her. She was sitting on the bed with her back to me as she reached back to unsnap her bra. Her back turned me on. I love taking her from an angle where I can see it or smooth my hand down it. That wouldn't go over well so I looked away.

Like a bug light, I was looking again, though. She was slipping on an old, black, muscle shirt with tie-dye circles and a Hindu elephant in the center. Her black panties rode low on her hips and I could see the dimples on either side of her spine above her ass. Now I was really turned on and that meant the beast was waking in my boxers. I adjusted myself and sighed.

This is the longest I've gone without sex. Yet, this was a self-inflicted celibacy! Where had my libido gone for two whole years?

She got back into bed, still keeping a continent between us with her back to me.

Then when I thought she was drifting, she spoke, "Hasn't this gone far enough? You've dragged me to your mom's now my parent's and everyone knows. I'm not changing my mind. I want out. We can't fix this- some things don't fix."

I turned over to her, since my boner was working its way down with every word she said. I moved over enough to rub her arm and it hurt deeper than ever when she curled away from my touch. I took my hand back and felt a little suffocated. I have lost the right to touch her. It was no better than being strangers. It's not okay to touch her when I want anymore because she's on her way to not being mine.

"I'm not doing this to you, to hurt you, Jenzy. Like I said, I want you to give me time to…earn you back, and yeah, I won't lie. That's what I want. There's something else, though. I really do want you happy, so while I'm using this time, I'm also trying to make sure I'm even capable of being what it takes. I did it for years before things got shitty, so…I just want time to see if, there's really nothing to save."

She didn't answer, and I rolled back to my side. Doubting myself hard, I wondered if I should just give her the divorce. I might have damaged her too much to ask for a second chance. I also wondered if she even heard me. Was she sleeping? She kept accusing me of falling out of love, was that because *she* had? I hadn't considered that. Oh, my God, had Jenzy stopped feeling everything?

I couldn't believe that. That's giving up, and she didn't need more of that from me.

JENZY

I came upstairs to get away from Chris and my parent's accusing eyes. I know my mom probably understood but I didn't want to chance a lecture. Then I felt sad and needed to cry without people closing in on me. Even if I wanted freedom, this was still Chris and the idea of being separated still scared me a little. He's part of me. He's the one I imagined my future with. It was his kids I wanted to have and his heart I craved.

When he came up for bed, I almost wept again hearing him picking up his things. I needed him close, so I offered for him to stay and in one sentence he proved why I was making the right choice with this divorce. That mean streak surfaced.

Then that fucker stripped, knowing good and well his tats make me horny. Now, as I'm drifting off, I hear him declare why he won't sign and all I see is false hope. Chris was always jerking my heart around for the ride and I was the idiot letting him drive. Just like college.

Falling asleep was a bad idea since my mind thought this was a good time to reflect.

Chapter Nineteen
JENZY
2008

"I got the transfer," Chris told me over the phone. I slowed my walk through the halls of my school as my smile faded. "I'll be in Sweden this time next month. They actually want me; my grades are pulling me right through."

I forced myself to sound excited, "That's great! I told you it would happen. I saw it in the tarot cards that one time."

"Yeah, your *cards,* were eerily on point, you should work for the government."

I laughed, "Then this is it. Did you tell Todd yet?"

"No, I'm going to his job now. Thanks for keeping this private."

"No problem. I'm really happy for you. This is…this is fantastic."

"Thanks, I'm pretty stoked. Think we can go shopping for the trip this weekend? It's cold there and I'm not a sweater wearer…"

"Yeah, sure. I'll check my work schedule."

"Okay, I'm at Todd's. Bye."

"Bye," I hung up and hugged my books to my chest. I knew we weren't a couple. Since sleeping together that first night, we had become as close as me and Todd. They were both my boys. Their mom loved me, and my parents loved them. I hung with Chris alone sometimes, but nothing ever happened. I just secretly hoped it would.

My roommate Mandy came jogging up the hall, "Ugh, girl I was so late for that stupid class. Get this, I still passed the test; because I'm awesome."

"Good for you!"

"Yeah, and Todd and I are going to the movies tonight, wanna come?"

"I think I'll stay in."

"You okay?"

I kept walking until we were outside, and she knew better than to press me. We walked the campus a while, which helped push down the lump in my throat. Our campus looked like Hogwarts, made of brick and stone and the fields were lush and full of big old trees. I sat on a bench under a bare looking tree and slouched.

"He's going…" I admitted.

"Pervy Chris got the transfer to Sweden?"

I smiled inside. Since walking in on him naked in our dorm, she called him Pervy Chris.

"Yeah. Thanks for not telling Todd."

"I know it's a secret. You okay with it?"

I shrugged, "Does it matter? He's going, I'm staying and we friend zoned each other after that first time."

"Well, it was best. No one has ever seen him with a girlfriend. He just sleeps around. Even if you started friends with benefits or dated, he'd never tell anyone or show any indication to the public. You want to be a closet lover?"

"No. I know how he is."

"He must care a little bit, he talks to you every day and sees you at least six times a week to hang out. I almost wonder if he wants you and is too scared to say. You did tell him no to it happening again."

"What's the point? He's leaving."

She hugged me and I leaned into her, "He's so annoying, hon, find someone better."

I smiled but didn't say anything.

That weekend, I helped Chris shop for Sweden. I had to endure the boy talk between him and Todd about how hot Swedish girls are, and how great this trip was. Then in a wink, the time came. Todd and I were driving him to an airport. I sat in the back seat and Todd drove while Chris sat in the passenger side talking to their mom on the phone. The hollowness of seeing him go was eating at me.

We waited at his gate later and while Todd stepped aside to buy us snacks, Chris sat back in his chair and looked over at me sitting next to him.

"You good?" he asked.

"Yeah," I faked a smile. "Nervous for you, but excited."

"You'll keep up with me, right?"

"Of course."

"There's like, a nine-hour difference. That's going to be a pain in the ass."

"I don't mind," I said honestly.

"You gonna miss me?"

I looked up at him and debated telling him how much I'd surely miss him. "You don't even know," I looked away because I was afraid my eyes would tell on me. He adjusted the beanie hat on his head and cleared his throat.

Then he stood up, "Todd just kinda, disappeared," he laughed.

I looked around and pulled my phone, "I'll try calling him."

"We have time to check the bathroom. Another 15 or 20…" I frowned at him. "Come on," he started walking and I followed while still trying to get Todd.

His phone was going straight to voicemail. We reached the divided hall where the restrooms were split women to men's and before I could stop to wait while he searched, Chris pulled me by the jacket front into the men's room. It was empty, thank God.

"What the hell, Chris?" I tried to skid to a stop, but Mr. Iron Pumper had no problem pulling me along. He shushed me then pulled me into a spacious handicapped stall.

"I've never been in a men's room before," I whispered as he locked us in. "Well, one time when I was five and had to pee. But my dad covered my eyes till we were in the stall, so I wouldn't see-."

Before I could say, he turned around and laid an intense kiss on me. My mind took a while to sink in the fact that Chris was kissing me. Chris! He was holding my face and taking my mouth and, and what did this mean? I dropped my phone into my purse and threw my arms around his neck.

His hands went down to my waist and he pressed me into him. I could remember the night we had sex so clearly in my mind now. He'd left me so satisfied and hot. It was the best sex ever and I hated that he was doing this to me now, when he was leaving.

"What was that?" I asked.

He searched my face, "I wasn't brave enough to do it when I wanted to but…I figured if you rejected me I could just…get on this plane…and forget you."

"You want me?"

"What guy on campus doesn't?"

"The gay ones," I teased.

"This was really stupid and I'm sorry, but I had to do it."

"Why?"

"I don't know." He stepped back and let me go. "Maybe cause, I think about you non-stop since sleeping with you. Because I haven't screwed around with other girls in like, way too long, since it happened. My game is so off when I try. Because, I hate being your friend, I really hate it. I hate watching guys talk to you and flirt. I really, really want to sleep with you again, bad. I've had a lot of sex okay, like a lot, but it was never, that hot, it was never like it was with us. It's not just the sex, it's you, you're in my head all the time."

"You're going to Sweden."

"I know," he took a breath. "I know this is the worst timing ever."

"What do we do? You have to go."

"Would you wait?"

"Until when?"

"I don't know, until I come home, change my mind, until you come visit, until- I don't know, but would you?"

I considered that. He didn't know but I wasn't seeing people either. I didn't want anyone. That night meant something to me too and now I was glowing inside. He wanted me too. I came up and used his open jacket to pull him in for a kiss. He bent his head and took my mouth again. He started gentle, just pressing tender kisses to my lips then hungry tastings.

He moved so my back was to the door and lifted me by my thighs. I was in a brown skirt and a tank that tied up in front.

His hands wrapped around my thighs, felt like fire. Our kisses went on and on and I smiled against his mouth. He was such a complicated thinker and I was so, *go with the flow*, that the two of us had misread the time. Now, when there was none, we were milking what was left.

"You'll fly home for Thanksgiving, right?" I panted.

"I will *now*." He kissed me again and soon I felt his hand pushing further up my thigh, under my skirt. I was open to him since he was keeping me suspended so there was no stopping him when he stroked me over my panties. My breath hitched, and we stopped kissing, so he could look me in the eyes. His fingers felt me through the material and the touch made my blood heat.

"You didn't say," he said in a honeyed tone. "Will you wait?" He worked his fingers into the sides of my underwear and found my telling body wet. He gently rubbed my clit then slid his finger into me and I gasped. "Tell me the truth," he bade.

I swallowed so I could make sounds, "Yes."

"You'll keep this safe for me?" he probed me deeper and found the place that rippled everywhere so I moaned into the side of his neck. He kissed my ear and then my neck. "Promise?"

"I promise," I ground myself into his hand because he was making me ready. "Will *you*?" I questioned. He slid yet another finger inside while massaging me harder. "You've said Swedish girls are pretty hot."

He laughed but it came out thick with lust, "Waiting for you isn't a problem, but only if you cum for me before I leave."

His request made my body burn to comply. I held the back of the door and rolled my hips. His rubbing and his penetration would bring it on faster.

He put his face in my neck and did that thing, the thing I loved with his tongue. Good God, it was my undoing. The flicking and the dragging timed perfectly with the thrust of his fingers.

I whimpered as the wave neared and he started whispering, like he knew his voice was key.

"Give me this, Jenzy give me this memory of you cumming at the touch of my hand. I need this from you, I want it. Let go and give it to me," he sounded greedy and I loved it.

I shuddered hard against the door and cried out when I came. It was too much to keep in and I didn't even care if someone heard. He kissed me when I finished, and I kissed him harder back. He slowly set me on my feet then crouched down in front of me.

"What?" I asked.

He smiled and held the back of my knee, "We need to clean you up before going back out."

I slumped against the door and waited for him to hand me paper but instead, his head dipped under my skirt and he licked a hot, wet line up the inside of my thigh and up the crotch of my panties. I panted when he went again up the other and hooked my underwear aside to drag his tongue over my sex. Then he took his head from under my skirt, stood and held my hand.

"I'm going to miss my flight, let's go," he unlocked the door and we stepped out to see we had an audience of like seven guys. They were all just standing there with either dumb smiles or wide eyes.

"Hey," Chris said nervously. We suppressed laughs as he tucked me under his arm and we fled. We walked hand in hand down the hall stealing secretive glances and giggles. We slowly took our hands away as we reached his gate and Todd came into view hanging in one of the waiting chairs texting, probably Mandy.

"I'll call you as soon as I reach my connecting flights, and again when I get there," said Chris as we got closer.

"Okay," I bit my lip to keep from smiling too dopily.

He hugged Todd goodbye then me and my knees felt weak.

Where did all that passion go? Why do people falling out of love, do things to each other that they would never do in the days they loved? It's like we forget. We completely forget.

Chapter Twenty
Present Day
JENZY

I woke up cuddled into something warm and firm. My eyes were heavy with sleep, but the room was so bright. Then I looked up to see it was Chris. We were lying facing one another and I was cocooned in his arms. His big, safe arms. He was still asleep, so I could look. He was the most handsome guy in the world.

His lashes were so thick I was jealous, it made him look like he wore liner. His nose was strong and shapely, and his jaws were prominent. Funny how bones are a turn on. Is that weird? I love his jaws? Then I freaked myself out because I wouldn't love his jaws if they were like Shark jaws and opened up with thousands of pointy teeth and ate me.

Wow, Jenzy. You really took it there.

I thought of sneaking away, but my knee was sandwiched between his thighs. I wanted us to stay apart but I think this cuddling thing was my fault. I move around when I sleep, but he doesn't. He's usually a light sleeper so I probably burrowed into him and he probably took advantage of the situation and pulled me in closer. *Dick.*

Then again, he hadn't held me like this in ages. I missed this.

I need to stop. I started to slowly pull my leg out of the trap.

"If you're trying to give me morning wood, use your mouth, not your leg," he murmured.

I froze and looked down. He was hard as a rock in his boxers and my body responded.

I retreated, "Sorry." I tried to pull my leg away, but he used his thigh muscles to keep mine trapped.

"I think you've got morning dew," he was grinning with his eyes closed, smug bastard.

"No," I tried to pull my leg free again because he was right. My crotch was damp. Probably from thinking about the past last night.

"Stay here a minute," he said. He still had his eyes closed and I felt annoyed but tired enough to stay put. He pulled me closer, "Listen. Between the ocean, the birds and the smells, it's like when we went to Hawaii."

Our honeymoon. Smooth move. He was trying to seduce me.

"Let me go, Chris or I'll seriously hurt you."

"You were terrible at that self-defense class I took you to. I'm not that concerned. Biggest waste of money."

I retaliated by trying a move on him but I found myself rolled on my back and pinned in the space of a second. "Get off, Chris!"

He held my wrists above my head and forced my hips to the bed with his own, "You're so cute with your empty threats. You didn't retain a damn thing from that class."

I made an effort to fight him off, but he didn't even strain at keeping me down. It was like worming out from under a rock.

I huffed, "This is stupid, get off!"

"Your sounds are adorable when you struggle too. They sound like your sex sounds but usually, I make you reach deeper. They aren't as high pitch."

I bucked my hips to try a move from that stupid class but I accidentally excited myself. Ugh! I could feel his boner and it was awakening my need of him. I realized how easy it would be for him to do it, right now. Panties and boxers were the only barriers and his demonstration of strength to keep me down was making me hungry for it.

In fact, now when I bucked or writhed it was to feel it, that rush to my sex that made me feel dizzy and receptive.

I have to watch it, though because those hazel eyes are keen to my body and the glint told me he was assessing my actions.

"Chris, I want to get up so knock it off."

"Why? Turning you on?"

Yes! "No."

"You usually liked it rough. Not so rough that it was painful but gentle bores you. Like," he tightened his grip on my wrists, "This is the pressure you beg me for, right? Tight, demanding, impossible to get out of, but safe, because you trust me."

His words were making so much moisture collect in my folds that I was sweating the idea of him checking, if he did he'd know he won.

He went on, "It's weird because what you want is what I need. Like I need you yielding to me this way after you've put up a good fight, and I need you panting with the effort, and squirming so your curves rub against me. I like the whole dynamic of you trusting your body to me, so I can pillage it but only by your will, and your equal want."

I'm so close to folding, it's insane. Every word he says has made the agony between my legs unbearable. I want him to take me, right here in this bed, without consequences.

He grinned at my silence, "Don't worry," he said, then released me and got off the bed in one fluid motion. "I'm just teasing." He said as he sauntered into the bathroom adjoined to our room.

Hours later after we visited with my parents from breakfast to long after lunch; I went up to change into my swimsuit. Chris and my dad were out fishing on some pier up the way and Mom is doing her meditation on the back veranda. I was meditating with her and it was great, until she stopped every two minutes to ask me why I was leaving Chris.

Every time it got quite a question popped up.

"Do you still love him?"

"Are you pregnant?"
"Are you sure about this?"
"How long does he plan to contest?"
"Was there a specific reason that made you feel like giving up?"

I stripped and pulled on the magenta bottoms with turquoise paisley print then pulled on the bikini top. It was padded enough in the cups to make my boobs look impressive, not that I wanted to impress anyone, just that a girl should feel nice about her boobs.

Then I was off to the shore. I wadded around and went into the deep to feel weightless. I even went under once or twice.

I brought my tote bag full of goodies. I laid out and read for a time then tried flipping through some dream interpretation books. I napped, and I even attempted at learning a new deck of tarot I found with Moses. All on the beach.

My mom shouted to me that she was going out with Dad for their swing dancing thing and I waved and blew a kiss. Now I really didn't want to go inside. No more alone time with Chris, thank you.

My phone buzzed in my tote and when I looked I smiled.

It was Moses.
"Hey, Sunshine how's the beach?"

I looked out past the waves. The sky was a cotton candy pink with dark purple and royal blues.

Then I typed,
"It's lucky. Lol."

The word bubble appeared, and I anxiously waited.
"Then it must be your colors then?"

He guessed right and that made me giddy.

"Good guess. You would like it here. My mom would love you."

He came back,
"Uh, oh, not dad too?"

I worded it carefully.
"Well, Dad and Chris are pretty tight, but he would be polite. Oh, and question! On the deck we bought I have a deity I can't place. You studied religions. Who is the Hindu goddess with all the arms?"

His bubble came up for a while as he typed for a bit. I loved this. Having someone to share my hobbies with.
"Parvati is usually with another deity called Shiva. Durga is a warrior goddess; she's usually on a tiger or a lion."

I studied the card still confused then typed back.
"This one isn't on anything."

He returned.
"What's she holding in her hands?"

I checked then typed.
"Weapons."

He knew right away.
"Durga."

I smiled.
"You're amazing."

I could imagine his rich laughter.
"I try. Lol."

But then I heard Chris coming and things got…really, really weird.

Chapter Twenty-One
JENZY

I heard the sliding door close and winced. When I looked back, Chris was coming out and munching on something. I faced the sea and hoped he would leave me alone but then I heard him getting closer.

He was in blue swim trunks and an open white button-down; the shirt sleeves rolled up. Tats everywhere, abs everywhere, he really didn't play fair but being out here, he probably felt comfortable showing his ink.

"Hey," I said trying to be friendly.

He looked down at me and stared a long time while he chewed his treat before his eyes brightened, "Hey! Jenzy! How long you been sitting there?"

I frowned, "You didn't see me?"

"Nope," he said around a mouthful.

"What are you eating?"

"Brownies," he stopped and looked at what was left. "Isn't that weird? Why are they called that? They aren't even the color brown."

I blinked at that one. *Okay.*

I started packing up my tote, "I'm going in." I felt intimate being in a two-piece with him around. Not that it mattered; I still don't think he wants me that badly. I stood up and bent to get my blanket.

"Are your boobs still real? They look bigger."

"What?" I blanched.

He reached out and felt one. He actually took a feel of my breast.

I slapped his hand, "What the fuck, Chris?"

He licked the fudge off his fingers, "They're still real, that's awesome," he laughed then finished his brownie, but he had fudge on his lips like a kid. Neat Freak Chris…? This man avoids Sloppy Joes and tacos in public to stay clean. He was eating this brownie, like he forgot how his mouth worked.

"Are you okay?" I wondered out loud.

"I'm really good," he laughed. "I feel so awesome. Just chill. So chill. Like…ice cubes, chill like ice, but I'm not see-through. I'm not transparent. Am I?" He looked down and patted his chest and stomach. "Nope," he laughed, "Just chill."

"Good for you," I shouldered my tote and set my towel under my arm.

He stared upward, "That is a really big plate," he crossed his arms and looked out with a dopey smile on his face.

I looked around and saw that the moon was appearing, "You mean, *the moon*?"

"Looks like a dish. A big plate that someone ate all the food and stuck it up there. I get what your mom said, it's so magical. Like, you feel that there's a full moon in your bones, you know? Like that energy thingy, with the zodiac and the flowers."

"Flowers? What are you saying? You don't believe in that stuff."

"Oh my God, Jenzy!" he clapped his hands together in excitement with an idea then came up real close; it was creepily animated for Chris. "We should make babies! Your mom said it would work tonight because the plate is full."

"You mean, *the moon*? Chris, you're really freaking me out."

"Our babies would be so beautiful, like better than Mandy and Todd because you know… Todd's ugly. We need to do this! We don't need to divorce, we need to make little babies and we can…oh my God, Jenzy we can build them fairy houses! Let's start now, so when the baby is born it has one. We can make them out of the sand!"

He knelt and started scooping sand up. Now I'm officially freaked.

"Um, Chris…?"

"I can sell any house. I could be a fairy realtor!"

"What's wrong with you?"

"We could name it- the baby- Moon Beam because, you know," he gestured at the moon, "And your mom almost called you that so it's like a sign." He went back to scooping but the sand wasn't wet, so it was just a pile. He stopped to look up at me, "You are so hot, like your stomach is long. I wonder where the baby will go…will it fit? But your legs are long too. I want to put my head between your thighs."

"Well, don't."

"You know what, if you're too skinny to bare the child, *I* can do it." He looked too excited, "Yeah, me, like a penguin! Or a- a- penguin!"

"Are you mentally snapping?" I asked. "Is this some sort of way to claim insanity because I can still divorce you if you decide to be insane." He wasn't listening, and I felt genuinely scared. "Seriously, what's wrong with you?"

He eyed the sand pile, "What was I making?"

"Let's go in, okay you're being weird and..."

"Yeah, maybe we can make whatever this was, later."

He got up and made slow zig-zagging lines to the back door, and he took the stairs at the pace of a turtle on Valium. He was distracted by everything, even the wood in the banister. Once in my parent's kitchen, he sat on a bar stool but fell off. I ran over to help him up, but he was laughing.

"Wow," he said between giggles. "That is a really low floor. That or it came up and grabbed my ass."

"Chris, did you take something?"

"I don't steal, Jenzy. I would never take stuff. Well, I take more napkins than I have to at restaurants… I took shampoo from a hotel once, but it was really good shampoo."

"No, I don't mean steal something I mean did you take a pill or something?"

He wouldn't stop smiling, "I feel so relaxed, like I don't even remember what was stressing me out. Oh, the divorce! Awe, yeah that still makes me sad. But I intend to change your mind, I have a plan. You are so hot! Who said that before? Was that me outside?"

I put some space between us to observe him.

He took a glass pan from the stove top and started forking more of whatever it was into his mouth.

I quirked a brow, "What are you eating now?"

"Brownies!" he turned and presented the half gone 8-inch pan. "You need these so bad, try one."

I laughed, "Can we be civilized and use plates and stuff? You usually yell at me for eating out of pans." I got two little plates and he cut me way too big of a piece and plopped it on my plate.

I went and sat on the opposite side of the island. "You don't usually bake," I said as I forked a piece. "When did you make these?"

He took a major bite of his; still from the pan, "I didn't even do it, your mom did. I found them on the stove."

I had just taken my bite but in the same second he said 'mom made them' I used my napkin to spit it out with wide eyes. "Chris! Stop!" I swatted the brownie out of his hand, from across the table.

"Hey," he frowned, "that brownie just literally jumped out of my hand- did you see it? They fly, Jenzy. Fuck!"

"Ugh, Chris, these are mom's *special brownies*! The pot brownies she makes sometimes. You can't just eat brownies you found in my mom's house, how many did you eat?"

His face fell, "You mean...there's a whole cooking pot in these flying brownies?"

"No!" I groaned, this was just great. "Concentrate!"

"Okay!" he looked excited then confused, "On what?"

"How many did you eat?"

"People?"

"*Brownies!*"

"Oh, I don't know, it was really full, like it was all there then I ate it."

"So, then you ate half the freakin' batch?"

"I don't know, Jenzy I wasn't there! You're making me nervous. Stop yelling at me!"

"It's okay, it's just…Chris, you're high."

"I am? Am I standing on something? Oh, fuck did I get taller? You know I don't like heights, is it bad? They say don't look down. I'm not gonna look down."

I sighed and tried to think what to do. I tried calling mom on my cell, but she wasn't picking up.

I left her a voicemail, where I could vent, "Mom! Are you freaking kidding me? You made pot brownies, and just left them out! Chris is high as fuck and ate almost the whole thing! What were you thinking? I'm going to-!"

Chris appeared behind me and loomed over my shoulder to talk into the phone, "I love you *so much,* mom! You are the bestest c*ook* lady ever."

"Shut up, Chris! See mom! Call me back, please. Hurry!"

I hung up and turned to look at my baked husband.

He shook his finger at me with glazed eyes, "You shouldn't talk to our mom like that."

"Let's get you upstairs so you can sleep it off."

"No, Jenzy I'm hungry, let's eat. Make something- no I'll do it." He raided my parent's fridge and came up with random things. "There's so much, let's just make all the things. There's butter, and hummus, something green, and a quiche!" His arms were full as he laid everything out on the counter. I didn't want to, but I laughed.

He looked up, "What? This is fine, we can lay all of it on the quiche! Look, they even have steaks! Oh snap, mustard."

I got up and went over to him, "Okay, just move over, I'll make you something."

"Yes! Thank you! Let's do this!"

"I'll do this; you just stand there and be high."

I grabbed the steaks from their packaging and took out my mom's cast-iron skillet. He started toying with his iPhone for music and settled on *Apologize* by *Charles Perry.* Like it or not, we had the same taste in songs. Our playlists were usually identical, therefore, this helped improve my sour mood over him being a victim of my mom's hippie madness.

Still in our suits, we made this situation work. I browned the steaks while he stood eating a stick of butter, watching me cook.

I had to wrestle the butter stick away, but only won when I promised he could have it back if he let me get what was left of the wrapper off first. He'd eaten most of it, paper and all.

Swaying while I cook to music is a habit, so there was mild dancing and he did too. It was a relaxed atmosphere; I knew he wasn't himself, I didn't concern myself with holding up pretenses. We were still two people who'd known each other a long time and were comfortable on a basic level.

"Will my job know?" he asked me for the thousandth time while I sliced some zucchini.

"Well, they do random drug testing, but I think by the time-."

He looked around suddenly spooked, "Are they coming here to test me?"

I didn't need him ending this trip paranoid, so I laughed, "No, just call out an extra day if you're worried."

"Maybe we should hide? Is there a basement?"

"Chill out, jailbird."

"This song makes me horny," he confessed.

I laughed at the ADHD quality of his thoughts, "The song? I should've used it all those times I wanted sex."

He came up behind me to grind while he danced, and I laughed because to see Chris this loose is extremely entertaining. His hands circled my bare waist and the heat of his palms instantly transferred his horny to me. His groin pressed into my hips and I considered for a split moment letting something happen. He was high, it would just be blamed on that, right?

The music wasn't helping or the lyrics, is that how he felt? We moved together in time with his front to my back while I cooked, and I leaned into him. Skin on skin, and he moved us with his chin rested on my shoulder as he whisper/sang the lyrics and it meant something to me. He was telling me with the song, under the honesty of the high how he felt.

His hands moved lower to hold my hip bones and I pressed my ass back because I wanted it. I could feel he was hard again like this morning and the excuse of his high would be what I needed to feel him without seeming weak. Chris was the best in bed, he was like an expert. He had the ability to make me feel better than even the high he had now, and it had been so long.

Then I heard the front door and got away from him. Wow, I almost fucked up.

When Mom and Dad came in I scolded them like I was the parent while Chris ate himself into a coma.

Chapter Twenty-Two
JENZY

The ride back from my parent's place was weird. It was raining the whole time and for some reason, rain makes everything feel intimate and closed in. Chris dropped me off at work and I expected a wisecrack about it like he usually did every single time.

"You want my umbrella?" he asked as he pulled to a stop in front of the family clinic.

"I'm good. You don't mind dropping off my stuff at Todd's?"

"No, it's fine. I can come back to take you home if you want. You can't walk or bike in this weather. We get off around the same time so…"

I paused with my hand on the door. "Oh, well, I have a ride…and plans so…"

He nodded, "Right, Moses?" I didn't answer that. "Okay, call if you need anything, alright?"

"Yeah."

"You need help looking for a place? I kind of have experience with that," he teased.

I smiled, "Thanks, but Todd and Mandy have admitted to liking my staying there. I help them with the babies and stuff. I'm looking but not seriously yet."

"Well, when you're ready we can apartment hunt. I know good spots that, would work for your income minus mine and they would be near your work… safer parts of town…"

I took the chance of setting my hand over his on the gear shift between us. "Thank you." It was him kind of acknowledging the divorce and he needed to know I saw that.

He looked like he wanted me to do more so I took my hand away and got out.

As the days went by, I found a settling feeling about life. In the transition from May to June, I started to adjust to being single again and being separate. I still wore the rings, which was like a habit I couldn't kick. I tried sleeping without them for a time, but I was restless.

I was getting closer to Moses, he and I talked every day like always; once in the morning before work, then the afternoon around lunch and before bed.

He took me on dates that thrilled me, and I was never bored. We would make out, which felt like a drug, but anytime it got heavy, we'd slow it down and I usually had a sleepless night after. Moses' patience honestly makes me like him more and more, and his ability to be my friend without making me feel guilty is applaud worthy.

Chris…that's an odd topic. He and I text a few times a day but now I feel like he's listening. He asks me about my day and though I give him filtered versions in fear he'll say something stupid, it's nice. I might even look forward to our interactions.

I also am beginning to think he's seeing why the divorce makes sense. I think he abandoned, 'the plan' to win me back and now we're just learning to be friends again.

I was at the desk in Dr. Mouser's office, when two of his patients showed. The doctor came up beside me and I forced myself to act natural. I was jarring some of his herbs and he gets picky about that.

"What's that there?" he asked but I know he knows.

"Ginger, for Mrs. Wiber's morning sickness."

"What else could she drink? Hurry up. Think."

I concealed a smile, "Peppermint, spearmint, lemon balm, chamomile of course-."

"Yeah, don't brag, Mrs. Clark."

"Can I send the next one in?"

"No," he frowned at me from under furry gray brows. "What do you think? Am I here for my own health?"

"I think, yes."

"Good job using your thinker. Alright then. I need lunch at one-thirty, don't screw up during your consultations, I don't wanna get sued."

"Okay, doctor."

"Hey," he pointed a finger at me, "still interested in Doula work?"

"Definitely-."

"Then here," he slid me a business card, "She's looking for an apprentice for midwifery, she partners with a doula. But if you take it, you're fired from here."

I waited until he left and sent the next patient in. Then I hurried to look down at the card. I knew this name. Bella's Bonding Birth was one of the most prominent midwives in the area. I pocketed it and shined through my workday. I love that old man.

I got a call at the desk and answered, "Good Morning, this is Dr. Mouser's office."

"Jenzy," I recognized Chris' voice and stilled. He never called me at work before. "I know you're on the job. Are you too busy? You can call me back."

"No…" I looked around, but no one was even paying me any mind. "What's up?"

"Do you have plans tonight?"

I thought fast, "Not really."

"Great, because I wanted to ask you out."

"Out where?"

"It's a surprise."

"Chris," I lowered my voice. "I don't think us going out is such a good idea."

"Okay, but I gotta warn you, I lost all my pens, so signing your divorce is going to be difficult."

I sighed, "Blackmail? To ask me out? Really?"

"It's just an outing."

"I don't think the risk is worth the gain."

"So strange because your horoscope said the exact opposite this morning."

I quirked a brow and blinked, "You read my horoscope?"

"You *didn't*?"

I started searching for the paper while I contrived a comeback, "Can't I at least know where?"

"Sagittarius' like spontaneity. Just go with it."

I came up fast from looking under the desk. Was he checking out astrology?

"Well, I don't trust you," I said as I finally got my hands on a copy and flipped to the horoscopes. "You have intentions. Just give me a hint."

"Hmm," his voice hummed down the line and made me shiver. "I figured you'd want a clue...check your bike."

I tripped on the wheeled leg of my chair trying to get to the window. Was he here? I looked but his car was nowhere in sight. "Whatever you're up to *isn't going to worrrk*," I sang that last part cockily.

"I'll pick you up at five."

I sighed and hung up. Then I let the guy in the waiting room know I was just stepping out for a second.

I ran to the lot where my bike was chained. Yeah, I tripped once. There was a little shiny gold box tied to the bars of my bike with white ribbon. I looked around still expecting to see him, then untied it and opened the lid. What I saw made me feel like a kid at Christmas. I had to stand there and weigh the balance between being offended that he bought me anything and freaking out over the gift.

It was a necklace! Not just any kind. At the middle of the fine silver chain was a circular silver frame that held the constellation of my sign, Sagittarius. A deep blue back with tiny twinkling stars all perfectly arranged! It was like having a 3D snapshot of my dimension. My universe.

I went back inside and was glad to see no one noticed my missing. I forced myself to stop staring at the gift, but I kept opening the lid and looking. Then I stopped to read my horoscope.

```
Dear Sagittarius,
    Today is a day of positive energy and
productive flow. Take chances, risks,
adventures, and new opportunities by the
horns. You'll be offered a choice today,
don't over think it. Go in like you usually
do, heart first, and the head will follow.
After all, you never know where romance
might find you.
```

Well fuck, how do you fight that one?

I ticked off the time by keeping busy, but my mind was gone. I had to stay strong on this or it was going to land me with tire marks all over my already road-worn heart. When I got off, I biked home, enjoying the balmy weather we had. I wasn't in the door more than a minute before Todd came at me with Connor on him, piggyback style.

"Auntie Jezzy!" Connor squealed. I love getting greeted that way by an enthusiastic four-year-old.

I smiled, "Good afternoon, Connor," I kissed his cheek. "How are you?"

He jabbered a minute and with his impediment, neither I nor Todd really knew what he said but loved listening.

"...And, how are you?" I asked Todd.

Todd pursed his lips, "Good but, I have something for you. You *can't tell* Mandy."

I laughed, "What is it?"

He handed me a box that looked identical to the one Chris tied to my bike with the necklace in it; gold lid, white ribbon. I checked around like Mandy was our mom and might catch us with alcohol. This one had a note attached.

"Read it out loud," Todd insisted.
I didn't want to, but I did.

Jenzy,

Figured you should have something lucky to wear tonight.

P.S.

You don't have to wear any of my gifts, but for each thing you refuse, I'm adding another month of contesting.

Chris

"That dick!" I snapped.
"He is pretty sly," Todd agreed.
Then I opened it right there in front of Todd. Damn. He's killing me. It was an elegant pair of oriental hair sticks made of purple glass. They were hand painted to have ornate Asian symbols and cherry blossoms.
I looked up at Todd, "What's he doing?"
"I'm only the delivery man."
"You know what I mean."
"I don't know." He let Connor down to go play and looked over my shoulder at the gift. "Maybe, the threat of you leaving…woke him up."
"But that's just it." I closed up the box and note, "What if I do give in, and I do stay? What if we do great, better than great, but then things go back? What if he goes blind to me again? I don't want that. You know Chris. He wants things until he has them then… I don't want…" I don't know, I can't think of a good word. Todd pulled me into his side and I held onto him.
"I think…the best advice I can give you…is the worst thing that Chris would want to hear." He set his cheek on my head and I closed my eyes. "Hold out. Don't shut him out anymore, but don't

let him too far in. Let him fight for you. If you're just another conquest, he'll run out of steam. If you're the real goal, he won't."

"How do I know when he's proved himself, *if* he proves himself?"

"Mom always says real love, loves with an open hand. It's not that love isn't somewhat possessive or demanding, it's that it balances those things with freedom for the sake of happiness. You'll know. If he does that one thing that's just purely selfless enough to bring you back, you'll feel it."

"Give him a chance in the meantime? What about Moses?"

"You're single, Jenzy and the bottom line is, you got two suitors. Moses knows you're in the middle of mayhem, he wants to stick it out and Chris knows you have options. May the best man win."

I laughed in his hug and he did too.

"Don't make it sound like *the Hunger Games*..." I said.

"Whatever, you better hurry up and get ready, he's coming in an hour."

Chapter Twenty-Three
CHRIS

I showed up at Todd's at a minute after five because I had to obsess about this plan. It wasn't like this was the biggest part, but it was a spoke in the wheel. I got out and went up to the door.

Mandy answered with Penny in her arms, "Where you guys going?" she asked with skepticism.

"None of your beeswax."

"Ha, ha. Shut up. Tell me."

"Nope."

"Just don't screw with her, okay. I'm serious; I'll tie your balls in a knot," she said around her gum.

"I'm not toying with her and keep your nose out of it."

"If I wasn't holding this baby, I swear to God."

"Just relax."

Mandy eyed me, "She'll be down in a minute, you can wait out here, pestilence."

"Really?"

But she shut the door and flipped me off through the glass. Bitch. Had to admire her though. That Mama Bear mentality meant she was being just as protective of potential love interests and I was thankful for that. I hope she drove Moses equally nuts.

I went back to my car and leaned my back into the passenger door. I was nervous. Wow. Nervous to take my wife out.

I heard her coming soon and watched the door up the steps. She came out wearing a short navy dress with tiny purple flowers. She had a denim button down over it but knotted the shirt tails at her waist. Her hair was up, and I was proud to see the necklace and the hair sticks. It made my stomach flip wildly to see her; it had been a while since the beach.

She hugged and kissed Mandy goodbye then came down to stand in front of me. I took a little long in responding. She had heels on, the kind with strappy ankles; she knows that's a weakness of mine.

"You look amazing," I got out.

"It's hard to dress right when you don't know where you're going."

"You did perfectly."

"Do I comply with all the demands?" she gestured to the necklace and turned so I would see her hair sticks.

"You wear all of it like royalty. Your hair looks, stunning."

She blushed a little and I smiled. I could do this; I could go back to how it was. It felt natural again.

"It's actually an Elsa hair-do. From *Disney's Frozen*. I found a hair tutorial for it. Cool huh?"

I laughed, "Looks better than hers," I let myself look, "Elsa wasn't as beautiful as you."

She shined with that compliment, but once it came off my lips I felt a dulling. Saying the words made me realize how long it had been since I said them. What a crime, to belong to someone this gorgeous and not tell her daily. And the way she looked at me when I said it. Because she's been invisible for years.

"Well, in her defense, Elsa didn't have a curling iron," she joked.

I opened her door, "Did *my* Elsa remember to unplug the iron?"

She instantly looked annoyed. I shouldn't have said anything.

She rolled her brilliant eyes, "Yes, I don't *always,* forget." She got in and I closed the door behind her before going around to get in.

I made light of it to recover from sounding like an ass. "If you were the real Elsa, it wouldn't matter I guess, ice castles and all that-."

She opened her door as soon as I started the engine and I tensed thinking I truly pissed her off.

"What's wrong?" I asked.

"Nothing, I just…-forgot something." I grinned then laughed. She swung her legs out, "No, not the iron. Something else. Shut up- Chris, stop smiling! Ugh!" She got out but not before I saw the smile on her face too. I laughed, knowing good and well she was checking the iron.

When she came back afterward, I reined some of the mirth in. "Ready?" I checked.

"Yes, and I'll have you know, I intended to leave it on, so I could touch up before going."

"Of course," I gave her the false belief with a slow smile and she pressed her lips together to keep from laughing. I reached over her to open the glove compartment and she sat back like she was afraid I would touch her. Grabbing what I needed, I made a point to graze her knee on the way out. "Here," I held up a necktie of mine.

"You already have a tie on," she said.

"This isn't for me."

Her eyes flashed with anger, "Oh my God, Chris! We aren't having kinky sex in your car! Asshole! What were you thinking? Really?" She tried to get out, but I put the child-lock on. "I get dressed up thinking you plan to do something fun-."

"It's not for sex, you spaz, it's for blindfolding." That didn't sound right either.

She stopped and frowned, "Why?"

"I don't want you to know where we're going until we get there."

"Oh…" she was bright red now.

"Yeah," I held it up and she turned her back allowing me to tie it on. "If I was intending for *that* it wouldn't be in a car and I would need more than the one tie."

She went still and I smirked. Once she was good, I put her seatbelt on which allowed me to skim over her breasts and I saw her swallow.

We took off after that and talked on light matters. When we made it to our destination, I went around to help her out. She stood and waited while I closed the door then I tucked her hand into my arm to guide her steps.

"Sounds busy?" she said like a question.

"Still not telling you."

She tripped and fell into me. Heels and Jenzy: great mix for appearance, not her ankles.

"Restaurant?" she guessed again.

"What a puzzler."

I made any exchanges quiet or done in a whisper. Then I opened a door and led her through. She still almost managed to hit the glass door front.

"Jenzy, walk straight."

"I am!"

"No, you walk sideways like a friggin crab."

"You *led* me sideways."

"You weave. That's why I keep you inside on sidewalks."

"That's what gentlemen do, you ass!"

"Only because the first few women were like you, and probably side winded into oncoming buggies." She snickered but then pressed her lips together, so I wouldn't notice. "Just hold my arm and trust me," I said.

"I already hit a door, while trusting you."

"Because you can't walk normal!"

"You walk too fast."

"Oh my-!" *Breathe Chris, Breathe...* This woman.

"I should just tie a cart to your back and let you pull me," she retorted.

"That or I should duct tape rollerblades to your heels."

We both broke the argument to laugh. The last time we tried in-line-skating was five years ago and Jenzy's clumsy led to disaster. She had collided with a priest that was walking by and fell on top of him...in one of her typical miniskirts.

Apparently, my skating comment brought us both back to the hilarity of that moment. It felt like magic to laugh with her again.

Once in the right part of the building, I found a seating spot more toward the center and helped her sit in the folded-up seat.

"Movie Theater?" she tried again.

"Possibly."

She set her purse on her lap and sighed, "Can't I look yet?"

"Keep your panties on."

She dramatically sighed and I smiled. When the lights went low, a very soft violin drifted off the speakers for atmosphere and I reached to untie the knot at the back of her head.

When it fell away, she looked around in curiosity then gasped when she looked upward.

"What?" She said in an excitedly loud whisper. "No way! You took me to the planetarium? For real?"

I took some time to soak up the success of the moment. "Only took me seven years."

"I don't care! We're here! Look! They say this is one of the biggest domes! It looks so clear, doesn't it? They'll show the constellations, you know? They usually show like-."

I heard her, I promise, but I also found this as another bittersweet moment. It was a memory she'd been begging me to make with her and a simple pleasure she craved, and I denied. Yes, I was making her happy now, but she waited too long.

I let my head fall back and let her jibber about what she saw, what she knew. There was a time I would have told her to calm down, or that I knew some of this, or that she was way too excited.

Not tonight. Tonight, I saw that her overreaction to little things was what kept me feeling alive. I have a tendency to go a little dormant and get caught in the grind. I don't spot beauty and seize moments like this that by appearance, seem so insignificant.

The dome was projected dark, mysterious blues full of diamond stars to misty pinks and streaks of orange and purple. The slides would turn slowly at times to make you feel suspended and Jenzy's giddy whispers about astrology and mythology actually held my attention. I felt excited to know what made her tick, smile, and excite. She even held her necklace while she told me stories, like the full worth of the gift had registered in her. We interacted back and forth.

Somewhere around the Milky Way, I felt like a galaxy expert and I also felt in need of her. Our shared armrest put her right at my distance. I risked touching her hand and tensed when she didn't move. I tried for her fingers, making my way slowly with my own. She didn't look but she quieted and sucked her lower lip. I entwined our fingers and she loosely did the same. This was like finding a thousand dollars in a coat pocket.

Jenzy looked at our hands but not at me so I kept my eyes on her profile, trying to read how she might feel. Our fingers stroked, brushed, and coiled, never settling long but it felt like magic.

Then she took her hand away and looked back up. Okay. I understand. I really do. I haven't given up, though. I just got somewhere, it might not be far, but it was further than where I was a minute ago, and to win Jenzy back it was worth the trek.

When the museum was done, and we'd visited most the exhibits, I suggested dinner. We went to a place called *The Coast*. It was in the side of a cliff near the ocean and I had a table reserved for us that was on the balcony.

The balcony itself, was carved out of the rock and below, the ocean crashed into the side and whipped all about. The air was fresh here and the upscale setting was classic.

"This is great!" she said as she looked down over the railing. "It's so majestic! I didn't know about this place, but you don't like heights, is this okay for you?"

I opened her chair then took my own seat. All while trying not to throw up when I inched past the open edge.

I settled my napkin across my lap and smiled with my lips tightly shut, "I'm good."

"No, you aren't. Let's eat inside. I'm happy either way."

"If I don't look down, I'm pretty happy too. Maybe I should sample more of your mom's pot at times like these?"

She laughed, "You *were* pretty relaxed." She looked at the menu. Out of habit, I knew what she was drawn to and filled her in over my own menu.

"The salmon has a tangy sauce, but the cook knows how to do sirloins, he'll know what color you want."

"Ugh, I like Salmon with asparagus… that sounds awesome. The sirloin with shrimp, though… but what's the-?"

"The asparagus is really what you call, *crunchy.* They'll make it tender if you want."

She blew air between her lips in indecision and I already knew what to do. "Go with Sirloin," I said.

"You think?"

"Yeah," I closed mine up and looked at her, "I'll eat your calamari side."

"Okay," she sucked her bottom lip and I had to look away or risk a turn on. When the waiter came, I gave him my order then hers and she did exactly what I expected. "Wait," she winced. "Maybe I want the Salmon."

I smiled at the waiter, "She'll have the salmon, but make the asparagus tender and put the sauce on the side so she can try it first."

He took our menus and with quick small talk left us alone. There was only one other couple out here at the table behind her.

She toyed with the necklace at her throat. "Thanks…how do you always know?" she asked.

"Easy, you're always more interested in the first thing. You get distracted by the second thing. Since you're a little defiant by nature, if I pick the thing you want less, you'll pick the thing you really want." I drank some water and she watched me.

"Am I that complicated?" she asked.

"It's not complicated, it's just careful. You always want what you saw first, purses, shoes, apartments, the second choice is you checking to see if you really want the first but when you leave it up to me, you're usually testing yourself. If I tell you, you'll do the opposite. You're not being difficult, you just like to explore, and carefully."

She looked intrigued at my knowledge, but I've loved her for years. I knew everything. Except how to keep her.

"Dr. Mouser gave me a card to a woman known in this area to be one of the best midwives," she said, changing topics.

Her statement came out of the blue and for a painful minute I stared in open 'freak out.' Did I get her pregnant? No, she and I haven't-. *Fuck!* Moses!

"You're pregnant?" I squeaked.

She frowned at me, "What? No! How would I be pregnant?"

Ahh, I see a trip up opportunity and I'm not losing it. "You and Moses…"

"We haven't-."

AH HA! I did the entire dance to *Uptown Funk* in my head but kept my expression indifferent. They haven't had sex! Thank God! I knew it! I knew she was holding out. I'd lost sleep being unsure.

She caught herself and recovered, "I'm not pregnant. Sorry, I realize how that sounded now. I've been considering becoming a Doula, remember? I have the herbal knowledge and now all I need is the apprenticeship under a midwife along with some heavy curriculum and a seminar and such."

Now it was my turn to be tested. I could easily tell her she was pipe dreaming again, or that she'd flake on this idea or that I thought home birth and holistic anything was stupid, but that's not what came to mind.

"You should call and make it happen."

Her eyes widened, and she tilted her head, "You don't think it's dumb?"

"I've never seen you stick with anything like you do holistic medicine and healing. You've been under Mouser for like what…how many years now? You were present for Mandy's births and you did great, and you loved it. You love babies…being a Doula makes sense."

Jenzy looked out over the cliff side and didn't respond for a bit. "You don't think I would bail?"

"Nope."

"Why?"

"It's the thing you wanted first."

Our food came out, but we kept one another's eyes while it was served. Like she was totally taken by me, but she didn't know I was feeling the same way about her.

"You always said home births or natural births were weird."

"I don't have a vagina, I think I'll keep my moot opinions to myself from now on," I laughed, and she did too. I lifted her plate and used my fork to swipe her sautéed onions. She didn't like onions.

She watched me for a long time afterward, even as I found topics for us.

Yes, I remember every little detail. I remember because I love you.

Chapter Twenty-four
JENZY

I got home feeling like a balloon. Chris was penetrating my armor. Tonight, was everything and I couldn't believe the romantic level he'd climbed, just to pull it off. Would it last, though?

I checked my phone for the first time this whole evening. There was one missed call from Moses and I felt a bucket of guilt dump on me. It was too late to call him back, but I did.

It rang and rang until the last, and then his sleepy tone floated over the speaker, "Hello?"

"Hi," I whispered so not to wake the family. "I'm so sorry; I was out longer than I thought."

"It's okay, did you have fun?"

I debated telling the truth, "It was good."

"Where did he take you?"

"The planetarium."

"That's awesome. Was it as great as you thought?"

"Better." I felt uncomfortable, "how was your night?"

"I taught a few classes, including the new prenatal one."

I laughed, "*You*? How did that happen?"

"Their teacher called out." He laughed sleepily, "I do a great pregnant, downward dog."

We laughed and then the silence soothed me a little. We were okay.

I sat on my bed, "I really am sorry about tonight. This must be weird for you. Why won't you admit that?"

"It's not weird. I think, even if you and Chris can't fix things, you could at least walk away with a close friend. It doesn't have to end in pain."

"You wouldn't feel jealous knowing he and I are friends?"

"No. He's part of you; my best friend is a girl, I have Chloe, remember? She and I never dated or anything, but I still understand. Oh, and I have a question." He sounded like he was sitting up. "I found a park today, it's not far from my house, it has incredible biking trails. Wanna go with me this weekend?"

"I'd love that."

"Great. I'll come get you Saturday."

"Sounds good."

"What's wrong?" His question threw me. "Tell me," he insisted.

"Nothing."

"Please."

I searched myself, what was wrong? "I'm falling for you, Moses." He always pressed for me to be honest, so there it was.

His breathing was all that came through and it was faint. I felt like I just walked down the street in my underwear, but Chris was confusing me. If I didn't commit to something- no- *someone* else, I might buckle.

Moses made a sound, something like a groan, "Please don't say that when I can't touch you."

"Sorry."

"Don't be sorry. I just…I feel the same way. I don't want to rush you. I'm trying not to pressure you."

"You never rush me into anything."

"Still. I…" he sighed again, "I don't think you really know just how much I want you. I live for my phone to buzz, I think about you all the time. Even without sex…I *want* sex but, you fill me up everywhere else."

"You're probably afraid I'll spook and run after the last incident."

"I don't need to have sex with you to know how I feel."

I put him on speaker but low, so I could get undressed. "Okay," I decided to lighten the mood. "You're right…we don't need sex."

"Hey now, I'm patient, I'm not dead."

I laughed, "Hold on."

"What are you doing?"
"Getting undressed, hold on."
"*Fuck.*"
I laughed, "Sorry."
"I don't think you are. You told me you had feelings then started stripping, that's…" he blew out air, "that's not a repentant move."
"When I'm not a damaged mess, I'll make all this waiting up to you. I promise."
"You already make it up."
"I think we'll be good together. Like…"
"Like natural?"
"Yeah." I felt a sudden ping. "I should let you go, so you can sleep."
"Okay, but call me in the morning."
"I will. Goodnight."
"Goodnight, Sunshine."

After hanging up, the ping worsened. I put on a Disney movie for distraction. Memories came uninvited to steal the moment and I let them because…well, I'm tired.

2008

My phone rang, and I startled awake to answer it. I had to search under my textbooks since I had fallen asleep on the bed. Chris' picture was pulsating on the screen and I grinned.
"Hello?" I said in a musical tune.
"Hello?" he checked.
"Can you hear me?"
There was a lot of static then, "You're lagging."
I moved to my right, "What about now?"
"Better- no, wait-."
And hence was the frustration of a long-distance relationship. It mostly consists of those few sentences.

"What about now?" I asked as I waded to the other side of the bed.

"Better. How are you, gorgeous?"

"I'm great! I'm bored in school and thinking of quitting."

"Jenzy, try to stick it out."

"Nursing is cool but…" I tapped my pen on a book cover. "I don't know, it doesn't feel right. I want to do something more…earthy rather than clinical."

"There's always the Peace Corps," he said. I went quite with the new idea. "No- Jenzy! I'm kidding. You aren't going to the Peace Corps."

"Okay, okay," I laughed, "what if I just be a vet? Can I even begin to tell you how amazing working at the dog shelter has been?"

"That would be really cool, actually. You're great with animals."

"Or I could be an environmental lawyer."

"Why not?"

"Or I could work at Disneyland. I've only wanted to go since I was two."

I could hear him walking in the background. The only service was outside his dorm, so he had to walk the campus to talk to me. Knowing he willingly made this nightly walk for me in the cold made me feel special.

"We'll go one of these days," he sniffed from the whip of the wind.

"Let's honeymoon there!"

"Only if you dress like Ariel, with real seashells."

"Perv," I laughed. "How's Sweden?"

"Cold. You wouldn't make it here."

"*That* cold?"

"We would have to snuggle for warmth."

"Oh, gosh darn, what a hardship," I teased.

"Yeah, and they say naked snuggling is most effective."

"I'll snuggle all you want if you speak Swedish for me."

"*Ja? Du lovar?*" he checked.

"Chris! You know that makes my knees weak."

"The snow is up to my knees," he sniffed again, "so I can't feel them." I could hear it crunching under his feet.

"That sounds fun."

"The people would probably kick you out. Swede's aren't that friendly, they would think there's something wrong with you. Jibbery little American Hippie girl."

"You've made like, thousands of friends," I corrected.

"Once they know you, they're the best people ever. You just can't walk up on a bus and tell them your life story. They'd call cops on you."

"My parents are from New York, they're pretty much the same way."

"But you were born in California; you have zero sense of stranger danger. You're still friends with that peddler on 4th Street."

"Oh, Steve? Yeah, he's great. He says *Hi,* by the way."

Chris' rich laugh gave me serious tummy flutters.

"Guess what I did today? I got that dragon tattooed down my spine," he told me.

"What? No way! Have someone take a picture." I gasped, "I can't believe you've got sleeves now. I wanna see all these hot tats for myself."

"Yeah, I'm getting addicted to ink, but it looks cool with the muscles."

"Okay, that's enough; my ovaries are having a seizure."

"Good, then you know my blue ball pain. Oh, and I have a complaint."

I closed more books and set them aside, "Here we go," I chimed.

"You haven't sent a nude since yesterday."

"You said to stop. You said you couldn't take any more sexual torture."

"I don't remember that."

"You said-."

"Don't listen to me when I speak nonsense," his teeth chattered on that one.

"I can send one now…since I'm sitting here …studying…naked."

His long pause had me silently giggling to myself. Oh, the joys of long distance. An oversized T-shirt and leg warmers aren't naked, but it's close.

"You're evil," he finally replied.

"I'm not."

"You're also lying because your roommate would never-."

"Mandy's at your frat house boinking Todd."

"Ew! Let's talk about something else."

"Like what I would do to you if you were here."

Long, agonized groaning went down the line and I laughed hard.

"Stop! Just, don't it's really mean," he started to sound genuinely frustrated. "It's also…just, pointless."

I lost the laughter and sat straight, "Pointless?"

The mood turned heavy and all the laughs that lit me up developed dark clouds.

"I'm not sure I see how this relationship makes sense. Sometimes, I'm not even sure…" he trailed off.

I felt a horrid sinking sensation. We'd been talking like this for three months since he left. We were in a top-secret affair, not even Mandy knew, not even Todd, and I told Todd everything.

Every so often Chris' mad passion about his liking me would fizzle while he ranted about how impractical this was.

I went the usual route, "You want to stop? We could…stop…" I always handled Chris with an open hand, but sometimes I wished he'd just close my fist.

"No, I didn't say that. Maybe. I don't know."

"Is it a sexual thing? Because…I could understand if something happened and you-."

"Jesus, Jenzy try not to be so irritatingly understanding, okay?"

"Okay."

"No, nothing happened, it's not just sexual. It's this shitty distance. I'm tired of being in a relationship with my phone. Our whole world revolves around cellular connections working."

I shrugged, "It will work out. You'll be home in November."

"I don't want to wait until November."

"It's only-."

"I don't share your *hippie optimism.* I'm realistic," he countered.

I felt irritated now but if he sensed that he would only get fussier.

I came at it softer, "I know, I read all about Leos. I know you need planning and solid ideas. However, it's not like we didn't discuss this all before. We knew when you left it would be hard."

He vented, "You really want this? Like last night when you wanted to tell me about your day and the phone died on us. That didn't piss you off? It pissed me off, I wasn't there for you. I couldn't hear you. Then there's the nine-hour time difference."

"You're worth most those things."

"What about the future?"

I wished I could hang up and claim bad signal. I just didn't pick at possibilities like Chris. I saw a glass half full, he saw it nearly empty and I wasn't sure how to help that.

His voice carried into my heart, "You said for a while you could move here with me, then you backed out."

"We were just talking, I would love to see it there and be with you but…I don't see myself living there."

"Then if I want to stay here and you want to stay there, what the hell are we doing?"

I went with a simple approach, I always used on him, "I miss you."

"See, when you say that it physically hurts me. I want to touch you, not this phone bull shit."

"I miss you," I repeated.

"What about the guys there? Are you beating them off with sticks? How am I supposed to sleep? What? Yeah… I miss you too, I guess. And what about holidays?"

I smiled because I already had him. He was such a complicated thinker that his mind hadn't even fully processed my words.

I interrupted his typical Leo rant, "Hey, Chris?"

"Yeah?"

"I like you."

"Yeah, I like you too, I guess."

I grinned. He was so wonderfully complex. I even loved how he said, 'I guess.' It was said more like a surrender to how he felt, which even though it sounded like a blow off, it was more of a confession and I almost needed it.

"If you were here, ranting on and on about this, I'd stand on my toes and kiss you."

"That might work," he confessed.

"Yep, and you'd still be ranting so I would just kiss you while you go on."

"That's actually getting really distracting then."

"Then imagine I'm doing that right now and stop talking."

He sighed, "Great, a little hippie girl is going to control my life with interrupting kisses and nudes." He mimicked my voice, *"Oh, you're mad Chris? Here's a nude. Are you upset? Let me kiss you."*

"Sounds like awesome fights."

"Keep that up and we won't fight at all."

"Be honest, though would you like to stop talking?" I asked.

"I didn't say that."

"You just said-."

"Shh! I don't want to claim I ever said that. No."

I smiled with a heart at ease. "I really do miss you."

"I miss you too."

"No," I went to lay on my stomach. "Tell me like you did before, I like that."

His laugh gave me butterflies again. "I miss you too…I guess."

"Better."

"When I get there, I'm going to assault you in the airport. I'm not physically letting go of you for shit. I don't care who's there."

Our relationship only grew from there. We were close and intimate and as each month went by, my excitement grew at the prospect of seeing him. Todd, Mandy, and a few of the boys from the frat house came to the airport when November rolled around. We were all that ready to see him. Chris was so popular it just made everyone want to be around him.

We were supposed to go from here to his mom's for Thanksgiving weekend with Todd and Mandy. I was buzzing with energy.

I saw him come out of his gate and primped. Then all of us jumped or waved. Todd came up first and the brothers did the quick 'brother' hug. Mandy got a side hug and they teased about not liking each other. One of his friends was in front of me so he got a hand-shake and guy hug.

When he saw me, I lit up like a Christmas tree and threw my arms around his neck. What should've been a great relief and comfort, turned into a steady fall from joy, when he stiffened, then let go with a distant squeeze to turn to his next friend.

I backed away as the smile evaporated from my lips and swallowed the rejection. We'd been friends for a year and lovers for eight months. Good morning calls, and goodnight, every day and every night, none of it meant anything when he all but shrugged me off just now.

I thought I was bearing the embarrassment alone but then looked up to see that Todd had noticed. I tried a fake smile, but he looked pissed and I wasn't sure if I was in trouble or Chris.

On the way to the car, Chris ended up filling in his friends and I fell behind the herd.

Mandy left for the bathroom and Todd fell back with me. "Something going on with you and Chris?" he asked.

"Not really."

"Jenzy, it's me. We tell each other everything."

"Don't be mad, okay."

I didn't have to say it. He did that kindergarten math and snapped.

"I am mad. Why Chris? Really? I told you, I warned you how he is with girls, tell me you didn't fall for it," he begged.

"It wasn't like that with us."

"Then why did you look so upset at the gate? Why hasn't he said anything about it or why didn't he say or do anything just now? I've said how he hates relationships and public displays. He's never, ever, ever going to be with someone like-."

"We've been talking for eight months," I shot back. Todd looked shocked. Maybe I was defending us even as I felt sure whatever we had while he was away mattered very little on American soil.

"Eight months? In a row?" Todd checked.

"Yeah. We…we were Skyping and stuff."

"I hate to tell you this, but the chances he wasn't…doing other girls, is really slim."

"He didn't."

Todd held back a 'yeah, sure' look. "Just count your lucky stars. It's not like you slept together or anything. Usually, he sleeps with girls, *then* breaks their heart."

I stopped walking and he did too. He saw the water in my eyes and closed his.

"Please, tell me this isn't happening," he whispered.

"Maybe I'll just stay at school for the holiday."

He opened his eyes and came to hug me, "Fuck that. Your parents are on that cruise, mom would die if you stayed here alone."

One of Chris' friends shouted back in the parking garage, "You guys coming?"

I looked past Todd's arm to see Chris was watching us. He looked almost concerned but a bitterness was growing in me that helped disguise the hurt. I plastered on a smile and Todd and I strolled that way.

"Coming," I called.

Todd pulled me closer as we walked, "Just do me a kindness and please, don't cut me out because of my brother. It's happened before and you're literally my best friend."

I rolled my eyes, "Your brother has nothing to do with my love for you."

He calmed and by the time we got in the car things felt awkward. Chris' friends had left, and Todd sat in the driver seat while Chris and I sat in the back waiting for Mandy. No one talked. It was awful.

When Mandy did finally show, she got up front with Todd and thankfully filled the car with chatter that blocked out the tension.

Chris used the distraction of Mandy and the loudness of the radio to look over at me. I kept my eyes out the window but felt him trying to communicate. He slowly brought his hand over to cover mine in the seat between us, but I took it away and put my hair in a ponytail to keep him away.

Yes, that's how it feels to be rejected, asshole.

Chapter Twenty-five
Present Day
CHRIS

I'm starting to really see a chance. A light at the end of the tunnel when it comes to Jenzy and I. As July approaches, one of the few plans I have, to turn her head, starts to fall into place. Our communication is already improving. I hate not seeing her every day, and I hate not sleeping next to her at night. I miss her legs across my lap while we watch a show (likely a show I was forced to watch). I miss her voice. No, I don't always listen, I just like her endless talk filling up the silence. I miss her presence in our home and the positive light she decks our halls in. I miss her messes. Five-star meals that leave nine-million dishes. I miss yelling at her over bills and the fact that she washed one of my work shirts without removing a stain first. I miss her screaming at me when I repeat something a guy at work said but she insists she told me dozens of times first. I hate that she isn't here nagging me about recycling. I miss her.

I think I might be seeing the point of astrology now, but only if it's from Linda Goodman. I'm still Chris. She seems like the only person that gets me.

I'm iffy on medical vs holistic points still, but if it comes up with Jenzy lately I take a less offensive view and listen more. I finally noticed that she isn't trying to make me do anything, she just wants to talk. She wants to hear what I think about what she thinks and maybe, not to mock it.

Over these months, I've realized something else too. Romance isn't like other things in life that are natural or responsible for the survival of mankind. Humans don't need romance to procreate or play a vital role in the day-to-day.

Romance isn't love. Love is a true instinct that evolves with a person, but romance, I made the mistake of thinking all this time that it wasn't still a necessity.

It is true that romance isn't natural, it's made.

Look at the evidence.

Knight's jousting, blind guys in books that make houses out of sticks to propose, those men I used to laugh at for all but laying in the dirt; allowing their chic to cross without ruining her boots… The vampire boyfriends that are willing to die for their lady friend, the Christian Greys… which I could teach a few things, by the way. The dudes that are so in love that they all but turn into women themselves (Moses). The men none of us normal menfolk can live up to.

I chucked the idea of romance because if sexes are so equal why should I kill myself to show her how I feel?

Now I'm getting it. Women love with all of themselves. They love in a trusting way that's fully invested. They put it all on the line. They may try not to fall hard but most do. They want to support us, they want to devote the time, and they willingly give hours on the phone, or planning weddings, or perfect gifts. Little girls want to grow up and know how to tie neckties because that's what being in love is to them. Being in love, to a woman, is being everything for us men. They hold the weight of loving a person in a three-dimensional way.

I'm not saying all of us guys are as dense as wood, or me rather, or that there isn't some out there that do all the above too, but it's the exception, not the rule. Moses men are random not a majority.

If a woman like Jenzy can love me so much that she was once reading books on preserving a marriage, asking me to go to counseling, dieting because she thought her perfect ass wasn't perfect enough, getting dressed up however many times only to take it all off in disappointment, reaching out to me but not being heard, calling because she cared and making the man she was divorcing a meal in a crock pot before she left, why couldn't I be romantic?

Was that such an inconvenience? Taking her to the planetarium had brought me so much personal joy, just to see her that happy, I was reaping from the romance too, so if she needed outward acts like that to know I wanted her and needed her, then for fuck sake, I'm on it.

Now more than part way through July, I've come up with something else just as awesome and as I ride in the back of a spacious rented limo, I can see Jenzy standing on a corner at a movie theater just as planned. She looks sexy as hell, wearing a larger gray tank with a super low scoop neck so you could see the indigo lace-cupped bra she wore underneath. Her hair was in messy curls and had that bed ragged look that made me hot.
She was about to be mad as a hornet.
"Alright," I told the driver. "That's her, can you do as planned and put up the divider… she's got the mouth of a sailor when she's pissed."
"Yes, Mr. Clark."

JENZY

When Todd said he wanted to go see a movie, but Mandy said she didn't feel like it, I already felt like something was up, but then Todd kept looking around like he owed a drug lord while we walked to the theater. This night was taking strange turns.
"What's your problem?" I laughed after he looked over his shoulder the hundredth time.
"Nothing," he tried to act normal, "just excited to see the movie."
"We didn't decide on one yet. Let's talk it over, you only parked *ten miles* away. We have time."
"It's dark and the street I parked on is safer."

"You're a nut, but I don't understand why I couldn't invite Moses. You are okay with him, right? Is it still weird? Chris is your brother so is it weird?"

"No, I like Moses. I think he's a great guy. I like him more than my brother, I would trade him for my brother."

"Then what's up? Do you need to talk?" he looked back behind him and I snapped. "Todd!"

"What?"

"What are you looking for?"

"Nothing. I just thought I heard someone."

"You're a terrible liar."

"So I've been told."

We came into view of the theater and there was only one dude, falling asleep at the ticket window. The light bulbs around the extended roof were bright gold and they lit the street in a comforting way but this was obviously a very unpopular theater.

I groaned, "This place only has foreign films…" I gestured to the line-up on the board up top. "No wonder it's a ghost town. Not only is it foreign, there are only two shows. Did you even look this place up?"

"Okay, you stay here and pick the movie and I'll run back to the car."

"What? For what? Are you freaking kidding me?"

"I forgot my phone," he stammered.

I gave him a flat look, "You're up to something. Spill."

"Jenzy, without my phone Mandy will worry. I'll be right back, you pick the movie."

I stomped my foot, because, I don't know, it felt good. "Todd! I don't know this street, don't just leave me here, it's shady."

"The ticket guy is with you."

"He's asleep."

"I'll jog," he hopped back and forth to make his point but was already winded.

"God, just hurry up, okay. I don't want to die here."

He ran off and I crossed my arms, feeling uncomfortable. This was too weird. I read and re-read the stupid movie titles and tried to pick between the two that I couldn't even pronounce. I stood further back on the sidewalk's edge and tried anyway because even though the ticket guy was asleep I didn't want him to think I couldn't spell.

Then I heard a car coming and checked over my shoulder before looking back up. In a slow but way too quick happening, I heard the car slug a little then the door opened. By the time I tried to turn, someone had a hand over my mouth and another around my waist. I freaked and screamed but behind the big hand, my cries were muffled. Then there was a yank and I fell backward into the car. Scratch that, it was a limo.

My initial need to panic turned into a spit-fire struggle when I felt the car excel down the street.

Chapter Twenty-Six
JENZY

I got my attacker in the jaw with a fairly good backward decking, but then there was a rumbling laugh and he hoisted me into his lap on the seat.

"Calm down, baby it's me," he said.

I set my head back since he was hugging me to him too tightly to move, "Chris? What the fuck is your problem? You scared me! I thought-."

"Again... I am so glad you didn't retain any of what you learned in self-defense."

"You're creeping me out, what is this?"

"A surprise."

I wiggled to get off his lap, but he kept me there. He looked like he just got off work, but his sleeves were rolled up. I at least managed to sit sideways on his lap, but he had my arms pinned down in a lobster clamp.

Now I argued, "You can't kidnap your ex-wife! I have a life! I have a job, a boyfriend, friends-."

"First off, *darling,* you aren't my ex yet. Second, I don't know why I used to think Dr. Mouser was such a shmuck, he's a pretty cool old guy. He's all for my whisking you away for a few days, *and* he's rooting for me, by the way, team Chris, just a little FYI. Thirdly, you're still married therefore Moses doesn't qualify as a 'boyfriend' he's a lover, and lovers just have to deal. Lastly, your *friend* aka my brother is in on this, as is his harpy wife. In fact, dear little Mandy packed you two bags, made sure all your personal effects were bagged and-."

"She did?" I asked.

He pointed across the vast inside of our limo. I found four travel cases laid there.

"No," I looked back at his smug face and made a bitch face in return, "I want to go home. You can't force me to go with you and if you don't pull this fucking car over I'll scream."

"No need, I'm more than open to dropping you off."

I frowned but then went back to bitchy, "Good."

"Of course, I'll just add another…" he swayed his head back and forth in thought, "Six months or so…to the contested status."

I grunted and got loose enough to punch him in the chest. He only made a 'puh' sound then laughed because who feels a tiny fist against rock hard pecks?

"You're a fucking asshole."

"You are so going to eat those words."

I felt my skirt was riding up my legs but if I looked, he would look. "How am I supposed to explain this to-?" *Moses*…I didn't want to finish that.

Chris shrugged, "He's not my problem." I looked away and crossed my arms. "Hey…" he said and rubbed my arms. His hands felt amazing. Warming me up. "We've been together for years, are a few days that big a deal?"

I softened but didn't want him to know, "Just don't try anything. I don't belong to you anymore, okay? I don't *want* to be your wife. This isn't a couple taking a trip. It's two people that know each other."

"Friends."

"Yeah."

He nodded, "Just friends going on a trip."

I squirmed out of his lap and sat as far down the seat as I could get. I texted Mandy to yell at her, but her response back was just,

"He said he'd take the babies for a whole weekend. Girls gotta do, what a girl gotta do."

That's annoyingly true.

An hour or so into the trip, I opened my kindle since the traitor Mandy had thought to pack it. I went back to reading what I now know to be my absolute favorite Author, *Martha Sweeney*. I'm in book three of her romantic trilogy *Just Breathe* and I'm madly in love with *Joe Covelli*. In fact, I'd gladly trade my dumb-ass husband for a Joe Covelli.

By the time I even noticed we were slowing, I was 70% through. I looked up to see a very expensive looking building and tons of lights. What was this? I looked over at Chris, he was looking out his window with his elbow rested against it and stroking his chin.

"Where are we?" I asked.

"Hmm, good question," was all he said.

I sat up and looked out my window. Then it hit me hard and I absolutely loathed the excitement that transferred into my voice. "Chris… Are we in Disneyland?"

"Huh…looks like it," he acted surprised.

I turned to look at him like he didn't understand the very big deal this was. "Chris, don't play."

"I'm not," he looked like he was barely containing the victory dance.

Hold up! "This isn't what will win me over, okay? I can control my feelings- Oh my God! Look! Is that the Sleeping Beauty Castle?" I squealed and climbed over his lap to look out his window.

He smirked, "What were you saying?"

I caught myself too late but damn it! Disney is my weakness and he knows it! I got off him and crept back to my spot further away. "All I'm saying, is though this is a grand gesture, don't expect one trip…to…" I got distracted again by the many attractions we were passing. "To…to…" so much magic.

"Right," he grinned and put on his suit jacket. "Let's get checked in, then we'll finish this little talk."

"Check in?" I looked out my window. "Here? At- at- at the- you mean the-."

"Yep," he opened his door when we stopped and stepped out. I stumbled out behind him, still a little stunned. He was leading me toward the hotel I had circled in my Wishlist book seven times. As if I didn't already look like a kid on meds, he had to basically hold my hand and tug me to the front desk because sorry, but my eyes can't take in all the awesome at once.

He was talking to the lady while I stared from floor to ceiling with an open mouth. He still had my hand like I was a wandering toddler. I kinda am. If he let go right now, I would follow all the pretty and get lost, then freak out.

I heard the words "honeymoon suite" come out of her mouth and I snapped to attention.

"W-what?" I choked.

He looked back at me as he tugged me along and a few bellhops came for our stuff.

"What's up, hon?" he asked like it was no big deal.

"Where are we staying?"

He got me in the elevator and hit the floor button. "Oh, right, just the fairytale suite."

Chapter Twenty-Seven
CHRIS

*O*kay, so I'm cocky as hell about how well this all unfolded. I've been planning the Disney trip thing, for a few weeks, but the suite was a means of chance. Jenzy always wanted to stay in that room, she even had pictures in her little wish book, but the real help to the plan was a co-worker and his intended bride postponing their wedding for family.

He gave me the tickets and I paid him back. It was a freaking miracle considering this place is always booked but as we walked into the room, one could see why.

This wasn't just a place, Disney doesn't just advertise being the most magical place on earth, they really are. I couldn't have found a better way to make Jenzy's eyes go any wider or those blues get any brighter. She stood in the middle of the bedroom and stared out the floor to ceiling windows at the surrounding greatness of where we were. All the buildings out there were lit up and buzzing.

Our room was dimmed and full of heavy mood.

I set her bag and mine down just as the bellhops showed with the rest. When I looked back, she was touching the thick blue bed canopy that was tied open on all four sides. Her eyes were taking in everything and I loved it.

She asked, "How did you-?"

"Doesn't matter," I came to look out the window and felt her figuring the next part out.

"Honeymoon suit, so I guess, no extra bed?"

"Nope."

"There's a nice sized settee-."

"Nope. We'll sleep there," I turned and nodded at the bed. "Together…as friends…"

"I guess if I fight this, you'll extend the contesting crap."

"Yup."

She sighed then looked at the bed. It was taking a lot not to push her onto it and show her I wanted her. I could communicate sexually, everything she needed to know, but that wouldn't make her stay. I had to keep the playing field fair. Sort of.

Jenzy went to the bathroom to change into her night clothes and I smiled to myself as I started stripping. She was in there way too long because she was probably openly gawking at the epicness that was the bathroom.

I was down to my trousers only when she came back in. She paused for a second behind me and I bit back a laugh. We were used to being naked around each other, but she was trying to be separate. I pretended not to hear her and unbuckled my belt, then pushed my pants down.

This isn't exactly playing fair, but it wasn't a foul, either. I pulled down my boxers and went to the bed where my bag was to pretend to dig around.

She knocked over her toiletry bag, everything came out, and I looked around, "Oh, hi," I said.

I acted like this was normal, but she looked flustered and scurried to stuff her bag, "Hey, sorry I was-."

"I'm not shy. No big deal," I crouched down to help her and she almost fell back on her ass.

"I got it."

"It's fine," I said. She stood up fast and clutched it to her chest while trying to keep her eyes north of my navel.

I put my hands on my hips, "You okay?"

"What?"

I smiled slowly, "It's not the first time you saw me naked, Jenzy."

"Well, duh, I don't care, I don't even- like- whatever, you know."

"Nice shirt," I set the collar of her nightshirt down and she looked at herself like she didn't remember what her body looked like.

"Oh…" she was in my shirt. It was a comfy, red, plaid, flannel button-down that had come with bottoms I still owned. She winced, "Shoot, I forgot. Do you want it back?"

I shook my head, "Nope, you earned it that day."

She frowned.

"You don't remember?" I checked.

She shook her head slowly from side to side while she tried.

I explained, "You bought me those pajamas our third Christmas Eve together. Christmas morning, you admitted you wanted the top to sleep in, but I told you, no way. You bet me my top, that you could make me cum without using your hands."

She went from confused, to enlightened, to memorable laughs, to 'oh shit what a memory.' Then her eyes involuntarily dropped to my dick and I smiled when she whipped her head up and rushed to the other side of the bed to put space between us.

She got in and I took the stress off her and pulled some bottoms on. Once in bed, I sat up a little and looked over at her on her kindle.

"Whatcha reading?" *Or attempting to block me out with, rather.*

"A book by Martha Sweeney."

"Ah, right. The one with your book husband. How do you balance all these lovers?"

She rolled her eyes at me, "For one, Joe Covelli isn't as demanding as you."

"Right, but he can't satisfy you…like sexually."

"Actually, he has and many times while you slept…"

"I think that's the only romance book I would ever really read."

"Because of the hot sex?"

"Obviously, but also because what's her name? Sweeney? She writes real people. Real guys. She wrote up a steamy novel about a couple that isn't dysfunctional as hell and still made it hot."

"Were you really listening when I told you about her first two books?"

I sank down into the mattress, "Yep." I set my arms behind my head and she stared at me a bit. *Open to me, open to me.* I want her to talk. I want her to tell me things and know I'm listening.

"Remember how the main character Emma, went through some trauma…?"

"Car crash."

Again, she held some surprise in her eyes, "Yeah…well, I was on the author's website and she said that the therapies Emma used in the book to counter her phobias in this last one, are real. She even lists the books in the back."

"You should try it with your bug fear," I suggested.

"That's what I was thinking," she set her kindle down and looked at me like the connection was everything to her. "Maybe I could take bugs outside for myself in the future? I eventually will need to do it myself."

"I never mind doing it."

"Yeah sure, It's annoying."

"No, it's cute. It would be good for you to work through the fear, but if I don't mind taking bugs outside for you, I'm fairly sure the next guy won't." It was a sacrifice to acknowledge there could ever be a next guy, but it got my point across.

She looked at me a long time and the urge to kiss her came on strong. If she held my eyes for three more seconds I might. But then she put her kindle away and turned over, "Goodnight," she said.

"Goodnight." I stared at the canopy until I heard her breathing slow. Sometime in the night, she snuggled her way closer and closer. Soon she was right up under my arm with her hand over my chest and her leg across mine. I brought my arms down and held her there.

Ugh, this is agony. True painful agony. I can't have her then lose her; I won't make it through that. I twined my hand up in her hair and gently massaged the back of her head and neck. She moaned in her sleep and pushed closer. I did the corny thing and used this moment to unburden myself.

"I know you can't hear me…." I waited to be sure but her breathing never changed. "I just need to tell you, without you cussing me out that I love you. I know I suck. I know this has been the worst two years. I know it's my fault. Just let me show you why you should stay." I turned my head to press a lingering kiss on her brow. "Because if you go, this is it for me, Jenzy. I'm not doing this again. I'm finishing life alone and I don't want that, but alone would be better than trying to find another you."

She spoke in her sleep and I went stiff. She was only dreaming. 'Joe Covelli's' name was murmured. Which is okay, I would rather share her with a fictional man crush than a real one. I kissed her head again then let myself fall asleep. Besides, I don't know how much time I have before I lose all this.

JENZY

Warning to self. If you read Martha Sweeney books, you *will* have naughty dreams and they will be great. Well, until Joseph Covelli turned into my husband and an already hot sex dream turned into a sex dream starring Chris. I woke up horny as a rabbit and in the bare arms of my hot, cover model husband. That's a bad mix. My thighs were wrapped around his and my sex was pulsing against his heat. I was so hungry for lovemaking, my brain felt fuzzy and I debated with a courtroom full of brain cells why sex with Chris would be a bad idea.

My pelvis shifted so my sex could rub against him and my stomach tightened. I needed to touch myself or I was going to go batshit crazy. His man smell wasn't helping, it was getting me intoxicated. I tried to shift my hips again in a sleepy way so if he woke up, I could blame not having control over my actions. The drag of his warm skin against my mound when I ground myself just a bit was heaven. My breathing got a little shallow and I forced it to slow.

Morning light made his skin glow golden and with my head so close to his chest, the need to slide my tongue over his nipple made me feel like a lizard. Ahhhh! What's wrong with me? I looked at his hand lying over his torso and sucked my bottom lip. I could easily imagine his fingers working into the top of my panties and fingering me until I screamed. What if I woke him and asked?

Hey, Chris, could you just fuck me enough to chill out my hormones? No way, I was asking that, he rejected me two years in a row. I groaned in my head. TWO FUCKING YEARS! I need sex, I'm not dead!

I bet Mandy didn't pack my vibrator. She's not that good a friend. I need something to release me or I'm going to explode. I need a dildo, dick, or an object close to those things. I pressed my sex into him again and let the ripple relieve me a microsecond. Mmmm….

He moved in his sleep and I froze. The arm under me tightened around my waist and the other went down to stroke my thigh before hooking my knee and hiking it higher. Mother of Christ, that feels good. Now my mound is against the hardness of his hip bone and my thigh can feel that he's coming erect. I ground my sex easily and almost moaned. What is wrong with me?

"Want me to pick you up and bring you down on my dick or is this foreplay?" he asked.

I scrambled away from him but fell off the bedside with a thud. I stood too quick and got lightheaded, "Don't be a perv, Chris."

"You were molesting me in my sleep. Who's the perv?"

"I was not! I was asleep."

"Sure, come here."

I grabbed my purse, "Why?"

"Just come here." I rolled my eyes and went his way. He sat up on his elbow and beckoned me with his fingers, "Closer."

I made one step and his hand snaked out to grab my shirt front. He gave a pull that landed me with my back on the mattress and my head was at his knees.

"Chris-!"

He glided his hand up my leg, "Yeah, I smell it…you want me."

"That is so not true," I sat up but his hand made it under the bottom of my shirt; the tips of his fingers then grazed the edges of my underwear. All the blood in my head drained to that region and it throbbed like mad. "Yep, dampness…I can help if you want."

I took too long to stop him, oops. He pulled me closer by the ankle then flipped to his stomach which put him right between my legs.

"Chris!"

I drew my knees back and sat up on my elbows, but I know I'm letting this go too far. Pulling my knees up only gave him a better viewing.

"Want me to take care of it before we venture out?" he asked.

I swallowed with a dry throat. His eyes were holding mine so steadily, "N-none of this is working, and I need to go shower."

"K," he got up slow like a cat and looked back at me with a smirk before going through his bag.

Fucker.

Chapter Twenty-Eight
JENZY

*O*nce we were showered and dressed for the day, we set off together. Chris even mapped out a plan, so we could see and do all the things on my Wishlist. I argued that only a Leo would plan out a vacation but as we went, I saw why. Between lines and stuff, a plan was a great way (and only way) to avoid missing out. His manic need to plot was what made this happen.

He took me all over! From rides I craved to shows, to shops and restaurants.

We met up with characters dressed in perfect costume and took pictures. I have a phone full of pictures with us and Mickey, Goofy, Cinderella and many more. We went through the Jungle Cruise, and Chris insisted on the Indiana Jones Adventure. He was so free and truly himself he was even wearing a T-shirt, no hidden tats. He was the Chris from years ago.

"What are you doing?" he asked as we walked down the main street.

I was walking on my toes, "Nothing, let's go find the Dumbo Flying Elephants!"

"Your feet hurt."

"No, they don't."

"We're here for three more days; we can quit today and go get dinner."

"Hell no! It's Disneyland, Chris! There is no quitting."

He laughed, "You're in pain."

"Then we go on rides and I'll be off my feet."

He rolled his eyes and stopped to bend at the knees, "Get on."

I groaned and cursed about my 'weak ass' before getting on piggyback style. Why fight him? I'm one more mile from crippled.

He hoisted me up. We used to do this all the time after college because I'm usually a high-heels wearer and when they start to pinch this was our method to get to and from. Chris also walks like Seabiscuit and I can't keep up.

"Where too first?" I asked, already feeling way better.

"Here," he reached back and took the map and directory from his back pocket. He handed it to me, "Look for the ride."

I found it a second later and we re-routed.

"I don't care if this is a kid place," I told him. "I threw hundreds of dollars' worth of pennies in wishing wells growing up to get here."

"Why didn't we honeymoon here?"

"I changed my mind last minute," I reminded.

He weaved around people, "Sounds accurate."

"I can't help that I'm indecisive."

"The only thing you can stick to is glue."

And our marriage, I stuck to that.

Scary part is, he's so ripped and in shape that even with me on his back, he's keeping a quick pace. He feels great under me like this, his neck is strong, and the tattoos are winding up the side. Let's not forget his hands are on my thighs and my feet don't hurt anymore.

We both got on the Dumbo ride and the motion brought me to life! This is the perfect day and Chris is the Chris I remember. He's fun, and invested, and aware of me in every way.

Not long after that, he was pulling me along to the next few rides. Stopping at a shop here or there. Letting me look. I caught him looking at his watch only once, but he stood there and let me turn over the same items ten times each.

The *teacups ride* was next, and I was dreading it and anxiously awaiting it at the same time.

"Let's go," he said and set me down when it was in sight.

"Nope," I tried to get away, but he took my wrist and brought me back.

"Oh, my God Jennifer! Your cousin Trixie threw up because she ate her weight in cotton candy and corndogs before getting on. Trixie brought that on herself. You won't throw up."

"But it would be horrific if I did. The throw up would swirl around with me."

He laughed, "We're getting on."

"Nope," I dug my heels in. "That's a nope idea."

"This is in the wish journal!"

"It's considered an optional wish. A whim, really."

"Bull, come on," he pulled, and I used all of my weight to fall back.

I let all my weight throw me back, "No, Chris! No!"

"Are you really trying to be dead-weight on me? Babe, I bench more than you daily."

"Your weights don't struggle."

He scooped me up in his arms bride-style and sprinted for the ride even as I thrashed about. My fight was pointless because I was laughing, and even when I told the guy manning the ride to help me, he didn't see the danger through my giggles. Chris was laughing until there were tears in his eyes but when it was time to go in, he dumped me into a brightly colored cup and then got in.

"This isn't funny! If I throw up, I'll do it on you; as karma," I panted.

He sat across from me and shrugged, "No worse than that time you threw up on me after trying whiskey."

"That happened *once*!"

The ride launched us into more laughs and a dizzy sensation that only forced funky sounding giggle/screams. This was the best experience ever and this day didn't need to end anytime soon. The swirling went into my soul and my hair hugged my face and neck in the wind until I convulsed with side-splitting laughs.

When it stopped, we stumbled out and Chris pretended to hurl just to freak me out. I was so dizzy that laughing at him made it worse and I fell backward into the cup again. He assisted me out but wouldn't stop cracking up and we kept walking like drunks from the motion.

Then we were off like bandits again. The sun is hot here but closer to the night it gets, the cooler it gets. We had an amazing meal surrounded by amazing people and staff members and I knew more than part way through dinner that Chris had gotten his foot in the door of my heart. It wasn't the trip, or the room, or the things, it was the togetherness, and the communication that we had back after what felt like decades apart.

The next day was the same and the next. We woke up together, we started the rolling ball of fun then we went to bed. We talked, we laughed, we played, it was bliss. Even the little fights were entertaining. Mostly over me spending too much time in the shower, him being a schedule Nazi, me leaving an iron on, him wanting to organize our room and so on.

We went to even more shops on the last day. I found so many wondrous Disney trinkets and memorable souvenirs it was crazy. Then it was time for more rides. Chris was deliberately saving the roller coasters till last. His fear of heights had me wondering if he would even give in and do it at all.

When we got in line for this more traditional roller coaster ride, I nudged him in line, "Can you handle this? It's pretty high…"

He set his hands on his hips, "I'm in line, aren't I?"

"It's not as high as the others."

"Your optimism does nothing for me. If I fall out, I'll still die."

"You won't fall out. I'll hold onto you."

"Says the girl with the upper body strength of a wet noodle."

"I can do plank longer than you."

He cocked his jaw, "This is like our *Fast and Furious* debates. Just stop."

"I will stop because otherwise, your snob will show."

"I'm not a snob- I believe in facts."

"The fact is, you have no imagination," I baited.

"A car cannot possibly drive through three buildings, Jenzy. That's a fact. They went way too far with that one."

I debated him, "Have you ever done it? No, then you don't know for sure."

"I studied physics! It was too farfetched."

"*Vin Diesel* can do anything," I said dreamily.

"No, his stunt double can."

"Fast and Furious is the best movie series ever, and I *could* hold you down on a roller coaster. Argument over."

He poked my ribs and I squealed because I'm highly ticklish there.

To the people around us, we were gathering the 'what a cute couple' reaction. They were smiling and laughing as they listened in, which made us laugh too.

Once we got on, Chris locked up with anticipation. He started murmuring about this being a dumb way to die when the braces came down and made me laugh. When the guy came to check our belts, Chris had to interrogate the poor guy.

"Is this on right?" Chris asked him again.

"Yes, sir."

"Securely?"

"Yes."

"You didn't give it a strong enough tug."

"It's on."

Chris wasn't convinced, "What about hers? Just check her again, the-."

"It's all good, you both are all set."

"Is the brace low enough? She's skinny, is that- what if she's too light?" Chris pointed out.

"Her belt is real secured sir."

"What about-?"

I pinched his bicep, "Chris! We're fine. Leave him alone."

The guy took his chance to run.

"Safety is no game," Chris reminded.

I was so excited to go that I was swaying in my seat while we waited, "Okay, *Dad.*"

"Listen, I don't tease you about bugs. It's not even a logical fear, you are billions of times bigger than a spider, but falling to my death and going splat is a legit fear."

"That's true," I wrapped my arms around his arm. "Sorry, you're a real gladiator for getting on a ride like this when you don't like heights."

"All for you. So, if I die, you need to feel irreversibly guilty. So guilty that mental-shrinks can't even fix you."

I laughed so hard it hurt so he went on, "Great, my death is funny." He smiled even though it was meant to sound sad and I buried my face in his arm as the laughter kept busting past my lips. "You'll make a shitty widow, laughing at my funeral. *Sorry everyone but Chris' death was so funny I couldn't even hold on like I promised.* You're as bad as Rose on Titanic and her 'I'll never let go,' bullshit. She let go at the end but at least she wasn't laughing."

His mockery made tears follow all the painful, side-splitting laughter.

Then I tried to hold it in, "You'll be okay, let's get your mind off it, okay?"

We heard the *clunk, clank, thunk,* sound as the cars started pulling down then upward to the top at a heart-stopping slow pace to freak you out for what was to come.

"Oh, fuck, fuck fuck, fuck…" Chris mumbled and set his head back before closing his eyes. His arm muscles tightened and became like rock. It's hilarious to see a big, strong man like my husband show fear over anything.

"It's okay," I tried to at least tame some of the laughter. "Look at me, I'm right here, it's not a long one and for real, it's not that high."

He made himself look down and groaned. "Oh, shit! Why the hell did I get in this- ahhh, Jesus Christ… not like this, ugh, I don't want to die like this."

I bit back the giggle bubble and took his face in my hands as we reached the top, "Just breathe, okay, look at me and breathe. It's going to be fun, alright. We're perfectly safe."

His gorgeous hazel eyes were sparking with gold. He growled annoyance but put his arm around me and held the bar brace; caging me in safety.

I held on with one hand and held his neck with the other. "See...? Just keep looking at me, not anywhere else..." He really focused on my eyes and I felt the air change between us. The slightest shift, I felt it go from playful teasing to intense attraction.

The ride held at the top before the drop to make us feel the adrenaline of falling that was right around the corner, but all I felt was Chris. I was very aware of his arm around me and his pulse under my palm at his neck. I felt him drawing closer and the electric current of hope when his eyes dropped to my lips. Then the softness of his lips came down on mine and my heart beat so fast it felt loose.

The ride started to plunge, and we paused but it was all blocked out. He kissed me again before we came back up, and we stopped when it took the jerky turns but as soon as it smoothed out to go up, or down we were on each other again.

His tongue pressed into my mouth and I opened to him. I could taste his lips, his teeth, his tongue, his everything. Chris, the expert kisser, he took control of the kisses each time and I gladly yielded. This man, he's too much.

When the ride slowed to stop, we attacked each other with more gusto. His hand tangled in my hair and I pressed my body into his. We would gasp in-between to catch our air, but I'd rather pass out than stop.

We finally quit long enough to get out, but then he had my hand firmly in his and led us off the platform to a deserted corner where he pressed me into a wall and kissed me harder. This was what I wanted for so long. His touch, his hands, it was so unreal. I set my head back into the stone and looked up, that way he could go deeper. His one hand on my cheek and the other at my hip; he pushed up until he was under my shirt and I could feel his skin of my waist.

I arched my back to press his front and pushed my hand up his chest and arm. I'm so hungry, for all of it, for him, for Chris, for my husband. I'm crazy with it. He sucked my lower lip into his mouth then bit lightly on the tip of my tongue. Every little thing sent electric signals to my sex and I couldn't control the need.

When we finally stopped he stayed close but took my hand. He led us back to the hotel and by the time I reached the door of our room, I remembered why this was bad. I took my hand out of his and he looked at me, but I didn't look back as he unlocked our door.

I went inside and made myself face him, "We can't." I shook my head, "We can't- I can't. What you're doing is wrong. You are using this place. All this to get me back, then what? What? We do good for five more years until you get bored with me again and tune me out? I can't live like that, not again."

"I won't," he stepped closer and held my face like I was precious gold. "I won't ever shut you out like that again. That's what all this is for, not to bring you back, to *keep* you. I don't want to go back to how it was, I want to do better."

"You can't even tell me what drove us to how things were. How do we avoid what we don't know? I made things hard, too. You had a reason for tuning me out, we haven't confronted that. This was the loneliest two years. I can't do it again and you were mean at times and it was like loving stone. You-."

"I know, I'm working on all of that. That's what I'm saying. I get that this is on me, I'm willing to fix it."

He didn't get it, "But it's not all on you. *We* failed, not just you. I obviously did *something*. You aren't even proud of me like I am of you. You don't like me. Even if we let this happen and had the best sex ever, it won't fix our problems. You might want me physically but what about after? What about at company banquets? What about award dinners? What about when you don't want sex anymore like before? What happens when we go home and there's no more Disney magic? What then?"

There was so much emotion in his eyes, he was hurting for me and it was good to see him recognizing the hurt but was that enough? He let go of my face and held my hands to his chest.

"I am so sorry, that I didn't invite you, and I'm so sorry that you think I'm not proud. I know those words can't mend this but Jesus, Jenzy I mean them. I don't know why I did those things. I hate myself. This isn't just physical."

"You want me because you can't have me. You've always been like that, we started that way. I don't belong to you anymore. I belong to myself, and whoever else I choose, and that person won't put me in a closet or cover me up like your tattoos. I didn't want this to be some ugly drawn-out divorce, I wanted us to face it like adults and just admit the end of a good thing."

He was refusing to take in my points.

I inhaled sharply, "All of what you're doing is amazing but Chris, it's coming too late." I took my hands back but tried not to jerk them away. I didn't want to slash his heart I just wanted out of it. I went into the bathroom and locked the door. My tears hurt they were so deep. They raked at my body and bruised me on the inside. I heard him leave the suite in a fury and let myself cry harder. It was like mourning a death.

Then my phone rang in my pocket and I checked it to see Moses' number. I silenced it and sat on the floor near the tub, but my phone went off again. I pulled it together enough to answer.

"Hello?" I croaked.

"You sound wrong. What's wrong?" Moses pleaded.

"Nothing," I hugged my knees and took a shaky breath. "I'm fine."

"Please, don't lie. What's the matter?"

I looked at the door and shrugged, "I just told him to stop. I told him it's too late."

Moses was quiet then, "Jenzy-."

"Don't. Just, please don't tell me how you understand his side or ask me if I'm sure or if-if- just don't. Stop being so nice to me, okay? I don't deserve it. I'm not so great and I-, you need to find someone less fucked up."

"You aren't fucked up."

"Yes, I am! I don't know what I want, like always, and I shouldn't be dating. I'm selfish for even trying it and what's wrong with you? You just handle everything all the time. I'm in a honeymoon suite with my husband and you still want to talk to me? Why? Why? Are you that lonely or are you desperate? What, you can't find a girlfriend? You don't need this mess! I kissed him, Moses we kissed, and it wasn't- I didn't even stop it. So just stop being such a nice guy and leave me alone. Get it?"

"Jen-," I cut him off and hung up. In a minute or so he called back but I shut off my ringer for a time and let myself cry some more.

Chapter Twenty-Nine
CHRIS

I walked the streets for a while to clear my head, but also to fight the feeling of drowning that I couldn't shake. I came so close and then I lost her. This woman is going to be the death of my heart. Worse than that, how do I fight what she's saying. I'm not even sure, if the roles were reversed, that I would take the risk I'm asking her to take.

I left her alone for two years, and you didn't have to hit a woman to abuse her. You didn't have to strike them to leave scars. Some of the ones she's dealing with now are old. I can feel it because the old ones from years back might not have healed properly.

I'm making all the same mistakes as when I was younger. Aren't you supposed to grow and learn from the past, not repeat it? When I got back to the suite, she was curled up on the little settee near the window with a blanket. She was also in deep sleep with her phone in hand.

Silly girl…didn't she know men took the couch in fights, women get the bed. Yeah, she knows, but even in a fit of anger she thinks about me, and she knows I hate couches. None are big enough for me.

Then I remembered how she'd been sleeping on the couch back home for a long while, and I hadn't even noticed. Wow. I need to be shot.

I took the blanket off and she shifted. Her nose was red, her eyes swollen, and tear stains were streaking her face. I hate myself at this moment more than I ever have. She doesn't deserve this. She doesn't deserve what I've done to her. Hearing her cry in the bathroom was enough to make breaking down the door seem right.

I lifted her up gently and she turned into me, dropping the phone. She's so light I could hold her like this and just soak in the feel. I walked with a light step to the bed and laid her down with care. Then I covered her up. She curled into a ball and didn't move again, and I went to get her phone. It buzzed in my hand and I looked.

I stopped with a sinking heart to read the messages were from Moses.

Moses.

My rival. I knew how wrong it was, but I needed to know, so I unlocked her phone, remembering the passcode was my birthday. She hadn't changed it.

Then I read. She wasn't responding to him so all the ones I saw were only from him, from about the time I left the suite, to one minute ago, all spread out. He must've pissed her off. Correction...*I* pissed her off, now she hated us both.

His first one was:

"Hear me out. I know you think I'm playing the nice guy, I'm not. It's just, I understand. I won't pretend it doesn't hurt to know you're with him, or that you kissed him. I'd love to be him right now. I'm so insanely jealous of Chris it's crazy. I lose sleep at night trying to understand how he could let you go. I think he's insane. I want to be the one you turn to, so I can take his place, that's my motive. It's just as selfish as you claim to be. No, I don't pursue you because I'm lonely or desperate, I pursue you because a man would have to be sick in the head not to. Just please talk to me."

Minutes later
"I only want a minute to talk, I know you're upset, but please."

Minutes later
"Jenzy, pick up."

Five minutes later
"**I don't care if you kissed him. I don't care if you're in a suite with him. You could sleep with him, I'd still want you. I want you that badly.**"

Two minutes later
"**If you want to just be friends again I'll do it. I told you when this started how I feel. I just don't want to lose you completely. Don't shut me out. I'd seriously friend zone myself so long as you were in my life. I knew the risk when we first went out. I'll wait if you ask me to.**"

This last one just came in when I moved her to the bed.
"**Jenzy, I feel things for you I haven't felt for a woman in a very long time. You're everything I could ask for and more. Please don't walk away from this without at least talking to me. I'm your friend first. Always.**"

I almost deleted every single one. Why should he have a right to say those things to my wife? I almost called him or texted him back.

Opting not to do any of the above, I put her phone with her purse on the table and sat there facing the window. Whenever she moved in her sleep I would take a minute to watch her.

There was someone out there that felt as mad and crazy about my wife as I did. Someone just as devoted, just as in love, by the sounds of it. The problem is Moses is better. He's better for her than I am. A real man would probably take that as a hint to let them be and give her the divorce that way she could have the life she wanted, but not me.

I see it as a challenge to try even harder. To prove to her I can be better. But looking at her now, I feel very small. This isn't the first time I fucked up on this scale. Moses' messages remind me of my own at one time.

2008

I lay in my bed at home for the first time in a long time and tried to block out the 90's kid theme, and the sound of Todd and Mandy going at it in the room next to mine.

Mom was never a conservative type; she didn't mind if we had a girl sleepover, so long as there were condoms involved. It wasn't the sound of my brother screwing a chic that was making me feel sick, though. Not that it was helping any.

It was really about today. I fought with myself all the way home about how to handle Jenzy at the airport. I have never been intimate with a girl so long. Jenzy knew my middle name. Girls don't stay with me long enough to learn that.

Trouble is, old habits die hard. I've been envisioning holding Jenzy, touching her, making love to her again for months. I had this whole line up for when I got off the plane. It was supposed to be, I see her, she sees me, she comes to me, I kiss her like life, and lift her up until her feet don't touch the ground. Then I attack her anywhere I can. The bathrooms, the parking lots, the doorway of the airport.

I even often wondered if I would feel emotional. She's been everything I could want in a girlfriend and I was coming home for her, but at the airport, my commitment issues surfaced, and I outright avoided her. The minute I saw my friends, I couldn't be myself.

Now, in the quiet of my room, I could relive the look on her face when I side hugged her like she was nothing and then ignored her. The scary part about a girl as amazing as Jenzy is she doesn't let you see her weakness. She handles it with positivity and acceptance and moves past it at neck-breaking speed. Inside, she might be torn to shreds, but outside, she's hardly affected. I only caught a glimpse in the parking garage when she was hugging Todd.

I took out my phone and started sweating as I tried to figure out how to breach this in a text.

"**Hey, are you asleep?**" I typed. It took forever before it went off.

"**Not yet,**" was all she said.

I strained to think up something else.
"**I'm sorry about earlier. I saw my friends there, and I panicked a little. I haven't told anyone about us yet.**"

Another eternity went by before she responded.
"**No worries. There's really no 'us' when you think about it. It's not like we've been dating. Just talking.**"

What! My rational mind couldn't wrap that one. Did she just belittle the fact that I all but sold my soul to her these months? Just talking? I haven't had sex in ages because I was 'just talking' to her. I came back with fire.
"**If we were just talking why did I think that meant no sex with other people like we agreed?**"

She took her sweet time coming back.
"**I'm sorry, I didn't want to make you upset. I just figured by how you acted at the airport that this was only casual.**"

Well fuck. I just buried myself.
"**I didn't want it to be like that. I'm sorry. All I wanted the whole way here was to be with you. I'm just not ready to go public.**"

She came back faster this time.
"**You don't usually go public with girls you talk to. I'm not upset. I think I misread what you said before, and that was my fault. No hard feelings. Your friendship means way more.**"

Friendship?! What the fuck was she throwing that F word around for? Christopher Clark does not get friend zoned. I jumped out of bed and crept out of my room. Jenzy was in the guestroom three doors down but mid-way down the hall, my mom came walking from her room.

"Chris? What are you doing up? It's after one in the morning."

"Hey, mom," I stopped and stretched, pretending I just woke up. "Had to go to the bathroom, that's all."

"Are you hungry? I'll make you a sandwich."

"No, Ma, I'm fine."

"You're too thin. Do you eat in Sweden? Do you need more money? You need more money, don't you, when-?"

"No, Ma, I'm doing fine."

"Your ribs are showing…" she poked me in the stomach with a frown.

I rolled my eyes, "Those are abs, Mom."

After finally assuring her I wasn't hungry or malnourished, she went on her way and I went to Jenzy's door. I checked the hall to be sure no one would hear and then knocked as softly as I could. Jenzy opened the door with a smile.

Have mercy.

She was sleeping in a long gray shirt that stopped high on her thighs and black knee highs. No bra, since one shoulder was falling, and I saw no strap, this girl!

"Chris?" She looked down the hall, "What's up?"

"Friendship?"

"I'm sorry?"

"You want to be friends?"

She scanned me from head to toe in my sweatpants and I hoped the lack of shirt, new tattoos, and added muscle might do something for her.

She hadn't seen my changes yet.

"Only friends?" I asked.

"Aren't we?"

"When we talked in Sweden, the *way* we talked, is that really all you want?" I tried again.

She kept the smile in place but now it was condescending. "Okay, I'm confused. You want me, but in private only? So, you don't want people to know we're together, but if I say we're casual, you get upset."

"Because we aren't casual!"

"I'm all for keeping things private, I like keeping people out of my business, but how long would you want to keep it that way?"

"I don't know...like I just don't want people to know."

"That way, if you get bored, you don't look like a jerk?"

I took a breath. That might be why, and I saw in her eyes that she saw that in mine.

She held the door and smiled again before rubbing my arm. "I think we should just backseat this. You have so much greatness happening, and I haven't told anyone, but I'm not going back to campus. My mom found this amazing Herbalist guy I can study under. I'll be working at the Animal shelter still, but this way I can start learning something in the field of what I really want to."

"Are *you* breaking up with *me*?" I questioned.

"No, silly we aren't even together. That's the beauty of a secret relationship, no one even knows when it's over."

"Jenzy," I held the underside of her elbow and stepped closer, "I don't want this to be over. You're not just another girl to me."

She stood on her toes to kiss my nose then smiled, "But you treat me like one." I felt a cut into my heart hearing her say that. "You better go now, someone might hear us. You don't want that, Goodnight." She kissed my cheek then closed the door.

I spent all of Thanksgiving staring at Jenzy across a room or table, checking for signs of sadness or bitterness or anger. She only smiled, laughed, made jokes, socialized and acted annoyingly natural. I felt like dying and she was blooming. Even now as I watched her with my mother as they cooked in the kitchen with a bored Mandy, I felt irritated.

I never had a girl just accept it like this. I usually got the whole, 'I miss you, I love you, let's try harder, why won't you tell people about me, if you don't tell people I'll break up with you.'

Jenzy was even polite to me! She would smile and joke like she did with Todd. No hidden anything. God, I want this woman, why won't she fawn?

When the holiday ended, Jenzy was supposed to go home to see her parents for a bit and I was due back in Sweden the week before Christmas. I would miss Christmas and New Year's but that was the plan. She avoided me like a plague and within two weeks I couldn't find her with a magnifying glass.

Until her Birthday on the 17th of December.

I got wind of the fact that Todd and Mandy were taking her out to a popular bar between our Mom's and Campus that hosted DJ's. I made my way out there and was assaulted by the boom, boom, boom of music when I hit the door. One of the year's hottest songs, by *Cobra Starship,* was blasting and people were jumping around and partying hard. The bar looked like a 20's warehouse with brick walls and lofts.

I spotted Jenzy up on the tables with Mandy and they were dancing like they were drunk but Jenzy isn't legal yet. I know that's just her being a free spirit. Everyone was cheering them, and I smiled despite the situation. She's hilarious and sexy all at once and I wasn't the only one that noticed. Guys were all too happy to show enthusiasm.

"I didn't know you were coming," Todd said over the music.

I turned to see him, "Hey, man. Yeah, I heard from Garrett."

He shook his head, "I mean because I didn't invite you."
"Great. I guess this means you know."
"I'm her best friend, I know everything."
"Look, I didn't-."

His face became sarcastic, "Hey, guess what? I don't care. I get it, okay? You pulled your regular shit and screwed her, hid her, and then broke her. I just find it funny you couldn't find someone that didn't matter to me too. Did it occur to you at all that you could've risked *my* friendship with her?"

"I don't like how things went either, Todd. That's why I'm here."

He remained the guard dog, "Leave her alone. Just, she's fine. She's got, six guy's numbers in her purse and a hot party, just leave. You want a grown-up relationship, practice on someone else."

"Shut up, Todd, you don't know shit about how I feel."

"And I don't care. How do you talk to someone for eight months and treat them like shit in person? What are you so embarrassed about? It's Jenzy! Half the state would kill to be her guy."

"Trying to say I took your chance?" Cheap shot on my part.

He looked at me incredulously, "Take your head out of your ass, Chris. Mandy and I are serious. We're talking engagement. If you looked outside your own shit, you would know that. I'm defending Jenzy because she makes a better brother than you sometimes. Don't fuck with her. Make a move or go home."

I hadn't expected a lecture when I came here tonight, but I might've needed one. Todd's a pain in my ass, but he didn't need to think I was a heartless dick. I looked up at Jenzy dancing and loathed myself.

I looked back at Todd, "This has been the most horrific few weeks of my freakin' life."

He looked back at me skeptically, "That's called feelings, stupid. Welcome to whipped."

He shoved past me and I made my way to the table Jenzy was dancing on. She had on tall black boots and skinny jeans that left little to the imagination with a black tube top. Her eyes were lined darker and her moves were siren calls.

"Hey!" I called up. She didn't hear me and with her back to me, she did a snake-like hip move that made me growl inside. I cupped my mouth to project, "Jenzy!"

She followed my voice, then smiled and waved without breaking stride, "Chris! Hey! Were you in on this party?"

"No, I came to talk to you."

"What?" She bent to hear me.

I came closer, "I wanna talk to you."

"Can it wait until after?"

I looked her in the eyes and shook my head, "No."

Mandy yelled from the other table, "Pervy Chris! Who invited you, dickweed?"

I looked over at a tipsy Mandy, "You missed me, don't lie."

"Whatever," she danced on. "I missed you like I miss the flu."

Jenzy was laughing but then looked back at me, "Why don't you go get a drink. You're legal! Or I have a friend you might like! Her name is Kelly. She's-."

"I don't want Kelly, I want you."

She frowned, "The music is loud, but people aren't deaf. Keep it down or someone's going to hear you."

"Good."

She straightened to dance but slower than the vibe, "You don't do public. I told you it's okay."

I leaped up on the table next to her and went under the guise of dancing, "I fucked up," I said over the music. "I should've sucked your face off at the airport."

She danced closer, so we could hear each other, and I spun her. She sighed, "Since that first night…when we met…I knew you would never be in it for steady. I'm fine with it."

"I'm not," I came even closer. "I need you."

"I'm not really 'under the carpet' material, Chris."

"You're right."

She smiled like she was glad I understood then stepped back to dance but I caught her around the waist and pulled her against me. I laid my lips down on hers. I broke every habit and every barrier to claim her in that minute as mine. I laid it all down to prove that she owned me too. When I took her mouth, I was writing my name there with my tongue, in front of almost every guy on campus.

She was stiff with surprise at first, but then when she heard the acknowledging hoots and hollers of peers that knew the breakthrough I made, she smiled against my lips and wrapped her arms around my neck. Yes! This was what I needed. Her. The support of those arms and the warmth of these lips.

She stopped us to look up at me but was grinning and still holding me close, "You realize half the school just saw this, right?"

"Happy Birthday."

She kissed me again like she was testing my new boundary and I kissed her back as I reached down to grab her ass. I lifted her against me and she locked her ankles to hold on. This way I could keep kissing her.

I kept kissing her, even as I hopped down off the table with her wrapped around me and walked us outside. Todd high-fived me on our way out.

Chapter Thirty

Present Day
JENZY

I had been home for three weeks and I was still avoiding Moses and Chris alike. I miss both of them, but I don't want to date either because it feels sloppy. Today I was walking into a home office owned by none other than Bella Snow. Bella was the midwife Mouser had directed me to that partnered with a Doula named Doreen. With a little luck, I might be their next apprentice.

The minute I met them, I felt a strong pull. Bella was a little shorter than me with long curly hair and a full-figured body. She hugged me upon meeting me and that warmed my soul. Doreen was taller than both of us and willowy with a pixie cut and she hugged me too.

"And how are you, Mrs. Clark?" asked Bella.

"I'm great!" I stepped back and sighed, "Nervous, though."

Doreen laughed, "Don't be nervous, I'm very happy to meet you, and I already feel anxious to start."

Bella stepped aside and turned to beckon a woman my age forward, "And this is Rachel. Rachel is like you, she studies under us."

"Hi, there," Rachel offered her hand but I'm a hugger. She switched gears and hugged me back. Then we all took each other in. "Funny how you feel instantly connected to some folks, right?" she said.

I sighed, "Definitely."

Doreen hugged me into her side, "We all have the same dream. We're kindred."

Bella poked Rachel's side, "Rachel only has seven more births and she'll be a certified Doula."

I smiled, "Congratulations!"

She blushed, "Thanks. I'm so nervous still, but I know this is what I want."

We went into Bella's office where the walls were filled with framed pictures of beautiful babies, mostly newborns. "Did you deliver all these?" I asked.

"Yes," she beamed. "Mommy's sometimes send me pictures and allow me to put them on my memory wall, I call it."

"Do you keep in touch?"

"Some mommy's visit and call, others sometimes don't. That's the saddest part, really. You get to know amazing women for nine months of their journey and saying goodbye is hard. I love all my Mommies."

"That's beautiful."

Doreen asked as we all sat, "Do you have any children, Mrs. Clark?"

I felt a shift of sadness. I didn't have children and I didn't have the potential mate to try. "No…"

"Do you and your husband intend to try?"

I could feel my mood crashing like a plane, "My husband and I are divorcing…"

"Oh no. I'm very sorry," said Rachel.

They all looked at me with sympathy, but I didn't want that.

"It's okay, but I love children and I do want them in the future."

Bella took over again, "That's exciting. Dr. Mouser says you were his very best, so I think that means I'm getting a winner."

We bonded over the course of an hour and when I left, I felt enlightened. Doreen and Bella are going to be the second-best teacher I've had. I called my mom, then Todd, then Mandy and my heart wanted so much to tell Moses and Chris but bridging communication with them would mean making decisions I just can't yet.

Days later, I was doing dishes at Mandy's sink when the doorbell rang. A few minutes later, Chris walked in with Connor on his shoulders and I forced myself to seem natural.

Mandy came in all dressed up to perfection and gave me a hug, "I really can't thank you guys enough for this. If Todd and I don't get out, we'll lose it."

"I know," I gave her a squeeze then went back to work. "We'll be fine."

"Are you mad at me?" she whispered when Chris started talking to Todd.

"Why would I be mad?"

"You have to sit my kids with *him* tonight."

"It's not high school, we can be civil. Besides, it was the tradeoff for the Disney trip. Date nights and eventually a weekend."

"I'm sorry it takes two people to watch my horrific kids. Connor is part ape and Penny still fusses all the time."

"Oh my God, Mandy. Connor just listens to Chris better and Penny is fine. You look hot as hell, go have fun."

"You sure?"

"Definitely."

"Todd told me upstairs…" she leaned in close, "That we might even get a quickie in on the ride home. He says I look that fantastic."

I laughed, "You guys are hilarious. Go get boinked. Just don't tell me about it."

She left us a list of contacts and emergency numbers then ran out after Todd slapped her ass at the door. Now I was alone with Chris and this was the first time since the trip to Disneyland.

"Are you hungry, Connor?" I asked as I set a plate in the dish drain.

"Yes," said Chris.

"No!" laughed Connor. "She asked me! I'm Co*w*or."

Chris looked up at him in surprise, "No way! I thought *I* was Connor."

"No, you Uncle C*wissy*!"

We laughed at his garbled words and he set our nephew down. Connor ran from the room to the hall over and over but in the lull of the third time he left, Chris came to stand by me, "Are we okay?"

"Yeah," I smiled up at him and then kept my eyes on the sink.

"Don't fake with me."

"I'm not. We're okay," I decided to lighten the mood, "We would be better if you signed."

He smiled, "I'll get around to it."

"Uncle C*wissy*!" Connor zoomed into the kitchen and jumped him. Chris held Connor up like an airplane and made perfect sound effects before flying him into the living room.

While the two of them zipped about, I made a dinner; a wicked dinner of organic veggie burgers and homemade apple crisp French fries to fool Connor, along with broccoli. Penny was asleep in her swing for an eternity.

When I was done, I checked in on the guys. They were building a tower of Legos that required Chris standing on the coffee table while they watched *SpongeBob and* stacked.

"Chris!" I snapped. "You don't stand on tables, it's bad manners. Now Connor will do it."

"He already does it and this tower is epic. We have no lifts, it's all manual labor."

"Could you not act five?"

Connor jumped. "Auntie Jezzy, *wook*!" he pointed up at the tower on his toes.

"I see!" I clapped my hands and came to kiss his head. "Good job!"

Chris carefully placed the next block and spoke under his breath, "I'm the one doing all the work, but sure, kiss the lazy four-year-old."

"The four-year-old isn't a D.I.C.K," I spelled for Connor's sake. "Can we find something educational for him to watch?"

"Why? He likes SpongeBob."

"It's not educational."

"Your face isn't educational."

"Really, Chris?"

They both started giggling and I rolled my eyes before tickling Connor under the ribs and poking Chris in the side. He jerked to avoid me and knocked over his tower. "Karma…" I sang as I returned to the kitchen.

"Karma takes the form of a B.I.T.C.H," he spelled back.

The boys followed a little after and I served them with glee. Until they looked at it like I served brains, "Come on Connor, it's a burger. Mmmm, yummy," I enticed.

"Wucky!" Connor grimaced and pushed it away.

"It's the same as other burgers. Just try it."

"No!" he pushed it further away.

I gave Chris a look and he tried, "Hey, buddy look." He took a man bite from his own that weirdly turned me on for a split second but then. "Ugh, Jenzy, come on." He said around a mouthful. "He's not gonna eat this. No kid would eat this. I can't even eat this. It's gross."

"I worked really hard on it, could you like, try?" I felt the well of disappointment.

He groaned, "Dude." He nudged Connor with his elbow and Connor stopped mashing his apple fries, "Just one bite, little buddy, just one."

Connor turned his face away and I glared at Chris.

Chris looked at me and shrugged, "It's a veggie burger and he's four," he said around a full mouth.

"Well, his role model just made it clear in front of him that is was gross, so…"

He looked guilty and irritated, "Connor," he tried sounding stern. "One bite to see if you like it. Auntie Jenzy made these just for you. Do it for Uncle Chris."

Connor took a tiny pinch of burger and chewed it. He grimaced again and spat it out. Chris pursed his lips. "Sorry babe, but it really is nasty. I'm chewing and it's growing in my mouth." He was joking but like always he didn't consider how I felt.

"Wuck!" Connor said again, spitting more.

I stood up from the table and took both their plates to the trash, dumping them. Chris was at my back suddenly and whispered as Connor ran off for the living room, "Hey, it's not personal-."

"Nothing ever is with you," I whispered back. "You undermine everything I do. You had no intention of even trying it with an open mind."

He fought back, "My mind was as open as Mandy's legs in college, the burgers have no shape, there are funky chunks of random things, and they smell like old socks."

"You're as bad as Connor, but he's got the excuse of being a kid."

"Are we really fighting because I don't like something?"

"Because you're an asshole about it. You're an asshole about everything."

I got ready to dump a batch of the fries I made but he took the platter back, "You overreact about everything!" he began. "It's food. How could you be that delicate? You messed it up, who cares, I'm not mad but I'm not going to lie. You can't cook healthy. So, what?"

"*So, what*? I made it, that's what," I threw the towel on the counter and faced him with a hand on my hip. "I tried something new, that's what. And I wanted to share it. I thought for a second that you wouldn't be a dick. You don't think about the fact that I have been in here trying really hard to make you both something special."

"Fine. Next time I'll lie-."

"There won't be a next time, if you sign the stupid divorce. This is yet another great example why-."

"Still, I'll just lie. You can serve weird shit no one likes. Sorry I didn't fake it like you do. Being positive about everything. If I told you the electricity was shut off. You'd say, *'oh, candlelight dinners.'* If I say, we have to live in a box, we were evicted. You'd say, *'oh good, we can move anywhere we want now, boxes are so easy to keep clean.'* Jenzy, the house is on fire because you didn't shut off your fucking hair iron. *'oh, that's okay we can make fucking s'mores!'"*

I want to punch him in the face but then a treacherous giggle bubbled past my lips at his morbid humor. He cooled immediately and saw the hilarity in his words. We laughed, and he wrapped his arms around me in a hug that reached my soul. He wasn't trying to be sexual just genuine.

He kissed the top of my head, "I'm sorry," he sounded serious. "You are an amazing cook, I just don't like your healthy stuff."

I sighed, "You don't even try it."

"I risk my life every time I do. Listen, I could stuff myself to obesity if you cooked the unhealthy way all the time. You're a kitchen goddess…but with the organic stuff your skills are off. I'm being honest."

I blocked that out, "I am *annoyingly* positive."

"Not annoyingly. I like you that way even if I want to strangle you at times. I get so serious and negative that I need the reminder things could be worse…"

I took in that he was still holding me, "Connor has to eat something."

"Can we call a truce and order pizza?"

I stepped out of his arms feeling defeated still. "Yeah, whatever."

He smiled and pulled his phone to call it in as I cleaned up my failure. "And steam the broccoli," he ordered. "No kid on this planet eats raw broccoli."

I saluted him like he was a General, with sarcasm.

"At ease, soliderette."

I tasted my veggie burger but when Chris wasn't looking, I spat it out in the trash. Damn it! He's right, I suck at making things organically. When I eat at organic restaurants I love it but when I cook it… Is it my measurements? This burger tasted like brimstone. It wouldn't even come off my tongue.

I looked back at Chris while he talked on the phone and noticed he was munching on my apple crisp fries. He was busy with the call, but he was actually eating them. When Connor raced back in, he climbed on Chris' arm while he spoke on the phone and to my shock, he ate one too. Connor took a crisp from Chris' hand and ate it, then two more.

When the pizza got here, Chris served it with my apple fries and Connor ate them without so much as a picky sniff… but so did Chris. I tried one and was happy to find I hadn't screwed these up, they were awesome, and the guys were devouring them. Then Chris pushed a broccoli on Connor's plate.

"No!" Connor tried to get down, but Chris pulled him into his lap.

"Nope," Chris cut it in half and stabbed it with the fork. "One bite."

"No! Wucky!"

"Alright, here it is," Chris shifted him on his knee as Penny started to cry so I went and got her.

I held her in my arms like the peanut she was, even though she was approaching six months. Then I listened in on the guys as I sat back down at the table.

Chris became theatrical, "This isn't broccoli. It's a tree. You…are a dinosaur. Dinos eat trees."

"No…." Connor sang the word in a laugh.

"Yes. They eat leaves. You must eat the tree, or you won't have the energy to run from the T-rex."

Connor eyed the veggie, "T-*wex*," he questioned. "How fast the T-*wex?*"

"Faster than you if you don't eat the trees."

Connor tried it and with some dying faces, he ate quite a few florets. I watched Chris while I snuggled Penny and smiled. He really is great with kids.

After dinner followed the crazy night routine. We had to get them baths, and that meant Chris and I chasing a half-naked Connor while pretending to be T-Rex dinosaurs. Not to mention we had a very fussy Penny wadding around during belly time. She was scooting all over and trying to crawl but unhappy about it.

Chris caught Connor in the hall with one sock on, one arm in a shirt, and no pants or pull-ups. Bath time left him and me wetter than our nephew, but the laughs were contagious. Penny was next.

I sat up in the rocker of their nursery to read with Connor in my lap, while Chris reclined on the other rocker and bottle-fed Penny the milk Mandy pumped for us.

Connor was out first, sprawled across my lap like a cat and Penny gripped Chris' shirt while she fed peacefully with her eyes closed.

"In air fist pump," Chris whispered.

I made a blowing up sound effect and we grinned. We made a good team with kids.

"He looks too cute on you right now," he said.

I looked down at Connor and ran my fingers through his hair, "I remember when he was born. Isn't it weird? Now he'll be five in a month or so."

"Speaking of birth…did you ever contact that midwife?"

He remembered? "Yeah, last week. She wants me, I start Monday."

"Congratulations. That's great."

I wasn't sure what to say to that, "Did you really like the apple crisps? Because it doesn't matter if you didn't."

"Then I have no reason to lie."

"Imagine, I guess we could've compromised with meals like we did tonight. Half healthy." I laughed but he looked at me with nothing but truth.

"We still can."

No, we can't. We're past that.

I searched for a way to steer us away from that but then was saved by the bell when Mandy and Todd came in.

Chapter Thirty-One
JENZY

*I*n the first week of August, I was biking a trail in the park and soaking in the sun and Mother Earth to clear my head. Things keep changing and I feel like I'm caught up in a blender of crazy.

The forest helped, the trees, the smell of pine, the dirt. I was a little creeped about the grasshoppers on the trail, but I needed the outside time.

Then I clipped a passing biker with my handle and we tipped over and slid across the ground. The clumsy star was late in coming, I should've foreseen an accident. When I sat up, I looked across the trail to see Moses. His eyes lit up seeing it was me and I felt mine do the same.

"Jenzy?" He stood with only a scraped forearm, "I wasn't looking."

"Neither was I." He came up and helped me to my feet. "You bike here?"

"Yeah, I was going to show you this place. I'm here with my friend Chloe…"

"Oh," we stood face to face with a heavy air between us. He looked amazing. He looked amazing in that way guys do when you still have feelings for them and they seem to get hotter from being away. I missed him and that made me feel like a mess again, "I should…go…"

He stepped toward me then paused, "Okay…"

I went to get my bike but then he touched my arm and I turned around.

He pulled me into him and I grabbed on. I missed him so much and he knew without me saying it. I curled closer and he tightened his arms. He smelled like man heaven. Crisp from body wash but manly from exercising. "Do you hate me?" I asked.

He gave me a skeptical eye then motioned for me to follow with my bike. We walked them off the trail before he lowered at the base of a tree and tugged me down with him. He lifted his arm and I snuggled underneath like it was a wing, huddling close.

He rubbed my back in soothing circles, "I could never hate you," he confessed.

"I said mean things. Things I didn't have a right to say."

"You were hurting."

"I called you desperate."

"Yeah, that was pretty mean."

I looked up in horror, but he was smirking at me. I sighed and set my cheek on his chest. "I was a bitch."

"But I know I seem weird. I've never been jealous by nature. It doesn't mean I care any less for you. I'm mad about you, I just don't-. I know you probably want me to act more disturbed by-."

"No, then we'd have drama. You make things so much easier for me by not being a typical male that needs to peacock. I just…" I set my head back to look up at him and stroked his short and neat beard. "I felt cheap, for kissing Chris. I almost wanted you to be mad and make me feel worse."

"I'm not blind. I know there's something still there with Chris, even if you two don't want to see it. I'm not seeing you and ignoring the chance this could end…with you and me being friends. I feel…*that word* that I'm not going to say, because it will complicate everything."

Love… I know what word. I'm starting to feel it too but the love I had for Chris feels like a door slowly opening too.

"Whatever you do, Moses, don't say that word, alright? You're right, sometimes I wonder about Chris, and if I hurt you like that I'd never forgive myself."

"I love with an open hand. I don't need promises or anything else other than to know you won't cut me out again."

I kissed his lips but with a touch of innocence. He kissed my nose next then my eyes and I relaxed into him. Moses is my safe house. He's my moving on, and my step out the door of my past. But I really need to let go if I'm going to go forward.

"Maybe we should be open…" he hinted.

I winced, "Like threesomes?"

"No, I did that once and it was a little too hippie even for me. For us, I mean… no exclusivity. You're married on paper still. If something happens with Chris, you shouldn't feel like you're cheating on *me*. We stay in an open relationship…"

I hated that idea. I'm naturally monogamous but until Chris signs, this would definitely be a better label.

Then I felt something crawl up my leg and screamed when I found a spider making its way over my knee.

Moses was on it right away and smacked it.

I held my cheeks, "Oh no! What if that was Louis Armstrong?"

Moses smiled and pulled me in to kiss my head.

CHRIS

Sometime after work, I was stuffing papers in my briefcase when a coworker, Alba Finner came to me with more for me to cram in there.

"You need a new case," she laughed.

"I need a new brain," I had to pull a handful out to refill it. Then I noticed she was still hovering. I hate that. Her suits always had an unprofessionally open collar and hence, her boobs were distractingly there. I saw another coworker go by our conference room and he slowed down a bit to peer in at us.

She was perceived as an office hottie. Something to do with the corkscrews of gold hair and tight fitted skirts over an ass considered impressive.

She sat on the table facing me as I sat in my chair. She set a perfectly manicured nail over a document, "Do you need the papers on that house over by 5th?" she asked.

I leaned back since I could see the blood coursing through the veins in her boobs, "Nah, I got em'."

"You're always on top of everything. Are you like that in all aspects of life?"

"Pretty much," I realized the tabs I had weren't matching up with the color coordination and swore. "Damn it. I just did these."

"I heard you were a neat freak…need help?"

"I don't know how much you know about neat freaks…but it pairs with control freaking too. You can't help my kind."

She smiled but I kept my eyes on my task.

I gasped, "What the fuck was I thinking, labeling the Petersons with yellow tabs? I use alphabetical *and* color codes, so they should be in Purple. Fuck everything, this is the ruin of my fucking day!"

Alba crossed her legs inward toward me, "Awe, that's sucky…" she winced. I mumbled but then she went bubbly again. "But, hey! Cheer up. Yesterday was your birthday, right?"

I considered flipping the table over with her on it. *Thanks for the reminder*. Jenzy had only texted me a 'happy birthday.' That's cold, considering she usually treated my birthday like a national holiday. Not anymore. I deserve it. I deserve every bit.

"Yeah…" I kept working. "What about it?"

"Are you free this weekend? It's Friday night. We could go with a group to get drinks or something."

"Not really a drinker."

"Oh, neither am I," cue flirtatious laugh, and she did, "I just mean to hang out and unwind."

"I unwind at the gym," it was a blow-off, but she was pretty relentless.

"Me too! I like swimming and the tracks. You look like you lift…how much do you…?"

"A lot, don't you have a house showing today?"

"Not until four. I have thirty minutes. What about your wife, does she go to the gym or…?"

I looked up at her and worked down my temper. "Are you really going to pretend you don't know when half the agency does?"

"God," she covered her full lips. "I thought that was a rumor. I had no idea it was true. When's the divorce final?"

"When I stop contesting it."

"You're still in love and she's letting you go? That's terrible. Some women are so heartless. She's going to see her mistake after it's too late, that's how it goes. You deserve to be happy. Was she difficult?"

"No, I'm a dick and she got tired of getting screwed. Do you have a purpose to coming in here?"

Finally, she gave me the 'you're an asshole' look and stood. "Jason wanted me to tell you to remember the banquet is October, he needs to know how many guests you're bringing."

"One. Me plus one."

She left in a silent huff like I would care, and I sat back. Yes, I could totally have gotten laid. All the passionate build-ups with Jenzy that came to nothing these days did have me fairly sexually frustrated, but no one could take me like Jenzy. If I want sex, it's her I want it from, not a bimbo that's only basic talent would be deep throating.

My body hummed with memories and I had to regulate my breathing and block them out. How in hell had I gone two years without sex? Whatever happened would have to be pretty big to have kept me from between Jenzy's thighs. What was it?

By the time I got home, I considered a cold shower but then my doorbell rang. I opened it to Todd and he came in to sit and chill on the couch.

"What's up?" I asked.

He rubbed his palms together like they were sweaty and was doing the foot jiggly thing, "Have a bottled water?"

"No…I'm not buying them…"

"Why, are you going green?" he teased. Then at my silence, he bugged his eyes, "Shit, really?"

"Just figured a refillable bottle made more sense." I watched him.

He nodded, and his leg went wonky again, then he avoided my eyes.

I stood in front of him and crossed my arms, "You're acting weird."

He sat forward, "I really hate being in the middle. I won't lie, I dislike the fact, that you both mean something to me."

"Something happened?"

He blew out a breath, "You remember I said they're dating again right? Moses and Jenzy."

Emptiness clawed up my throat, but I nodded, "Yeah, I remember."

"So, you told me to just keep you informed on how they're doing…which is morally wrong and very shady, I might add. However, if I were in your shoes…I'd want to know even if I didn't need to… I guess."

The more he built toward it, the more I felt my world shrink, "Say it, Todd."

"I heard from Mandy that…tonight… Jenzy plans to…make it…more official."

My voice thickened, "Official how?"

Todd stood up and worked how to put it. While he debated a delivery, I crossed my arms tighter and tighter until I thought the sleeves of my shirt might rip.

"She plans to sleep with him. They haven't…yet. She says, she thinks she feels ready… I didn't- I'm not sure telling you was right. Was I wrong? Tell me because-."

"It's fine." I felt a wave crash on me that stung all angles of my heart, "I'm fine. Thanks, Todd."

"You're not fine."

"I'm fine." I nodded at the door. "I'm tired, though, Todd. Work was long, I didn't even stop at the gym ...maybe head out."

He stayed, and I debated throwing him out, so I could deal with how I felt.

He jabbered, "You want me to thwart it? I can tell her we need a sitter or… I don't think it's a good idea…or start a rumor that he's got *the clap*."

"Nope," I shook my head and the emotions twisted my heart painfully. "She's an independent woman; she can sleep with whoever she wants. It's not like I was doing what she needed. I wasn't doing anything."

"They're going out tonight first. That dancing nightclub, Rapture Pulse. We could-."

"I need to sleep, Todd."

He got the hint and nodded before clapping my shoulder and heading out. I couldn't breathe again once the door was closed. I knew this was coming, it's Jenzy, she would never be single long because men would never not pursue her. Still, the news was tearing me apart. Her body was mine like mine was hers and if she shared it with someone our bond would shift.

I need to sleep.

Chapter Thirty-Two
JENZY

I feel gorgeous, but I also feel like I'm readying myself for a sacrifice. On one hand, I'm dressing for Moses, I want him to want me tonight because like I told Mandy, I want to take the next step with him. I need to push myself to move on or I won't. I trust Moses, and the least I can do after all the drama he's survived through is give him this part of me.

On the other hand, I think of Chris and my body starts to revolt the change in ownership. I'm so in need of touch and intimacy, I feel like my head might explode. I want someone to break the sexual fasting that I've been on and I can't even satisfy myself anymore. I want the electric that passes between two people. I want the sweat, the breathing, the unpredictable-ness of a partner.

I feel like Emma from the book *Just Breathe*. I just wish I could have her kick-ass resolve…and her money…and her guy…and this could go on for a bit.

I checked my reflection and was satisfied but anxious. I found a nude-colored dress that was embroidered with glimmering silver designs. The neckline was a deep V and the hem was high above my knees. It had long sleeves, but the material was thin, fitted, and it sheathed me like a glove. Silver strappy heels finished the look and dangling earrings.

I took off my wedding band and took an extra hour to straighten my hair. The bangs fell partway over my eyes in a smoldering way and I put warm waves from top to bottom for a sleek but bodied look.

I went with Mandy for a wax pretty much everywhere there was body hair and I took an extra half-hour perfecting the winged liner look. By the time Moses showed to pick me up, I was feeling like an expensive but classy escort. I came down the steps to the living room, and when I turned the corner Moses stopped talking to wow over me.

"Jesus," he took my hand. "You look like everything women want to be."

My heart pattered out of control. That was a compliment I could never forget. "Enjoy, because the chances of me not falling and messing the masterpiece up, is thin."

"I'll catch you," he brought me to his side and I moved closer with my hand on the firmness of his chest. Now that I was touching him, sex didn't seem so scary. I need what he has, and he wants what I have.

Looking at him might give me an orgasm alone. He had a black blazer over a steel-gray button-down that had a short, upturned white collar and cuffs, with jeans. He was stylish, but the hippie was never too far, he also had a silver necklace with an Asian symbol for luck.

"Have fun guys," said Mandy with a wink. "You make the best-looking couple ever."

I smiled, "Thanks, lovely," she came to kiss my cheek and Todd shook Moses' hand before giving me a quick side hug.

Todd whispered, "You okay?"

That made me stiffen, I was okay until he asked. What did he know? Did he know what I told Mandy? If so, how did he feel about it?

"Fine. Why?" I asked back.

"No reason. Lookin' out for you is all. You look amazing."

I smiled but then I left with Moses. He went to open my door but then stopped and looked back to make sure we were alone. "Hey," he smiled and leaned down to kiss me now that we weren't under watch.

I smiled and held the back of his head, "Hey," I kissed him back and my body lurched into desire. I need sex now. I don't think I can keep up the interactions with two hot men, one of which I know is the best in bed, and not have sex soon. Two years and God knows how many months. I'm going to die if I don't have it soon.

I think all this was communicated in my kiss because Moses pressed me against the car and worked with me like he understood. His hands were on my hips, but I felt them like they were on my sex.

"Maybe," I turned my leg out, so I could feel his thigh against my mound, "Maybe we should forget the club and," I gripped his blazer and kissed him harder.

Moses and I are still learning one another's bodies and signals, but he's starting to see I like force. I like to feel dominated in sexual matters, whereas everywhere else, I like the liberty to hold the reigns or be flighty at will. When a man kisses me, though or takes me, I need to feel invaded, ravished, pillaged. I need the high of being aggressed to get off and Moses is trying to learn all this but he's still too careful with me, too gentle, too much romance, not enough animal just yet. I sense he can be rather dominant but he's afraid to try my limits.

His kisses are getting harder and his hands bolder, but he still seems afraid to let go on me, "I would love to take you home, right now," he admitted. "But all this work you did," he slid his hands down my sides. "It needs to be appreciated. We don't have to stay long."

I was glad he said that. I did work hard and even if it was just for him, I did want to dance, and I did want to feel free a while. "Okay," I smiled and set my arms around his neck. "Thank you, let's go."

He kissed me again, "After you, sunshine."

Sadly enough, I think he also senses my readiness comes and goes. That's why he matters so much to me. He understands.

CHRIS

I rolled up in my car to Rapture Pulse and stepped out. This place had valet parking, it was that elite. The name came from the popular urban legend that the music the DJ's played, had a pulse and it could be heard from the street. There was a strictness to who got in. Your looks, clothes, and such all had to add to the atmosphere. I wasn't exactly dressed for the select; in a black fitted T-shirt and dark jeans, but between the expensive watch, my years of frequenting, and the fact my looks were golden, I got in with no problem.

    I walked the inside of the club in a slow and watchful stride, taking in the darkness with flashes of light and the massive dance floor filled with beautiful people. They danced erotically with their partners or invitingly by themselves. The DJ's on the platform was completely in their zone, as they put out music that shook the floor under my feet and made the rhythm of my heart stronger. The bar was long, it nearly wrapped around the room in a semi-circle with multiple bartenders, and people sat there and flirted, waited or drank.

    I made my way around to where the regular seating was and used my eyes to scan the loft where more dancers were. The darkness was only penetrated by light in intervals with greens, and blues, and silvers. The floors were a shined black and the walls had abstract art in frames.

    Still no sign of them, I took an easy walk to the right but then I spotted her, and my heart tripped. She was on his arm and looking like every man's wet dream. They were talking to a group near the dancefloor and I found myself a table. I can tell just by how she's dressed what she wants. It's like a call out.

    Right as I came upon a table, she looked out and locked eyes with me. Her smile faded, and she took a quick assessment of me. I know what she's thinking. I'm full on myself, no cover-ups, and that's my call back to her. This is the pitfall of having lovers.

They know the language of your eyes, your body, the telling signals in your movements. Hers are telling me, she's at an almost combustible point in sexual need and I'm telling her back with my eyes and my body language that I'm more than willing to fulfill her.

To make up for every time I did not.

I dragged a metal chair out slowly and sat down with my legs open and my shoulders straight. I kept watching her and when she realized she was looking back too long, she hid on the other side of Moses. When she did chance glances, I stayed steady.

Yes, I know what you plan for tonight, and I dare you to not think of me.

Sometime after a new beat started that I know she has in her playlists, *Paradise Circus* by *Massive Attack;* she whispered up to Moses and he bent to hear her, then kissed her ear and set down their drinks to follow her out to the floor.

He didn't know I was here yet and I doubt she intends to tell him. She initiated dancing and Moses kept up with her well. I saw how they made a pair, I didn't like it, but I saw it.

She was an excellent club dancer, always had been. She's brought me to a brink of cumming just by dancing for me and I'm sure she remembers. Moses does better complementing her from the rear with her back to his front. He can predict her moves that way and roll with her.

They talked over her shoulder at times and she faked smiles with him but now and again her eyes were on me and mean it or not, they were glowing with want she couldn't hide. She wasn't giving Moses those eyes.

They danced the majority of the eight-minute song but toward the end, she was holding my eyes more and I was touching her with mine. Moses spoke to a friend while they moved around but then she whispered something else and kissed his cheek before walking away. He drifted off the floor to continue his talk with friends, but she was making fast tracks to the back where the restrooms were.

I followed but she didn't look back to see or seem to suspect. By the time she got there, *Animals* by *Martin Garrix* was pounding through in a medley from the first. She swung the door of the bathroom open but before it could close, I used my shoulder to push it open. Hearing it jolt, she turned around to see me.

"Chris!" I walked in and held her face in my hands. I pressed my lips down over hers. She shoved me, but I didn't really feel it and came down harder, instead. There was only one white lightbulb above the sketchy sink and mirror that kept flickering in the darkened, gray room. It made this feel dirty and wrong, but also hot and thrilling.

She might've been shoving at me, but she was also opening her mouth and taking me in.

Some guy all in leather tried to come in and said, "Move out guys-." But I let go of her long enough to slam him out with the door, using my shoulder again and locked it.

"What the fuck, Chris?" she whipped.

I turned her roughly by the arm and pushed her into the sink with the length of my body. She pushed herself back and her ass woke the erection in my pants to full mast. She felt it and I pressed harder before reaching around to cover her mouth and hold her waist.

I spoke against her neck, "Shhh, I have a few questions, I'll be quick. I know you need to get back." Her head went back on my shoulder and she looked at me from the mirror. "If I'm going to let you go to someone else, I need to be sure about some things first."

I forced my hips into her and smoothed my hand down her long torso, "Does he know how you like it? I can't tolerate the thought of you dissatisfied." I stroked her thigh all the way down then up and brushed over her sex to do the same with the other. Her eyelids drifted closed and I felt a hunger gnawing. "See, I know how you like being had, you won't cum if you don't get pounded hard and fast. His hips have to carry that speed to push you over."

I traveled my hand under her dress to press and glide over her flat belly and used my finger to circle her navel. "Tell me," I still had my hand over her mouth, but her eyes fluttered open. I nuzzled behind her ear, "What about his tongue? Does he do that thing with his tongue you like? One time I held you down and made you cum just by," I stopped to demonstrate. I flicked the tip of my tongue over that place on her neck, just under her ear, over and over, then dragged it down to the shoulder and bit.

Jenzy whimpered and pressed her ass into my groin. With my hand still over her mouth, I jerked her head to the side and licked a sweet line back up her throat, biting at her jawline until I reached her earlobe. I flicked my tongue over it multiple times and she shivered which made my cock twitch and strain.

"That, does he do that, Jenzy?" I asked again. With measured control, I let the hand on her stomach move down again until my fingertip curled under her panty line. I pulled the top outward and zipped right and left so she'd stress over when I'd go in; all with my mouth on her neck. "Can he make you drip?" I let my fingers touch and tickle down over what felt like a freshly waxed bareness that made me fight for control tough again.

I smiled, "You might've done this for him," I made a V with my fingers and pressed in and up, "But you were thinking of me."

She gripped the sink so tightly her knuckles were white.

Her breathing on my hand was sharp and shallow and I stroked her entrance just as more wetness was making her slick for me.

"Has he been here?" I asked as I put a finger inside her. She moaned into my hand and stood on her toes. Her shoulder blades poked into my chest and I almost bent her further over and just took her.

I slipped another finger inside, "No, he hasn't, has he?" I watched her bathe in the moment from the mirror and then took my hand away from her sex. I hooked what felt like a thong and yanked it down under her ass. "Does he know how to ride you from the back?"

I let go of her mouth but before she could say anything I grabbed a fist full of silky, auburn locks and drew her neck back sharply. "He can't just bury himself, that won't do it for you. You need," I made a better ponytail with her hair in both my hands; using only one to pull back. I slid the back of her dress up exposing her rear and rubbed against her. I switched to the other side of her neck to nip at her flesh and she panted and pushed into me. "You need suspense," I murmured into her ear.

I released her so fast she fell forward into the sink a little, but I caught her by the arms and turned her around to face me. Her breathing so labored she didn't seem like she could speak, and her eyelids were hooded.

I teased her lips with mine like to kiss her but didn't let her close enough to reach. Then I wrapped my arm around her back and set my hand at her throat. I glided it down her neck, chest, and stomach then cupped her sex. She rubbed herself into my hand and clawed at my shirt to brace but then I moved her back again until she was sitting off the side of the sink but still standing.

I sank to my knees and bit her knee. Keeping my eyes boldly on hers, I took the side of her black, lace, thong between my teeth and pulled back only to let go so they could snap back.

"I hope for your sake," I bit them again, "That he can lick you the way you used to beg me for. You have a sweet taste, but the key is your clit. He has to come down on it while he makes a humming sound deep in his throat, the vibration gets you every time."

She moaned louder from my words. Then I pushed her dress up to lick and suck at her inner thigh. I moved up far enough to have her lips brushing my stubbled cheek and sucked the skin of her thigh harder. I moved to lick a fine line up the center of her and she spread her legs further.

Jenzy dragged her nails through my scalp but I smacked her hands off me and she gasped. I turned her by the hips and slammed her against the sink again. She made a noise that had me so ready to cum I had to work it down. I held her wrists behind her back and still on my knees, I kissed the underside of her ass cheek then bit it.

"Your body needs alpha love, babe," I led her panties down off her legs and took them from under her heeled feet.

Fuck, these heels are killing me. I stood, and she turned to face me on weak knees.

I shredded the panties like they were paper, and said, "Oops," I shrugged, and then tossed them in the trash. Her eyes were so ablaze with lust I debated giving in already. I gripped her under the ass and sat her on the sink. She was so spelled, she wasn't fighting me anymore, she was yielding the way I liked and accepted me as her sexual dominant.

I held her dress front and pulled it down over her breasts, another weak spot of hers. She arched her back over the sink like she was serving me, and I dipped my head and tasted the edge of her bodice over the black, pushup-bra that once matched the damaged panties.

"Maybe this is what our marriage needed," I held her breast up from underneath and pushed my tongue under the cup to run across a taut nipple. "Me dragging you into a filthy club bathroom and fucking you speechless?"

Jenzy groaned and reached for my belt. I let her play at opening the buckle while I engaged plan B. I pulled the shoulder of her dress further down and there, by the strap of her bra, and the top of her breast, I sucked and laved. The harder I drew her between my teeth, the more she squirmed and fought to open my pants. She wants me on her nipples so I'm purposefully avoiding them even as she presses them out to me.

"Do you want me to fuck you, Jenzy?" I brought my face up to hers and brought the cup of her bra down to let her breast free. She kissed me in a fiery wetness of teeth and tongue and I caressed her nipple, pinched and tugged. She was like putty in my hands now, but the leash was tethered to me too. "Say it," I broke the kiss. "Say you want me to fuck you here, right now. Unless you think he can fuck you better…"

"No," she finally spoke. "No, fuck me. Chris, please, do it."

I smiled and put the cup back over her breast, "Nah, you have plans tonight, don't you?"

She frowned, then I saw her remember. "Oh, shit! Moses!"

"Yeah," I stroked the long lengthy side of her neck with the back of my fingers, "Might want to wait on any new steps in the relationship, though. At least until those go away."

Her frown deepened, and she followed my eyes to a sizable hickey I left on her breast.

"Oh, my God!" She figured it out and lifted the hem of her dress to look between her thighs where two more were right beside her sex. "Christopher!" She got down off the sink and turned to look in the mirror. Another was appearing under the other at the edge of her bra cup.

I righted myself and backed toward the door, "Goodnight, Jenzy."

She turned and threw the soap dispenser from the sink at me, but I was laughing and already out the door.

Chapter Thirty-Three
JENZY

I'm not even sure how I got out of going home with Moses. I made something up about feeling sick, but to be fair, I was just dazed and confused. My husband attacked me in the bathroom and I needed time to figure out how I felt.

First, I was pissed. That fucker busted in on me and dared to molest me in a public place while I was on a date.

Second, I was hornier than a rabbit on boner pills. Chris and I have always been animals in the sack but what the fuck?

Thirdly, I was indecisive. I wanted to call him and demand he explain himself whilst throwing me on the nearest surface and having his way with me. However, that gave him a lot of control he didn't need, and I had a boyfriend.

Fourth…do you say fourth or fourthly? Fourthliest? Whatever. The fourth feeling was sadness. Now my body was humming but my soul missed him too. I came close to having sex with another man and I don't know how he knew, but the idea that he knew made me sad.

The fifth feeling was anger again because the little bastard left marks on my body. His so-called 'territory', which is both hot and infuriating. Like he said, I can't do anything too intimate with Moses and risk him seeing the hickeys. Moses has been a real champ but I'm not that brave.

The sixth feeling was general desire to weep a little. Yes, that was hot as hell, and yes, I could easily go back to him but what if it went back to how it was? What if he just wanted me still because he couldn't have me? We still hadn't figured out what drove us apart. Sex wasn't what would hold our marriage together. I can't fold now.

A few nights later, I was sitting up with tea and my new adult coloring book, *Bookish* by none other than Martha Sweeney; this woman does everything. I was lucky enough to win this in one of her giveaways. Lucky me…my life falls apart at times, but I won a mind-blowing coloring book.

Then my cell rang. I put down my pencils and muttered since the coloring book was bringing my stress levels way down, but the ringing phone brought them way up. All that faded when I saw Doreen's number. It was eleven at night, so I jumped into an alert position and answered.

"Hello?"

"Hello, girly," her voice was soothingly calm. "We have a mama in labor. Interested in overseeing your first birth?"

My eyes went buggy. I wasn't qualified to assist yet, but I was already learning, and this was a hands-on way to learn. "Yes! Oh, yes, that would be awesome." I looked around for a pair of pants since I was only in my sleep shirt.

"Wonderful," she gave me an address and I scribbled it in my coloring book, hung up, and got ready.

I don't have a car and I wasn't going to wake the family, so I left a note and called a cab. I waited outside on the steps even though it was chilly.

When I made it to the house of the woman having the baby, I knocked softly. Rachel answered and let me in with a grin. I knew quiet was the key. She'd already taught me no noise, quick movements, or raised voices. I heard soft moaning coming from the parlor and Rachel and I made our way there.

The woman giving birth, I had only met once. Her name was Stella and she had a long braid down her back and big blue eyes. She was in a tank top and sitting in a big birthing tub set up in the center of the living room. Her husband, I think his name is Rick, he was behind her, holding her up under the arms while Doreen knelt on the side whispering encouragement. Meanwhile, Bella was observing from the opposite side.

Stella saw me between contractions and smiled, with a weak sounding, "Hello."

I whispered back, "Hello, I'm so honored to be here. Thank you for sharing this."

She put her hand out and I came closer to grasp it. She had amazing energy and she was very confident and at ease with what her body was doing. I let her grip my hand as tightly as she needed while I came to sit at her side.

Her touch tensed as another labor pain came and she groaned deeply in her throat to ride it out. Her husband held her up from behind and she handled it like a pro. The sleeping six-year-old girl on the couch behind us told me she was indeed, a pro.

The hours went by slowly, and soon her newborn was crowning. The sounds she made intensified and her position changed a few times. Doreen was ever encouraging as was Rachel and though this wasn't my first birth, it was my first home birth, and it was making me fall more and more in love with the process. All the training, and reading, and seminars couldn't put it plainer. How beautiful this moment was...

There were a few times over the months I wondered if I would stick with this career move. Even in college, I had gone through so much studying and changing my mind, but being in this moment, I was never surer.

"Push mommy," Bella instructed. Stella groaned, and Doreen came from her side to pull Stella's leg further back.

Doreen nodded, "Tuck your head, lovely that's it, push."

Rachel and I stayed close and I noticed all of us made a rising noise with Stella when she moaned that seemed to help spur her on.

I saw the baby's shoulders slip out from under the water and I cried.

Bella was guiding the baby out gently and smiled up at Stella, "That's it, my love, one more, come on."

The baby made its way out in time and Doreen scooped the new person up to set upon mommy's chest. Stella's husband wrapped his arms around both his wife and his new baby and the two of them cried. The baby was active; fusing, and stretching, and reaching out. The commotion woke big sister, and she excitedly joined her parents to greet the new soul.

Bella went about her business, checking them without being invasive and Doreen took the pictures they requested. Rachel and I started cleaning up with dopey smiles and happy whispers. We got mommy into bed with the family and within another hour or two, we were leaving.

I fell asleep in the taxi, but when I got to Todd's I stumbled out half awake. Chris was coming down the steps from the house and we stopped to look at one another.

"Jenzy?" he came all the way down and looked me over. "Are you okay? What are you doing out this early?"

"Yeah," I forgot for a minute why I was mad at him. "I just witnessed my first *home* birth," I told him with a dim-witted grin.

He grinned back, "Congratulations! How was it?"

"Magical. I mean, wow," I sat on the steps because I really need to, my knees are giving out. "Chris, it's so special."

He sat with me in his work suit and listened, "Mandy's were definitely something," he agreed.

"It was just like that," I nodded. "It was just in someone's home, not a hospital, so it was quiet and calm. This mom had candles lit and music. She was so strong. She embraced each contraction and oh, Chris…" I propped my elbow on my knee and set my cheek in my hand, "It was incredible."

He smiled and nodded, "I didn't think Mandy would want me in the delivery room the day she had Connor, we don't like each other but I'm glad she let me in. Both times."

"You held her hand through most the labor that first time, right?"

"Yep, she has a grip, let me tell you. She might've been trying to break my hand on purpose."

I laughed, "You really don't get along."

"Yeah…but you should see what would happen to a person who was dumb enough to try bitching about her. She's a sea witch but she's family. I love her."

I watched him watch traffic go by and digested that. That might be the kindest thing I ever heard him say about Mandy.

"That was sweet," I told him.

"Don't tell her I said that. Anyway, I'm glad for you. I can tell by how you're glowing that you found your passion."

I smiled and shook my head, "It is definitely it for me. I feel it."

"And the baby?"

"*Cute!*"

He laughed and groaned, "Boy or girl?"

"Boy."

"Tiny?"

"So small, Chris. He was a nugget. His dad was there, supporting mom. He was part of everything and so happy to have a boy. He didn't leave the mom's side once."

Chris shook his wrist to adjust his watch, "I wouldn't want to miss anything either."

We sat together in quiet, "Why are you here?" I asked.

He looked down at me and I saw he'd been holding a little cream-colored envelope. "I was dropping this off, I thought you'd be home."

I looked at the time on his watch, it was six in the morning. I took the envelope and opened it. It was an invitation to a banquet for his real-estate company. It was a suit and tie affair.

"Let me guess…" I slipped it into my purse. "If I don't go, you'll contest longer?" He only smirked and I rolled my eyes. "After that shit, you pulled at the club, why on earth would I go anywhere with you."

"You're just mad I didn't give you a mind-blowing orgasm and because I left you all hot and bothered."

"Shut up."

"Did the vibrator I bought you help? You know, I noticed back home, you left the other's we bought together, behind. Should I drop them off? No, wait, I should contest their ownership in the divorce. We could go to court over them like normal couples do over pets and children."

"You have a twisted mind."

"Custody of Coitus equipment…"

"I'm really tired, Chris; my sense of right and wrong is fuzzy. Pushing you into traffic seems justifiable."

"Don't be mad," he tried.

Anger boiled under my skin, "You marked me, so I couldn't have sex! What am I? A tree? You basically pissed a circle around me, you dog!"

"I am a dog and you were in heat. I didn't have a chance against the urge to make you my bitch."

"This bitch is going to tear your throat out if you try that again."

"So, you're going then? To the banquet? I'll come at six." He stood up and headed for his car.

A thought came to me and I stood up, "Wait."

He looked back and made his way over.

"Why?" I questioned. "Why invite me when the last time, you-?"

"I don't like to be stupid more than once. I want you there. I *need* you there. Forget what I did last time. Get a dress, all expenses on me, make me go broke for revenge if you want."

Forget? Easy for him to say. He wasn't the one left behind last time.

He came closer, "It's not the airport again…" his reference to our past made me feel weird. I guess we have both been reflecting.

He lightened his tone, "Oh…and put your rings back on… that's part of my conditions.

Chapter Thirty-Four
CHRIS

There was an eternity in the time between that day we talked on the steps, to October when the banquet was being held. Jenzy didn't talk to me as often, as get back, and though I worried her, and Moses had gotten closer, I knew thanks to Todd, they still hadn't had sex. It was a nightly holding of breath for me.

When I got to Todd's the night of the banquet, I waited in the living room with Connor. Even dressed sharply, I couldn't resist a chance to play with him. I think the only reason I like my brother now is because he gave me a nephew and a niece. Connor sat high in my arms and jabbered about things until I heard Jenzy coming. When I looked, I did a double take.

Her dress was a fitted, floor-length, pristine white. It laid over her figure like a flowing sheet with long sleeves. When she stood to the side, to take her clutch off the hall table, I saw that her dress was wide open; exposing her back. It all led to a flawless rear end. She glided up to me and Connor, and I drank in my wife.

Her lips were painted ruby red and her hair was up with long wavy curls down each side of her face. Best part of her attire? I'd say that was the constellation necklace she had around her neck. My gift was proudly lying against her chest and it turned my insides to lava.

"So?" She stepped back and did a turn. "The sleeves are long, that way my Sagittarius tattoo on my wrist won't show. I won't talk about holistic crap, new age crap, or basically anything at all. I will say I'm a nurse, not a doula in training. No hippie babble. Will I embarrass you or gratify you, Mr. Clark?"

I put my hand under her chin and turned her face up, she was avoiding my eyes and I hated myself for ever sewing such insecurities into her free spirit, "You'll outshine every wife there." Her eyes searched my face, and I tipped her chin higher. "You are perfection and you can discuss whatever you want."

It looked like that made it into her heart and mind where I wanted it. Connor distracted us a minute. I let her go just as Mandy showed.

Mandy smiled at us, "Hey guys. Todd says good luck tonight. He's still lying down. His sinuses are acting up."

Jenzy made a sad face, "Tell him to feel better."

"Tell him to take a shot of whiskey and get over it like a man," I grumbled.

Jenzy laughed.

"See you around," I said, putting Connor down. He wasn't a foot from me when Mandy came up and hugged the stuffing out of me. I frowned but then I saw Jenzy's face and realized the little twit had told Mandy what I said about her being family. I rolled my eyes and hugged her back, kissing her forehead before letting go to open the door for Jenzy.

The banquet was held at a very elaborate hotel ballroom. There was a small dance floor where some couples were, and catered food and drinks were floating in all corners. The room was mostly maroon with gold trims and a massive chandelier hung over the middle of the ceiling.

I opened my jacket and Jenzy's brows raised, "A gold waistcoat? You look handsome."

"I'm a royal Leo. Red and gold are lucky for me."

"Are you really getting into astrology?"

"Only Linda Goodman, so don't get too excited. She says my kind are charming and we can't argue that, now can we?"

We mingled with the crowd and she shined like a bright star.

None of my co-workers mentioned the divorce rumors. I don't know if they were scared to or if they thought all was well again. She was wearing her rings, I was wearing mine and she was here, all appeared well.

I noticed something else, too. When Jenzy talks about me with others, she makes me sound like a hero. She sounds genuinely proud but I'm not. Her enthusiasm throws me. She highlights all my talents and abilities like she looks up to me.

Mid-way through, I lost her when I got sidetracked by a co-worker, but when I found her she was surrounded by half my division and conversing with them like old friends. Now, I'm not sure why I hadn't brought her to all of these. Why hadn't I?

"Mrs. Clark, you sound very accomplished for a lady your age," I heard my bosses' wife, Debbie, say as I moved closer. "I'm so impressed."

"Thank you!" Jenzy shook her head, "But I wouldn't be where I am if Chris hadn't supported me. I was lucky."

Supported her? Maybe financially. I haven't supported her in any other way for years. Why would she even bother to make me look good after what I put her through? I kept on the outside ring of people but listened.

Debbie touched her own chest, "You two sound like you had the most romantic start. Now with all these wonderful career doors opening, do you intend on starting a family or waiting? It's so hard to balance, but you don't want to put it off too long."

Jenzy stumped on that one but opened her mouth to answer when my boss Cole, came to Debbie's side. Ever being the wannabe joker, he reminded me why I didn't bring Jenzy to my work events.

His eyes twinkled with mirth and the man old enough to be my father, spoke as unwisely as a teenager. "Mrs. Clark is what Mr. Clark called, a toddler at a tea party of choices," he laughed and one or two others with him but Jenzy tilted her head. Lost.

"I don't get that one?" Jenzy tested.

I started to push my way closer, but Cole was still talking. "*I want that, I want that, I want that,*" he cracked himself up. "Christopher gets me every time, with his imitations of you. He said to me once, 'no kids until I'm sure she realizes there's no off button on their back'. Like a baby doll, they have those buttons, you know? My sides were splitting."

They all laughed but Debbie looked a little disturbed by the vulgarity of the slander and Jenzy was slowly understanding what Cole was implying.

Jenzy used her old tact, indifference, but the hurt was visible to me, "Well, that's true. I change my mind a lot." She smiled but it didn't reach her eyes at all.

Cole kept talking and I started to push my way in as he said, "What was the other one he told me? Oh, yes!" he snapped his fingers with the memory. "'When she stops believing in fairytales and only tells them, I'll know she grew up enough to have kids'. That man's humor is so infectious! Stand-up comedy is Chris' calling." Cole tilted his glass at her, "He's right, though. Kids are a big commitment. You gotta be totally invested. You can't be indecisive with having babies like he says you are in steady jobs and where to have dinner."

I came up from Jenzy's right and she sided me a very wounded look, "Good advice," she agreed. "Excuse me." She smiled at my boss and his wife before leaving but Debbie looked at me with something akin to disappointment. The group kept talking but I followed Jenzy to where the halls were that led to the lobby. I caught up and took her wrist.

"Listen," I started. "What he said-."

"It's true," she nodded then shrugged, "It's fine. I get it now. I do. It's okay. You made me a joke to your work people and that's why you didn't want me to come to these events."

"No," I came closer and grasped at ways to put this. "Yes." I looked her in the eyes to face the clusterfuck I made, "Yes, I made you sound-."

"Stop," she sighed. "I'm not being sarcastic or jabbing you back. I'm admitting to being a flake. I'm not organized or forward thinking like you and the people in that room. In your own weird way, you were just…keeping me from embarrassment by keeping me separate. These are definitely not my sort of people. I feel like an alien."

"After what we went through, why even tell them all that bull about me? You never lie, so why tell them how great I am-?" I asked.

"You are great. You're a brilliant man, with a heart that's really big. When you aren't being an ass, anyway. I've always admired you. You can do anything."

"No, I can't."

"Yes, you can. To me, you can. You know the answer to everything and you make things happen even when there's no visible way. You're an incredible salesman that's honest and dedicated…"

"Why'd you tell them I support you?"

She tilted her head, "Chris, you did at one time. If I told you I wanted to be a bird, you would fashion my wings. The last two years we grew apart, but before that…I'm like the kite and you're like the string."

"Can't you get pissed or retaliate at all? Sometimes I think you just pull that 'it's all good' shit to make me feel like an asshole!"

"I just don't have a problem admitting I have problems. I'm almost thirty and I *just* found the career I want. I'm aimless most times. I switch motivations and have trouble settling on ideas. Half the time I wear multiple necklaces and bracelets because I can't decide which one to wear. I change course at the last minute, I'm sloppy with choices like I am with keeping the closets clean. I'm not always 'good' with everything I just don't have trouble facing stuff. No lie, the jokes you told Cole…they make me feel shitty, but they're true. You are the main provider because I don't stick to a cause. That's a lot of pressure and even when you admitted that to me, I didn't act."

"That's not an excuse for me to have broadcasted it like I did."

"No, it's not, but you did, and what's done is done. I came out here to gather myself, now I'm going back in."

I licked my lips and tried to mend this, "You would make an incredible mom."

"That part was disturbing."

I shook my head and skimmed the back of my fingers down her neck, "That was a nasty joke to make. You're the only woman I ever imagined having children with."

"Thank you…"

I saw in the far back of my mind, this is where she and I differ greatly. I don't like being wrong or risking things or seeing my faults. I go into denial or I bury the problem I have so deep even I can't see it. Jenzy embraces her issues.

Suddenly I felt a hard slap to the side of my face and as the sting cooled I realized the little twat hit me. She looked perfectly collected, though no frowns or tears.

"That was for mocking me to your work friends," she said with a smile. "Are we good now? Was that pissed and less positive enough for you?"

"Yeah, loud and clear."

"Good," she slipped her arm into mine and walked back with me. "And I'm telling your mother."

"Fuck!"

JENZY

It really did hurt like hell to know that Chris had been using my ways as a punch line with his jokes, but I saw the utter freak-out on his face when he heard it. I also get that I don't fit in here. I'm not goal oriented like Chris and though we come head to head on education, our ethics and values differ.

The people in this room didn't want to hear about my night helping a woman give birth in her parlor, or how I read tarot cards that foretold Chris would get a job here, or how I felt about the elections or any of that jazz. In raw truth, this wasn't my thing. Chris had been afraid my mingling with these people would result in confrontations, debates, heated arguments, embarrassment…

It doesn't justify his lying to me or making fun, but in the long run of our relationship and life; the ending of this marriage; this union we had, his joking about my ways didn't really matter anymore.

He already proved by bringing me tonight that he saw the wrong. I looked up across the ballroom to see him getting us drinks. While he waited, a woman with curly golden hair and a stunning black dress came up and smoothed her hand down his arm. He turned to see her and stepped out of range of her touch with crossed arms.

She was slightly aggressive, following him back into his space to talk and set her hand on his. There was a thin needle-like sting to my gut, but then he casually took her hand off and turned his back to her with a cold shoulder. I have seen him do this before while we were married.

She rolled her eyes then walked away and I went to him.

"Hey," I said. he saw me and smiled then was handed our drinks by a caterer, "Who was that?"

"Oh," he shrugged, "Alba…"

"Alba is very pretty."

"Alba is very annoying," he echoed.

"She just likes you, I think."

"Oh, joy."

"It wouldn't hurt to look. You're single now."

"Not in my mind."

"You used to look at me like that."

He creased his brow, a little confused and I bit my tongue. That was a careless slip.

"I'm not interested in Alba," he repeated more firmly.

"I know, that's what I meant. These last couple years…that is kind of how you treated me too. Not interested. I feel sorry for her, I guess. She wants to be seen by you. She's not really doing anything wrong."

He was staring at me and I was so uncomfortable I sipped my red wine to avoid looking back.

"I'm married, that's what she's doing wrong," he answered.

"You won't be soon, and you haven't been in *the whole* sense for two years prior."

"Five good years of marriage to you isn't so easily erased for me. Even the additional two bad years."

"I'm just stating that she's attractive, and you shouldn't turn her down for me."

"It's not *for* you, it's *because* of you."

"I don't want you to turn things down because of me. I want you happy that's all I ever wanted. Turning down a woman as beautiful as Alba is like…turning down…" I looked up to see his lips part and his brows creased. "What's wrong?" He looked past me like he was seeing things in his mind very clearly. "Chris? What is it?"

He looked back at me, "Let's leave?"

"Leave? It's not over."

"I don't care. I need to talk to you." He took my wine and his and set them on the banquet table before tucking my arm and leading me out. He wasn't even slowing down to say goodnight to people.

He helped me into his car and then sped off toward Todd and Mandy's. When we got there, he parallel parked us across the street and when I tried to get out he held my knee. I stopped and looked back at him, but he was staring at the steering wheel. We didn't say anything for such a long time, but then he started.

"I know what happened," he said.

"With what?"

"With us…with me."

Chapter Thirty-Five
JENZY

I straightened and twisted the wedding rings on my finger to cope. Was it me? Was I ready to hear it if it was?

"Tell me," I said. He took his hand off my knee. "Chris…if I did something I should know-."

"It's not like that," he sighed and turned off the engine. "What you said about Alba…turning her down… do you remember why I left for Sweden?"

"You wanted to break the mold. You didn't want to stay and get caught up in 'how things go' you called it. Sweden was one of many places you were going eventually."

"I turned down a job," he dragged his eyes to mine and I tried to understand. "I didn't go into marketing and finance to be a realtor that was…I was as indecisive as you are. I wanted options and marketing is broad. I was offered an internship at a major digital marketing company. It was a travel industry division. I would've had the best of both worlds. Stability and freedom."

"When did you turn this opportunity down?" I felt sick asking.

"Once when I came back to stay, right after we met up that Thanksgiving… your birthday when I stayed for us."

"When was the second time?"

He sat back, "Two years ago, right after I made that life-changing sale…"

"So…" I felt my face flushing with color and my heart was beating at a slow and sinking throb. "When you excelled in real estate at the same time as this offer reappeared…you started to resent the work…and me?"

He wouldn't look at me, which told me I was right.

"Even when you say that I hate myself," he replied.

"You felt…stuck? Like you settled, and you didn't want to tell me-."

"No, I didn't know. I didn't realize I was feeling that way."

"So, I've held you back?"

"You saying that, is seriously making me ill, Jenzy. Please, don't say that."

"Why? So, you can sweep that under a rug too? You always do that, you put things you don't want to face under a rug but then when it is time to clean, the mess is out of control. At least my mess is out in the open. For a neat freak, you should know that."

He kept up, "I'm not proud of those feelings. It is not your fault that I stayed. I chose to stay. But yeah, on some level that's why your sudden steady work at the clinic bothered me. You're so freaking flighty and even you settled without a problem. But even your indecisiveness drives me crazy. You put more thought into which necklace to wear or what dinner to order than I did about coming home."

"You think it was impulsive and a mistake?" I asked him

"Yes- I mean, no. No, I love you, I wanted to stay."

"If that was the truth, you wouldn't have shut me out."

He gripped the wheel and looked out, "When I saw you sometimes it reminded me of what I gave up. What I wanted but didn't get."

My stomach lurched. I was the reason he was unhappy? I put my hand on the door to the car, "Okay…" I nodded. "Then…you shouldn't have stayed."

"Don't say that. This isn't your fault."

I felt a tear slide down my cheek, "It sounds like it is."

"No, I'm the one that pursued you. I'm the one that started this the day of my flight, over the phone, on your birthday; I came for you over and over. You even said…you offered to stop talking or to stop seeing each other, I just-."

"You made a mistake," I brushed the tear back. "You um…you settled because you thought you had to. That's why…us…*we*…we don't make sense anymore. It's time to… you can start over."

He turned in his seat and unbuckled so he could hold the back of my head and lean close, "No," he rubbed down my neck. "No, Jennifer that's not what this is."

"Now I get why you hate romance." It all dawned on me, "These men in movies and books, they give up things to be with the woman they want, and they're depicted as happy. The truth in real life- in our story… giving things up to be with me didn't result in happy. It resulted in resentment."

"I don't resent you; I resent the way things turned out."

"You resent me for being the icon of why your wings were clipped. No travel, no career, no going forward in the manner you sought to avoid. You were on a fast track to regular nine to five work, a wife, children, a house payment…you're stuck, and I was the live-in reminder." I turned to him with more hurt, "That's why you didn't want to talk about home birth versus hospital birth or why you pushed about me taking the pill instead of condoms. You may love kids, but you didn't want to be more stuck with me…"

"Listen-."

"That's why there was no sex, you were afraid I would get pregnant. If I did, you would never be able to leave; you love kids too much to do that. So, instead, you've been making me feel like an unattractive rock in your shoe. You intended to leave." He's not denying anything I say. There's not enough air in here.

Even his hand on my body feels forced. I pulled from under his touch, "The lawyers are just waiting on you, Chris. The sooner you stop all this and sign, the sooner we can grow the way we need to."

His eyes darkened, "Wow," he took his hand back and smiled to himself. "You really don't get it, do you?"

"Me?"

"I just said that's not what this is and you're finding a reason to call it quits."

"You aren't breaking your neck to tell me I'm wrong. I'm not right for you, Chris. You keep trying to make this fit. I'm new age and earthy-."

"I know what the fuck you are, Jennifer. We've been married seven years! Don't come up with some shitty excuse to-."

"I'm not!" Our voices were booming in the car and making my head throb. "You tell me to be real! Then when I'm real you can't take it. You want things you can't have with me and over time, you've only discovered how little you even like me. That's why you told your boss that. You don't *want* someone like me raising your kids."

He looked ready to explode, "I'm crazy about you! I proved that! I'm proving it now. What else am I supposed to do? Fucking bleed? I dragged you to the banquet, I'm doing the best I can! What do you want? A parade? I'm, here aren't I?"

"Here because you have to be," I jabbed.

"Yeah! I'm still here!"

"That's not what I want. Love doesn't mean being happy off the back of your partner's sadness. I want you happy too. I'm not enough."

"That's-," he looked out his window to avoid me.

"Answer this…" I turned a little and when he didn't look I tugged the lapel of his suit, "Please." He looked but with anger and impatience. "If you could go back in time…and had to make this decision over… what would you do?"

"I would go, okay!" He shouted it at me and the words sliced through me like a sharpened blade. "I would go back to Europe and pursue you later. Later. Jenzy! I said- don't look at me like that. I didn't say I wouldn't, I would just do it, later. Stop- don't fucking look at me like I said-."

I opened his car door and expected to see a red heart tumble out and shatter.

"Jennifer!" He took my arm but after a struggle and ripping his hand off me, I got out. I was barely making it to Todd's door because I couldn't see through the water-filled eyes I was holding back.

I heard Chris slam his door, he was out and grabbed my other arm, "For fuck sake, Jennifer! I meant I would still make you mine just not so fast. What's wrong with that? You're overreacting again! I would do what I had been planning and then maybe a couple years after that-."

Maybe? Later? Years? These words don't exist in my vocabulary for Chris. I wouldn't give up a single memory with him or so much as a kiss or hug. Every moment he and I have loved has been sacred to me. If later meant losing a lazy day memory or even a night of arguing memory, I wouldn't choose *later.* I don't understand *maybe.*

"No more contesting, no more conditions and no more romancing," I managed in a breathless and calm comeback. "We're done now. You need to accept that, so we can move forward. If you can honestly look back at all that time, all those times we…kissed, or touched, made love, held each other, laughed, cried, argued…and be ready to trade even a minute…our wedding day."

I gasped for air because my pain was making it hard to breathe, "If you can trade my dress getting caught in the limo door. Your mom getting tipsy and forgetting her speech, the- the dress I wore…my Dad, gifting you his chess set, the one that's been in our family for years… he did that because your dad is dead, and your step-dad couldn't make it."

I'm rambling now but that's how I sort shit out, "If you can erase being there for our niece and nephew's birth, coming to the bar on my birthday to claim me, all that and more, for a chance at better. If *this* relationship wasn't what was *better,* then…" I backed away from him.

His eyes were wet as he nodded and bit back, "Fine. Then you go your way, I'll go mine, and we'll pretend this- that us- this seven-year car wreck, wasn't a total loss of fucking time."

His words curdled in my stomach like sour milk. Tears ran freely down my face now, "You're a horrible, horrible person, Chris."

"Yeah, I'm horrible," he mocked.

"You are because I tried very hard to make this divorce painless. I moved out slowly, I told you the truth before Moses and I got serious, I made steps to preserve a friendship, I cared about you as someone meant to be in my life. I gave you respect in how we handled the damned properties and the splitting of shit. You're a selfish asshole! I didn't have to ever know this. This heartbreaking truth that you so greatly discovered, I didn't need to know, if you had just signed the stupid fucking papers!"

I was openly screaming at him from outside Todd's apartment. It had gradually been going from a talk to me screeching. There was still more to say, though because he'd wanted real and now he was going to get it.

"I've given you outs!" I shouted. "I've opened doors since the time I was eighteen-damned-years-old to leave! That first night, you were the one coming back to kiss me, or coming back to my dorm after leaving. I always followed your lead and kept my hand open and you-you always came back, and I thought…*it's because he loves me*…but…." my chest heaved with hollow nothingness. "You don't love me, Chris…you settled." My voice came down, "You don't even say it our special way because you know it's true."

He stood with his hands in his pockets and his head high even as tears were blinking over. Ever the proud Leo lion, he wasn't about to show he'd made a mistake.

I left him like that in the street and went inside where Mandy and Todd had been standing by the door, awake. The kids were down but it looked like the two of them heard everything.

"Jenzy," Mandy tried. "Honey, I'm so sorry."

"Don't." I set my clutch under my arm and let my hair down, "I'm going to bed."

"Why don't we talk about-?"

"No," I sounded mean as hell, "No, I said *bed*. I want to go to *bed*. I would like *someone* to actually hear me and fucking get it!"

"Babe," Todd tried to approach me, but I stepped back to go around.

"I said don't!" I busted into tears that raked my body and Todd came up to swallow me in his arms. I clung to him because I did need this, but I didn't know I did.

My knees felt weak and I started to sink to the floor, but Todd came down with me and then Mandy was holding me from behind. The harder I cried the more she worked to soothe me and Todd stayed strong. I never lose my temper to this degree, it is so rare that it has sapped me. For the first time ever, I hated Chris. I worked so hard to avoid it, but now along with this gut-eating hurt, I felt angry.

My anger burns hot, but it also burns fast, though. By night's end, I was cuddled in my bed alone with my thoughts.

Chapter Thirty-Six
CHRIS

I've never felt quite this alone. No, that's a lie. I remember one time when I was five and my mom decided to teach me a lesson in the grocery store. I was always running from her, apparently. Todd was a fatty and a mama's boy, so he rarely strayed far, but I was her 'little demon.' I was one of the first kids to have a leash put on, I think.

Anyway, I bolted from her in a store and to teach me a lesson, she hid; keeping an eye on me, but enough that when I turned to see if I could see her, I couldn't. I actually remember freaking out. I thought she left me or I was lost and as evil, as I was, I had no desire to be separated from mom.

It's a lame comparison, but that's how this feels. It's falling down a dark and scary place where the woman that was my foundation is missing; hence, there's no bottom. That fight was October, and this is December. I haven't heard from Jenzy at all and my family is treating me like a plague.

Christmas shit is decorating all the stores and playing on TV and radios, but all I see is the most void future ever. I'm not putting a tree up that was Jenzy's passion. The music makes me nauseous, she loves this music, but it reminds me I'm alone.

I've tried calling, texting, she won't respond and still waits for me to break, and sign. I tried grilling Todd a few days after the big fight, but he made it clear, in a definite way that he wouldn't be telling me anything regarding Jenzy.

His exact words were, "*If you want us to stay close as brothers don't bring her up to me again.*"

I had fucked up so badly, I lost every shred of his respect and Mandy of course, pretty much banned me from the house. I haven't seen Connor or Penny.

All I know is *she's* seeing *him*…Moses. They go steady, and I only know because he and I share gym buddies. Other than time with Moses, she was becoming a successful understudy to that midwife and studying hard.

As her birthday approached, I started to calculate ways to at least try reaching out.

I tried calling this morning but got her voicemail. At the beep, I took a breath, "Hey, it's Chris…" I had this planned out, but now all I could see was her face. Mostly the night of the banquet when I told her my love was a mistake. "I know I sucked at remembering this twice now…it's a significant day…for you but…for us…I'm sorry I-." I inhaled deeply. What was I doing-saying? "I'm just calling to say, happy birthday…I hope…" I don't know. What did I hope? I don't have much hope for anything. "I hope today is as special as you…" I waited then hung up.

Later that night, I left our place to walk. No car, just some movement. Without knowing it, I let my feet carry me to a place full of memories. They all played in clips because I was distracted but then I saw her there and stopped. She and Moses were walking and laughing, and a pit grew in my stomach when I saw where they were headed.

They were coming up on the bar…our bar…the bar she was dancing in on her birthday the night I kissed her in front of all those people. This was our memory, our place, and our history.

There was a small line to get in and I kept hoping they would pass it, but then they turned toward it and waited.

I don't know how long I stood there watching them interact in line. They tease a lot and she holds his arm. God, that…that hurts. She holds my arm like that.

Moses kissed her lightly on the lips then went inside the bar without her to reserve them a spot. She wandered to an iron bench beside the door and sat back. She was in black jeans and a black turtleneck with a tan coat. She looked like home. She looked like all the good things in my life.

I approached slowly and kept my hands in the pockets of my jacket. When she saw me, she smiled at first thinking I was a passerby, but when she registered who I was, she sat straighter and the smile fell away.

"Chris?"

"I'm not here to ruin your night…" ugh, this hurt. It hurt like hell. "And I know I don't have a right to ask you anything…" She waited for me to finish. "Please, not *here*…" I saw her eyes light up with memories and my veins rubbed together in desperation. "I don't deserve much…but please, not here… not tonight. Not of all nights. Can you understand?"

She took a minute then nodded. "Yeah," she said in a huff and I could see her breath.

I looked when someone on the other side of the street spoke too loudly, then at her again. My wife. My girl, "Thank you," I said.

She nodded, and I walked away. When I looked back, Moses was coming out and reached for her hand. She smiled up at him and shook her head as she spoke. I'm too far to hear, but he looked unbothered when she pointed to another bar and he brought her close as they made that walk. She didn't tell him why, I can tell from her face, but I was grateful she at least changed course.

As I made my way home, I let that night…our foundation replay in my mind. Sad thing is, now that the memory is allowed to play out, I see how much damage I've done. Forgetting her birthday twice in a row, a day that meant so much to both of us…that was just plainly unforgivable. Here's why…

2008

I carried Jenzy out of the bar with her legs wrapped around my waist and her arms around my neck. When we got outside, I devoured her mouth against the brick building and under the soft glow of Christmas lights they had slung overhead. It was cold but not freezing and with her body against mine, I didn't feel much else.

Her kisses made my retreat from her at the airport, and the last couple weeks not talking seem ridiculous. I belonged in her arms and she belonged in mine, and I didn't care anymore if all the people I know found out. I wanted them to know. Now they do. I kissed this girl on a tabletop in front of most our peers. It's over for me, I'm branded, and I love it.

She untangled her legs and stood while I kissed her over and over.

"I can't believe you did that," she said as we finally slowed down.

"I can't believe I didn't do it sooner."

"You were kinda in Sweden, to be fair."

I lost the happy for a minute and set my head back with a growl.

She reached up and brought my face down, "What's wrong? What?"

"Sweden…I go back in-."

"Don't ruin this. It's fine. We'll keep calling and Skyping."

'That's not enough," I whined. "It doesn't compare with this," I kissed her; held her hands so our fingers could lace, palm to palm. "I need to touch you, not my phone."

"I can't leave my parents, Todd, my friends… I like it here. You shouldn't give up what you like either. We'll just compromise until you get sick of me."

"That's just it; I'll never get sick of you. I can't leave now. It's going to be worse than before. Especially, if I sleep with you tonight, which I fully intend to do. If I couldn't get you out of my head the first time, the second time is moot."

"We'll visit back and forth, and-."

"That's expensive," I countered.

She shivered, and I shrugged out of my coat. Only she would try a tube top in December. She slipped her arms into the sleeves and I held it closed in front.

"Chris…" she tried.

"What if there's a problem or one of us is hurt?"

"Chris…"

"What if I got you knocked up?" I panicked.

"Hey, Chris…"

"I don't wanna miss my baby being born. How would I even be here to support you?"

"Chris…"

"This is where I freak out. The future is too blurry, there's no plan."

"Chris," she came up real close and kissed the underside of my chin.

"You don't intend to move to Sweden. That's clear," I assessed.

She kissed her way up my jaw, "Chris…"

"If I move back that defeats why I left."

She came to stand on her toes and spoke into the corner of my mouth, "Hey, Chris?"

"What?"

"I love you…"

"Yeah…" my mind didn't process the beauty of the moment since I was busy contriving plans, "I love you too I guess."

She giggled, and it caught my attention.

"What?" I asked her.

"I just told you, I love you," she kissed my mouth.

Oh, love. Is that what this was? I need her all the time and when she isn't there I want to kill myself…I guess that's love.

"What did I say back?" I asked into her mouth.

She laughed and mimicked my voice, "*Yeah…I love you too I guess.*"

I laughed, "Did I really?"

"Yep, but I love it. You should say it that way all the time."

"No way, I sounded distracted," I frowned at my own stupidity.

"That's the beauty of it," she leaned back to see me and stroked my jaw. "You said it without thinking. Like it was so natural like you've been feeling it a long time and saying it was obvious."

I smiled and backed her against the wall again to kiss her harder, "You're crazy and weird, and strange, and over the top optimistic, and I love it," I confessed. "You control me completely. Did you notice? Where's my nude? I thought we said when I rant you would present me with a nude."

She was laughing, and her cheeks were pink from it and the cold, "If you get me indoors, I'll just take off all my clothes. That's better isn't it?"

I thought about the internship and the doors to travel. I thought about Sweden and I thought about my desire to break the mold, but all I saw was the future I saw here, in my arms, in front of me.

"I'm not going back," I bent to put my forehead to hers. "I can't, I won't. Fuck my plans. Fuck the job-."

"What job?"

"It doesn't matter. This gorgeous girl, that's kinky, smart, funny, clumsy, sexy, weird as hell girl, she just said she loves me. I can't pass that up. Say it again. Say it slower."

She kissed me first and held my eyes, "I…love…you."

I smiled and kissed her, "Yeah…I love you too…*I guess*."

Chapter Thirty-Seven

Present Day
December 24th
JENZY

My mom and Dad don't just have a beach house; they also have a log cabin in the mountains. It's tradition for the whole family to go on Christmas Eve. We stay until the day after Christmas. This year, I'm going up with Nona, so she doesn't have to drive alone. Mandy, Todd, the babies and my parents are already there.

Chris' mom avoided any and all topics of Chris on the ride up. We laughed and filled the time up with anything but him. When we got there everyone was hanging out between the kitchen and the living room. This cabin is enormous but it's cozy. It's six bedrooms and three stories including the basement/men's cave my dad made.

There's a hot tub in the back and a library. The wall that connects the living room to the kitchen is vast and all window glass that overlooks the forest. It's divided by a stone fireplace and in the center of the ceiling is a hanging light made of deer antlers. There's another fireplace in the living room and the two master bedrooms, one of which is where Chris and I used to stay.

The place was decked out for Christmas this year; garlands, two trees, one in the main hall and one in the middle between the kitchen and parlor. There were wreaths above the hearth and gifts galore under the tree. Looks like Connor and Penny are going to be spoiled as hell. With my help, of course.

"It's snowing!" My mom said excitedly at the window in the kitchen. The whole place smelled like ham since she had begun the holiday meal. "Oh, thank goodness. I needed a white Christmas."

Chris' mom sniffed the pot on the stove full of goodies then replied, "It's colder than a witch's tit out there."

"Nona!" I laughed and jerked my head at Connor. He was busy zooming toy cars across the spacious floor.

Nona shrugged, "He's not listening."

My mom waved me off, "Leave Nona alone. Connor survived off tits for months. He can handle the word tit."

Todd came up and gave me a peck on the cheek, "Can we all stop saying tit? Thank you," he requested.

Mandy came up from behind and hugged my back and I smiled, "Not sick of me yet?" I asked. "I live with you."

"You're my soul sister," she squeezed tighter and it felt amazing, "I never get sick of you."

"Todd, how's work, honey?" My mom asked him. They were close, we all are.

"I want to quit, and be a stay at home dad," he replied.

We all laughed and then I heard the front door. I could hear my dad talking to someone but couldn't make out who as I tied on an apron to help mom and Nona.

They were all chatting but as the voice got closer I tensed up. Chris walked in, talking deeply with my dad and he had an overnight bag on his shoulder and another bag full of gifts. I looked back at my mom like she was a traitor, of which she was.

Mom set down the cranberries she was pouring and came over to me just as Chris met my eyes.

"Jenzy…" he said. He looked rougher. He was letting his facial hair come in enough to shadow his jaw. "I thought…you weren't coming," Chris explained.

I looked over at mom, "*I* was told *you* weren't coming," I dug.

"I can drive back," he volunteered.

My mom frowned, "Like hell, you will. It's snowin' and it's Christmas."

I glared at her, "Then I'll go."

Chris stood in my way, "No, you can't even drive; you would need a ride down. I'll leave. This is your family's cabin."

My dad frowned, "Penny and Connor should see their uncle on Christmas. You two's shitty problems shouldn't change that."

My mom tossed oven mitts on the counter, "This is my fault, I invited both of ya," she admitted.

Mandy set her hands on her hips, "After what he said to her, he should be the one to leave," she cut.

Then Todd, "Apparently, he would trade all the holidays we've spent together for a job he was offered years back, why spend it with us now?"

"Like our babies' first Christmas'," Mandy raised a brow. "Scotty, why should he need to be here this time if he would change all that from before?"

My mom held up her finger, "I get how this seems-."

Then Nona jumped in, "I don't want you driving back down, Chris but for Christ's sake, coming here wasn't a brilliant idea."

Everyone went into an uproar about what should be done. I avoided all eye contact with the man that ripped out my lungs a couple months ago, but I could feel him looking at me.

My dad shook his head, "Eh!" he shouted. My dad doesn't shout; not unless it's at mom, so all of us chilled out to listen. "No one's leavin' this friggin cabin. Same as in *The Shining*, it's snowin' like your mother said, and it's Christmas. End a story."

"Daddy!" I bugged my eyes at him. This was going to *end* like *The Shining* too. I was hurt that Dad would pick Chris over me. "Dad!" I said again.

Nona stepped forward and pointed at Chris, "You stay. It's not safe to be driving, but if you do one stupid thing, you're sleeping outside with the bears. Got it?"

Chris vented, "I'll leave! It's fine. Jenzy," his addressing me made me look up. "I swear I didn't know. If you want me to go, I'll go."

I stood with my arms crossed debating, but then my mom stepped in.

"Alright, listen up," Mom faced both of us. "This is hard. We all know that. I'm mourning the fact that a love like yours…is gone, but that don't mean caring gotta be gone too. You spent many years making each other happy. Loving each other." She set her sights on Chris, "You may have said you'd trade the time for something else, but you didn't. You loved my daughter, at least at one point."

He held her eyes because mom silently demands that of people, but he looked like her words were eating at him.

Then I was next, and she addressed me, "Something happens to him on the way down the mountains, could you live with that?"

Just the thought made a cold shiver go down my spine. I shifted my eyes to Chris and the love that came from habit took the weight. All it took was one vision of him in a car accident because I sent him home, and on Christmas, "Stay…" I said below a whisper.

He nodded once in thanks and then we went separate ways. My Dad came to me while I was setting the table and I refused to acknowledge him.

He sighed, "I know you're mad at me," he began, "your mother said we should invite him, and I says… I says to her, well yeah, cause' he's family."

"Not if he would just sign the freaking divorce," I hissed.

"Christopher will always be family, Baby Girl. Papers ain't gonna change that."

I turned to leave, but he held my hand and with very little persuasion, got me to hug him. Even if he was a Benedict Arnold I guess it was Christmas. Even my husband doesn't deserve to be home alone.

Dinner, I thought would be tense, but people talked and laughed and there were enough people to cushion our interactions, which were thankfully limited. Connor was overjoyed to be with his uncle, sucking up every moment he could. Us girls cleaned up afterward and then Mandy and my mom went to the hot tub and my dad took Chris into the man cave with Todd. I put the kids to bed with Nona's help and then I retired too.

The crazy part was no matter how hard I tried, sleep wasn't coming. I tossed and turned constantly, and even after talking to Moses I couldn't get my eyes to shut. I checked the clock on my phone and huffed. It was already almost two in the morning.

I must sleep in t-shirts to be comfortable, but even with the fire and the warmth, I'm used to cuddling into Chris for heat here. I've never slept in this cabin without him.

I whipped the bed covers off and padded my way down the hall. The house was sleeping, not one sound except the hum of appliances, fires cracking and the wind gently caressing the cabin. Mom's white Christmas lights lit each room like when I was a kid and I tiptoed into the kitchen for water. Then I tiptoed to the living room to sit.

When I sat down, and something moved under me, I jumped up and looked down, "Chris?"

"Sorry," he sat up long ways on the couch and took his feet down, so I could sit.

I did but at the way other end of the sofa. All I had was an oversized t-shirt, panties, and socks, but I had been smart enough to remember my robe; I shut it.

"Can't sleep?" he asked.

"My mind is just busy. You?"

"My uh…" he sat forward, and my heart raced. "My head is killing me. I forgot to pack meds."

Chris looked amazing, even heartbroken. He also ran a hot body temp so even in the mountains, in December, he was wearing a dark gray tank and boxers. The firelight and glow from the tree lights made him look irresistible and my body was thrust into awareness.

"I have-," I looked down at my water and berated myself for talking without thinking first.

"Go ahead, you have what?"

"I don't know. Just, mumbling."

"Tell me."

I looked into the fire, "I have stuff with me. That's all I was going to say, but it's- drop it."

"Your herbs?" his question didn't come out snide. I shrugged. He sighed, "It feels like a vice squeezing my head." His eyes were rimmed in pink. I wonder why.

"A tension headache..." I wondered out loud.

"Sounds right," he came further forward and held his head between his hands. Then he came up and turned his head to me, "I would... be open to trying anything, really. If you don't mind."

I was a little stunned, "Okay, yeah, hang on." I left and went into my room to find my pack with all my 'on the go' remedies. I returned, and he was lying on the couch again rubbing his face. I knelt by him and presented a tincture.

"Do I drink it?" he asked.

"No, we'll put it on your hairline."

"What is it?"

I opened it and put it under his nose.

"Hmm, peppermint," he guessed.

"Yeah," I dripped some onto my finger and without over thinking, I smoothed it over his hairline. There's supposed to be a touch barrier when you separate, but he and I...

I sat on the floor and put my back to the sofa. We sat for maybe an hour with no sound and then he sat up and I took my eyes from the fire to look, "How do you feel?"

He shifted and sank to the floor; sitting next to me. I moved over an inch away and drew my knees up.

"I feel great. It's working, headache is almost gone," he rubbed the back of his neck. "It was a mean one, too. Thank you."

"No problem..." I was still shocked he tried it and even more shocked he admitted to it working. "I think... I'm going to bed."

"Okay," he smiled at me and took his jeans off a nearby chair.

"Aren't you going to try and sleep?"

"Nah, now that the headache is gone, I think I'll sneak out before our parents get up."

"Sneak out where?"

He took a long-sleeved shirt from his bag, "I'm going home. You were here first, and you need a Christmas without mayhem."

I frowned, "Chris, the snow-."

"I'll be fine. I can drive in snow. I have four-wheel-drive."

He went to pull the shirt on, but I held his wrist.

When He lowered it to question me, I held his hand, "I might not want to be your wife anymore; it doesn't mean I want something to happen to you. Mom was right. No one should be alone during the holidays."

"Thank you for thinking of me, but-."

"I'm asking you to stay," I kept his hand until he caved. Then I took my hand back, but I didn't want to. I had a sudden urge to ask him to hold me. I made a move to get up, but he tugged the hem of my robe.

"If I'm staying, can you just… humor me for a minute?" he asked.

"What's up?"

"Nothing… I want to talk to you. You don't answer my calls anymore, and I get it. I understand why, but I uh… I miss you. I would like to just hear how you're doing." I pressed my lips together and he hurried on. "I know nothing's changed. I know you're mad and hurt. We don't have to talk about all that, I just want… talking."

I agreed then waited for his first question, "How's the doula training?" he tried.

"It's great. I've witnessed ten deliveries now, two were in hospitals. I love it."

We talked back and forth about work then it lulled, and I felt his next question.

"How are things with Moses?" he looked terrified to ask since he kept his eyes averted, but when he did finally look, I gave him a '*must we venture there?*' expression.

"I'm not asking to be a dick," he clarified, "I'm trying not to be in denial, I guess."

I hugged my knees, "Things are good."

"He's still… good to you… he….?"

"Yes."

"Good. What about…? How come you didn't bring him?"

"He has family in New Mexico. He and his Dad are visiting them along with his best friend."

I could hear his true question. He's too afraid to ask me so he went with another, "Have you met his family?"

Nodding, I said, "His sister. I have spoken to and known his dad at the bookshop. He met my parents two weeks ago."

"How was it?"

"Mom is Mom; friendly, open. Dad is…" I laughed, "Always on your side," he laughed. Then I realized now was a time to bridge a major question. "There's something else… I found a place."

He brightened in a sad way, "You did? That's good. How is it?"

"I like it. There's an obstacle, though…"

"Is it financial? Because-."

"No… I would have a roommate."

"Nice, so then… what's the obstacle?"

"Our divorce."

His handsome brows came together, "How exactly is that an-?" And then he realized. The beautiful golden eyes I admired, dulled considerably; it was almost scary.

"Moses and I want to move in together. It just makes sense for us. We've been talking and stuff for almost a year and we're friends, you know? We have a lot in common, living together would be a smooth transition for us." He wasn't talking so I kept talking, "It's not like I need the divorce to move in with him. That's Moses… he feels like it wouldn't be right to start, with me still married. He knows you never have to agree with this, but he doesn't want you to feel… he wants you and I to be okay. I guess like a blessing to move forward out of respect."

Now he was staring at the fire and the room felt small and dark.

"Chris?" I checked.

He shook his head slowly, "No, I'm sorry." I was disappointed but also curious. "Sorry, I can't," he stood up to sit on the sofa again.

I looked up and stood as he sat on the sofa, "How long do you plan to contest, Chris? Forever? Do you understand what you told me in October? Don't you see how that changed things? I would have moved mountains for you, and you basically told me that love wasn't good enough that *I* wasn't good enough."

He told me something then, "When we went to your parent's beach house this year, and you went upstairs to sleep. Your mom said something I kind of hated. She said the reason everyone thought I would cheat is because I always want what I can't have. Then when I get it, I basically have a timer on how long I'll want to keep it." He rubbed his face and then said, "Yes, I wanted that internship and I wanted the life that came with it, but I never wanted anything the way I want you. I said that I would do it all over differently, and that was a lie. I wanted it two years ago because I couldn't have it, not because I actually wanted it. Two months without you has been like two months without a soul. If I made another choice, then I'd be nothing now."

I listened but I had walls up.

He went on, "It may not be the career I was aiming for, but I love my job, I like real estate. I'm good at it and I wouldn't have known love."

He stood, and I backed up a step. He kept his distance but kept going, "I can't believe, no matter how many times I re-live it that I told you I would do it differently. I can't believe I lied that well to myself as to even let that be said. My years with you have been the best years of my life and for the last two, I treated you like shit for something that wasn't even your fault."

I felt tears pooling in my eyes and the break down upset me. Was he ever going to not matter? How could I make Chris nothing?

"The baby thing?" he asked like he could hear my thoughts had gone there. "I don't want a future with anyone else but you."

He stepped forward, but I leaned back a little, even as his words filled the air.

"You asked how long I plan to contest. Jenzy, I don't think I can ever sign it. I don't want a divorce. I don't want this state and the law to tell me you aren't mine anymore." He gestured to the bareness of my left hand. "You took off the rings but," he turned his own ring. "I'm getting buried with mine because whether you leave me or not, I'll love you till the day I die. To my last breath. You didn't just give me your love, you brought me closer to my own family, your family, you led me to this amazing career. I don't want what could've been in Sweden, I want what could be with us."

His profession was tearing my insides out and shredding them to bits. My fortress of control was one hit from condemned and if he touched me or said one more thing I would fold.

I backed toward the steps, "I'm going to bed…" I rasped. "I can't do this again. Sorry," I hurried up the steps and into the safety of my room before crying myself to sleep. What am I supposed to do with all that? It's too late. He's just too late.

Chapter Thirty-Eight
March
CHRIS

*I*t's been a full year since Jenzy filed and I still can't put pen to paper. Sometimes it feels like I'm going crazy in this house. She's moved more of her things out since then and I finally stopped sleeping with the picture, and the bra, and I finished the book.

I'm slowly getting used to doing simple things alone, even driving. There's no one to call to tell stupid little things, and no one cares about those things anyway. If I get hit on, I still use the ring as a means to be left alone.

Today I'm driving out to the park where Todd is meeting me with the kids, so Mandy can have a free day. When I get there, Connor runs to me and I grab him up to swing him around by the back of his pants. Penny is a walker now, but unsteady and she makes her way over but one careful step at a time, and with her daddy right behind her. My mind still runs things through about the empty road of my future.

I can't see myself with another woman, does that mean I'll never have kids? I'm fighting jealousy toward my little brother. He adorns his wife with the affection and commitment that keeps her. They fight and have plenty of problems, but the problems don't outweigh the need to be together and because of that, they have two children to be an icon to that love.

All the times I berated Jenzy for her whimsical beliefs have turned into a joke on me. She was going to make a dynamite mother. She would've given my children, imagination, wings, and creativity. She would be in our garden, (the one I would have to maintenance because she's afraid of bugs) teaching them to build fairy houses. She would be the one collecting rocks with them and though I would be the disciplinarian in domestic chores, she would be the teacher of heart.

As Penny came up to hug my leg for support, I saw the chance at holding Jenzy's first baby fade. I saw the chance at holding her hand through labor, disappear. Someone else would be coaching her, debating about home versus hospitals, fighting her on names like John versus Agamemnon, feeling a child move in her for the first time, cutting the cord.

My future was going to be lived by another guy. My holding her hand down streets, my gathering her in my arms at night, my chance at making her body shake with pleasure, my making her laugh, my inside jokes, were all up for grabs now.

I lost all of it by my own hand, and though it ruined me, I was learning to live with it.

"So, guess who likes to come up and grab women's boobs for no reason," Todd asked me.

I laughed and turned Connor upside down, "Not cool, little man," I said as I swayed him back and forth. "You can't do that. It's a lawsuit."

Todd lifted Penny, "Yeah, he grabbed his teacher's and now he does it with everybody."

"He'll get over it," I said.

"Before or after he's labeled a pervert?"

"When he was whipping his wiener out randomly, you thought he would never get over that phase too."

Todd gagged, "Ugh, I forgot about that one. I hope this next one isn't a boy, I think girls are easier."

"Whatever man, girls are just as- wait," I set Connor down and he took off for the slide as I raised my brows at Todd and looked at him over my sunglasses. "Did you just say *next* one?"

He grinned at me, "Yeah man, Mandy's pregnant."

"What? Holy shit! Again?" I shook his hand and we half hugged, "Congratulations. Wow. Three. I'll be an uncle three time over. Most days I want to duct tape your wife's mouth shut, but I sure do love her for being a babymaker."

"Yeah, don't say that when you see her at Mom's this week."

"She loves me," I said cockily.

"Still, don't push it."

"How are you feeling?" I asked.

"I'm stoked. Scared shitless but stoked."

"Don't you guys know about condoms?" I taunted.

"Shut up."

"They're latex, they come in a box, you can find them at drug stores," I goaded.

He smirked, "*Shut up*," he sang.

"You can even find flavored ones, they're like," I held up my hands to measure length, "This size, well, but in your case," I made my hands almost touch and he punched me in the arm as we laughed.

Connor tried the monkey bars and while Todd held Penny, I went and kept my arms out under Connor to be sure he would make it across.

"How are you these days?" Todd asked.

"Can't complain. Made a closing on two houses with a serious commission."

"Good for you! Well done."

"Thanks…" we walked, following Connor, and Todd let down Penny. "Uh…" I chanced it. "I know I'm not supposed to ask, but how's she doing?"

He stayed open and easy, "She's really good. She's moving out, though this weekend."

My throat went dry and my heart took a plunge, "She moving in with him?"

Todd didn't say, but I knew, "You need to sign, Chris. He's good for her. They really do work. He treats her like a queen and she lights up when he's around. Don't ask because I don't know if they've been together yet. I assume so if they want to live together unless it's just a roommate agreement. Either way, she deserves to be happy. You broke her heart, you should at least give her the okay to heal. We've all hung out with Moses and you know I wouldn't let her into harm's path, but he's really great. He's even great with the kids."

Replaced, wasn't a strong enough word. He didn't just have my wife, he had my niece and nephew too. Moses was going to have the bounty life had offered me on a silver plate, but he was apparently, grateful where I hadn't been.

I didn't want to talk because the tightened cords in my throat weren't relaxing enough. I made it through the visit and somewhat through the drive, but when I got home, I lost it.

I picked the lamp up by the door in the living room and hurled it at the wall. Next was the paintings, I tore them down and smashed them. The coffee table didn't have a chance, I flipped it over, candles, magazines and all. I kicked the ottoman over too, this felt amazing. Wedding picture on the end table… I banged it into the wall, and when the glass broke I ripped the picture out and tore it to bits. I put my fist through the wall over the couch. I had a fugly hole there now and fucked up knuckles, but the release of temper and suffocating sadness felt healing.

Then with all that heat and all that rage, I sat down at my kitchen table and took a pen from my shirt pocket. I wrote a letter. It was the first 'handwritten' letter I've written since school maybe. I wrote everything down, all of it, and then I stuffed it into an envelope with something else and got in my car to deliver it.

JENZY

Moses had rented a truck for us to load my stuff in. I don't have too much therefore, it's easy. Keeping an eye on Mandy, to be sure she won't lift something heavy in her condition is harder. Moses called while I was taping a box shut. I fished the phone out of the back pocket of my overalls.

"Hello?" I answered.

"Hey, Sunshine, I'm done with class. I'm heading to the locker rooms now then I'll be coming your way."

"Excellent! I'm almost done boxing the little stuff."

"Perfect. Do you need anything?"

"Just you and your man bod for lifting." We laughed, "You're still sure about this, right?" I checked behind me to be sure no one was listening, but I was in my room alone. "Moving in with a girlfriend is already daunting. You're moving in with one, you have yet to test drive."

"I still would've preferred you to be divorced in full first," he admitted. "Out of respect, but I also don't have much backbone with you."

Mention of Chris made my gut twist. I found a new way to cope. Not so new, it was Chris' method. Block everything you should face.

I brightened, "This might help him see it's time to sign."

"Maybe. As long as you are okay, I'm to the brim with happiness."

I smiled and almost asked him a moving question when he mumbled the word, "Weird."

"What?"

He paused before answering, "There's a letter sticking out of my locker."

I frowned, "Who's it from?"

"Don't know… no name. It only says *Moses* on the front."

"Hmm, I'll let you go so you can check it out and get here."

"Okay, can't wait."

"Me too."

We hung up and I pocketed my phone.

Chapter Thirty-Nine
JENZY

$\mathcal{M}$oses showed up a half-hour later, and when I heard him talking to a truck guy outside, I checked my reflection. I'm wearing a printed crop top under my bibs and Chuck Taylors, but I managed to not look like a wreck with my hair in a ponytail.

I bounded down the stairs with a lighter box and out the door. On the steps, I stopped as he was coming up.

"Hey, there!" I said with cheer. He looked up at me and I saw the sadness plainly. His face was so burdened, and I cupped his cheek from the step above his, "What's wrong?" I joked, "Cold feet?"

He took my hand and kissed my palm, "No, but we need to talk first."

Ew, does anyone in history like those words? '*We need to talk*,' is sign language for, '*bad shit is flying everywhere.*' I bet before Caesar was stabbed, Brutus said, '*we need to talk*,' but in Roman. I have a clear vision in my head, of King Henry VIII telling each wife on the eve of their beheading, '*hey, so we need to talk.*' That's why when Moses just said it, I considered tossing the box and ugly-running down the street, but there are cell phones now, that wouldn't work.

"What's going on?" I checked.

He took my box and set it down before he sat on the steps. I sat next to him and waited. He pulled an envelope from his pocket and pulled it easily through his fingers at each angle.

Then he started, "So, I would be lying if I said I didn't debate hard with myself, the whole way here if I should show you this. A pretty big part said, 'no' but a voice in the back of my head said, 'yes'. Before I do, I want to tell you something."

He set his warm eyes on me and laid his hand on my knee, "I haven't said these words because I didn't want to rush you or make you feel pressured. I also didn't want to get hurt…but…I love you." His words made something in my mind spark. "I don't need to sleep with you to see that I love you. I know I love you because you made it so easy to feel this way-."

"Moses, I-."

"Wait…" he swallowed hard, "Don't say anything back yet, just listen." He smiled sadly, "I know that is death to a Sagittarius, but try."

I smiled and listened.

"This has been beautiful, us," he motioned between us. "Even without sex, I connect with you in ways that I've never connected before. The only thing is," he set his attention on the letter. "I still don't view you as mine. Whenever I try, it feels more like, I'm caretaking. Caretaking your heart for someone else. It may sound like a crappy job, but in truth, it's awesome."

He licked his lips and the emotion in his voice brought forth my own as he said, "I want you to read this… all the way through. If in the end, you can say you love me, then I'll literally throw you in my car." Despite the heavy feel of the moment we laughed then turned somber again. "If not…then… then know it doesn't change anything. You matter to me, you always will."

I accepted the letter with tears in my eyes and a raging need to know what was inside. He pulled me close and kissed my mouth, but it felt like a farewell and pleading at the same time. Then he got up and went inside the house. I steeled myself and then pulled out the letter. I unfolded the papers; there were a few. By the handwriting, I knew it was Chris and prepared for something very brash.

Then I read, but it was hard with eyes so full of water. It also started raining or only misting and I heard distant thunder. It read…

Moses,

This is the most important letter I think I'll ever write. My handwriting might get sloppy and my grammar might suck but listen up because if I find out you didn't read this, I'll shove it down your throat 'hypothetically'.

I know about the move and I won't say I'm happy for you, I'm not. I was you only a few years ago. I still remember the day Jenzy and I moved in together, it was the start of my life. So, I know how you feel. But the fact is I fucked up, and the only reason you're happy right now is because I made the biggest mistake of my life.

Another hard-fact is that I can't change it. I tried, I gave it all I had but some things can't be fixed. So, in light of all that, if I'm going to let her go, if that's my only option then I want to know I'm letting her go to better. I need to know she's happy, loved, worshiped. I need to know you'll do a better job than me. She's too special, too beautiful, too kind. She's too good for any man on this planet but she's picked you, so make yourself the best.

Here it is. All I know about Jenzy that you need to know now.

She's terrified of bugs. Not just regular girly scared, I mean full out, level-trauma. She'll turn into an indoor cat during summer to avoid them but then she'll get unhappy, so make time to take her out. If she's holding your hand or arm, she won't freak as much. If one gets in the house, for the love of God, don't kill it. She believes all creatures have a purpose or are reincarnated so just capture it and take it outside.

When you eat out, she'll sit over the menu for an eternity. Don't get impatient. If you do, look at it this way. It's time with her that I'll never have again and would kill for. When she gets stuck between two choices, pick the second for her. She wants the first thing but she's testing herself and just got distracted with the second. She'll override you and pick the first. Problem solved.

She can't sleep in complete darkness, so let her keep her candles and stuff but stay up long enough to blow them out when she falls asleep. Unless there's moonlight, she likes that.

The woman is a walking fire hazard, so please, check all female devices pertaining to hair before leaving the house. Curlers, straighteners, blow dryers, crimpers she leaves them on and plugged in. Incense, candles, and wax warmers apply.

Whenever you go to get Chinese food, it's the 'chew mei fun' noodles she wants but even after years of ordering, she never remembers the name.

When you shop for gifts, she's going to check the item by turning it over and over and over to find flaws. Don't rush her, it won't go any faster but gifts matter to her.

Same with shoe, purse, or jean shopping. Take a seat, it's going to be a while. Don't say a damn word. Remember, it's time.

We both know she's inhumanly gorgeous, but she doesn't. Tell her constantly. I stopped, and I may have ruined her confidence, so you have repairing to do.

She's a terrific cook. If you don't stay in shape, you'll end up the size of a house, but when she cooks healthy, things get scary. Just eat it. Offer a suggestion maybe, but don't put it down. Eat it. She made it for you because she wanted to serve you, that's all that matters.

She's clumsier than a flamingo on Ritalin. If she wears heels, stay close, a fall or misstep is definite. In antique shops either carry her purse or stay close enough to keep it in. When she shops, it's like Godzilla's tail. She forgets to hold it back and has wiped out entire aisles.

She can't sleep in clothes.

If you go to her mom's, <u>do not</u> eat any brownies setting out. I just learned that one.

Her ambitions change, but I think she's found her calling with the doula work. Support her and don't mock anything she changes sides on. One week she might be 'save the whales', the next is 'global warming'. Either way, your life will never be boring.

She's a little too trusting sometimes. She stops to talk to homeless people, which is fine, but she has no sense of stranger danger. Keep her near in dark alleys. Jenzy jaywalks and will not even check both ways. Keep her on the inside when walking sidewalks, just like the old days.

She'll talk about ex's a lot and you'll get a full report of men she's interacted with when you weren't around. She's not trying to make you jealous she thinks she's preventing it because she's being honest. Besides, she is not with her ex's, she's with you and the guys she saw today didn't stand a chance, but she doesn't want you finding out from someone else and accusing her. Trust me, that woman will never betray you once you have her heart.

She's positive about EVERYTHING, if you were shot in the eye, she'd say 'well at least you have the other one.' There are worse flaws. She'll be positive about you too. That means you're like a superhero to her. Don't blow it.

She will use your razors. Just buy more. Don't bitch.

You want to impress her Dad, buy him tickets to a game. Any game, he loves sports, but his football teams are the Giants, Steelers, and Eagles. Change teams if you have to. He still won't like you like he did me, but you'll have a fighting chance. Making his daughter happy is the real test.

If I ever find out, you hurt her physically your face will end up on a milk carton. If you break her heart, I'll break your face. Not hypothetically.

Lastly, don't screw up like I did. Nothing and I really mean nothing is worth losing her. Nothing is worth losing the possibilities of being her man. Nothing is worth never touching her again. Losing her optimistic support, the smile, the laughs, the nothing days, the goofy hippie girl that gave you her heart, will break you.

I didn't believe in them before but now I'm really praying there is such a thing as past lives because if I get another chance, I'm never letting her go. So, don't let her go.

The divorce is signed, and I have it enclosed. Give it to her but don't let her read this. This was for you. Only you.

Chris

Chapter Forty
CHRIS

I stood in my kitchen and stared at the damage I had done to my living room a couple days ago. Considering this was Saturday, I would venture a guess that Jenzy was moving today. Ok, so maybe the mess had a purpose. I hate clutter and this menagerie needs a purpose, so there it is. I'll use the mess as an excuse to start clearing Jenzy's presence out.

Yeah, that works. Box any stuff that's hers, then…burn the whole place down. That's what it would take. So, fuck it, the mess can wait another day. I'm already in hell and going crazy, maybe the house should look like it too.

I went to the kitchen table, where my briefcase looks like it threw up. I have documents everywhere because I don't want to organize the house, but I need to organize something, so I'll do this. I have a house to show later, but for now, I took off my jacket and vest and loosened my tie. I always feel like I'm choking lately, loosening the tie doesn't help much.

I took a drink from my coffee and set my hand on my side while I tried to focus on this distracting task, but nothing made sense anymore, and I need to shave soon. The light scruff on my face is annoying. Not to mention far from orderly, but razors make me think of her. Everything does.

I heard the front door open, followed by what had turned to hard rain, then it slammed shut and I frowned, "Todd?" I yelled. Did Todd have a key? My question was answered when Jenzy came in with a furious gait to her walk. She was in a long lilac-colored raincoat and matte gray heels.

She pulled her hood back and tossed her purse down. Her breathing told me she was pissed but her beautiful fire was making my heart do crazy twists. Her hair had gotten wet at some point and now it was drying in that sexy, wild way I loved.

"What the fuck was this?" she held up papers and I knew what they were. "You tell me right now, why you sent this to Moses. Chris, tell me."

"Calm down... you weren't ever supposed to ever see it-."

"That's not what I asked you," she came further in and held them up again. "Chris, why?"

I shook my head not sure what to say and set my coffee in the sink, "I can't answer that."

"Tough! You have to. Tell me. Why? What was this supposed to do? What was the point?"

"If you read it, you should know."

"You want this...? Y-you want Moses, to do all these things to know all this?" Now that she was closer I could see the tears. "You- y-you want... is that what you're telling me? Is that why you signed these? You're-."

"No, I don't *want* it. I don't want any of this but I'm doing it. I'm giving you what *you* want." She shook her head at what I said but her tears were so heavy she couldn't speak. The shaking of her head lit a match in the dark abyss of my hope and I straightened. "What? You don't-? You don't want-?" I couldn't get it out. She shook her head even harder and I all but broke my neck to get to her and seize her in my arms.

She pulled me close like she would fall if I let go and I squeezed to the point of crushing her.

Jenzy pulled her head back and I kissed her. This is the best kiss of my entire life. I've been drowning for months and she was like oxygen. I moved until her back was to the wall and just kept touching her, pressing into her, like I was trying to figure out how to mold to her body.

"Chris," she whimpered my name and I stopped crushing her mouth, so she could talk. "If you shut me out again-."

"I won't. I won't. I swear to God, I won't," I kissed her because I can't be apart from her too long. "I'm sorry, I'm sorry.

Forgive me, please, please, Jenzy." I'm not crying but maybe I am because she's blurry to me.

Her hands are on my face, "I did already."

"Don't leave me."

"I'm not."

I'm swallowing her again. I hope I'm not hurting her, but I have to have her, all of her. "I need to be inside," I clenched my jaw a second and took in the burning in her eyes. "I need to feel like I'm part of you. Can I-? Do you want me? I know it's been a long time," I thought of Moses, "A long time for me."

"Me too," she clutched my collar and relief rolled in.

"You didn't-?"

"No. I couldn't…because…because…I love you, and…I love you, Chris, I love you."

"Yeah," I wiped the tears from under her eyes with my thumbs, then smiled through my own. "I love you too…*I guess…*"

I could see her mind light up with fireworks when I said it our way. Our special way. Then I took her mouth again. She stopped to race past me and up the stairs. I ran after her and caught her when she stumbled on the steps. *Yes, I want to be the one catching you, always.*

Once in our bedroom, she turned to me and kissed me. I reached for the zipper on her raincoat, but she stopped my hand.

"What's wrong?" I checked for a change. "Did you bike here like this? In the rain?"

"No… I took a cab. I also changed before I came here."

My imagination went places. What did she change to? "Can I see?"

"You need to know something first," I let go of the zipper. "I offered myself to you, so many times before…you didn't…and every time you rejected me you took a little of my confidence, okay? Like you said in the letter. I'm not telling this to hurt you or pick. I'm telling you because now I'm almost scared."

A punch to the gut wouldn't cover it. This was more like a knife to the heart. I did that to her?

I took her zipper between my fingers, "Let me show you... how I really feel... let me give you back that confidence... okay?"

She wiped under her eye and nodded. I slowly unzipped her to find she was in nothing but underwear. Sexy, seductive underwear; A pink bra with gray designs and cream lace feathering across the bodice. The panties matched and rode low on her hips.

"Christ, Jenzy," I reached inside to hold her hips and pull her near. "You're too damned sexy... but please, don't go out, in public, in a friggin *cab* no less..." her saddened tension broke and she rolled her eyes. I waited till she looked at me again, "I'm going to lose it on you, Jenzy. Right here, in this room, I'm going to let go on your body. Can you handle that? Can you ride with me?"

Her breathing picked up, "Yes."

I kissed her and tore the coat off her shoulders. She yanked my necktie and pulled at my shirt until the buttons popped loose and went flying. My hands ran along her body while she jerked my belt tongue and opened my pants. I'm so hard it's in pain. She wrapped her hand around my shaft and pumped me sending heat everywhere.

I shoved her chest; she fell back on the bed. When she sat up, I straddled her and pressed her down into the mattress by the throat. I came down on her and turned her jaw, so I could lick a path up the length of her neck. A moan slipped past her lips that delivered straight to my groin.

"Do the thing you do, Chris please..." she presented her neck and I smiled.

"You want my mouth on you?"

"Yes."

"I need to make up lost time. Tell me what you want."

"Lick me."

I dragged my tongue over her collarbone then up behind her ear where I flicked at her skin with the tip and again, "Who knows your body best?"

"You," she whined. I took my hand from her jaw and glided down to her breasts.

The bra hooked from the front, "You're mine." I unclipped it and it sprung apart so her breasts bounced free. "Everything here is mine," I grasped a breast in my hand and spoke over it. "This is mine," I tasted the erect tip with a lick, then again. "And this one?" I grasped the other.

"Yours," she panted.

"Right," I sucked only the nipple into my mouth and the rigidity made my cock strain to madness, "Touch yourself."

Jenzy put her hand between us to do as I asked. Pressing and stroking herself. Her breathing was ragged, and I pinned her other hand above her head before moving back to her other breast and teasing the nipple with my nose. She moaned and went stiff under me.

Watching her while I worked was euphoric, "Touch yourself *under* the panties," she obeyed right away. "Good," I assaulted her nipple with powerful sucking. I could feel her hand working her clit under my hips and I moved up her chest to her neck again.

"I'm cumming…" she warned.

"How close?"

She gasped, "Really, really c-close."

I took her hand from inside her panties and pinned it over her head with the other.

"No," she groaned. I laughed into her ear and sat back on my knees, letting go long enough to take off my boxers. She tried to touch herself again, but I held her wrists.

"I said stop it," I barked.

She oozed of defiance, but I pushed back on my knees and spread her legs around me. I pulled her panties down her thighs but then she set her foot in the center of my chest. The cool touch of her heels tipped my control. She was smiling wickedly.

"You wanna play games right now?" I asked.

She bit her lip but when I resumed pulling down her panties she gave my chest a playful kick.

I grabbed her ankles and spread them around me.

She giggled.

"Behave," I cautioned.

"Why?"

"Because if you ever want to cum, you'll behave."

She took off her bra the rest of the way and fondled her breast while biting the tip of her fingernail, "Like this, Chris?"

"Better," I took off her panties and then parted her folds and looked. I love the way her lips down there are shaped, the color, the passionate pink that blushes with wet want for me. "You didn't invite him here?" I drew my finger down her slit and she pulsed at my touch.

"No."

"Tell me why…"

"It's your home," she spread her legs wider around me and reached down at her sides to pet at my thighs. "Come home to me."

I wrapped my hand around my cock and pressed the head against her entrance. One thrust and I would be where I belonged. She put that troublesome foot against my chest again, though.

"You need a condom," she remembered.

I placed her ankle over my shoulder and loomed over to kiss her. My flexible little hippie. My hand teased from her folds to her nipple where I rolled it lightly between my fingers until she groaned.

"Not today, I want to feel everything, your heat closing in on me, the throbbing that comes before the spasms, the warm wetness of my success. I want what's mine, in full."

Jenzy pressed her hands down my chest and then held my arms and looked into my eyes, "There's no other prevention…I don't take things. You want to risk that?"

"I want to risk everything with you," I pulled back enough to watch her beautiful face as I let my head penetrate past her lips. Her eyes fluttered closed and her body hugged around me; welcoming me further until I was fully engulfed. What an exhilarated feeling. She's right, I'm home.

She opened her eyes and I sat back on my knees to put her other leg over my shoulder too. Then I let go. I went my speed, I withdrew over and over only to plunge back inward with enough force that she was gliding all over the bed. Jenzy and I have never been one for slow lovemaking, not unless we're half dead with exhaustion.

However, this is her first time letting me back in. I tested her with strong strokes but lingering ones.

She wrapped her hand around the back of my neck, "You're holding back…" She dragged her nails down my chest. "Harder, Chris. I need it the way you give it."

I don't need more encouragement. I cut loose on her with thrusts that didn't move her around; instead, they drove her into the mattress. Her sounds echoed off our walls and made me crazy. Her sounds are like touches. I sat back and held her ankles apart to my sides. I could roll my hips deeper and she grasped the bedding above her head and pushed her head back, baring her body to me.

Her body laid out before me like this is a sight. A blush is fanning across her breasts and she's glistening with our sweat. Her breasts bounce with our movements and she creates thunder in my chest. She brought her hands down and I took one in mine and held her stomach down to quicken my pace. She held onto my hand and forearm, taking me in.

I felt the throbbing within her that ensured a coming orgasm and pushed her to the brink before withdrawing.

"God, damn it!" She slapped my chest and I laughed.

"Almost," I laid over her with kisses then rolled us so she was on top, "I'm making up, remember?"

She pulled her long hair to one side of her neck and I crunched upward to kiss and suck at the long lovely pillar. She took hold of my shaft and worked me with her hand while I bit at her ear and squeezed her ass.

Jenzy slid down my body until she poised herself with her ass arched high like a tigress ready to pounce. She kept my eyes as she teased her own breasts with the end of my dick. Here was perfect proof of why, without Jenzy, I would die alone. She's in every way, made for me, especially the dirty workings of her mind.

If I didn't stop looking, I would cum all over her. I laid back and closed my eyes. I could feel her circling her nipple with me. I was still slick from being inside her and sensitive as fuck. Then she pressed her tits together and I brought my hips up to drive between them.

Not being able to trust my imagination, I sat up on my elbows and watched. She didn't look to care if I watched or not, she was enjoying herself and that made the ache to be inside her again unbearable.

"Come here," I said.

"No," she sat straight up on her knees and touched herself over me.

"I can't, Jenzy," I watched her slip a finger into herself and my cock pounded. "I can't do this. Get the fuck on." She intensified the rubbing of her clit with one hand and slipped a second finger into herself. If I wasn't holding her eyes, I was glued to her hands on her body. I grabbed my dick to alleviate the oncoming blue balls, but she slapped my wrist. "Don't test me, Jennifer."

"I just did."

My attention caught on the rings. She was wearing them again. Thank God, "I think you're forgetting who rules in here," I arched a brow.

She bit her lip and I realized she was getting herself there. I snorted, "No, you don't," I sat up and caught her hair in my fist. She panted harder and I pulled her head back and then sucked her throat. She groaned, and it vibrated in my mouth.

"Don't stop-," she pleaded. She was that close. I seized her wrists in one hand to stop her and she cried out in need. I took her hand and sucked the fingers she had pressed into herself. The sweet taste of her, transferred to my mouth and I growled. She lined my lips and I gently but aggressively snapped and bit the tip then released.

I leveled a look on her, "I said, get on." When she took too long I gave her scalp a slight jerk. She positioned herself over my cock and hovered. "Come down on it."

She rebelliously lowered herself enough to take my head but no more.

"Fuck me or I'll fuck you," I threatened.

She grinned under my grasp, which told me that was exactly what she wanted. I love this woman.

I released her hair, grabbed her hips and forced her down. A scream of pleasure ripped out of her and I fell back with her ass in my hands.

I fucked her as hard as she wanted, staying in control of her but she has an ability to move her pelvis in that damned figure eight that makes me have to think about rainbows to keep from cumming. She dug her nails into my chest like a wildcat and when they dragged over my nipples, I cried out.

I remembered her sexy-ass shoes were still on and held them by the 6inch heels. They were like handlebars and she screamed my name with the new angle they tipped her into. She had to lay chest to chest with me and I held her eyes to bring us higher.

I could feel it again, by the pitch in her voice and the frenzy of her movements she was close. So was I. I don't want this over yet, though. I let go her heels and rolled us again. Now I was on top.

When I pulled out of her, she turned her head and bit my forearm in anger, "Chris, I'm going to seriously kill you! Why?"

"That wasn't very nice," I flipped her onto her stomach and crushed her with my body. "Now, why would I give you anything after that?"

She tried to press up, but I laid my full weight on her and used one hand to restrain her hands in front of us and with the other, I guided my dick against her entrance. She made whiny whimpers that had me biting my lip. She rubbed her ass into it and the smoothness of her back against my chest made me groan.

"Why are you torturing me?" she said into the bedding.

"Because I want to make sure you remember who owns you," with my dick in position, I pulled her hair again, knowing what the sting did to her. "I want to lay claim to all my favorite parts." I dove in and she cried out. I let my hips pump her at that speed that was wild. She stoked to a fire quickly and her silky walls closed in on me, causing my cock to swell. "You own me too…" I licked at her ear and felt her climax. "Always," I went harder and just as her high had ebbed it built a second time.

My body was ready to combust and our sweat mixed to create a sweet vanilla and spice aroma. Her ass being ground into by my hip bones was heaven and I felt her walls grabbing at me again. "Yes," she tried to get her wrists free, but I kept her down. "Fuck, Chris…I can't take it again."

"You don't have a choice," I came up off the bed and she tried to cuss me out, but I wasn't actually trying to tease her, I wanted more. I took her by the hips and dragged her to the edge of the bed. She brought her knees up and looked back, but I shoved her upper body down and put one knee on the bed before plowing into her. She cried big tears when she came this time. I saw tears of passion rolling down her cheeks and I felt her spasms last much longer as I intended.

When I felt mine arriving, I knocked into her until the bed was chipping into the wall. She started to come again but I released into her with a hot blast. Still, hard I put my hand under her and massaged her clit with gentle strokes of my dick until she shuddered in my hand and spent herself a last time. I bent forward and set kisses up her spine.

"I love you," she whispered.

"I love you too…*I guess.*"

Chapter Forty-One
JENZY

*I'*m lying here with my husband, feeling happier than I can recall. We're laying the way we used to. Him on his stomach with his arms folded under his head, and me on top of him with my head lying between his shoulder blades. We're naked and the skin on skin is feeding my soul. I'm tracing his tats with my fingertip. He took my other hand and kissed my fingers.

"Did you mean everything in your letter to Moses?" I asked.

"Every word."

"And the internship…you really wouldn't change the past if you had the chance."

"No, Jenzy, I would still change it."

I tensed over his body and felt like crying. "Oh…"

"I wouldn't have gone to Sweden the first time," he said. My heart inflated. "I would stay here and make more memories with you."

I smiled and hugged his shoulder into my chest, "Will you watch romance movies with me now?"

"Not the sappy ones, but yes."

"Books? What about the *Just Breathe* trilogy by *Martha Sweeney*?"

"Nope," I grumbled but he continued. "I'm busy reading the husband's book."

I gasped, "*Tom Sweeney*? You're reading *The Harem Book*?"

"Yes. You spoiled most of *Just Breathe*."

"What about my holistic alternatives?"

"I like that peppermint thing you did. I can't promise to eat wheatgrass to fix a bullet wound or something, but I'll try your way sometimes. Just don't nag me."

I'm so excited right now my head is spinning, "What about healthy eating?"

"I like those apple fry crisp thingy's."

I kissed his ear, "What about my sloppiness?"

"I'll just whip you when you fall behind on housework or take you to a dark club bathroom and leave you hot for an orgasm."

We laughed, and I nuzzled closer, "Oh! What about babies…? If we have babies and I say I want them born at home…?"

"Well, usually I would say, we'll cross the bridge when we come to it, but after just now you might very well be knocked up." I pulled his earlobe between my teeth and then sucked it as he went on. "As far as the home birth thing… No vagina, no opinion. As long as you're safe, and the baby is safe, you can have it in a barn if you want."

"Hmmm."

"No. That was a joke. No-. Baby, please don't have my kid in a barn."

I laughed, "I'm just toying with you," I assured. He stuffed his face in the pillow. "What about your razors?"

"Fuck."

"Pleeeeease?"

"Just put them back!"

"Deal."

He moved to get up and it feels like lying on a lion. My Leo Lion. I came off him and laid back down. He came over me and kissed my lips, "You can have whatever the fuck you want. Just stay here, make me babies and cook human food on occasion."

I giggled and kissed him back. Then he got up and walked to the closet, naked. I admired his ass. His ass and his back. He looked over his shoulder and laughed, "Didn't have enough yet?"

"It's been a long time. Sorry…"

"Don't be," he pulled on new boxers and came over; kneeling by the bed to kiss me. "My gorgeous wife is a nympho. Every man's dream. I'll just have to fuck and fuck and fuck until I make up the time." I breathed in his kisses and the taste of his tongue. "I'll be back." He went downstairs, and I went to his closet for a shirt. I found a pinstripe white and blue but left it unbuttoned to my navel. Then I went and sprawled on our bed.

He came back with plates of different goodies and wine. He sat against the headboard and I knelt across from him as we ate. Everything tasted amazing but it's because we're together. It's because sex with Chris wakes me up to living.

"Not to be nosey, but what happened to Moses?" he asked.

I winced, "He understood. He said he felt like I always belonged to you. Like he was just guarding me. I hate myself for even trying to date now."

"I made you feel alone…you did what anyone would do."

"What about you?" I didn't really want to know. "You were alone when I left. You didn't do anything to feel…less alone?"

"I masturbated a lot, does that count?"

I laughed and shoved his shoulder, "You're a perv."

"Not really, I used that video of us to do it."

"What video? Oh-." My eyes widened, "You still have *that* in your phone? That was three years ago."

"So? You rode me like a porn star and it's my husbandly right."

"I can't judge. I touched myself while thinking about that time at Rapture Pulse a lot."

"Liked that, then?"

"Aside from the fact that you marked up my skin…yeah."

"It was just to keep you from doing something you'd regret."

I wanted to swat him again, but I already felt bad about Moses.

If I had slept with him, it would be worse, "I guess… if you do it in places people can't see…you could mark me now too."

"I intend to," he drank his wine but watched me over the rim of the glass and my body heated.

"Can you attack me in a public place again?"

"I'll be attacking you in a lot of places," he brought up a chocolate candy and I took a bite. He watched my mouth and when I dropped a small piece between my thighs I felt sloppy and swore. His eyes dropped with it but before I could wipe it…

"I'll get it," he set the wine and the plates on the nightstand and crawled my way.

The chocolate had melted there; he bent his head and lapped it with his skillful tongue. Even after it was clean, he started sliding his tongue further up. I wasn't wearing panties, so when his tongue tickled over my lips and parted them to lick within, I opened my thighs. The chocolate I hadn't finished was melting on my fingers, but I was too hot and too turned on to finish it.

The growl that hummed in his throat, in a steady, long note while he sucked at me made me dig my fingers into his scalp with my free hand.

He rose up on hands and knees to bite the treat out of my grasp and his teeth made wetness pool between my legs. Then he sucked my finger into his mouth, cleaning it before going to the next and the next.

Chris is a master at sex and I learn from him every time, but I think he thinks I'm his equal.

He laid on his stomach in front of me and pushed at my thigh, "Open wider."

I sat straight up on my knees and did as he asked. He rubbed his thumb over my clit and unbuttoned the shirt I wore the rest of the way. "Now touch your tits," I set my two fingers at his lips and he read me and sucked them again. Once they were wet, I cupped my breast and circled the nipple with the fingers he soaked.

He groaned his appreciation of the sight and rubbed quicker. He bit and sucked at the place just under my navel and I moaned and tried to breathe easily so I wouldn't pass out.

"The other one," he demanded, and I switched breasts. He left a nice hickey on my stomach.

While I was busy with that, he rolled onto his back and pushed back, now his head was between my legs.

My husband…he really does own me, he's proving it again right now. We might quarrel and be opposites in most things, but here, in our marriage bed, he's king, and I'm his queen.

He clutched my hips and pressed me down on his face. I heaved with the oncoming tide and he moved his evil hands up to take over the work on my breasts. He was pitching a tent in his boxers but when I tried to lean forward to sixty-nine him, he kept me upright and went harder. Sliding his tongue into my folds and humming for vibration as he gently assaulted my sensitive clit.

Too many orgasms in a day lead to one really Earth-shattering one. I came in his mouth and he cleaned me. Then before I could blink, he was out from under me. He tossed me down on my back and buried himself in my body to bring me to another whirling high and this time he came with me.

He laughed to himself when we were done and held me close in his massive arms.

"What?" I asked.

He stopped but was grinning, "When we met and had sex, I said, *'just tonight'*."

I smiled and burrowed closer, "Silly boy."

"I also had a house to show today."

I stopped, "Oh my God."

"Oh, well. I feel sick…guess I should call in."

"That's bad Karma. You'll really get sick."

He rolled his eyes, "No, it's not!"

"Yes, it is."

"Shut up."

"You'll see-," he tickled my side until I cried, and I lost control and a will to debate. Besides, I don't want him to move. Not ever.

Months Later

Well, here we are...on track and when I say, 'on track,' I mean we fight a *lot*. However, there's an upside, we fuck a lot too. Usually, we start with the fighting, like foreplay. Then we remember what it was like to almost lose each other and one of us folds to apologize. Then we make love like we're trying to collide into one being.

    Today as I serve him sushi in our kitchen, I feel very good about us. We grew up, I think. We aren't going to always like each other. He's an arrogant, asshole and I'm a flaky bitch. The love outweighs that, though.

    "This is great," he said around a mouthful of sushi. "This is...awesome!"

    "Really?" I came up behind him and hugged his neck then kissed his cheek, "You really like it?"

    "Almost as much as that sundress," he reached back to tug my dress. "Still, prefer naked, though."

    Yes, he noticed me again. All the time. I never dolled up for no reason anymore, it was fantastic. I don't even have to doll up, yesterday he caught me doing yoga in the banged-up parlor. Downward dog is a must try I never considered.

    "Maybe I should take off the dress and *feed* you the sushi..." I suggested.

    "Maybe you should," he took another bite.

    I rubbed his shoulders and kissed his jaw.

    "This really is great! You made this? With organic stuff? You're amazing," he fawned.

    "I didn't make it, babe I bought it."

    He stalled and dropped his chopsticks, "Where?"

    I frowned, "The grocery store. They sell it there now."

    He bugged his eyes and spit it into his napkin, "Oh my God, Jenzy!"

    "What?"

"You don't buy sushi from a grocery store! Are you trying to kill me?"

"Don't be such a snob! You just said it was good."

"You can't trust raw fish-," he squeaked.

"You're just saying that because it's healthy."

"Not if it has fucking bacteria!"

"Fine," I took his plate and threw it in the sink. "Never mind, you prick!"

"What the hell's wrong with you?"

"They make it right there in front of you," I argued.

He made an incredulous face, "So if they chop rat there, you'll eat it as long as you can see it?"

I started the dishes, "Want to borrow a tampon, Chrissy?"

"I'm not being unreasonable here. It's called research! Nobody eats raw fish if they don't know the source. Take your head out of the damn clouds and check shit sometimes."

I sprayed him in the face with the sink sprayer and cocked my brow like to say, '*yeah...I did it...fuck you.*'

"Really?" he snarled.

"Yeah."

"Okay."

I turned back to the dishes and tried to work the hot anger coursing through me. Then I felt him pin me to the sink with his body but before I could react he pulled the sprayer and squirted it down the inside of my dress. Cold water shocked my front and I screamed bloody murder. I tried to wrestle it from him, but we ended up spraying half the kitchen and each other.

As a last resort, I whipped it from him, turned and squirted it down his pants.

He yelled, "Fuuuuuuuck," at the cold and I laughed my ass off at his horror-filled expression.

"Oh, it's funny?" he asked. I couldn't answer because I was bent way over, laughing. "You think giving me literal blue balls is funny? That was ice water." I still laughed until he got that look in his eyes.

"Okay," I tried to dry my eyes. "Sorry, I'm sorry."

He turned me around and bent me over the sink. He kicked my legs apart and shoved my upper body down further.

Anger turned to mirth, which turned to sexual arousal. My stomach came alive with butterflies and I rubbed my ass into his groin.

"Admit you're wrong," he demanded in my ear.

I fought a giggle and decided I would rather infuriate him to a fuck. "Nope, and don't touch me, snob." I pressed my rear back further in contradiction of my words.

He whipped the short skirt of my dress up and trailed his fingertips down my ass cheek, "I'll touch you where I want when I want, you're mine, remember?" He yanked my panties down my legs and held my hips tight. "We order pizza, those are my terms."

I laughed but then bit my lip, "No, we eat what I served."

Chris jerked the tie on the halter top of my sundress behind my neck and pulled the front down. The coolness of the sink, and the ice water he sprayed me with, and the strength in his touch all made my nipples pucker out.

"One more chance, Jenzy. I'm not an ice cream truck of chances."

Oh, it was hard not to laugh at that one, "Whatever, we eat what I made, asshole."

He shoved me forward again since I moved and then I felt and heard him opening his belt and the front of his pants. He leaned over me to bite my shoulder then licked the same spot before reaching around to grasp my breast and rub the nipple between his fingers, sending an involuntary orgasm to my sex. Hearing me moan tipped him off and he slipped his other hand into my folds and pushed his fingers inside me.

He hummed the word, "Hmm," then I felt his cock pressing. "This feels like it's been served warm…and ready…" he used my wetness on his fingers to slicken my clit. "Maybe I *should* eat in?"

"Chris, come on, stop playing and…" I thrust my hips back to make my point.

"I'm not giving you anything until you fold. I could have my way, use your body and just zip up my pants; leaving you in misery."

His other hand was still tweaking and pinching at my nipple. I can't fight all this, those words. When he used the head of his dick to line the lips of my sex I groaned.

"Okay! Alright! I fold now do me."

"Pizza?"

"Yes, I don't give a shit just do me."

"And I was right, no raw fish from-."

"Chris!"

He shoved into me and I closed my eyes because it felt so amazing. He took me that way, banging my hips into the sink and holding my hips to drill deeper. Over and over he buried himself in me.

Then when we came, he withdrew and held me to him. Safe and bonded ever more than before.

"Go order," I said.

"I did it last time."

"You were the one that wanted pizza."

He jabbed me with his finger in my side and knowing it was a tickle spot, I leaped away and held up my dress front.

"Sorry babe, what now?" he asked.

"It's not funny, Chris I'll laugh too hard. I can't breathe when I laugh that hard."

He shrugged, "Shouldn't have sassed," he said as he zipped his pants, but his boner was returning and so was my turn on.

"Don't, you have that look. I hate tickling. I hate it."

"You have three seconds."

"Chris, wait!"

"Time's up."

I bolted, and he took off after me. All through the kitchen, living room, guest bed, then up the stairs and into our room, where he showed me why this fight, like all the others coming, didn't stand a chance at breaking us again.

~Bonus Chapter~
CHRIS
March 2009

When I decided to make Jenzy my wife, I went straight to my mom first. She was so in approval that she looked down at her left hand and gently pulled the diamond from her finger.

I frowned and asked what she was doing. Her answer was to put the ring in my palm and close my fist around it, "I want you to give this to Jenzy."

"No, Ma, I can't. This is the ring dad gave you."

"That's why I want you to give her this one. I loved your dad more than any man in this world. I did love your stepdad, but no two loves are the same." She wrapped her hand around my knuckles and tears started to fill her eyes. "It also feels right because your dad would be so proud of you. If you do this, it will be like he's with you. I adore Jenzy and I can't think of a better gift."

"Why didn't you…?" I struggled with this a little. "Are you sure you don't want Todd to have it for Mandy, Ma? They were engaged first."

"Todd and Mandy have a ring that suits them very well and even though you don't remember, you had two years with your father before he died. Todd never laid eyes on him. You are the son he knew about and you are also the oldest. It's yours by birthright."

I opened my hand to look at it. I know how much my mother cherishes this ring. It was in my dad's family for ages and even when mom remarried, she never took it off, she just moved it to her right hand.

As we stood there in her kitchen, I imagined Jenzy wearing it. I saved a lot of money to go to Sweden for the internship but once I realized I was staying, I was going to put that money toward her engagement ring. Now I would only have to have the ring sized and cleaned.

"Unless you think she would hate it," mom questioned when I was quiet too long.

"Are you kidding? She lives for antiques. This thing is over one-hundred years old, isn't it?"

She nodded with that look mom's get when they know they just saved your life. "Then you'll take it, yeah?"

I stared at the ring, "Would dad like Jenzy too?" I tried to imagine a father figure telling me to go for it or avoid it, but Mom always played both roles fairly well.

"Your dad would have been fascinated by her."

"Yeah?"

"Oh, yeah, he loved hippies, his closest friend was a hippie," she laughed. "He would think she was exactly what you needed. Jenzy belongs in our family. Trust me, Jenzy earned your dad's stamp of approval."

That was a weird way to say it. Jenzy never knew my dad. What would make mom say that?

I smiled and rubbed her arm instead of asking, "Thanks, mom."

She hugged me. The sappy hug I hate but I let her do it because I'm honestly a little terrified. Jenzy is a free spirit and I'm not sure that she will accept what I'm offering.

Three weeks later, I was driving her to her parent's house from campus after her classes. Over the last few years, while Todd and Jenzy were friends, our families have woven together. Since she and I met, I became a part of that weave. Her dad loves me. He legit, thinks I'm the best thing since the wheel and her mom is so cool.

Now we can have a free weekend. No work for me and no classes for her.

She doesn't know it, but in my duffle, is the ring and I keep going into long silences, rehearsing how to ask her.

"Chris?" she called my name and I turned my head her way for a second before returning my attention to the road. "You seem really quiet, what are you thinking about?"

I shook my head, "Nothing."

"Guess what?"

"What?"

"I have a surprise for you while we're at mom and dad's, I'm the best girlfriend ever and you will love me until I die."

I smiled because whatever she did can't equal up to what I have planned. "What is it?"

"It's a surprise," she repeated.

"Does Todd know? Because if Todd knows I can squeeze it out of him."

"Nope, only your mother knows, and she knows how to keep a secret."

True story.

Her mom and dad live in a three-story home out in the suburbs, built like a perfectly modern paradise. There's a big Japanese garden in the backyard and a stone wall surrounds the property. Todd and Mandy were already there, so was my mom. I carried our stuff into the house and was immediately caught up by Scotty. He took me down into the den. I forced Todd to come with us, which made Jenzy arch her brow.

I usually exclude Todd because he's more a woman than a man, but I shrugged as I grabbed my duffle, "Guy time," I told her and shoved Todd forward behind Scotty.

Jenzy watched us leave suspiciously but then our moms and Mandy pulled her into their chatterbox and hen house known as the kitchen.

"Chris," Scotty told me as we made it to the last step downstairs. "Show me how to set up this widescreen thing. I don't get it, you're smart, you do it."

I waited until we were all in the den and then shut the door, locking it for good measure.

"I can help too," Todd said rolling up his sleeves.

"No thanks," Scotty waved him off. "Last time I asked for your help was with the futon and the damn thing closed up on me like a Venus's Flytrap."

"Guys," I threw my bag down on one of the desks and faced them. "I have something big to tell you."

"You have an STD," Todd joked.

"Shut, up," I glared and bounced my eyes between Scotty and him. Did he forget we are in the same room as the guy whose daughter I'm dating? You can't throw around words like STD. Dumb fuck.

"Uh, sorry," Todd coughed.

After Scotty and I were done staring at him, I went on. "I uh… so…" I dug out the little, crushed, velvet box with the ring inside but then stopped. Maybe I should explain first. "Um…" I looked at her dad. "I know we don't live in the seventeen hundreds or anything but… I really think highly of you and… you're really cool, I mean... I like hanging out. So... I wanted to ask you first... you might say no."

Scotty laughed a little as he put his hands in his pockets, "You either wanna borrow money or marry my daughter," then he laughed again like it was all so funny, and I started to sweat bullets.

He stopped when I didn't say anything and just looked at me blankly.

Oh, shit.

"No fucking way," Todd said in a huff.

I just kept watching Scotty. I can't tell if he wants to agree or jump the desk and pull my lips off.

"My Jenzy?" Scotty asked.

I swallowed and picked up the box. My hands kept shaking, it was awful, "Y-yeah, I have... um... I want to ask here, around everyone she cares about but, but I wanted to-."

"You asking me?" he asked. "You didn't ask her yet? You comin' to me first?"

I nodded.

Long, horrid pause.

He came my way, but I couldn't read his face, so I felt my eyes bug out. Scotty is a big dude and Jenzy is pretty much his reason for existing, so this really could go either way.

After he went around the desk, Scotty held my eyes like he was trying to read behind them. It was a tense minute.

"You askin' me to marry my baby girl?" he asked again.

"Yeah..."

He grabbed my shoulder and frowned but then he patted my cheek, "Welcome to the family, son."

I felt sucker punched with breath. He hugged me. It was weird, but it felt great. Acceptance.

"Does this mean yes?" I said over his shoulder.

"Hell yes, it does," he pulled me back to look at me, "Absolutely."

I grinned until I saw Todd by the door. I narrowed one eye at him, "You good with it?" I questioned.

He raised his brows, "Why are you asking *me*?"

"You're her best friend."

He turned womanly.

"Don't look at me like that," I whined. "You are such a pussy. I'm not trying to be all sentimental. I'm just acknowledging that you matter to her."

"You're a dick, but this is awesome, and you definitely have my okay."

I showed them the ring and they hovered around me to look at it. Todd didn't act frustrated or wounded by the fact that mom gave it to me. Maybe he finally realized I'm the favorite.

When we finished in the den and were headed up the steps I threatened Todd with his life and a wedgey that would put all over wedgies to shame. He was not to tell a soul not even Mandy. Before I could leave, Scotty called me back inside.

I set my back to the door and watched Scotty pocket his hands again, "While we're alone," he began. "I wanna ask… all this talk about marriage… I know you were close to your stepdad, but it sounds like he's not active in your life."

I felt unsettled in my chest at the mention of fathers, but I answered anyway, "After he and mom divorced, he kept up but by the time I was in college he and I didn't stay connected as often. I think Todd talks to him more than I do."

"Well, I only brought it up because I want ya to know that you can come to me about anything. I like you apart from your connection to Jenzy. And what you did today," he lifted his chin at my duffle. "Coming to me first, you got my blessing. I want you to know that."

I needed to know that. He didn't realize how much it mattered.

We rejoined the rest of the family and I let my nerves settle. One look at Jenzy and all my doubts evaporate.

JENZY

On the way to mom and dad's, Chris was quiet. Too quiet. It worried me. When we first got into the car, he was carefree and goofy. We blasted music that we love (we love all the same music) all up and down the highway. *Metro Station's Shake it* was on at least four times. We screamed the lyrics until we were hoarse, and we shared road snacks.

He held my hand most the way or he would place mine over his strong thigh. Sometimes he just stared at me during traffic or at stoplights. He was always finding reasons to touch me; my hair, my legs, my upper arm.

Chris was alive with energy and was making me laugh so hard that I cried most my mascara off, but the closer we got to our destination the more inward he became. He didn't seem angry, just off. He's been off for weeks.

As soon as we arrived, he disappeared with my dad, but he brought Todd too. They were down there a fair amount of time and while they were gone I enjoyed Mandy, mom, and Nona.

"What's the matter with you?" my mom asked in front of the others. I was pulling at my lip while we all gathered on the sofa looking at a magazine with hot pictures of Johnny Depp. But I wasn't looking, I was frowning while I thought about Chris.

"Me?" I asked.

"Yeah," Mandy nodded, "You do look a little weird."

"I'm fine."

Nona shut the magazine, "No, they're right, you look upset."

"I'm not," I tried to think up a lie, but none came. "I'm…" I flicked my hair back, it was suddenly annoying. "It's not a big deal, I'm just thinking."

"About what?" mom pressed. "Your aura is a dishonest color."

I bit my lip.

Mandy tilted her head, "Is it school?"

I shook my head, no.

"Is it that bitch that debated with you about global warming at the beach?" Mandy tried again. "Because I put a crab in her purse. Justice is served."

"I think..." I took a breath and then whispered, "I think Chris is acting funny."

Nona sat up straight and drank the glass of water in her hand rather quickly.

"How so?" asked mom.

"Well," I checked over my shoulder but when the den door is closed, you can't hear a thing from the room. If it's open the acoustics carry. I can't hear the guys, so it must be closed. "He's been... kinda needy."

"Chris?" Mandy arched her brow. "Pervy Chris?"

I tried to explain, "He says, I love you to me about everything. All I did was tell him his phone rang while he was brushing his teeth one morning, and he was all, '*that's why I love you, so attentive. I love you, Jenzy,*' yes, he said that. I told him that I forgot to mail a letter, he took it and goes, '*I'll do it because I love you. I love you so much, Jenzy even when you're forgetful.*' It was a *bill,* guys. When I forget to mail bills, he would be capable of clubbing kittens, not telling me I'm cute. Plus, he's always jumping up to do stuff. He never sits still, he sits with or near me everywhere we go, and he even watched a crapload of Disney movies with me last week. Didn't even complain."

"Ew," Mandy grimaced, "It's like invasion of the body snatchers."

My mom sat forward, "Maybe he just feels like connecting."

"But mom," I shook my head. "Chris isn't a clingy guy. He's also asking me weird things." I tried to recall some of them. "He asked me where I saw myself in five years? If I still plan to stay in school. He asked if I would stay and finish school even if I got pregnant? Why I wanted kids one day? He asked if we could survive on one salary. That got me thinking..."

Nona stayed quiet but kept itching random parts of her body.

"Oh, my God," Mandy guessed it. "He's gonna break-up with you, that little douche canoe!"

I felt my stomach knot up, "I'm starting to wonder."

Nona waved her hand at us, "No, no, no, stop it. He's not… he would tell me. He would say something and honey, he really, really loves you."

"But," I couldn't help the doubt. "What if he wishes he went to Sweden? We've been living together in an apartment off campus that we both love, so why ask if we could live off one salary unless…"

Mandy followed my thoughts, "Unless he's planning to leave you. He wants to know you won't be poor and evicted. He also sounds worried he'll knock you up before graduation. That will probably be his excuse to call it off."

Hearing Mandy voice my fears was awful.

"Honey," my mom held my hand. "You're stressed out and stress makes people overthink."

"Exactly!" Nona all but screamed it at me. "You can't overthink. Chris is very committed to this relationship. *Very* committed."

I eyed her.

"The surprise I have for him," I whispered again. "I'm giving it to him tomorrow. Maybe it's too much right now."

Nona shook her head, "Jenzy, you can't go back on it. What you have planned, he needs now more than ever."

"Why?" I asked her.

She hesitated, "Just trust me on it, honey?"

Before I could say, I heard the guys coming, "Alright. Just don't tell him what I said."

"You should do something to unwind," mom stood up and beckoned me, "Come on, upstairs."

"For what?"

"Some relaxation." She motioned to the steps. "Off your tushy, let's go."

When Chris came upstairs I saw only love in his eyes, but then I saw a little nervousness. I smiled at him before following mom upstairs.

CHRIS

Alright, it's go time. I have the ring, I have the balls, and I have the location. I texted Jenzy an hour ago to meet me in the Japanese garden. It feels like she's been avoiding me since we came here. She was upstairs for a long time with the women and then she came down for dinner in a weird stupor.

I walked a slow circle around one of the smaller trees in their yard and tried to breathe. When I heard her coming out the back door, my brain went there. It asked me that question I had not allowed it to ask since I decided to do this.

What if she says no?

"Hey, babe," I said so she would know where I was.

Jenzy tripped down the last step but recovered and walked my way. There was something odd about her gait; slow, sloppy, incapable of staying straight. "Hi!" she said in a low voice; she drew out the 'I' like it was a million 'es'. "You look so good," she laughed a little and fell into my chest.

I caught her and bent to see her face, "What's making you so happy?" I held her to me and assessed her reaction.

"I feel…" she squinted until it looked like she was hurting herself. "I feel…enlightened."

"About?"

"About… love…" she wrapped her arms around my neck. "I've been… really… concerned about… us…"

I paled, "Why?"

"Because I was overthinking it. I mean," she held the front of my shirt and pressed herself closer, "I wanna love you. And… and treat you right. Everyday… and every night…"

"You do that already."

"We'll be together with… the, the roof over our head, same room…"

"Are you quoting Bob Marley lyrics?"

She looked off into the distance, "He's so deep. So, deep. He's like… like a… black Jesus."

I pursed my lips, "Are you feeling okay?"

Her big eyes shifted on me, becoming giant orbs of innocence, "Chris, if Bob shot the sheriff and not the deputy… who shot the deputy?"

I opened my mouth to ask again if she was alright, "Um…" I tried but then I got lost in her eyes. I love when she's like this, all girl, maybe a little less woman. She hasn't seen as much of the world as I have, and she might be sexually adventurous, but she was naive everywhere else. It brings out this sleeping bear in my chest.

"I love you," I blurted.

"Awe," she held my face with both hands. "You've said that over three-hundred-twenty times this month."

"You counted?"

"I know what you want to tell me," she nodded more to herself. "And… and… it's okay… if…" she was crying.

I started to feel terrified, "Hey," I forced her to look at me, "Baby, don't cry. I can't handle it when you do that. Talk to me. You knew? You know what I want to tell you? Did Todd tell you?"

"Todd knows?" she sniffed. "Oh, God. I feel so stupid. You probably felt like telling me forever ago and you held off, afraid I would react like… *this*!"

I laughed and nodded, "Yeah, I think every man worries his girl will react like this. I don't want to make you cry. I don't want you to feel like you have to agree. I just, can't keep living day-to-day like I'm satisfied with how things are. I need more, I need you to-."

"I know!" She buried her face in her hands. "I love you, so much, you are everything to me, but I totally get you need to do this."

I froze, "Well, I don't need to do it, I want to do it. Do you want me to do it?"

"No!" she yelled it at me. "Why on Earth would you think I want you to do it? I've never been this happy in my life. I love how things are with us, but I want you to be happy..." she couldn't get the rest out. "Obviously I'll do it if I *have* to."

I felt stabbed in the heart by her words. She didn't want me to propose. She felt like she had to say yes? Maybe I should feel let off the hook but instead, I feel totally deflated. Why doesn't she want to be mine?

"Okay..." I stood a little straighter. "Then... I won't ask." I rubbed the back of my neck and then I got mad. "I need a better reason, though."

The twinkling lights were making her look angelic and her hair was a softer red than brown.

She held herself, "I don't think there's a way for me to not be in love with you, Chris. If we break-up, I don't think I would make a whole person by myself."

My heart took big painful thumps of joy, "That's how I feel too," I held the back of her neck. "I feel like I need you to do anything, everything. You..." I stopped and frowned. "Why would we break-up?"

"I don't know, but you want to and I... I need..." she started to cry. "No woman, no cry..."

Jesus, more Bob Marley.

"Jenzy, I'm not breaking up with you, I think we've been on separate pages. I'm trying to marry you."

Her head came up and she looked at me, dazed for a long time. "Me?"

"You. I want you. I want you forever. I want a house and kids, and maybe if you promise not to get ten, maybe *one* dog. I want..."

I heard the back door to the house open and close, so I realized I needed to hurry before anyone interrupted us. I slipped to one knee near the roses and reached for the ring in my back pocket, "Jennifer-."

"Stop!" Mandy shouted.

We both looked but by the time I turned my head, Mandy sprung and threw her whole body against me, knocking me to the ground like a football player. The box went flying.

"What the hell are you doing?" I bellowed.

"Stop! Listen to me!" She hissed in an urgent whisper. "You can't do this tonight."

"What?" I moved under her, "why? How do you know what I'm about to do?"

"Todd just told me, Chris, you can't."

"I'm going to break his face."

"I love seeing you guys hugging," Jenzy smiled with fog in her eyes. "So beautiful. Love is..." we waited forever for her to stop blinking and then she said. "Love just is."

"We aren't hugging, she's pinning me," I growled. "With her airbag tits."

Mandy used her eyes to point at Jenzy in code, "You can't do *this tonight...*"

"Why?" I snapped.

"Because she's high as fuck, that's why. Didn't you notice, stupid? Her mom served up some fresh cannabis upstairs to chill her out. I also think she could do better than you, but the point is that she's high."

I looked up at Jenzy and it all made sense, "Damn."

"Yeah," Mandy stood, deliberately kneeing me in the nuts on her way up and smiled at Jenzy, "How are you, honey?" she asked her.

"Chris loves me," Jenzy held her chest in admiration. "He wants to get married one day, then we can die together..." she turned serious. "We're gonna die someday. We'll be married dead people."

"That's a morbid turn," I muttered. "Maybe I should get you to bed," I said more cheerily, swiping up the open ring box. I pocketed it discreetly.

"Maybe sleep is death practice," Jenzy told me. "Maybe if you never sleep you never die because you didn't practice."

I looked at Mandy.

Mandy shrugged.

Yeah, my girlfriend is high.

I went to Jenzy, "Come here," I offered my back and she climbed on, piggyback-style. "To bed," I ordered.

"Okay," she snuggled into the back of my neck, "Thank you for not breaking up with me."

"I can't break-up with you," I said as we walked to the house. "Silly little hippie girl."

When we went inside everyone almost yelled congrats. Mandy signaled to them not to and I carefully took Jenzy upstairs. After lowering her into bed, I started to take off her shoes. She was already almost gone.

"How could you think I wanted to break-up?" I asked her.

She didn't answer because she was falling in and out.

I knelt on the bed and unbuttoned her jeans next; tuging them down her thighs, "You must be really, really high, to think I could do that," I pressed a kiss to her hipbone.

"Mmm," she hummed.

I peeled off her top and whispered over her lips, "I've just been scared. I'm not scared in moments like this one, though."

She stroked my arms in her stupor, "You want to marry you."

"I want to marry *you*."

"You want to wife me..."

I reached under her back, between her spine and the mattress, to unsnap her bra, "Yes," I pulled the straps down her arms and kissed her nose. "But don't answer me right now. I'll do better asking tomorrow."

Jenzy opened her eyes and gazed at me sleepily, "I have something for you. It's a secret. Shhh..."

"Okay," I kissed her lips and she brought her hips up to mine.

"No, not tonight, you need to sleep," I told her.

"Don't you want me tonight?"

"I want you every night for the rest of my life."

JENZY

I woke up feeling warm and safe. Chris was sleeping on his stomach and I was laying across his back. His skin gave off this delicious scent that made me blush. My big Leo lion. My bare chest to his bare back, the heat, the safety.

Then last night came rushing into my mind. Did Chris break-up with me? No. Marriage. I remember the word 'marry'. I looked at my left hand, but it was empty. Hadn't he knelt at one point?

I shook my head and pressed kisses to his shoulders. We didn't break-up, I remember him saying that was not his plan. I remembered my surprise and jumped up.

"Hey," Chris rolled to his side and watched me tie up my hair, so I could shower. "Get back in here." His voice was groggy from sleep.

"I have to get something…ready…" I winked and then left to get in the shower.

He rolled onto his back and put a pillow over his face to sleep more.

After my shower, I sought out Nona and we started preparing my gift.

Last night was a blur but I feel better. I feel sure.

CHRIS

"You can't even propose right," Todd taunted.

I looked at him from across the dining room table, "Shut up, booger."

He smiled over his coffee.

"What exactly happened? Cold feet?" asked Scotty. He was behind us, frying bacon. A mountain of bacon.

I shook my head, "No, your wife had her tripping to Bob Marley."

Scotty rolled his eyes, "Edna and that damn weed stash of hers. She thinks it cures everything."

"Jenzy thought I was trying to break-up with her," I told them. "So, the whole time I was talking she thought I was doing the opposite of a proposal."

Todd laughed.

I gave him a death-glare.

"It's all good," Scotty served me a plate of bacon with nothing else because menfolk don't need other food groups. "It will all work itself out."

Todd tried to take a slice off my plate, but I stabbed him with my fork.

"Owe!"

"No touchy," I took a giant bite of *my* bacon.

Scotty defended me, "Todd, don't. The man needs his strength for tonight." Scotty looked down at me, "Try again this evening. I'll lock up Edna's pot."

"I don't know…" I sighed. "What if it was a sign? Maybe it's too soon. Jenzy likes freedom."

"You can't bow out now," Todd argued.

"You told Mandy," I realized I hadn't made him pay for that yet. "What part of 'secret' confused you?"

"It was a mistake!" He said around a mouthful of Scotty's pancakes. "Like your conception. I was planned," he told me, pointing his fork in my direction.

"You want to taste floor?"

"I did you a favor," he argued. "If I hadn't told Mandy, you would be engaged to a space cowgirl with a fuzzy recollection of the biggest day in her life."

I put my elbows on the table and rubbed my hands together. I wish I had someone to talk to that wasn't my brother or her father. I love them both but… I considered calling Todd and I's stepdad, but that feels weird. We don't talk enough. I want solid advice from… I don't know.

Later in the day, I talked to my boss on the phone. I have found my knack as a realtor. My commission has kept us afloat and my boss bounces ideas off me like an equal. Maybe I should ask his advice? No. Just because he's old enough to be my dad, he isn't.

I sat long ways on the couch with a *Men's Fitness* magazine and my earbuds in listening to *I Got a Pocket- Got a Pocket- Full of Sunshine* (don't judge). I was turning the page when Jenzy held both hands over my eyes from behind.

"Guess what?" she said excitedly.

"What?"

"You can have your surprise now."

I laid my head back on the arm of the sofa and looked up at her, "Cool." There it goes again. My heart is doing flips because she's close.

I pulled my buds out and reached back, over my head to grasp her hips, "Spiderman kiss…"

She giggled before bending to kiss me upside-down. I made it lengthy because I feel like my logic and my heart are constantly at war, and the only time they call a truce is when she's touching me.

She tastes like spearmint and Carmel.

I stood, and she led me to the guestroom my mom was staying in. Mom was bringing up her blinds on the window as we stepped in and the television was on, reflecting a blank blue screen. Below it was a giant antique, "Is that a VCR?" I asked them.

Jenzy made me sit at the edge of mom's bed and dropped down next to me, "Yes," she said. "My gift has two parts. The first is this one," she pivoted, and mom handed her a big flat book. There was a picture of a firetruck on the front.

"A book?" I asked, curious.

"Not just a book, a scrapbook," Jenzy shifted to face me and Mom stood to her side with an expression that said she was holding back a bucketload of feels. That alone made me uncomfortable. "Last month, was your real dad's birthday and that got me thinking. You've admitted that you feel cheated about him being gone. Maybe a little guilty that you don't remember him."

"I feel guilty too," Mom said. "Jason… your dad… he didn't like pictures, and this was obviously before cameras were right there on our phones. I had nothing to give you and Todd. All I could tell you is that you look very much like him, but I know that wasn't enough."

"That's okay," I retreated a little from the conversation. "I know all that."

"But," Jenzy sat up more. "I decided to do some digging. Your mom told me your dad was a volunteer fireman in a county up north where they met. Once I looked up the county, I found the station, and once I had the station, your mom and I drove up there…"

Mom held Jenzy's shoulder, "Jenzy thought of something I never did. By going back to his old station, we found out they had a scrapbook of the gang, from the year your dad was active. There's only a few pictures in there," she tapped the scrapbook, "but Jenzy kept asking around. She found something…" Mom started to cry, and it made my hair stand on end. "Something lost, that I didn't even remember…"

Her voice broke so she stopped.

I don't know why I flee emotions like I do, but now I'm burning with curiosity all while needing to get out of this room. Jenzy touched my back and made soothing circles with her palm, "Your dad had a best friend named Todd. Yeah, he named your brother after him. He was a Fire Captain. They were so close that when your dad moved away with your mom to southern California, they stayed in touch. Your dad sent him something a year before he died, and he was glad to pass it back to you."

I rubbed my knees and got out the word, "Okay," but in an apprehensive way.

Jenzy looked at mom and then got a big remote from the nightstand. She sat back down near me and held the remote to her lips, "I could have gotten it put on DVD, but I was afraid something could happen to the VHS in the process. I couldn't risk it. That's why I'm using a VCR."

I nodded and looked at the screen as she pushed play.

All those Stone Age sounds came rumbling and clicking from the player. It sounded like a hungry electronic beast. Then the screen turned to that old snow, made of black and gray before it evened out. There was a yard and it was filled with sunshine and vibrant green grass. The fence looked familiar but distantly. When whoever was holding the camera turned it, you could see a ton of fanfare. Big balloons were tied to tables and the support beams of a house. There was a long table of gifts wrapped in colorful paper, a kitty-pool, sandbox, cake; it was a birthday party. The film cut to black but when it came back on, the yard was full of people and babies.

I heard my mom's voice behind the camera, she was thanking someone for recording the party.

I crossed my arms to keep out my vulnerability. I don't know where this is going but I sense it's going to throw me for a loop.

In the next clip, a guy that looked eerily like me walked past with a baby in his arms, "Hey!" The guy holding the camera whistled. "Jason!"

I swallowed.

The camera jiggled all around while the guy ran to catch up to my dad, "Stop being such a scaredy-cat! It's just a camera!"

"Do *not*, put that in my face," my dad warned in a voice so similar to mine that I got goosebumps.

"Who do you think you are avoiding the lens? Tom Cruise? I'm not the paparazzi. Come on! Do it for the boys at the station," the guy bargained.

My dad sighed as the camera swung up to his face and then zoomed out, so we could see most of him. He was still holding a baby. "Fine," he tried not to smile. "What's up?"

"No one has seen your son yet because you moved to the middle of nowhere," the guy teased.

My dad laughed and then held up the baby, "Hi, everyone, this is my son, Christopher. As you can see, he's as perfect as I am."

Some people in the background laughed and I stood up. I don't know why. It's not like it will help me hear better or see better but my eyes feel glued to the television. I've never seen my dad and yet, here he is holding me and moving and breathing.

"Hey, little buddy," the guy holding the camera said before grabbing my toes.

My dad held me up higher, "Chris, say hi," dad prompted me. He waved my hand at the camera before putting his mouth in my neck and blowing raspberries to get me to laugh. "Chris is," he stopped to adjust me in his arms, "One-year-old today," he told the camera. "One," he then told me and held up a finger.

"How do you like being a dad?" one of the people passing by asked him. It was a woman with very frizzy hair to fit the 80's.

"Hey, Barbra. I love it, I plan to keep doing it," he teased.

"Maybe a girl next time," camera guy suggested.

"Nah, I want all boys. If you have boys, they grow up to love girls, then you can have daughters. If I had daughters of my own, I would get neurotic," he laughed.

I studied everything about my dad's features. Mom wasn't lying, the differences are subtle. Otherwise, we appear almost as twins.

"What about married life?" camera guy asked as a younger version of my mom came to put her chin on my dad's shoulder. "Any regrets? How's the ol' ball and chain?"

Mom laughed in the video, but she wasn't laughing now. Her eyes were overflowing with tears. She's always been pretty to me. She's pretty in this time capsule video too.

"Fear is stupid, so are regrets," said dad.

"Marylin Monroe," mom said in the video before kissing his cheek and then mine. "She said that once…"

"I guess that means you aren't moving back to work at the station again," camera guy sighed dramatically. "Nona, you ruined him."

Mom laughed again in the video and hid her blushing face behind dad's shoulder, "Sorry guys."

Dad bounced me in his arms, "I don't wanna risk not seeing this guy get bigger than me."

"You say that like fighting fires is dangerous or something," the guy teased.

"Right," dad grinned. "He's smarter than other babies," he explained, swaying with me. "He passed all his milestones. The ones in that book… very smart kid."

"Jason!" Mom growled and poked his side since there were quite a few babies my age at the party.

"He is," dad defended. "He has my eyes too, but Nona's brain."

The video steered away from dad and became more about the party and when it ended, the screen went to snow again.

And there it was. I wanted a sign, advice…

And I got it.

From my dad.

The person I wanted it from.

Fear is stupid, so are regrets.

Mom hugged me, and I squeezed her. I don't know what it's like to lose the love of your life. I don't really know what it's like to lose a father either, I was too young to understand.

But I can remember December when I made Jenzy feel like I didn't want her, and she disappeared on me. I remember that void. I don't want that again.

When mom let me go I grabbed up Jenzy. I think I said, thank you, but the word seems so small and unable to carry the weight of what I mean. Now I know why mom said that Jenzy already won dad's stamp of approval.

All this…

She's *the one*.

JENZY

I've never seen Chris that emotional. He kept thanking me, kept kissing me, kept telling me how much this meant to him. It was worth every sleepless night of research and investigation.

After dinner, we all went into the living room to chill. I was about to sit down when a mighty roar erupted in the kitchen, where Dad, Todd, and Chris were all clearing the table for the girls.

"SON OF A BITCH!" Chris hollered.

All of us frowned at each other.

"Chris?" Nona called. "What's the matter with you?"

"Nothing, MOM!" his voice went so high he sounded like a girl.

I stood up and went to see, but Todd blocked me from the kitchen, "Hey, bestie, what do you want? What's up?"

I tried to see past him, "Chris sounds pissed."

"He stubbed his toe. It was bad. He's just trying not to cry."

I nodded, "Can I see him?"

"Nope." He shook his head, "He's got a big ego, he doesn't want you to see him crying."

I heard the back-door slam shut and crossed my arms, "What's wrong with him?"

"Haven't you ever stubbed your toe, Jenzy? It fucking, hurts. He needs a minute."

CHRIS

I LOST it. I LOST my mother's ring. I can't propose without it and I can't face my mother without it. I took it from my back pocket in the kitchen to check on it and the box was empty.

Scotty implored me to retrace my steps, but I couldn't think of a time I was lax with it. Then I realized that when Mandy tackled me to save me from declaring myself to a high girlfriend, the box went flying. It must have come out. I left the house to crawl around in the yard in search of the ring. There wasn't enough light, so Scotty brought out two flashlights and helped me look.

My head is spinning and for just a second, I wondered if this too was a sign. I felt so sure after the video that if Dad was looking out for me, he wanted me to make this move with Jenzy, but now…

I checked between every blade of grass where the ring box fell but nothing glimmered or caught my eye. It was just gone. An heirloom that was in my dad's family for over a century was gone. I had been on all fours near the place Mandy tackled me by the roses, but I sat back on my knees to take a breath. I screwed this all up.

"Chris," Scotty said from somewhere to my left. "Now, don't give up. It's out here. We just gotta look. You gotta put on your head. Think. Where else can we look?"

I shook my head, "I don't know." I stared at the red roses in front of me. "I wish there was a better way to know I'm not fucking everything up."

"Ask for a shooting star or a billboard, or a miracle…" he checked a patch of grass with his flashlight. "I'm serious, you might get a sign. I did when I asked Edna. I hit a big yellow butterfly with my windshield. Figured that was a good sign because they mean transformation, she said. Then again, I killed it so maybe it was a warning."

I let the corner of my mouth tilt up from his unintended humor but then I felt hollow again. Until I caught a twinkle of light. I turned on my light and aimed it at the roses. It happened again so I moved the light slower. There, in the very center of a red rose in full bloom, was my engagement ring. The diamond was gleaming and shining like a winking eye. It was perfect. Just sitting upright, looking at me, not in a conventional box, but presented in an unconventional flower. Unconventional. Just like the love of my life.

It was a sign.

"*Thanks, dad*," I said in a whisper.

JENZY

When Chris came into the living room, he looked more relaxed than he had in weeks. His hair was disheveled as if he had run his fingers through it non-stop. His jeans had grass stains on them and he was biting his lower lip. He looked like a little boy to me. Maybe it's because I saw the video with him, I saw a one-year-old Chris, and all it did was put a burning in my soul to make no less than three more little Chris'.

Chris was holding a fresh rose from my parent's garden and in a blink, he was a man again not a boy. My man. Tall, handsome, kind, complicated but beautifully so. His t-shirt had a dirt smear on it and his hands kept the rose upright, careful of the thorns.

"Where did you go?" I asked him.

He didn't say anything as Dad and Todd came into the room from behind him.

"Um…" he licked his dry lips and looked down at the rose before looking back at me. "I was looking for… well, I wanted to tell you something."

I waited but he never finished. He looked past me to where my dad was, and Dad nodded at him. What was going on?

"Are you okay?" I asked sitting forward on the couch.

"Yeah," he nodded a lot, "I'm more than okay, especially since I met you. I've been better than okay since… that day at the bus stop."

I smiled but frowned a little, unsure of where that came from in his mind, "Me too," I said and patted the sofa near me. "Come sit."

"Actually," he looked so scared again, coming further into the room but then stopping. "Can you, uh… can you come here? I would go to you but I'm thinking I might not make it. My knees are weird right now."

I stood right away and walked over to him, "Hey," I rubbed his forearm, "Tell me what's wrong."

"I love you so much that it kinda hurts right now." He bent his head like to kiss me but paused near my lips. "It's too much love to stand, so…" he whispered, "I'm gonna kneel, okay?"

And he did. He came down on both knees right in front of me and the rose he presented had a diamond in the middle that I recognized. My breath caught painfully in my throat and I had to hold my mouth with both hands.

The world fuzzed out. I know I'm in a room full of family members, but it feels like just me and Chris are here, and it doesn't feel like he's offering me a ring; it's his heart and an eternity.

"Jenzy…" he looked terrified but so brave about it, "I want to marry you. I want to marry you because… I love you… I guess…" he waited. "Will you be my wife?"

I tried to stop crying but when a man like Chris comes down on his knees, there's a poetic elegance that overwhelms the room. The regal Lion, submitting himself to a so much larger entity like love. He's the king and my heart is forever his kingdom.

I held a hand to my stomach to keep the swirling down.

Then I smiled, "Yes... *I guess...*"

He laughed and blew out this tight breath. Did he really think I would say no? What universe could we exist in where Chris was not mine?

He slipped his mom's ring on my finger and everyone applauded us. He came to his feet and kissed me so hard my lips throbbed.

"Let's do this forever thing," he said near my nose, so the others wouldn't hear.

I went on my toes and kissed him, "Forever."

Thank you for reading my book!

I hope these characters came to life for you as they did for me.

This one meant something special. Divorce is a difficult process and it rarely ends like Jenzy and Chris' did. The love can fade, and time can change people but if it's meant to be, little will stand in the way.

Either way, Divorce is a new beginning…so here's to new beginnings.

You can follow me and my writing on my Facebook, Twitter, Instagram and Pinterest sites! I post things about the era of my books and the characters to keep you well in the loop of my next idea. Also, you can email me at nicolesbooks@yahoo.com. I try to make sure I answer emails in a timely fashion so if you have any questions message me! I love to hear feedback from my readers so if you wouldn't mind writing a review on my websites or wherever you purchased my book from, it would be greatly appreciated!

www.nicolesbooks.wix.com/authorpage
FB:@nicolestrycharz
IG:@nikkiwrites2
TW:@asag4jupiter
Pinterest:@nikkiwrites2
GR: @NicoleStrycharz
www.amazon.com

**CHECK OUT THE Q&A ON THE NEXT PAGE! →

#TheRelationshipQuoSeries

~Q&A/BOOK DISCUSSION WITH NICOLE STRYCHARZ~
MOST ASKED QUESTIONS ABOUT *THE DIVORCE*.

Was *The Divorce* based on a real couple?

Yes, many. I didn't write Chris and Jenzy specifically after certain individuals. They were a collage of situations and a blend of rich personalities. Divorce, even usual break-ups share something in common; heartbreak. Most of us will experience at least one in our lifetime. I did pull from real-life, personal and otherwise, to make this book poignant. I did have a 'Chris' in my life and I did fall into Jenzy's role at times. I have had a lot of people tell me that they see their own relationships reflected in this story and I believe that's because we are all a lot more connected than we think. Hence, this series is doing what it was meant to do. Make you feel understood.

Who was at fault in *The Divorce*?

It was always my intention to make Chris appear to be the obvious problem where Jenzy was the less obvious. The divorce was actually a 50/50 fail.

Chris was holding his wife responsible for his missed opportunities and failed to communicate his struggle to her. He also became callous and shut her out of his world to cope. He became disrespectful of who she was because he let the animosity fester.

Jenzy, on the other hand, was aimless and even when he expressed her lack of direction was beginning to put pressure on him, she remained uncommitted and too wavering to rely on. Jenzy's cute quirks for disorder and financial frivolity, were as disrespectful to Chris as her husband dropping her crystals into the waste bucket.

It's only natural that readers choose sides while reading the book, but the truth is that their marriage lost communication and mutual respect.

Did Chris and Jenzy have any sex at all during the rough two-year stretch? They seem too sexual to have gone so long without it and why?

No, Chris completely withdrew and here's why. Sex begins in the brain. Our minds respond to images, thoughts, and touches… No matter how sexual a person is, they need to be in 'the mood'. Imagine your partner looks at you and says, "I don't find you attractive anymore." Even if you were turned on prior to his/her statement, your libido would take a plunge. The same goes for unresolved anger or pain. Chris loved his wife, but she had become a reminder that he did not take the road he wanted for himself. People grow, and, in that growth, our desires and goals sometimes change with us. Chris didn't see that his life took a positive turn and that he was equally content with the outcome, so he attributed that negativity to staying in the States to be with Jenzy. Therefore, Jenzy became a mental anchor to regret, lowering his libido.

Also, I hint in the book that though he wanted children, he was concerned about Jenzy's indecisive nature and children would lock him into the life he was suddenly doubting.

Was Jenzy a cheater? Did she cheat with Moses?

That is a subjective question. It's a personal judgment that is gray; not black and white because it depends on your own morals and creeds as the reader.

Jenzy did not cheat in the traditional sense. She and Moses developed a friendship and did not go on their first date until she told Chris she wanted a divorce. She also made Chris aware that she would never lie or act behind his back, but that there was a person of interest. Moses was aware from the start that she was in the process of splitting from her husband, so he was never lied to either. In the middle-to-the-end of the book, Moses suggests they have an 'open relationship' so that she could be free to weed out her feelings toward Chris versus Moses. That too removes the element of dishonesty or the raw portrayal of infidelity.

However, cheating does begin in the mind and Jenzy felt neglected, so she did entertain the idea while they were married. Though they had been estranged for two years, Jenzy was still *legally* married when she went on her first date.

So, it is an internal question and answer to you as an individual.

Didn't Jenzy jump into a new relationship with Moses too soon?

Yes, it was much too soon. Jenzy's character is impulsive, passionate, and curious. It was not in her nature to be prudent and I, as an author, believe in committing to characters even if that means letting them do brash or unwise things. Why? Because characters are people and people do brash and unwise things sometimes.

Humans tend to go one of two ways; jumping in too fast or lagging forward too slow. We are either hasty or hesitant.
I bet you can look back right now on your life and remember a relationship that you leaped into with both feet into shallow waters, only to hit a rocky bottom. No, then you are remembering a time you dipped your toe into deeper water too cautiously and missed a perfect opportunity.

Jenzy was pushing herself forward to secure that she wouldn't fall back and during that time, Moses became a rebound but at his own hand as well.

Why was Moses so tolerant of Jenzy's situation? He was too good about everything all the time, why?

Ah, yes. Moses and his never-ending lenience. Wasn't it awful? He was too perfect and, in the end, kind of a pushover. Why does Moses annoy some of us? Because we either know a guy/girl like him or we *are* the guy/girl like him. Moses only appears perfect in Jenzy's story but in book two, *The Friend Zone*, we see how Moses' endurance complicated his personal life and how he too carries many flaws unseen from Jenzy's perspective in book one. Moses is based on a real type of person and he only aggravates us because he appears perfect and come on, we humans are never perfect. Whether you are a fan of Moses or not, I invite you to read book two to see his dynamics as an individual.

Who did you want Jenzy to end up with as you wrote The Divorce? Did you know where you wanted the story to go?

I had no clue as I wrote the book, who Jenzy would settle with. I didn't even allow myself to work toward one man or the other in the rough draft. A lot of readers can't predict who she will choose, because the author couldn't either! I wanted the outcome to be organic and I didn't allow myself to make a choice until after Chris' letter was written.

There's a scene toward the beginning where Todd says to Jenzy, "You'll know. If he (Chris) does that one thing that's just purely selfless enough to bring you back, you'll feel it." When I wrote that it was more for myself. I needed to see if Chris could do something to prove that their marriage would not revert to the dark ages and the letter was it.

Will Chris and Jenzy last? Will their marriage make it, or will they fall into the same old habits?

Again, that's a little subjective. I can say this, they both now know what they stand to lose if they fail to communicate. They are born opposites, so the struggles will never end. Relationships and marriages between opposites will always be a little turbulent and the key to success will always be mutual respect. Even relationships between two people with everything in common will have ups and downs and conflict, but Jenzy and Chris have been depicted in the end, to be willing to work past them.

Do you believe in Divorce?

I believe that people, the human heart, is complicated and that in our time here together we undergo changes. Some loves grow with us, expanding and deepening, keeping us rooted while making us into better people.

Other times we outgrow love and the people it came in the form of. It can grow stale and most of all requires maintenance. This book was an exception, not a rule. Most divorces do not end the way Chris and Jenzy's did. The lesson in the book is that if you cannot imagine your life without your significant other, then you need to work hard to regain the love. You must rise to the challenge of overcoming the difficulty, be it through counseling or other proven methods. Go back to where it all began, and ask yourself if given the choice, would you change anything? Is that love worth fighting for? If the answer is yes, then fight. Win or lose, at least you know you tried.

On the flip side, it is also important to recognize when the time to move on has come, so that you can go separate ways in a healthy break.

Divorce can be a new beginning but please remember this; even enemies can demonstrate respect. Call a truce. Remember that no matter how ugly things might have become that there was a time this person mattered to you. There was a period when the love existed even if it was short-lived. It taught you something about yourself, about what you want, about who you are. Lay it to rest with reverence and then press forward with an open heart but a wiser one.

~REFRENCES~

In 'The Divorce' I mention a true Amazon Bestseller, and Close Friend, Author Martha Sweeney and her Husband Tom Sweeney. Their books are available in eBook and Paperback.

The Just Breathe Trilogy
Breathe In
Breathe Out
Just Breathe

Yes! Jenzy's Coloring Book by Martha Sweeney was real! And you can own one too!
Titled:

Bookish
Adult Coloring Book

You can connect with Martha in the links below!

Website: www.marthasweeney.com

Facebook: www.facebook.com/Author-MarthaSweeney

Twitter: @MSweeneyAuthor

Instagram: www.instagram.com/MarthaSweeneyAuthor

Goodreads: www.goodreads.com/MarthaSweeney

To Connect with Tom Go to: Facebook:
www.facebook.com/theharembook
Instagram: www.instagram.com/theharembook
Twitter: @theharembook

About the Author

Nicole has been writing historical romance for over ten years. Her passion for history fuels the creativity for her novels and she finds the tools there to create a compelling plot.

However, she's evolved into writing contemporary romance as well, with more modern stories to come.

"The Divorce" was nominated in the 2016 Indie Book Awards! "The Divorce" also won second place in the 2016 Best Cover Design in 'Urban Literature Magazine.'

Nicole lives in Virginia with her three children and their amazing Grandparents. She is always reading or working on the next book between mommyhood adventures.

Here are other books by Nicole! You can find her Paperback & eBook copies at Amazon.com.

<u>(Historical)</u>

<u>Short Story Novellas</u>
<u>The Gift Keeper Series</u>
Nollaig Shona Duit; A Christmas Tale
Bealtane; Tales of the Fae
Midsummer's Eve; Tales by Moonlight
Samhain; A Ghost Tale
Coming Soon More Maura and Shea

<u>The Maybrook Trilogy</u>

The Maybrook Prequel
(A Letter for Randal)
1881-1886

Book One: A Valentine for August
Book Two: A Passion for Henrietta
Book Three: A Song for Giselle
1902-1913

Printed in Great Britain
by Amazon